THE BANCROFTS

ON AND OFF THE VICTORIAN STAGE

MARIE and SQUIRE BANCROFT

THE BANCROFTS

ON AND OFF THE VICTORIAN STAGE

Caroline Blomfield

with an introduction by
Sir Michael Holroyd

cover design by
Lyn Keay

Leyborne Publications
Kew

Published by Leyborne Publications,
7 Leyborne Park, Kew, Richmond, Surrey TW9 3HB

ISBN 978 0 9520515 7 5

CONTENTS

ILLUSTRATIONS

ACKNOWLEDGEMENTS

My thanks are due to many people, but especially to Sir Michael Holroyd for his very kind and generous introduction; to Frances Hughes, Chair of the Irving Society, for her support and encouragement throughout and for sharing with me her books, her files, her boundless knowledge of all things theatrical; to John Didlock for his enormous help with getting the book from computer file to printed page; to Lyn Keay for her lovely cover design, and Tim Keay for his technical expertise in setting up Lyn's cover for printing.

I also thank Brenda Bancroft for allowing me access to her family papers and use of portraits; Jennie Bisset and the late Richard Briers CBE for their expert knowledge and for the loan of their precious books containing photographs that I have used; Ian Brooker for sharing his knowledge of the Kendals, for his permission to use his pictures, and for helping me 'win' pictures of the Bancrofts on eBay that might otherwise have got away; Brent Fernandez for unearthing a mass of material that I would never have found by myself; Matthew Lloyd for allowing use of material from his website http://www.arthurlloyd.co.uk – a mine of information on the theatre; Margaret Muntz for sharing her in-depth research into the Wilton family.

Thanks are also due to countless other people. The following are just a few of them: Alex Bisset, Prof Jacky Bratton, Diane Conrad, Chris Gare, Al Gregg, David Lloyd, Christopher May, Melanie Millington, Marcus Risdell (Curator and Librarian, the Garrick Club), Helen Smith, Christina and Jules Wolfreys. Thanks are due also to RADA, the V&A Theatre Archive, Westminster Public Library.

Above all I thank David Blomfield, without whose editorial expertise and calming help and encouragement this project would not have started, nor ever have been completed.

Caroline Blomfield

INTRODUCTION
by Sir Michael Holroyd

Of all the actors belonging to the early Victorian age, the one I would most like to have seen is Marie Wilton. She began her career as an 'infant phenomenon' who gave extraordinary recitations in her childhood. But she was to gain fame with brilliantly audacious and impudent performances in breeches roles which greatly excited Charles Dickens. 'The girl's talent is unchallengeable,' he wrote. 'I call her the cleverest girl I have even seen on the stage in my time, and the most singularly original.'

Besides being a natural comedienne, she had courage, ambition and a good business sense about the management of theatres – indeed she was the first woman to establish herself as a successful actor-manager. Until the mid-nineteenth century, members of the theatre profession were generally seen as no better than gypsies and vagabonds living beyond the law. In her early twenties, Marie Wilton took over a rowdy and disreputable theatre known as the 'Dust Hole' which specialized in 'blood and thunder' entertainments. By giving the place new seats, curtains, carpets and decorations, she transformed it, with royal permission, into the smart and comfortable Prince of Wales's theatre.

'I was successful in a modest way from the very first,' she later wrote, 'gradually but surely my lucky star led me on to fortune.' This was the beginning of a quiet revolution in the theatre. The two most fortunate decisions she made there, in her late twenties, were to employ the actor Squire Bancroft and then, in 1867, to marry him.

Squire Bancroft was a popular actor who became increasingly well-known for playing 'swells', flourishing his eyeglass, bristling his moustache and filling the theatre with his tremendous exclamations: 'By Jove!' But it is not for his acting that he has gained a permanent place in the history of the British Theatre, but for his remarkable and what seemed counter-intuitive financial decisions as a theatre manager. He was, as Henry Irving observed, 'the only actor since Garrick who made a fortune purely by management of his own theatre – I mean without the aid of provincial tours or visits to America'.

Almost all Bancroft's innovations seemed to run contrary to the spirit of the times. He did away with the enormously long evenings which contained a farce, some burlesque and then violent melodrama in declamatory blank verse, and replaced all this with a single light comedy (often written by his favourite playwright Tom Robertson). The Bancrofts took off successful plays when they were still bringing in crowds and brought them back later in repertory. They put the orchestra below the stage and did away with the pit, placing the cheaper seats in the upper balcony. Altogether they changed the status of the theatre and made it open to all classes of society.

Squire Bancroft's most egalitarian change was to see that, instead of relying on benefit performances, the actors received decent wages discreetly brought to their dressing-rooms. The most visible novelty lay in the natural authenticity of their productions. Doors with actual knobs on the handles opened into rooms with real rugs, ceilings, chairs and tables on which real tea was served from china teapots into cups and saucers. It became known as a 'cup-and-saucer' revolution.

In 1879 the Bancrofts took possession of the Haymarket Theatre in London and remodelled the interior. Henry James was to praise 'the excellent device by which the old fashioned and awkward proscenium has been suppressed and the stage set all round in an immense gilded frame, like that of some magnificent picture. Within this frame the stage, with everything that is upon it, glows with a radiance that seems the very atmosphere of comedy.' Within four years at the Haymarket, the Bancrofts (then in their mid-forties) had made enough money to retire. Twelve years later, in 1897, Squire Bancroft was knighted. He and Lady Bancroft lived in great style into the nineteen-twenties.

'We more often need to be reminded than informed,' stated Dr Johnson. Caroline Blomfield achieves both these useful services in her comprehensive and well-researched book. What Ellen Terry called 'the brilliant story of the Bancroft management' is too often overshadowed by dramatic stories of Shakespeare's Globe, the permissive age of Restoration Comedy, Garrick's and Sheridan's reign at Drury Lane, the invasion of foreign playwrights from Molière to Ibsen and the occupation of the Royal Court Theatre in Sloane Square by Bernard Shaw and then John Osborne in the twentieth century. But, as this necessary book informs and reminds us, audiences and actors during the twentieth century have taken for granted, while greatly benefiting from, the Bancrofts' *ensemble* productions in the previous century.

Michael Holroyd

PROLOGUE

In the second half of the 19th century, Squire and Marie Bancroft were theatrical royalty. They were then as famous as their friends and contemporaries, Henry Irving and Ellen Terry. Irving and Terry were certainly the finer actors, but the Bancrofts arguably made the greater impact on the development of the British theatre.

The Bancrofts' supreme achievement was to transform the theatre of their day, from a raffish milieu where no respectable woman would venture to a glamorous, yet wholly respectable, place where audiences from across the social spectrum could feel at home. They turned the interiors of their theatres into comfortable, inviting surroundings. At the same time they improved pay and working conditions for their actors, while commissioning plays that pioneered realism in place of the ludicrous plots and posturing that had cheapened the theatre in the past.

Their success was founded on two priceless assets. Marie Bancroft was a brilliant comedienne, so popular that in any play she could fill a theatre with her admirers for month after month. Squire Bancroft was equally talented, but in a very different way: he was both a man of the theatre and a man of business. A shrewd judge of plays, he rarely misjudged their artistic worth or his audiences' tastes, and never misjudged their monetary value.

The Bancrofts came from very different backgrounds: Marie was the child of travelling actors while Squire was the son of a middle-class oil-merchant. They married in 1867, from which time they were a partnership like no other in the theatre of their time. In management together for almost twenty years, they took early retirement when they were still only in their mid-forties, having made a fortune, largely by providing London

1

audiences with plays they wanted to see, in comfortable surroundings.

The mystery is why the Bancrofts have had to wait so long for a reassessment of their place in theatrical history. There is no doubt about the respect in which they were held in their day. Marie was adored by her audiences and the critics, as well as by literary lions such as Dickens. Squire received a knighthood – being only the second to be so honoured for services to the theatre after his friend Henry Irving. He then became the GOM of the theatrical world, acting as chair of almost every theatrical institution between his retirement and his death in 1926.

There is also no lack of material. In retirement the Bancrofts wrote two volumes of memoirs which give a colourful picture of their own lives, of their friends, and of their theatrical achievements. (These provide much of the context for this book, complemented here with quotes from the columns of comment and criticism in contemporary newspapers and journals of their day.) However, their memoirs deliberately avoid any reference to their children or their domestic life. This has perhaps deterred theatrical historians, aware that they cannot easily present a fully rounded picture of what were clearly complicated relationships.

Certainly, despite the eminent position they attained in the theatre and in society, Sir Squire and Lady Bancroft had secrets in their past that they determinedly left hidden. It is far from certain how Marie was able quite suddenly to move from her popular, but ill-paid, career as one of London's stars of burlesque to managing her own theatre. Who lent her the money? Could this mystery be linked to the paternity of her two illegitimate children? She left no indication of who might have been the fathers. And why did one of those children marry his sweetheart, only to have the marriage dissolved within six months for non-consummation, yet go on to father a child whose descendants are still alive today? It is in dealing with these issues that theatrical research has to be supplemented by family papers and the rapidly expanding techniques of family history, along with information that has only recently become available via the internet.

It is thanks to this that the Bancrofts can now emerge from the elegant but staid shadows of the Victorian theatre as fully rounded characters with a tale to tell. They have waited too long to make their entrance.

1

A CHILD OF THE BOARDS

Marie Effie Wilton was born in Doncaster, Yorkshire, the second of six daughters of a travelling actor, Robert Wilton, and his wife Georgiana, probably in the year 1839. In Marie's very early youth her parents worked on the northern theatrical 'circuit', moving with their family from place to place all over the north of England, and in East Anglia.

In the 1830s the theatrical circuits, a system of theatre organisation that dated from early in the eighteenth century, still played a valuable role in promoting theatre in many parts of Britain, although they were in decline. The circuits had been established to forestall possible clashes when more than one travelling company of actors might arrive in the same town at the same time. A circuit theatre manager would control a company based in a major city such as Liverpool, Lincoln or Newcastle, with its principal theatre often being called 'Theatre Royal'. The manager might be responsible for several more theatres spread around a wide region. The Lincoln circuit in the 1830s, for example, included, among other towns, Grantham, Peterborough, Newark, Huntingdon and Stamford. The East Anglia circuit covered so many towns that it was eventually divided into two, the Norfolk-and-Suffolk circuit and the Norwich circuit. If a large circuit had enough actors the company itself would sometimes be divided in two, with its actors visiting different towns simultaneously.

Some towns boasted their own theatres or playhouses, where the actors would perform for seasons of perhaps three or four weeks, but many smaller towns did not have a theatre and the actors would then perform in assembly rooms, in booths set up in the courtyards of coaching inns, in

3

barns or even in tents. Circuit managers would try to plan their companies' visits to coincide with important events in the towns they were visiting, such as race meetings, fairs, or the assizes, which would guarantee large audiences. The actors travelled mostly on foot, with the scenery, costumes and properties being transported in horse-drawn carts. As the railways spread, the transport for travelling players became easier, but it was many years before the railways reached the smaller towns of England, and by then the growth of rail transport was itself contributing to the collapse of the circuits and their companies of travelling actors.

In 1844 the Wilton family were with the Norwich circuit, based at the Theatre Royal, Norwich, which was large and significant enough to attract many 'star' actors over the years, including Edmund Kean, Ben Webster, Madame Celeste, Fanny Kemble and others. William Charles Macready visited Norwich no fewer than three times. Marie's father was not a particularly successful actor, usually playing supporting roles, and his children's early years were spent mostly on the road, moving from place to place with the work, living in a variety of lodgings, many of them squalid and dirty and sometimes, but not always, run by kindly landladies accustomed to the travelling actors and willing to mind the children when the parents were out at work.

The Wiltons – the women of the family at any rate – were a superstitious lot. This dated from Marie's infancy in Yorkshire. She fell ill one day and her small body was covered with a curious rash that looked like pinch marks. Naturally the baby was crying and could not be pacified. An old woman passing by asked what was the matter and the distraught Georgiana replied that she thought her baby was going to die. Looking closely at the strange marks, the old woman told Georgiana to stop worrying and that she should 'gi' thanks, for t' bairn's bewitched!' Georgiana screamed in horror, almost dropping the infant. 'T' bairn's bewitched, I tell thee,' repeated the old woman. 'At sunset those marks will disappear and 'twill be the luckiest bairn you ever know'd of. She'll bring good to them she wishes to, and woe to them as wrongs her.' The old woman went on her way and sure enough, by sunset the marks had disappeared, just as she had prophesied. The story spread quickly around the village where they were staying and many local people called to kiss the baby, believing that she would bring them luck. In later years Marie would say that she was often told that when she visited a shop in the morning the lucky shopkeeper would have good trade for the rest of the day.

Certainly Marie was gifted with a precocious talent. Before she was five she was learning poems and dramatic scenes by heart and at a very young age she began contributing to her family's meagre income by performing in public, as did her sisters in their turn, and most small

4

children of acting families at the time. At the age of just five, in Norfolk, she appeared as Tom Thumb, and as Cupid in a 'burletta', a short comic opera. 'It was thought a great achievement to stand alone on a big stage and recite,' she was to write many years later in her memoirs. 'What a nuisance I must have been!' She recalled a childhood that was happy, but full of work. For the children of travelling actors there was little time for toys or games with other children. Marie owned one doll, which she never had time to play with, except occasionally on Sundays. She thought of it as an invalid who spent its life in bed.

Marie described herself as being 'impetuous, wilful, enthusiastic, ambitious; easy to lead, difficult to command; a long speech in anger would fail to affect me, but a few gentle words would quickly conquer me.' On one occasion the spirited little girl was in a rebellious mood. On stage, playing a gypsy child, she was seated by a camp-fire with a kettle hanging over it. Georgiana was in the wings at one side encouraging her daughter by demonstrating to her the facial expressions she was supposed to be assuming. Her father was on the other side ready to prompt her, should she forget her lines. Sure enough, Marie muddled her words, which annoyed Robert, so defiantly she proceeded to mimic his irritated expression when she should have been smiling like her mother, and smiling happily when she was meant to be looking sad. Then, to her parents' horror, when she was supposed to move to the front of the stage and tell the audience's fortunes, Marie spotted their landlady, of whom she was very fond, sitting in the front row, beaming with pride at the little girl's performance. Marie dropped the basket she was carrying and stretching out her arms to the familiar face cried out a greeting, demanding to be lifted off the stage to join her friend in the pit. The next time the landlady came to watch the Wilton family perform she was persuaded to take a seat up in the gallery, out of sight of the unreliable small performer. The young Marie sounds rather like Mr and Mrs Crummles's daughter, Ninetta, the 'infant phenomenon', in *Nicholas Nickleby*, though she turned out to have more genuine talent than that precocious child, and she was certainly never made to drink gin-and-water to arrest her development.

Many Victorian plays included parts for children, and audiences had a great enthusiasm for watching children perform, the younger, smaller and prettier the better. The life of child actors was undeniably hard. Very young children would often have to walk for miles with their families throughout the day to reach their next destination and be ready to appear on stage as soon as they arrived. There was little or no regulation as to the hours a child might work. Frequently cold and hungry they would be on stage at all hours, often until well past midnight.

By the age of seven, when the family was with the Theatre Royal, Manchester, Marie was the principal child actress of the company, appearing as the 'Emperor of Lilliput' in a pantomime version of *Gulliver's Travels*. In the same year she found herself performing less glamorously in a small fishing town on the Yorkshire coast. A temporary theatre had been constructed on the beach: the stage was erected on a platform above a 'dressing-room', whose floor was the sand of the beach itself. Suddenly an unexpectedly high tide came rushing in and the dressing-room area was quickly awash. 'I hurried upstairs,' wrote Marie, 'but not before my thin shoes had been well filled with sea-water.' She went on stage and sang and danced as best she could in her squelching shoes and her performance was wildly applauded by the audience. Then, greatly to her alarm, herrings were flung onto the stage! 'Pick them up. Acknowledge them!' someone hissed from the wings to the horrified little girl. Far from indicating disapproval, the offerings of fish were the highest praise the audience could offer, the more usual flowers not being available. Marie did her best to gather up the slippery tributes, all the while smiling and bowing to their donors. The audience enthusiastically called for more and returning to the stage she danced an encore. She had barely begun when things got even worse. 'Before I had got half way through an alarm was raised. "The sea is on us! The sea is on us! Save the wee lassie!" The lights went out, and the scrimmage was awful.' In the gloom, Marie felt herself being snatched up by a burly fisherman and thrust into a large fish-basket in which she was carried to safety. 'I can smell those herrings still, and have never cared for fish since!'

The young Marie had no formal education: she was taught the bare essentials by her mother, and, clearly a bright child, she learned to read young, by cutting letters out of her parents' playbills and arranging them into words. She learned to write by copying both her mother's and her father's writing: to this she later attributed her mature handwriting, describing it as 'an untidy mixture of masculine and feminine hands' – a flattering description of her adult hand, which was almost illegible.

Georgiana was clearly a talented teacher, particularly of elocution, which, being a regular branch of education for nicely brought-up young ladies of the early nineteenth century, she would have learned in her own schooldays. She coached all her daughters in voice techniques from their early childhood, and to this training Marie attributed the power she always had of making every word she spoke from the stage heard by the entire audience, at a time when sound amplification was undreamed of. Georgiana impressed the importance of this on Marie by telling her a story of a poor young man who had saved up sixpence to give himself the treat of a ticket to the theatre. The only seat he could afford was in the very back row of the gallery, from where he could barely see or hear. 'Think of him when you are acting,' Georgiana told her daughters. Throughout her stage career Marie never forgot her mother's story. 'I addressed myself to the "poor man" at the back of the gallery, as if *he* heard me, the rest of the audience must.' In later years, Marie's son, in his own memoirs, would write of his mother's advice when herself coaching young actors, words directly learned long ago from her mother:

> Always make a point of pronouncing all your final consonants, and never gabble. She would advise any public speaker, upon rising, never to start off at once, but to survey his audience first. By that means, she held, he would command their attention. Then as to gesture, every one must have meaning and must be broad and bold, never cramped and only from the elbow .... Often have I heard her say that a wrong or unnecessary use of the hands could enfeeble the spoken word. 'If you feel they are in the way or that you are conscious of them,' she would add, 'lock them behind your back.' She would always say that the best advice she could give to any actor .... was to study deeply Hamlet's advice to the players.

While still very young Marie had to learn the child-parts in various plays as well as pieces for recitations, including extracts from Shakespeare such as the balcony scene from *Romeo and Juliet* and the sleepwalking scene from *Macbeth* – rather inappropriate speeches for a child, it would seem today, but much appreciated by Victorian audiences, and Georgiana worked tirelessly to drill the words into her small daughter's head.

In her memoirs Marie wrote that her mother never appeared on stage herself, but there is evidence to the contrary from surviving playbills. Indeed it would surely have been necessary that she help her husband to support their growing family. Marie also believed, or at any rate wrote, that Georgiana's father, Samuel Faulkner, had been proprietor, or perhaps editor, of the *Morning Chronicle*, an influential radical London newspaper. However there is no evidence of him being in any way connected with the paper. In fact her mother had, like Marie, been born into the theatre. Samuel Faulkner originally came from the Tynemouth area of Northumberland, where he was married in 1813 and where his five children were born. For part of the first quarter of the nineteenth century he managed, together with a partner, the theatre in Sunderland. In around 1815 this partnership ran into considerable financial difficulties and eventually Samuel joined another partner, Thomas Downe, of the York circuit. Together they managed the Theatre Royal, York, as well as theatres in Leeds and Hull.

For years Faulkner suffered from mental illness. His own father had died in an asylum for the insane in Gateshead, where Samuel himself had also been confined more than once suffering from 'signs of a disordered intellect'. He and his Sunderland partner had invested what was then a substantial sum, around £500, in a bank that failed and Samuel was also bearing some heavy financial burdens that he had inherited from his own late father. He was heavily in debt and was being pursued by his Sunderland creditors. Then in around 1823 his wife, Maria, died and Samuel plunged into deep depression. The loss of his wife, coupled with the severe legal and financial problems with which he was beset, drove him to total despair.

One evening in the spring of 1826 two of Samuel Faulkner's colleagues from the Theatre Royal, York, who were lodging in the same house, became concerned about the state of his mind. He was talking incoherently and threatening to take his own life; in his distress he had asked his friends, 'Whatever will become of my poor children?' The landlady told them she had overheard him saying to his young children that 'tomorrow the breakers will come and I shall be ruined'. He was living with the terror that his creditors would seize everything he possessed and that he would be sentenced to the York debtors' prison. As a precaution, his friends removed his razors and anything else they could think of with which he might harm himself.

Gradually Samuel grew calmer. His friends stayed with him until he fell asleep and then they retired themselves. At around six o'clock the next morning, Saturday 1 April, 1826, one of them was awoken by the sound of the front door being softly closed. Rising, he anxiously checked Samuel's room, to find he had gone, leaving his gold watch, his snuff box and his ring lying on his dressing table. Alarmed, he called for help. A search began and at about seven-thirty Samuel's walking-stick and gloves were found lying beside the River Ouse. The river was dragged and Samuel Faulkner's body was found in the water about 100 yards downstream. It was taken to a nearby public house. A coroner's jury was summoned and at six o'clock that same evening an inquest sat in the inn where the body lay. The verdict given was that he had 'drowned himself in a fit of insanity', brought about by the 'undoubted pecuniary embarrassment, arising from the pressure now made upon him by creditors in Sunderland, where he for some years managed the theatre .... and where he had contracted debts to a considerable amount.'

The remains of Samuel Faulkner were buried in York, in the churchyard of St Mary's, Castlegate. (Burials of suicides at that time were permitted in a churchyard if the death was due to insanity. Otherwise, the unfortunate deceased could not be buried in consecrated ground.) There were suggestions in some newspapers reporting Faulkner's death that there had been a major disagreement between him and his partner, Thomas Downe, but one newspaper insisted that Downe, knowing of Faulkner's problems, had offered him financial help. Nevertheless it seems that Marie and her sisters grew up believing that her grandfather had 'been deluded into joining a partnership, and putting his money into the management of the York Circuit; but knowing next to nothing of theatrical matters, and owing partly to the treachery of others .... lost all he possessed.' Probably their mother, Georgiana, being a small child at the time of her father's suicide, never herself knew the full story and simply told her girls what she herself believed.

Following Samuel Faulkner's death Thomas Downe immediately announced that the Theatre Royal, York, would be closed until further notice, 'on account of the awful and sudden death of Mr Faulkner'. Three of the five children, aged between five and thirteen, were away at boarding school in Hull. The two youngest girls, including Georgiana, were still in Faulkner's lodgings and were immediately taken by Downe and his wife into their own home, where they were cared for until relatives could be found. On 25 April a benefit performance was held at the Theatre Royal in aid of the children. The house was full and well over £100 was taken, the equivalent of about £4,500 in today's money. Among the pieces chosen to be shown on the night was one entitled *The Adopted Child.*

To ensure that the orphaned Faulkner children were not entirely destitute, Thomas Downe arranged for them to receive their father's share of the profits in the theatres until 1828 when the leases were due to expire. Eventually a wealthy brother of Samuel Faulkner was found living in Brussels. He became guardian of the children and he also settled all Samuel's outstanding debts.

While she was still in her teens Georgiana Jane Faulkner met and fell in love with the much older Robert Pleydell Wilton, a handsome, charming travelling actor from an old-established Gloucestershire family. His father, Charles Henry Wilton, was a violinist, born in 1761, who had spent a couple of years in his youth studying music in Italy. He composed for the violin, viola and piano and he is known to have conducted for the Three Choirs Festival in Gloucester Cathedral on several occasions. In 1785 he was leader of the orchestra in a performance of Thomas Arne's oratorio, *Judith*, at the Haymarket Theatre in London. Wilton's compositions, which included settings for the psalms, were well-known in their time; one of them, a short, very simple 'Sonatina' for the piano, was to remain familiar until comparatively recently to generations of young piano students, as for decades it often cropped up in the Grade I piano syllabus. Wilton also taught music – a good musician could make a decent living as a teacher in those days as it was essential for any well brought-up young lady to learn to play the piano and sing. Charles Wilton and his family lived in various places around the country, including Liverpool, where Robert was born in around 1799; then while Robert was still a young boy, they moved to Brentford in Middlesex. Now a densely populated suburb of west London, in the early nineteenth century it was a country village. Prosperous middle-class households in the area would have included potential pupils. There were also several great houses nearby, such as Osterley House, Syon Park and Boston Manor, which may have needed his services both as a private teacher for their young ladies, or at soirées where Charles Wilton might have played to the assembled guests following dinner. However, it seems that Brentford was not considered a suitable place for a musician of repute to be based. When Wilton was proposed for membership of the Royal Society of Musicians in 1805 he was rejected by twelve votes to nine, as some members felt 'he was not eligible from his Residence being at Brentford.'

The respectable Wilton family may well have been concerned that Charles Henry was pursuing what they would have seen as a career unworthy of their status as prosperous citizens of Gloucester, but it would have been far worse when his son Robert left home to become an actor, then regarded as a most disreputable profession. Not long after his father's death in 1832, Robert met Georgiana Faulkner, many years younger than himself, and they ran away together. Robert was now totally rejected by the rest of his family, as he already had a wife living when he eloped with Georgiana. He had married Margaret Huson in 1817, when he himself was no more than eighteen, and they had three children, two girls and a boy. Two years after the birth of their youngest child, a son, Henry, in 1828, the names 'Mr Wilton' and 'Mrs Wilton' appear in a programme of 1830 for the theatre at North Walsham, one of the theatres on the Norwich circuit. This 'Mrs Wilton' probably refers to Margaret, as Georgiana Faulkner would have been no more than seventeen in that year.

There is no evidence that Robert and his first wife Margaret were ever legally separated, nor that she died young, and although Georgiana and Robert lived together for many years and brought up their large family together, the probate document attached to Georgiana's will many years later reveals that she and Robert were never legally married. In this document, Georgiana is described as 'spinster'. As a charming, ever-optimistic dreamer, Robert Wilton never achieved any great success as an actor. The height of his career seems to have been when he played the part of Tubal to Charles Kean's[*] Shylock in the *Merchant of Venice*. In those days when a famous actor arrived to 'star' in the provinces he expected the resident company to be totally familiar with any play he might choose to perform. The players attached to the circuits or with the provincial stock companies had to know many parts and be ready to play them at short notice, usually with little or even no rehearsal alongside the star. On the occasion when Robert Wilton was to play Tubal, Kean unusually insisted on rehearsing the *Merchant* with the company before the first night as he wanted the cast to be familiar with his powerful acting style.

---

[*]Charles Kean, 1811-68, son of the great nineteenth-century tragedian Edmund Kean, 1787-1833, was himself a fine actor.

He was anxious that they might be frightened by his, Kean's, ferocious performance, and Wilton was indeed quite alarmed by the famous actor's passionate portrayal of Shylock.

Later, in her memoirs, Marie described her father as the eternal optimist. 'Dazzled by the surface glitter of the stage, he went his way, building castles in the air, living in dreamland, and hoping for a position which never came to him.' He always looked on the bright side, however bad things seemed to be. Often when his family was in low spirits, usually due to severe shortage of money and consequently hunger and deprivation, he would cheer them up by telling stories of his early days on the stage.

Robert and Georgiana's first child, Emma, was born at Selby, in Yorkshire, on 14 January 1838. It is more difficult to establish with absolute certainty the birth dates of the rest of the Wilton girls, as apart from Emma, their births do not appear to have been registered, and the ages they later gave in successive censuses are wildly inconsistent. However, other evidence indicates that Marie Effie Wilton was the second daughter, born in Doncaster on 12 January 1839. The third child, Ida, was born in Worksop, Nottinghamshire, in 1840, and the last three girls were born in East Anglia when their parents were with the Norwich circuit. Georgiana (known as Georgina, to avoid confusion with her mother) and Augusta were born in Norwich in around 1843 and 1847, and the youngest, Blanche, was born in Woodbridge, Suffolk, in 1848.

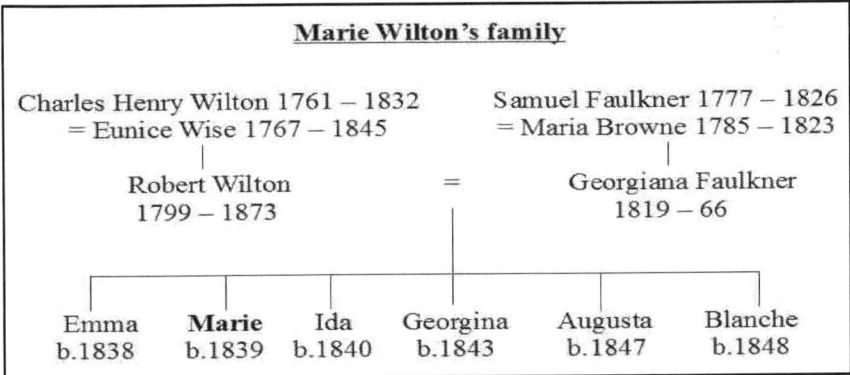

Marie Wilton's family

Charles Henry Wilton 1761 – 1832   Samuel Faulkner 1777 – 1826
= Eunice Wise 1767 – 1845   = Maria Browne 1785 – 1823

Robert Wilton   =   Georgiana Faulkner
1799 – 1873   1819 – 66

Emma	**Marie**	Ida	Georgina	Augusta	Blanche
b.1838	b.1839	b.1840	b.1843	b.1847	b.1848

Marie's sisters all followed in their parents' footsteps as children and when they grew up, with the exception of Georgina. She suffered from epilepsy, which was then untreatable, so it is unlikely that her parents would have taken the risk of letting her appear on stage. During their travelling years, the family was invariably and inevitably short of money, and the girls would have had to provide necessary additional income. They would possibly have had more work than their parents, because of the popularity of child actors, particularly girls, with mid-Victorian audiences.

However, Marie was made aware at a very young age of just how actors were regarded by 'the quality'. In her memoirs she told of a time when she was engaged to take part in a private entertainment in aid of a charity. She performed some recitations to the delight of a smart audience, especially the ladies present. She wrote of the occasion many years later: 'After the entertainment was over these ladies kissed and petted me with such remarks as, "What a sweet child!", "Dear little thing!", "How clever!" and "What lovely hair!"' Someone suggested that the assembled ladies and gentlemen might care to contribute a small sum to buy a toy for the little girl who had given them such pleasure, and purses were eagerly opened. Then one of the ladies asked 'whose dear child' Marie was. On being told that she was the daughter of an actor, 'the smiles vanished, and the expressions changed in a way to have turned even lemons sour. Bags were closed with a relentless click and the owners muttered between their teeth (for fear, doubtless, of breathing the same air as myself.) "Oh gracious!", "Horrid!", "Unfortunate child!", and drew back from me as if plague-stricken.' The young Marie was deeply upset by this episode.

Some members of the moneyed classes felt it their duty to try to rescue some of these unfortunate child actors from the disreputable lives that lay ahead of them, and at some time early in Marie's life a wealthy, childless Roman Catholic lady took a great fancy to her and came up with a proposition: she would adopt the child and ensure that she received a good education at a convent school. Marie would be allowed to remain in contact with her parents and even visit them occasionally. The condition was that Marie should take the lady's surname and never again set foot on a stage; in return, she would be left a considerable fortune. Robert and Georgiana may or may not have been tempted by this offer of a secure, comfortable, but certainly restricting, future for their daughter, but they turned it down.

It would have been a hard and restless life for the Wilton family, and Marie could not recall a settled home at any time in her childhood and described her parents' life as being 'for many years little else than toil, anxiety, and care' as they constantly travelled from place to place around the country, with several small children and often the latest baby in tow, staying at one lodging house after another. The programmes of theatrical entertainment that were performed at that time would have been mixed bills of melodrama and farce, with plenty of song and dance and recitation thrown in. Travelling actors contracted to one of the circuits might be expected to play as many as twelve different parts in one week. For this they were paid a pittance and had to provide their own costumes and personal props such as swords, daggers or walking sticks. Absence for any reason such as sickness or injury resulted in pay being forfeited, and lateness or non-appearance for any reason resulted in the actor concerned being fined.

While the Wilton family were working in Manchester Marie took dancing lessons and during one of these she injured her foot: she was in a lot of pain and could not walk without a limp. When she was unable to perform, she would have forfeited her meagre contribution to the family's income. She was on crutches for some weeks and during this time the only part she was able to play was that of Tiny Tim in a dramatisation of Dickens's *A Christmas Carol*.

Marie was fit and well again by October 1846 when the renowned actor William Charles Macready[*] was making his final tour of the provinces before retiring from the stage: his final farewell performances were in London in 1851. The play was *Macbeth* and the seven-year-old Marie played two parts, Banquo's young son, Fleance, and also the apparition of a child conjured up by the witches. After the curtain Marie was summoned to Macready's dressing room. Afraid that she must have done something wrong, she knocked at the door and waited anxiously until she was admitted. Inside she found the great actor sitting in an armchair, looking tired and cross in the dimly-lit room.

'Who is it?' he demanded of his dresser, who replied, 'It's the little girl you sent for, sir.'

'Oh yes! Turn up the gas.'

Macready held out his hand and regarded the awe-stricken Marie kindly. 'Come here, child.' She went across to him and he patted her on the head and kissed her. Then he said: 'Well, I suppose you hope to be a great actress some day?'

'Yes sir!'

He smiled. 'And what do you intend to play?'

'Lady Macbeth, sir.'

Macready laughed out loud and said, 'Oh! Is that all? Well, I like your ambition; you are a strange little thing and have such curious eyes; but you must change them before you play Lady Macbeth, or you will make your audience laugh instead of cry.'

He then asked whether she would like half a sovereign to buy a doll with, or if she would prefer a glass of wine. Boldly Marie replied that she thought she would rather like both, at which Macready laughed and gave her the wine as well as the coin – it has to be hoped that for such a young child the wine was well watered. 'I am sure you will make a fine actress,' he said. 'I can see genius through those little windows.' He placed his hands over her eyes. 'But don't play Lady Macbeth too soon; begin

---

[*] William Charles Macready, 1793-1873, was one of the finest actors of his generation.

slowly, or you may end quickly!' Marie drank her wine and left feeling 'as proud as any little peacock'. The great man had patted her head and kissed her. She did not want to wash her face ever again.

William Charles Macready as Macbeth

Also while in Manchester Marie met another famous actor. This was Charles Kemble[*], the younger brother of the great Sarah Siddons and John Philip Kemble. He had retired in 1840 and, now in his seventies, was on one of his rare visits to those who laboured on the provincial circuits. He was watching from a stage-box when Marie played Prince Arthur in *King John,* with a well-known Shakespearean actress, Isabella Glyn[*] as Queen Constance. In the scene where the young prince falls from the battlements Marie thought she heard a voice call out from the audience. The next day a story appeared in the press, headed 'The Veteran and the Child.' The report said that:-

Charles Kemble sat anxiously watching.....he seemed saddened, perhaps by the memories of those halcyon days when his great brother was the King and he the gallant Falconbridge; but the scene between Hubert and Prince Arthur awoke his approving smiles. More than once he clapped his

[*] Charles Kemble, 1775-1854. His own acting career benefited from those of his famous brother and sister.
[*] Isabella Glyn, 1823-89, a celebrated actress who played many Shakespearean and other dramatic roles.

hands, and as the little prince fell from the battlements, exclaiming, with exquisite pathos,

Ah me, my uncle's spirit's in these stones;
Heaven take my soul, and England keep my bones!

Kemble was so carried away by his enthusiasm as to rise to his feet in his box and exclaim: 'By heavens! That girl will be a great actress.' He sent for Marie after the final curtain and complimented her warmly: 'You spoke your lines beautifully,' he said. Cheekily Marie replied, 'Oh, but you are deaf, sir; you could not hear me.'

He laughed and replied, 'I could see your words, child: your little face spoke them.' Then, strangely, Kemble repeated Macready's advice: 'Climb not the ladder too quickly,' he warned, 'or you may come suddenly to the ground again.'

Marie was aware from her earliest childhood of how essential it was for actors to turn up when and where management demanded. Fines, which her parents could ill-afford, were often discussed with dread in her hearing, and as a result she developed a real fear of being late and so being responsible for her parents being penalised. Once, when the Wiltons were attached to the Norwich circuit, Marie's services were not going to be needed for a couple of weeks, so she was left in the care of the current landlady in Norwich while Robert and Georgiana went off to play in another town, some distance away. This certainly points to Georgiana being needed as an actress: she accompanied her husband rather than staying to look after the children, though she may have taken the smallest ones with her. Robert and Georgiana had been gone for about three days when management changed its mind about the programme and decided it wanted John Baldwin Buckstone's play *The Green Bushes* to be performed instead of the production originally planned. In this popular melodrama of the American frontier, which had first been seen at the Adelphi in London in 1845 and had been performed many times since, there was a part for a child-actress; so Marie, who must by then have been around ten or eleven, was urgently sent for as she was needed for the following night's show. She was hurriedly got ready by the landlady and rushed to the station, just in time to see the last train of the day steaming out of Norwich. The landlady tried to persuade her that the first train the next morning would get her there in plenty of time, but she was so distressed at the prospect of missing the morning's rehearsal that she insisted that somehow she must go that night. Never mind that she knew the part so well that she did not really need to rehearse it. All she knew was that a fine would be her punishment for absence from duty and that she must go at once.

A carter was found who was going that way and he agreed to take Marie. The landlady's husband went along too, to keep her company, and she was tucked up at the bottom of the cart on a pile of flour-sacks where she slept contentedly with the carter's dog curled up beside her. Very late they stopped at an inn for refreshment and to rest the horse. When Marie was lifted from the cart she saw a group of rough-looking men drinking around a camp-fire. 'You ain't been a-kidnapping, 'ave you?' they jokingly asked her two protectors and, on being told that Marie was a child-actress, the men demanded that she 'do a piece' for them. Reluctantly at first, she nervously recited a few lines of verse. The response was so enthusiastic that her confidence grew and the small actress readily carried on with her performance, while her two guardians sat smiling proudly as if they were themselves entirely responsible for the juvenile talent displayed. Word got around that something unusual was going on, and soon the landlord of the inn and his wife, the potmen, stable-boys, farm-labourers and a crowd of villagers had gathered around in the firelight, smoking, drinking and enjoying the unexpected entertainment. When the time came to depart, Marie was smothered with beery hugs and kisses before being lifted back into the cart to complete her journey. She arrived at the theatre at first light after a long night of unmolested travel, covered in flour, straw and dog hairs but in good time for the rehearsal.

The Wilton family sometimes had to split forces, going in separate directions to wherever there might be work for them. When Marie was about twelve she was in the west of Scotland, with her father and three of her sisters. Her mother was in Lancashire with the two remaining girls, 'fulfilling an engagement'. While Robert Wilton needed to go away for a couple of days, leaving his girls in the care of their landlady, a message arrived saying that Georgiana was seriously ill. Marie, convinced that her mother was going to die, determined that she must go to her at once. Knowing where their father kept a small amount of cash hidden away, she helped herself to the money, packed a small bag and, with her sister Ida and another of the younger ones in tow, crept quietly out of the house, so that the landlady should not catch them. The epileptic Georgina was left behind as they did not dare risk taking her. (Marie refers to her sister as being 'mentally afflicted': epilepsy at that time was widely misunderstood and regarded as a mental condition.)

At the pier they found a boat bound for Glasgow. The sea was rough and the smallest sister, who can have been no more than six or seven years old, cried and begged to be allowed to get out and walk. On their arrival in Glasgow, Marie discovered that her pocket had been picked and that they were penniless. They found a steamer that was about to leave for Liverpool and Marie asked to be taken to see the captain. She told him their story and at first he said that they should return to their father at once, but when Marie wept and told him how ill their mother was he reluctantly agreed that he would take them to Liverpool for no charge, along with the other poor passengers who travelled free. He even gave them some sandwiches. It was another rough voyage and the confined area below deck was so full of tobacco smoke that the three little girls sat on the steps where the air was fresher. Marie related that 'The language amongst the "free passengers" became so dreadful that I covered the children's heads with their coats to prevent their hearing.' The distressed Marie was crying as she tried in vain to sleep when an officer came by and found the three children. He took them to his own cabin where they spent the rest of the night, all three tucked up together in his bunk, and in the morning he brought them some breakfast. On their arrival in Liverpool, the captain, concerned for their safety, allowed the officer to escort the girls to the address where their mother was staying. Believing her daughters were safely in Scotland with their father, Georgiana had a terrible fright at their sudden unexpected appearance, but the shock seemed to have done her some good, as the next day her health improved and word was urgently sent to Robert that the girls were safe.

A terrible commotion had been caused back in Scotland by the girls' disappearance: the poor landlady had the town crier shouting 'Lost, stolen, or strayed' around the streets, and Robert was understandably distraught and raged at the unfortunate landlady for her neglect of his children. In later years he often told Marie that he had never really forgiven her for the terrible scare she had given him. It is hard today to imagine three small girls undertaking such a journey on their own, and surviving it unmolested at a time when there were no means of speedy communication as to their whereabouts.

Many years later, when Marie was a successful young actress, she was again in Liverpool, on tour. A note was delivered to the stage door for her and to her astonishment she found it was from the young ship's officer who had come to her rescue all those years before. Full of gratitude, Marie met with him a few times and he eventually asked her to marry him. She wrote, 'I wished I could have said yes, for a man with such a heart must have made a good husband. My feelings, however, were only those of gratitude, not love, and I was obliged to tell him so.'

By the spring of 1852, when Marie was thirteen, she was back in Scotland, at the Theatre Royal, Edinburgh, in Horatio Lloyd's[*] production of *Belphegor; or the Mountebank and his Wife*, a sentimental melodrama translated from the French that had had its first London performance at the Adelphi in 1851. The *Caledonian Mercury* described a heartrending scene when the mountebank and his young son, played by Marie, were 'broken-spirited and worn out with fatigue and hunger .... here let us do justice to

---

[*] Horatio Lloyd, 1807-89, a well-known actor, who worked mostly in Scotland. He was the father of the famous music-hall comedian, Arthur Lloyd, 1839-1904.

the acting of Miss Wilton as the boy Henri. In its varied phases of joy and grief we have not seen a more beautiful or interesting representation than that of Miss Wilton. There can be no question of the talents of this young actress.'

In 1853 Robert Wilton, with his family in tow, was taken on at the Theatre Royal, Bristol. With at least three of his daughters already seasoned performers, Robert would have been a welcome addition to the company. The Wiltons were to remain in Bristol for some years, working for James Henry Chute[*], considered to be one of the greatest provincial theatre managers of his day.

By the middle of the century the circuits were dying out, to be replaced by the stock companies. A stock company was made up of a group of actors each of whom had a specific type of role they would regularly perform, with a wide repertoire of plays. The leading male members of the company would be the Tragedian, who would play the major roles such as Hamlet or Macbeth, and the Low Comedian who played the leading comic parts. There would be the Old Man and the Old Woman, who would play such parts as the nurse in *Romeo and Juliet*. The various other categories included the Walking Gentleman and the Walking Lady, who would take on whatever minor roles that they might be called on to play. Robert and Georgiana Wilton would have been Walking Gentleman and Lady. They would not have been well paid and bringing up six children would have been a struggle. However, those children certainly contributed to the family's finances; many plays included parts for children and at Christmas there would usually be a pantomime which would call for dozens, or even hundreds, of children.

The Bristol company was large enough for Chute to run the theatre in Bath as well as in Bristol, sometimes with performances in both cities on the same night. Bristol was one of the largest cities in England at the time, and when they had star actors visiting they would usually play for twice as many nights in Bristol as they did in Bath. In *The Bristol Stage*, published in 1919, G.Rennie Powell described how after a performance in Bath, for which they received a small extra payment, the actors would return to their lodgings in Bristol late at night, their fares and any refreshments coming out of their meagre pay. They would '[squander] the balance on a glass or two of ale or "a cup of the beverage which cheers" whilst awaiting the arrival of the midnight train to Bristol.'

Marie's first part in Bristol was at a wage of £1.15s a week, as Fleance in *Macbeth*, the role in which she had so impressed Macready, but she was to be reminded only too literally of Charles Kemble's warning about

---

[*] James Henry Chute, c.1808-78, actor and prominent theatre manager, who married into the Macready family.

climbing ladders when she appeared in Chute's Christmas pantomime. In the opening scene of this production she made her first appearance as the 'Sprite of the Silver Star' from the 'flies' high above the stage, with her long blonde hair hanging loose, dressed in a costume of pale blue silk covered with twinkling spangles. She accompanied her hazardous and terrifying descent from the 'clouds' with distinctly pedestrian verse, spoken in a quavering voice:

Weary of the little progress here we're making,
A trip to Earth, this night, I think of taking.

Old front of
Theatre
Royal
erected 1766.
Pulled down
in 1904.

the Theatre Royal, Bristol

To undertake this 'trip to earth' Marie was strapped into a rickety metal contraption that jolted and jerked alarmingly as it lowered her to the ground. She was petrified and, instead of the joyful smile she was supposed to display as she descended from on high, her expression was more one of terror and her eyes were stinging from the smoke of the gaslights high above. When she was eventually deposited safely on the stage her voice was still shaking as she spoke her first words on *terra firma*. The machinery that was used to 'fly' children was truly frightening

19

and accidents were not infrequent. The playwright Tom Robertson, who was also a journalist, once wrote of the hazards involved when children were made to 'fly' above the stage. He considered that theatre managers regarded their child performers as little more than animated props. His account so closely matches Marie's description of her experiences as the 'Sprite of the Silver Star' it is clear that she described the terrors of 'flying' to him when they met some years later:

> [In an] ingenious piece of cruelty …. the poor, pale girl is swung up to terrific heights, imprisoned in and upon iron wires, dazzled by rows of hot flaming gas close to her eyes, and choked by the smoke of coloured fires. Sometimes the silver-robed victim faints or goes into hysterics, and so incurs the odium of affectation. The scene-painter is relentless, the stage manager is relentless, and the manager must make a fortune speedily. 'Hoist 'em up!' – fill their minds with fear, their lungs with foul vapour. They are young and strong; and it won't kill 'em, unless, indeed, a rope break or a wire give way; and if so, the spirited and enterprising lessee will behave with that accustomed liberality which has ever characterised etc., etc. He will bury the girl at his own expense, and for the parents' tears, they may be d----d with a £5 note.

There were many other mechanical devices used to achieve startling effects in pantomimes and extravaganzas. In the days of gaslight, and with minimal concern for health-and-safety issues, effects could be achieved that would astonish even present-day audiences. As well as descending from high above, various hazardous 'traps' in the floor of the stage were used, along with clouds of coloured smoke, to enable demon kings and the like to appear and disappear as if from nowhere. The notorious 'star-trap' was divided like a pie into hinged segments that would fly open, and by means of springs, weights and counter-weights below the stage the performer was projected at speed up through the floor to materialise on stage in an instant. It was the cause of many injuries until its use was eventually banned later in the century.

In spite of her shaky entrance Marie's performance for the rest of the pantomime went down well. The *Bristol Mercury* described her in elaborate words: 'The "dark vaulted ether" suddenly discloses a brilliant star, from whose effulgence emerges the Sprite of the Silver Star, which character was played by a clever, and we must add exceedingly pretty girl, who made a first appearance – Miss M.Wilton.'

James Chute's pantomimes at Bristol and Bath were famously spectacular. When preparing for a production of *The Babes in the Wood* in 1858, he advertised in the Bristol press for 'a host of children', between the ages of seven and nine years old, to appear as extras – fairies, sprites, elves and the like. On the appointed day the Theatre Royal was besieged by hundreds of aspiring young performers. They swarmed all over the theatre, finding their way into every corner and crowding the passages, making them so impassable that Chute could barely move around the building. Eventually they were all auditioned and the successful applicants were selected: these children were quickly trained to take part in the pantomime, their wages doubtless contributing much-needed extra funds to many poor households.

The number of children working in theatres grew as the nineteenth century progressed and by 1887 there were hundreds of them involved all over Britain, throughout the year but especially during the Christmas pantomime season. The Victorians had an insatiable enthusiasm for seeing children perform. This seems to have been a mixture of sentimentality and often far less healthy interests. It was not until 1889 that legislation was passed that prohibited the employment of children below the age of seven and restricted it between the ages of seven and ten. Until then no concessions were made for their age and they would be expected to perform until late at night. They might then have to leave the theatre well after midnight and make their own way home, often with no one to take care of them. Their nightly journeys through large cities to their homes often some distance away could be seriously hazardous for unprotected young children. They would then be expected to reappear promptly the following morning for rehearsals.

A year or two before Marie arrived in Bristol, she and her family were in a small country town, probably somewhere in the north. She wrote that she was thirteen at the time, although the playbills claimed she was twelve, and that she had become quite a pet with the local audiences. 'Attractions must have been at a very low ebb,' she wrote, 'when the manager conceived the idea of my playing Juliet.' The audience were assured that Shakespeare's Juliet would not have been much older and would have been considered marriageable at that age. Marie described herself as being then 'a pale, thin, delicate-looking child, and tall for my age. Everyone thought at that time that I should, if I lived, be a remarkably fine woman; but since playing Juliet on that memorable first occasion I have not grown an inch …. I sometimes think that my tragic efforts gave as great a shock to my system as to my audience.'

In a shop window Marie had spotted a pretty necklace, three rows of pearls that she longed to have. Its price was five shillings – 'a fortune to me then'. She had managed to save up half-a-crown – two shillings and sixpence (12½p) – from her wages and tried to persuade the shopkeeper to let her have the necklace for half-price, but he would not agree. Her father promised he would buy it for her if she studied Juliet thoroughly and learned her part quickly. 'The labour of learning the words seemed light indeed, compared with the joy of possessing those little pearl beads.'

The first night arrived and her anxious mother helped to dress her.

Marie wondered why her mother was so worried. 'I was not. I was of that happy age that knows no responsibility. I had on a pretty white dress, trimmed with narrow silver lace, my hair hanging in large waves over my shoulders; and the best adornment of all was my beautiful pearl necklace. Oh! how everyone would envy me those beads!' All went well until near the end, when throwing back her head to drink the poison, her feet got tangled in her elaborate long train. In her attempts not to fall one string of the necklace somehow broke; beads scattered all over the stage. Marie was so upset at this that she started to cry. The audience, thinking this was wonderful acting, applauded wildly. Then in the middle of Friar Laurence's speech, she saw that he was about to tread on some of the scattered beads. The supposedly unconscious Juliet then disgraced herself by reaching out to rescue them, wrecking the tragic scene. The manager was understandably furious as were her father and mother. As she was leaving the theatre with her parents, in deep disgrace, a military gentleman approached them. Introducing himself as Captain --- (Marie never named him) he addressed her father: 'I have been impressed by your little daughter's acting. It was, for one so young, remarkable. Take care of her, sir; there is a bright career before her.' He then asked if Marie would give him the remains of her beads. She hesitated, not wanting to part with what was left of her necklace as she had hoped to repair the broken string, but reluctantly she parted with it. After that she watched out for the captain every night but he did not turn up again.

A couple of years later, by which time she was in Bristol, Marie was once again leaving the theatre with her mother after the evening's performance when suddenly the captain was there and, 'My heart jumped at the sight of this man.' Georgiana, however, was less pleased to see him, acknowledging him coolly, fearing that his admiration for her young daughter might become something more serious now that Marie was a bit older. He remarked that he had been right and that her career was flourishing as he had predicted. 'Mark my words, the next step will be London,' he said. He then produced the pearls from his pocket and said, 'You see how I have treasured these. I don't intend to part with them unless you ask me for them.' Many years later Marie was to write: 'It seemed like taking away my heart when he first asked me for them; and now he *had* taken it away.'

Every night, during his leave in Bristol, the captain sat in the dress circle, and every night, during the curtain call, he would hold up the broken necklace for Marie to see. He would then wait outside the stage-door to bid her goodnight. They could do no more, as Georgiana was sure to be watching from the window of their lodgings, which were right across the road from the stage-door, to ensure that her daughter came straight home and, mistrusting the captain's intentions, she would not allow him to call on her at home.

Marie Wilton was in love, for the first time in her young life. To her, the captain was not young, probably in his late twenties which would make him many years older than she was, not good looking, and poor, with just his army pay, but 'How everything else in the whole world suddenly dwindled into nothing! Father, mother, sisters, theatres, acting – all seemed to be shut out by a curtain, and only one being was in view.'

Then one night she received a note from her captain telling her that he was being posted to Ireland. The note ended, 'Goodbye. I wonder if we shall ever meet again. I shall never part with your pearls. I love you, little one. I wish you loved me; but it is better for you that you should not.' Marie showed the note to her mother, begging to be allowed to see him before he left, but Georgiana refused, telling her that she was just a silly little girl. 'Surely,' she said, 'you cannot wish to destroy all your professional prospects! Let me hear no more of this nonsense! Thank goodness he is gone, and you will forget him in a few days.' But Marie was desperate not to lose him. 'Forget him! and in a few days! Oh, mother!' she wrote years later. The captain had left her an address in Ireland and she wrote to him, telling him that 'I loved him more than anything else in the world, and that if he really cared for me as much, I would run away, and go to him; that if I did not marry him, I would marry no one else, that I could do nothing but think of him.'

The captain replied that he wanted to be certain that she was absolutely sure. He said that he was reluctant to take her away from a profession in which she was destined to shine, and that he should never be able to forgive himself if she regretted her decision when it was too late. But the more Marie reflected, the more determined she became, and eventually he agreed that she should come to him, saying that he was sure that once they were married, her mother would forgive her. So, it was decided, and Marie prepared to elope with her captain. Each day she managed to intercept the post before her mother found his letters.

The night before she planned to run away, Marie could not sleep: she lay awake, agonising over whether she was doing the right thing and hoping and praying for some kind of a sign or a dream that would tell her what she should do. (Being very superstitious, she was a strong believer in signs and omens.) 'I felt how I was deceiving my dear mother, to whom I owed everything and who was now dependent upon me. If I went away, what would become of her and my young sisters? How I wept and prayed that night! I implored God to help me and to give me some warning in my dreams.' Then early in the morning she heard the postman's knock. 'My heart seemed to stop beating. I could scarcely breathe .... and as I crossed the room to open the door, a voice, as if in great haste, said quickly, "Don't go." A thrill, first of awe and terror, then of thankfulness, came over me. I fell on my knees, and said, "I won't go."' The directions had arrived, along with the promised ticket and money for the journey. Marie immediately sat down to write to her admirer: 'Don't expect me, I cannot go. I have changed my mind.' She enclosed the money and slipped out to post the letter. Then she returned to her bed where she lay and cried bitterly. Only a few weeks later Georgiana, with a smile of satisfaction, showed her the marriages column in a newspaper. Her captain had married. 'I threw my arms around my mother's neck, had a good cry, and told her everything.'

Despite this sad outcome of her first love affair, Mary was happy in Bristol. Chute inspired loyalty among his actors who would often stay with him for many years, or return to Bristol after a period working elsewhere. He was an efficient administrator and was known to be a strict disciplinarian, imposing fines for minor misdemeanours. However, he and his actress wife were always kind to the younger members of their company and he had been known to return penalty money surreptitiously to those he knew could ill-afford to pay it, saying: 'Do not say anything about it, and do not be late again.' The company was large enough for Chute sometimes to send his actors on tour and in 1853 Marie was among a group from Bristol who went over to Ireland where they played in Cork for a few weeks. The other Wilton girls were also appearing on stage at Bristol. The oldest sister, Emma, performed there in 1854, and in the 1856 Christmas pantomime Ida Wilton played a cat, presumably borrowed from Dick Whittington, as that year's pantomime was *Jack and the Beanstalk*.

Chute's young actors were encouraged to stage their own entertainments when they were not needed on a particular day, and on at least two occasions in 1854 Marie starred in a programme of one-night 'entertainments' in the Broadmead Rooms, the largest public rooms in the city, which would be advertised in the press. These would have been a way of earning supplementary income for those involved, one of whom, in June 1854, was Walter Montgomery, who became a well-known Shakespearean tragedian. His own life ended in tragedy when he shot himself in 1871, one day after his marriage.

On a similar occasion, Marie's youngest sister Blanche also featured. She clearly had some musical talent, as she was billed as 'The Infant Pianiste, only 7 years of age', when she appeared with Marie and some others in a 'Dramatic and Musical Entertainment' in August 1856. As part of this 'Entertainment', which the Lord Mayor had promised to patronise, it was also announced that 'Miss Wilton [Marie] will deliver an Address to her Friends'. What this 'address' consisted of is hard to visualise. Maybe it was some kind of a recitation; an address from a seventeen-year-old does not sound like much of an attraction.

Chute's theatre served as a kind of stage-school for many young actors and actresses who had to play every kind of part from farcical comedy to high tragedy, melodrama and pantomime. Among the young actors who worked there were several whose names were one day to become extremely well-known, including Kate and Ellen Terry, Madge Robertson (later Mrs Kendal), and a young actor called Charles Coghlan.

BROADMEAD - ROOMS.
Under the distinguished Patronage of
SIR J. K. HABERFIELD, KT.
MISS MARIE WILTON,
Of the Theatres Royal, Bath and Bristol, has the honour to announce that, at the suggestion of her Friends, she is induced to present an Entertainment on
TUESDAY EVENING, June 20, 1854,
Consisting of a Series of
DRAMATIC READINGS, and a CONCERT,
On which occasion she has retained the valuable Services of
Mr. WALTER MONTGOMERY,
Tragedian, of the Bath and Bristol Theatres, who will Read and Recite from several Popular Authors, positively FOR THIS NIGHT ONLY. Several talented Vocalists of Bristol have also, in the kindest manner, tendered their Services.
Pianist, Mr. CHARLES CAIRD.
Doors open at Half-past Seven, and commence at Eight o'clock. Reserved Seats, 1s. 6d.; Front Seats, 1s.; Back Seats, 6d. Tickets to be had of Miss WILTON, 19, King-street; Mr. HOLESGROVE, Drawbridge; and of Mr. WALTER MONT-GOMERY, 36, Prince's street.
Full particulars in Small Bills.

from the **Bristol Mercury,** *17 June 1854*

It was in Bristol that Marie, who was later to concentrate entirely on comedy and burlesque, played her last serious dramatic roles. She played Ophelia more than once, and also the tragic heroine Adrienne Lecouvreur. But comedy was already beginning to emerge as her strongest suit. A couple of the boxes at Bristol were then described as the 'Bachelors' Boxes', from where high-spirited young men would often call out to the stage during a performance. One day Marie was performing a song called 'Buy a Broom', made hugely popular in 1826 by Madame Vestris, the first star of burlesque, who performed the song both as a solo and as a duet with the comic actor John Liston[*]. There were prints made of the pair of them singing the song – with Liston in drag – of which there are copies both in the British Museum and the Victoria and Albert, as well as Staffordshire figures of Madame Vestris as the broom girl.

'Buy of the wandering Bavarian a broom. Buy a broom! Buy a broom!' sang Marie.

A voice called out from the Bachelors' Box, 'How much?'

Quite undisturbed by the interruption, Marie held out one of her brooms, and called back to him, 'Six and eightpence to you, sir.'

Sometimes comedy might be taken a step too far, as when the Bristol company was touring in a country theatre somewhere in the southwest. A

---

[*] John Liston, c.1776-1846, one of the most popular comic actors of his time.

25

well-known 'star' actor was engaged to play the main character 'Claude' in Bulwer Lytton's popular play *The Lady of Lyons*. The actress who specialised in old ladies' parts, and who was supposed to play Claude's widowed mother, was taken ill, and at short notice Marie was told she would have to do the best she could with the part. She was given a grey wig and a mob cap, neither of which fitted properly. These immediately began to slip and the audience began to titter. Someone in the wings stage-whispered at her, 'Put your cap on straight - it's all on one side.' In her efforts to correct it, Marie disturbed her wig even further and it became all lop-sided. The audience began laughing out loud. When the star actor made his appearance Marie's efforts to portray an old lady, with her young voice addressing him as 'my son', so enraged him that he could scarcely say his lines. When the first scene was over, he demanded an explanation and declared that the whole piece was destroyed. When Marie did her best to explain, he said, 'Well, it is not your fault. But surely they could have got someone to look more like my mother. I am dreading the next scene.' Somehow they got through the rest of play, until they came to a supposedly moving moment when Marie spoke the words: 'Claude, Claude, you will not desert your poor old mother!' At this the audience fell into an uproar of laughter. Nothing more could be heard and 'Claude', embracing his 'poor old mother', gave her an angry shove, dislodging the wig and cap entirely. The curtain fell amidst shouts of laughter and curtain calls for 'Claude's mother' − to which the mortified Marie did not respond.

Charles Dillon[*] was a well-known actor who had worked extensively both in London and in all the major cities in Britain. He came to Bristol to star in *Belphegor; or the Mountebank and his Wife*, the melodrama that Marie had first appeared in four years earlier, in Edinburgh. The diminutive Marie was once again to play Belphegor's young son, Henri, whose mother has deserted her family. In rehearsal Dillon, as Belphegor, raged and wept inconsolably for the loss of his wife, with exaggerated dramatic gestures to illustrate his distress, while Marie grieved in a more restrained but natural way, sobbing pathetically and shedding real tears. Dillon, concerned that she might upstage him, objected, telling Marie that she should fall on her knees and, with her hands clasped in prayer, appear overwhelmed with *silent* grief. 'But Mr Dillon,' protested Marie, 'I can't *imagine* my tears – I must mean it and cry in earnest.' 'You can mean your grief, but keep it to yourself,' Dillon insisted. Marie pleaded that if his performance was powerful enough really to make her weep, surely this

---

[*] Charles Dillon, 1819-81, actor and theatre manager whose London career was only moderately successful. He later spent many years touring the USA, Canada and Australia.

could only enhance the drama. She begged Dillon to let her play the scene her way in rehearsal the next day, when Mr Chute would be there: *he* could decide which way was best. The next morning Marie's performance reduced Chute himself to tears, and so, with everyone weeping copiously, her interpretation of the part was agreed.

When the piece was finally performed to an audience it was to rapturous applause. 'Dillon's "Belphegor" was a truly fine performance,' wrote Marie in her memoirs. It also seems that he was big enough to admit that her rendering of Henri did indeed enhance his performance and following *Belphegor* he told her that if he should ever be in charge of a London theatre he would send for her. Not long afterwards, Charles Dillon did become manager of one of the most important theatres in London, the Lyceum. True to his word, he wrote to Marie inviting her to come and join his company. Daunted at the prospect of going to London, Marie approached Chute and told him that for even a small increase in her salary she would really prefer to stay with him in Bristol. But telling her that he believed she had a great future ahead of her and that she was now more than ready for London, Chute encouraged her to accept Dillon's offer. When they parted he urged her to have courage and belief in herself. He also promised her that if she failed in London, or if she was really unhappy there, she could return to him in Bristol.

With that reassurance Marie Wilton, aged just seventeen, left the security of Bristol behind her and set off for London in 1856.

2

TOUJOURS CUPID

For the seventeen-year-old Marie Wilton, London in 1856 was a terrifying place and at first she found the capital overwhelming. Her description of her first impressions, written more than thirty years later, could easily apply to central London today:

> How big London seemed to me! I felt as if the houses were going to fall on us; and in the vast city, with its turmoil, there seemed to be no room for me. A restless, crowded, get-one-before-the-other city, I felt it an impertinence to try for a place in its rushing stream of humanity.

Marie had arrived in the London of Charles Dickens and Henry Mayhew. Little had changed from the city roamed by Fagin's boys in *Oliver Twist*, and even less from Henry Mayhew's *London Labour and the London Poor*, which had first appeared in book form just a few years earlier, having originated as articles in the *Morning Chronicle*. The main thoroughfares of the West End were often gridlocked with horse-drawn vehicles of every kind, even harder to extricate from traffic jams than modern motor traffic – it is hard for horses pulling a jumble of carts, carriages, cabs and omnibuses, all mixed up with small hand-drawn carts, to reverse out of trouble. Only the main roads and the smart streets and squares where the rich lived were kept relatively clean. The cobbled back-streets were filthy, covered with a mixture of refuse and horse manure; ragged boys earned pennies sweeping important crossing points, hoping for tips from pedestrians; everywhere else you had to pick your way around as best you could. There was constant noise: along with the rattle and clang of harness, hooves and metal-rimmed wheels, drivers would be shouting at each other and street vendors crying out their wares; small workshops operated noisily day and night; barrel-organs and other street entertainers would contribute to the din. Delivery boys would rush by on foot only to be shouted at by the pedestrians they jostled from the wooden pavement into the filthy gutter; beggars called out for small change. After dark many thoroughfares could be dangerous places: away from the gas-lit main roads, the side streets and alleyways were the haunt of pickpockets, robbers, prostitutes and beggars. A snowy scene and backdrop from Dion Boucicault's play *The Streets of London* at the Princess's Theatre presents a vivid impression of a busy London street of the time. The view of St Martin-in-the-Fields on the left and Trafalgar Square and Nelson's column beyond is quite recognisable today. Representing a smart part of London, the set was brightly lit with real gas street lamps. A group of 'peelers' is marching past the shops on the right and a small boy turns a cartwheel alongside them. Street sellers are doing a brisk trade: the knife-grinder is busy at his wheel and the hot chestnut seller at his brazier; a woman sells bowls of hot soup while a shifty-looking man tries to entice smartly-dressed passing gentlemen to take what might be a playbill.

engraving, from the **Illustrated Times,** *of a scene from*
Dion Boucicault's play,* The Streets of London, *1864

Georgiana Wilton accompanied her daughter to London and they found lodgings south of the river in Lambeth, then as now a more inexpensive area to live than in the centre of town. From there they could walk across the old Waterloo Bridge to the Lyceum Theatre, in Wellington Street, just off the Strand, where it still stands today. Robert

Wilton remained in Bristol and Marie's sisters stayed with him while their mother was getting Marie settled in London. Emma and Ida, who would soon follow Marie to London, must have taken much of the responsibility for looking after the three younger sisters.

The Lyceum was by far the biggest and grandest theatre that Marie had ever seen and the resident company much larger than any she had worked with. She was accompanied to her first day of rehearsals – her first part was once again to be Henri in *Belphegor* – by her mother but still she felt intimidated by her reception at the theatre. The other players did nothing to make her welcome and indeed appeared positively unfriendly to the young girl from the provinces.

> When I went to the first rehearsal everything around me looked so grand that I felt quite ashamed of my poor country clothes. Some of the people looked me up and down with a kind of sneer, wondering, I dare say, where I and my clothes had been picked up, and as if it were presumption for me to stand too near them. I had never seen so many people all at once upon a stage before; but I felt as solitary and chilled as a room in winter seems without a fire .... I felt nervous and shy, and kept close to my mother's side, who every now and then whispered some tender words to give me courage.

Marie's starting salary at the Lyceum was £3 per week, even in those days a small sum for two people to live on in London, and on their way home after this alarming first rehearsal she remarked to her mother that the other actresses must all be on much higher salaries than she was, as they were all so well dressed. Georgiana pointed out that they were established, popular actresses and that one day Marie herself would surely be earning similarly large amounts. When that time came she must not forget this day, and if she should see a poorly-dressed new arrival standing shyly to one side, hoping for a friendly face and a kind word, she was to remember how she had been treated herself and welcome the newcomer into the company. It was not only her fellow-actresses who were unfriendly. The stage-manager at the Lyceum, whom Marie herself forgivingly declined to name, was then a man called Barrett. He was positively hostile to her, finding fault with her at every opportunity. At that time the stage-manager's position was second only to the manager's, equivalent to that of the director today, as he controlled the entire production of the play that was being rehearsed. Georgiana had known Barrett some years before in the provinces, when he had been going through some difficult times. The Wiltons, although desperately hard-up themselves, had assisted him financially and Georgiana had also helped him during an illness. She suggested that if Marie let him know who her parents were, then he would surely be kinder to her. However, he clearly did not want to be reminded of the past, and his treatment of Marie remained unchanged.

A leading member of the company was John Lawrence Toole, who was to become a lifelong friend and the best-known comic actor in London. Born in 1832, just seven years before Marie, he became almost a father-figure to her at the Lyceum. He had also started out in the provinces, making his first London appearance in 1854. Toole was always kind and encouraging to Marie: during rehearsals, if she appeared despondent, or upset at her treatment by the stage-manager, he would attempt to cheer her up with a joke and once whispered to her, 'Twenty pounds a week .... I think, after the first appearance.'

For a while during the rehearsals Barrett was off sick for a few days. The atmosphere lightened and everything went smoothly and enjoyably. Marie hoped that his illness would keep him out of the way at least until after the first night. But this was not to be and he soon returned. She confessed that she was 'uncharitable enough to own that never was I so sorry to hear of a recovery.' But the next time he raised his voice to find fault with Marie Charles Dillon himself came to her rescue and things improved for her a bit.

Then, at short notice, Marie had to learn another part. Every bill at that time had at least three pieces playing on the same night, so that an evening at the theatre was something like an evening in front of the television. On the same bill as *Belphegor* there was to be a burlesque by William Brough called *Perdita, or the Royal Milkmaid*, based on the legend that had inspired Shakespeare's *A Winter's Tale*, with Toole playing the part of Autolycus. The actress who was to play Perdita at the Lyceum had been taken ill and Dillon told Marie that he would like her to take over the part.

Victorian burlesque had now reached its heyday. It had its roots in the satires that had flourished in the seventeenth and eighteenth centuries, such as Buckingham's *The Rehearsal* (1671), which mocked John Dryden and the heroic drama of the Restoration period, and Sheridan's *The Critic* (1779), which made fun of the sentimentalities of his day. Consisting of parody and satire, complete with popular musical numbers and much risqué cross-dressing and double-entendre, it was usually based on contemporary opera or drama, or on familiar classics, myths and legends. Nineteenth-century burlesque, far from being dismissed as superfluous to the legitimate drama, was probably the most widely enjoyed form of popular entertainment. By the mid-nineteenth century burlesque had lost its critical edge and was becoming less subtle. Complete with appalling puns and verse, it aimed to attract larger, less educated, audiences, while at the same time continuing to appeal to more sophisticated tastes. Today, although it appears excessively lightweight and trivial, it is considered significant enough to be the subject of academic research by theatre historians, with several theses written on the subject. It would gradually go out of fashion during the second half of the nineteenth century following the rise of the music-halls, while becoming hugely popular in America, its female performers eventually evolving into the raunchy stars of burlesque as it is known today.

Brough's *Perdita* is regarded by modern scholars of Victorian burlesque as a charming parody of Charles Kean's production of *A Winter's Tale* at the Princess's Theatre that same year, 1856, in which Shakespeare's original had been much corrected to iron out the bard's historical inaccuracies. Marie had just a few days to learn the words and the music. What was more, she was expected to provide her own dress out of the meagre £3 a week that she had not yet even begun to receive. Knowing that she had nothing suitable in her basic wardrobe of costumes, she went home in tears to her mother who reassured her, saying that she would make a dress for Marie, which she did by cutting up one of her own. The next problem arose when Marie was told that Perdita must wear pink boots, with stockings to match. First she tried a shop that specialised in making boots for the stage and, knowing that almost nothing would be left out of her first pay packet when it eventually arrived, ordered a pair, only to be told that as they did not know her she would have to pay in advance – impossible, as Marie and Georgiana between them had not nearly enough ready money to pay up front. They then walked around every bootmaker's shop they could find: at each they were told that boots could not be made in time. They were heading home in despair when they passed a dingy shop in the Waterloo Road. In its window was what Marie described as a pair of 'great heavy ugly boots big enough for me to live in and receive friends'. Georgiana said they should not bother with such an unpromising place, but Marie insisted on one last try. In she went and asked the shopkeeper if he had such a thing as a pair of pink silk boots. Laughing, he replied, 'No, we don't make your fancy fal-lals here in the Waterloo Road.' Marie had turned to leave, when a woman's voice called out from a back room: 'Stop miss. Did I 'ear yer say yer wanted pink boots? I believe I 'ave the very thing. There was a girl what was to 'ave acted a fairy at the Surrey* more'n a year ago. The poor little thing took ill, and 'er mother put 'er into an 'orspital. I bought all 'er things from 'er, and sold them – all but the boots, for they was too small for anyone. 'Ere, Billy! Bring them pink boots down: they're up on the top shelf in the cupboard. They'll be too small for you though, miss.' At last Marie's luck was in. The boots fitted her own small feet as if they had been made for her. She waited anxiously while the woman thought about a price, then

---

* The Surrey was a large theatre south of the river in Blackfriars Road, famous for melodramas and circus. It was burnt down in a fire in 1865 and rebuilt, but was finally closed and demolished in the twentieth century.

she said, 'You can 'ave 'em for three-and-sixpence.'

With her Perdita costume sorted out, Marie went happily over the bridge to rehearsals the next morning – but things did not go well. She knew the music and sang it correctly, but her small voice could scarcely be heard above the noise of the large band accompanying her. Her *bête-noir*, the stage-manager, stopped her: 'You don't call that singing, do you? Louder! Louder!' She tried again, and again, until her voice began to give out. Her lack of experience and untrained singing voice were letting her down badly and Barrett was furious; the crosser he got the more distressed Marie became and less capable of singing as he wished her to. 'If you don't sing better than this,' he snapped, 'you must be taken out of the part.' This caused a flutter of excitement among the other girls who were hanging around, each of them hoping that Marie would be sacked and that she would get the coveted part of Perdita.

At this point the musical director, seeing how upset Marie was, stepped in. Stopping the band, he demanded of Barrett, 'Are you the musical director here, sir, as well as the stage-manager? Allow me to know whether Miss Wilton is right or wrong. Her voice is not strong, but it is true to time and tune; I wish I could say the same for everyone.' There were murmurs of agreement from the orchestra. 'Now, Miss Wilton, you are too much distressed to sing again this morning, so we'll try again tomorrow and when your part comes, the band shall be more *piano*, and then you will be heard beautifully.'

On the opening night, in September 1856, the house was full. Marie Wilton's first appearance on a London stage was with Charles Dillon as Belphegor, Toole in his comic role, and Marie as the boy, Henri. Toole had the audience shouting with laughter before he had been on stage for more than a few minutes. Marie's moving scene with Dillon came towards the end of the first act and when the curtain fell there was tremendous applause.

Dillon and the hugely popular Toole took many curtain calls while Marie waited in the wings, hoping that Dillon might call her to join him in front of the curtain. But her enemy the stage-manager spotted her and packed her off to the dressing-rooms. Then a call-boy came running along shouting for Marie: Mr Dillon had sent for her. She ran back to the stage from where she could hear her name being called by the audience: 'Miss Wilton! Miss Wilton!' She was pushed out alone to the front, where she curtseyed several times before slipping back behind the curtain. The audience continued shouting for her to come back, but Barrett was having no more of it and grabbing her by the arm he insisted, 'That will do; we shall never get the piece over if this goes on.' She ran back to the dressing-room where Georgiana was waiting for her and flung her arms joyfully around her mother's neck. Among the audience was a young

33

lawyer of around twenty-five called Thomas Edward Crispe. More than half a century later he wrote his memoirs, *Reminiscences of a K.C.*, in which he described Marie's 'Henri' in *Belphegor* as 'an exquisitely pathetic performance'.

Perdita followed: 'I looked very nice, I think, with my hair hanging loosely over my shoulders, a pretty wreath of blush roses, a charming little dress of white cashmere, which my mother made, a bunch of roses at my waist, pale pink silk stockings, and *the boots!'* A small '*carte-de-visite*' photograph was produced of Marie as Perdita. Measuring approximately 2½ by 4 inches, *cartes-de-visite* were, despite their name, never intended as calling cards. They were produced as 'collectables'. Millions were printed and the collecting of them became known as 'cardomania'. They would be given as gifts, were widely swapped among friends, and many a Victorian parlour would contain an album full of the little cards depicting well-known people. Sometimes the cards were hand-tinted and there was at least one print where whoever did the tinting had clearly not seen the show, as Marie's white dress is coloured pink and her boots are – *blue.*

carte-de-visite of Marie Wilton as Perdita,
probably the earliest known photograph of her

Perdita went well, even the singing, Marie's songs and others from the show becoming so popular they were soon being played on barrel-organs all over London. At the end, Marie was again called for by the audience and flowers were thrown onto the stage for her, enough 'to fill my little milk-pail'. These flowers were certainly an improvement on herrings. Marie was elated by the reception she had received from her first London audience, but she was anxious about what the notices might say, as some of the other girls in the company warned her that the critics would often condemn what the audience had loved. But when she arrived at the theatre the next day she was surrounded by people congratulating her. Her friend the musical director passed her a handful of newspapers, saying, 'Here, my dear; take these and be happy.' She was especially pleased by her notice in the *Morning Post*:

> Miss M. Wilton is a young lady quite new to us, but her natural and pathetic acting as Henri, the son of Belphegor, showed her to possess powers of no ordinary character, which fully entitled her to the recalls she obtained at the end of the second act. She appeared also as Perdita, the Royal Milkmaid, and made still further inroads in the favour of the audience .... she is a charming debutante, who hails from Bristol. She sings prettily, acts archly, dances gracefully, and is withal of a most bewitching presence.

Despite her good notices, Marie's months at the Lyceum were not happy and she would have been totally miserable had it not been for the kindness of John Lawrence Toole and of the musical director, who helped her develop her singing abilities. She was cast in several more plays and burlesques but, as she herself acknowledged, with only moderate success, until she once again had the good fortune to land an important understudy part. Charles Dillon and his wife were appearing in *Virginius,* a melodramatic tragedy by James Sheridan Knowles[*], based on a story, told by Livy, of a noble Roman soldier who killed his own daughter in order to save her from a fate worse than death. Dillon's wife, Clara, who was playing the daughter, Virginia, was taken ill and Marie, as her understudy, had to take over at short notice. Fortunately the part was not too demanding (a review of a later production describes the role of Virginia as making '…no demand on the powers of passion or tragic force') and Marie felt pleased that she got through it quite well.

Charles Dillon was happy with Marie's performance, saying that she had 'a pretty, natural style of acting'. He added, 'I should like to see you one day play Juliet.' She told him that she had in fact played Juliet when she was 'quite a child'. Dillon replied, 'Those are exhibitions I would

---

[*] James Sheridan Knowles, 1784-1862, an Irish dramatist who was a cousin of Richard Brinsley Sheridan. *Virginius* was first produced in Glasgow in 1820 and later that year the title role was played by Macready at Covent Garden.

rather not witness; I am glad I was not present!' Marie was hurt by this remark at the time but later realised how right he was: roles such as Juliet, however young she might have been, demanded a mature experience of the theatrical craft that juveniles could rarely grasp.

Marie Wilton's time at the Lyceum was to last less than a year. Benjamin Webster, who was then leasing the Adelphi, offered her £5 a week to join his company, an offer that she gladly accepted. However, this was not to start for three months so she was able to accept another offer that came her way. John Baldwin Buckstone[*], the famous and popular manager of the Haymarket Theatre, offered her a short engagement there which filled the gap nicely. Buckstone was at this time one of the best-known figures of the London theatre scene, as an actor, a manager and as a dramatist. (He was the author of the melodrama *The Green Bushes* in which Marie had often played in her childhood.) He was also a popular comic actor: just the sound of his voice off-stage before his entrance would have the audience laughing even before he appeared.

The production Marie had been engaged to play in at the Haymarket was called *Atalanta and the Golden Apples,* in which she was to play the part of Cupid, the god of love. *Atalanta* was an extravaganza based on a story by Ovid. Extravaganza, like burlesque, was a popular form of entertainment that flourished in the mid-nineteenth century. It was closely related to pantomime, being usually based on myths or fairy stories, and featured spectacular costumes and musical numbers.

Needless to say, Marie was not sorry to leave the Lyceum. The Haymarket was a complete change: she was met with encouragement and friendship from everyone and the stage-manager there was quite the opposite of her old enemy, Barrett, at the Lyceum, encouraging her in every way possible. She also scored a real success as Cupid, including the musical aspects of the part, as her singing voice was growing stronger, perhaps along with her confidence. During her time at the Haymarket, Marie ran into Barrett. With a wide smile he greeted her effusively and held out his hand – which she declined to take. With all the dignity she could muster and drawing herself up to her full five feet, she said to him, 'Sir, you almost broke my heart at a time when I sorely needed help and support; now that I am successful, and beyond your reach, you can offer me your hand in friendship. I refuse to take it.' He laughed and replied, 'Oh, my dear little God of Love, don't be severe.' Years later Marie wrote, 'I have long ago forgiven, but have not forgotten him.'

Not long after she arrived in London Marie met, one more time, the soldier she had loved in Bristol. The circumstances of their meeting again

---

[*] John Baldwin Buckstone, 1802-97, theatre manager and much-loved comic actor. He also wrote many plays.

were decidedly theatrical. Not long after she arrived in London, Marie was walking along Regent Street, where there was a marble workshop, with headstones and other monuments displayed in its window. She had paused to look at this window when she heard a voice behind her speak her name. It was her captain. He told her that after she had rejected him he had married a wealthy widow, who had since died. 'I am rich now and can return to my old young love. I wonder if my little Juliet loves me still?' Then, out of his pocket, he produced her pearl necklace, just as she had last seen it, still with the knot she had tied in it to stop the last of the beads from falling off.

The captain was shortly to sail to India and, before he left, he called to ask Marie's mother's permission for them to correspond and then to marry on his return to England in a year's time. Georgiana reluctantly agreed, secretly hoping that something would happen to prevent him from ever returning. When he departed he swore that he would never part with Marie's broken necklace. She wrote to him by every mail for six months and every return mail brought a letter from India. Then one day the expected letter did not arrive. The next mail from India came, and the next – still no letter. Georgiana, sad at her daughter's distress but secretly relieved, said it was no more than she had expected: 'Ah! The old, old story ....' After a while a heartbroken Marie began to believe her mother must be right. 'He had seemed to be my guiding star ever since I was a little girl and all my first and purest love was his. Oh, it was dreadful to bear!'

Some weeks later Marie was once again walking along Regent Street and paused at the marble workshop, remembering how they had met there. In the window, she saw a large white headstone. Engraved on it were the words: 'Sacred to the Memory of Captain ------ who died suddenly at Kurrachee.'*

A date was given, but Marie did not reveal this, as she never revealed either his identity or any fact that could lead to it. Devastated she hurried home, where she found her mother, with a letter that had arrived that day from a fellow-officer. The captain had died soon after writing his final letter to Marie and his friend had found her letters among his papers. The broken pearl necklace had been buried with him. The headstone must have been on display while waiting to be shipped out to India.

A problem that many attractive young actresses have often been faced with, and probably always will, is unwelcome pursuit by obsessive and increasingly persistent admirers – stalkers, as they would be called today. A deeply disturbing episode occurred during Marie's short time at the

---

* *Kurrachee*: an old Anglicised spelling for Karachi, then in India, now in Pakistan.

Haymarket, when she attracted the attention of a young man who began bombarding her with letters of admiration, accompanied by posies of flowers which he demanded she wear. Hoping he might then leave her alone, she did eventually go on stage one evening with the flowers attached to her dress and nothing more was heard of the young man for the next two weeks. Marie hoped that her unwelcome fan was gone for good. But one night, following the performance, Marie received an alarming letter from him. He wrote that as she had worn his flowers once, this proved that she must care for him. He went on: 'I shall be here again tomorrow night, and if you do not then wear the bouquet I shall send you, I shall wait outside the stage-door, and as you pass me in your cab, I shall shoot you dead.' A terrified Georgiana insisted on accompanying her daughter to the theatre the next night, and they were advised to leave the theatre by the front entrance rather than by the stage door; meanwhile the stalker would be watched out for and arrested if he was indeed armed. However, there was no sign of him that night and Marie and her mother arrived home safely thinking the whole thing must have been some kind of a hoax.

A few days later, a worried-looking woman called at their lodgings asking to see Marie. She had a sad tale to tell: she was a widow and her twenty-one-year-old son was Marie's pursuer. The mother had become increasingly anxious about her son's recent behaviour: he would pace up and down in his room at night, talking to himself. While he was out one day, she had gone into his room and found a note threatening Marie's life. That night she had locked him into his room and sent for a doctor who declared that he was insane. However, the young man had insisted that if Marie were to tell him in person that she could never care for him, then he promised he would never trouble her again. His mother begged Marie to see him, in the company of his doctor. Marie reluctantly agreed, but only if her own mother was present as well. A day or two later the young man and his mother arrived, accompanied by a doctor. Marie described him: he was a 'pale, fair-haired young man, with a very freckled face and odd, light-blue eyes, which he fixed on me the moment he entered the room, and never took them away until he left the house.' She was terribly frightened by him.

The doctor asked Marie to tell him about the notes and flowers that had been sent to her and as she spoke with him Marie could hear the young man muttering to himself. 'I could not injure that which I loved,' she heard him say. Then the doctor said that his patient had agreed that if he heard from Marie's own lips that she could never love him, he promised he would never trouble her again. Marie said firmly, 'I can never care for this gentleman, and I ask him to trouble me no further.' Crossing the room to stand in front of Marie, the young man stared at her wildly for a moment and then he rushed out of the house and vanished in the direction

38

of Waterloo Bridge. To Marie and Georgiana's relief the others hurried away after him. Shortly afterwards Marie received a message from the mother informing her that her son had been confined in an asylum. Clearly he was seriously mentally ill.

But that was not the end of the story: many months later they heard that the young man's doctors had decided that he was well enough to be released from the asylum and his family had packed him off to Australia accompanied by a minder. While at sea, he had thrown himself overboard and drowned. Years later, in telling the story of her stalker, Marie wrote that 'I often wondered whether his inherent madness or *my beauty(!)* was the cause of this sad episode. After .... several references to my looking-glass, I concluded that it must have been the former.'

In the autumn of 1857 Marie Wilton took up her engagement at the old Adelphi Theatre, a small house in the Strand, then under the management of the celebrated Benjamin Webster and Celine Celeste, always known as Madame Celeste. The Adelphi had first opened in 1806 and was named after the Adam brothers' elegant 18th-century riverside buildings opposite, the word 'Adelphi' coming from the Greek word for 'brothers'. Webster and Madame Celeste had been in management together, and living together, for some years. Celine Celeste was born in Paris in around 1811 and started out as a dancer before becoming an actress. She then came to England, making her first London appearance at the old Queen's Theatre in Tottenham Street in 1831. She was of striking appearance, with dark hair and black eyes. Parts were often written for her that incorporated the strong French accent that she never lost, and in 1860 she created the part of Madame Defarge, knitting away at the foot of the guillotine, in the first dramatized version of *A Tale of Two Cities*. Benjamin Webster was born in 1798. He ran away from home to become an actor when he was seventeen, playing in theatres all over England, as a 'walking gentleman'. He arrived in London in 1818, and at the same time began writing plays. In 1837 he took over the Haymarket, turning it into one of the leading theatres of London. In 1844 he also took on the lease of the Adelphi, putting Madame Celeste in charge. Webster joined her there in 1853, John Baldwin Buckstone going to the Haymarket.

At the Adelphi, once again Marie found herself in a well-established company, but there was not a lot for her to do there. She was given several small parts but, following her success during her short time at the Haymarket, she was now full of ambition and felt frustrated to find herself spending much of her time standing around in the wings watching the rest of the company rehearse. She had parts in just two plays between October 1857 and Christmas. One of these was a dreadful-sounding vampire melodrama, called *The Legend of the Headless Man* by Buckstone, described by the critic E.L.Blanchard[*] as 'a very bad piece'. It ran for only eighteen performances.

Despairing of ever getting any better roles, Marie soon asked to be released from her contract. Webster, although always kind to her, insisted that she should stick to their agreement and that her opportunity would come if she would only be patient. It came when she was cast in the Christmas pantomime extravaganza. In *Harlequin and the Loves of Cupid and Psyche* the curtain rose on the gods of Mount Olympus indulging in a Bacchanalian orgy. Marie was the love god, Cupid, and his lover, Psyche, was played by Mary Keeley[*]. With elaborate special effects, they were magically transformed into Harlequin and Columbine. Transformation scenes in Victorian pantomime, with their use of complicated and dangerous machinery, were the high points of the show. The most famous and spectacular pantomimes of all were those produced at Drury Lane, with huge casts and dozens of stage hands to operate the machinery.

The two girls performed 'with great éclat', according to the *Standard.* Together they sang duets and danced a polka, a hornpipe, an Irish jig and a waltz, all choreographed by Madame Celeste. The show also featured a clown on a slack wire and performing dogs and monkeys, and the goddess Venus made her appearance in a golden coach pulled by doves. Unfortunately the first night, on the evening of Boxing Day, 1857, was something of a fiasco: much of the machinery that was supposed to produce the breathtaking special effects went badly wrong. 'Scarcely a trick was successful,' reported the *Standard*, 'while the scene-shifting was so badly managed that the scenes themselves were frequently mixed up in the most incongruous manner. The good-natured audience, however, bore all patiently, although in consequence of the delays caused by these mishaps, the performance was not got through till half-past twelve o'clock.' During February, fortunately after *Harlequin* had ended, Marie was very ill with congestion of the lungs. She believed this was caused by standing around in the cold, damp passages beneath the stage in her scanty costume in the middle of winter, while waiting to make her spectacular entrance via the star trap in the transformation scene. London's theatres were unhealthy, insanitary places, cold in winter and sweltering in summer. The toilet facilities were minimal, often with no more than a single lavatory for the entire cast and backstage staff. Marie's illness was serious and she was off work for several weeks, all through February. This

---

[*] E.L.Blanchard, 1820-89, theatre critic for newspapers and magazines, including *The Era*, the *Daily Telegraph* and the *Observer*. He also wrote numerous works for the stage, notably pantomimes for Drury Lane.
[*] Mary Keeley, 1831-70, was a daughter of Mary Ann Keeley, 1805-99, one of the most acclaimed actresses of the first half of the nineteenth century, who played 'Smike' in the first stage production of *Nicholas Nickleby*.

was no trivial matter, as an actor's salary ceased to be paid from the moment a manager was deprived of his or her services, and although Marie's sisters Emma and Ida had now joined her in London and were both working as actresses, the loss of Marie's earnings had significant impact on the family's finances. It is more than likely that they could not afford to send for a doctor, and relied on whatever medicines could be obtained over the counter.

Marie returned to work in March, but her engagement at the Adelphi ended at the beginning of June 1858, when Benjamin Webster closed the theatre for six months. He had the old theatre demolished and a beautiful new one built in its place, brilliantly lit with glass chandeliers fuelled by gas. Marie had now turned nineteen and felt she was no closer to realising her ambition of making a major impact on the London stage. Then her luck changed: she was offered an engagement at the Strand Theatre. She also had a very welcome offer from her old friend at Bristol, James Chute, to go there for a fortnight before starting at the Strand – to play Cupid! Her friends teased her, declaring that she must have been born with wings.

On her return from Bristol in 1858 Marie joined the company at the Strand Theatre. It had that same year been taken over and rebuilt by William Swanborough, the head of a large theatrical family that included his daughter, Ada, the leading actress in the company. The theatre stood on the south side of the Strand, where the disused Aldwych underground station now is. Marie was to work with the Swanboroughs, on and off, for more than six years and it was there that she made her name in London, quickly becoming one of the most popular stars in the burlesques for which the Strand Theatre was famous.

The two of Marie's sisters closest to her in age were also offered contracts at the Strand. Emma and Ida both appeared in several of the Swanborough productions in around 1858 and 1859. The three sisters appeared on the beautiful, large Strand playbills, printed on flimsy paper about 800cm long, as Miss E. Wilton, Miss Marie Wilton and Miss Ida Wilton, with Marie in better and larger parts than her sisters. There were usually at least four separate productions each evening, a mixture of farce, comedy and, most popular of all, burlesque. It would be a long evening, often not ending until around midnight. In most theatres tickets would be reduced to half price or less after nine o'clock.

In his *Reminiscences of a KC* the barrister Thomas Crispe, who memorably nicknamed Marie 'Toujours Cupid', has left an illuminating picture of the Wilton household at that time. As a young man, before settling down to his studies for the bar, Crispe attended an educational institute that put on lectures and occasionally, on a very limited budget, short runs of plays, using professional actors. Crispe was involved in the

41

casting of these, a task he seems to have relished, as 'the engagement of the actresses was always left to me'. It had been suggested to Crispe that Miss Emma Wilton, 'a young lady of promise', might be just the girl he was after for a particular role, and he was warned, 'But you'll have to see Marie.' Marie clearly acted as a sort of agent for her sisters.

Arriving at the Wilton lodgings, a modest house just south of the river in the Waterloo Bridge Road, Crispe was shown into a small parlour, sparsely furnished, but 'enlivened by a few ornaments and flowers', where he was welcomed by a young girl, Ida Wilton, who he guessed was about fifteen. She was in the middle of giving two children a piano lesson. Crispe was very taken with Ida, who was wearing 'a neat print dress, low at the shoulders as the fashion then was for young girls' and he considered that she must be 'the prettiest of the Wilton girls'. Ida told him that her sister Emma was out working, her mother was shopping and her father was not very well, but that 'Nothing can be done without Marie' who was also out. Crispe settled down to wait, happy to chat with Ida while her two small pupils were given a break from their music lesson.

When Marie arrived home, Crispe was even more smitten with her than he had been with Ida: 'I can only describe her as altogether charming …. her simple, piquant beauty, her vivacity, her archness, and the sparkle of her merry eyes.' But when they got down to the matter in hand he quickly discovered that she 'was a very good little woman of business'. The absent Emma was duly engaged, Marie negotiating a good wage for her sister. She then suggested that Ida would be ideal for another part in the play, but unfortunately that part had already been filled. When Crispe met Marie again, very many years later, he reminded her of this first meeting. Marie had forgotten it entirely but Crispe wrote that it was a 'compliment to her that it has remained fresh in my memory.'

London audiences in the mid-nineteenth century had a huge appetite for burlesque and the productions that were usually shown alongside it, such as farce and pantomime. In those days before cinema and television, theatres and music-hall were virtually the only forms of entertainment available to a wide public, apart from drinking in the thousands of public houses. More serious drama was produced in a few theatres, but for the most part audiences wanted light entertainment of the kind supplied by the Strand and many other theatres in London. One of the main attractions of burlesque, to the predominantly male audiences of the time, was that it provided them with a legitimate opportunity of getting a sight of attractive young women showing off their legs, in parts known as 'breeches roles' – or what Thomas Crispe and his friends called 'leg-pieces' – where the girls dressed as boys, in tights and short tunics, so that as much leg as possible was on display. These burlesque roles were gradually to evolve into the thigh-slapping principal boy of the twentieth- century pantomime.

As soon as she joined the Strand company it became clear to Marie that she was almost invariably to be cast as a 'burlesque boy'. She was not happy about this as she had hoped for more variety in the parts she would be given, but it was as a 'Queen of Burlesque' that she was at last to find fame in London. One of the first roles she was offered at the Strand was that of Pippo, in *The Maid and the Magpie*, written by Henry James Byron, a young man who was to become the most prolific writer of burlesques in London. He was distantly related to the great poet, Lord Byron, and took care to remind everyone of this fact. This makes him sound pompous, which he was not. Byron was later to figure significantly in Marie's career and he was distinctly upset when she made it clear that she did not like the part of Pippo, as she had had enough of playing boys. Byron insisted that he had written the part expressly for her, that there was no one else to whom he could entrust the part, and that this burlesque could make his name. Actually Marie had little or no say in the parts she was allocated by Miss Swanborough, and certainly could not afford to turn them down, so, of course, she played Pippo as was demanded of her.

The Maid and the Magpie was an instant success and as a result Marie was established overnight as one of the favourites of the London stage. The part of Pippo involved singing and dancing, and the songs became immediate hits. Encore would follow encore each night: the equivalent of the chart successes of their time, the songs from the burlesque could soon be heard from the barrel-organs played by buskers on the streets of London. It was also in *The Maid and the Magpie* that Marie came to the attention of no less a theatregoer than Charles Dickens, although she was unaware of this until many years later, when Dickens's friend and biographer John Forster wrote his *Life of Charles Dickens*, first published in 1882, twelve years after the novelist's death. In it Marie read for the first time of a letter the great writer had sent to his friend describing her performance:

I went to the Strand Theatre, having taken a stall beforehand, for it is always crammed .... to see *The Maid and the Magpie* burlesque there. There is the strangest thing in it that ever I have seen on the stage – the boy Pippo, by Miss Wilton. While it is astonishingly impudent (must be, or it couldn't be done at all) it is so stupendously like a boy, and unlike a woman, that it is perfectly free from offence. I never have seen such a thing. She does an imitation of the dancing of the Christy Minstrels – wonderfully clever – a thing that you *cannot* imagine a woman's doing at all; and yet the manner, the appearance, the levity, impulse and spirits of it, are so exactly like a boy, that you cannot think of anything like her sex in association with it .... I call her the cleverest girl I have ever seen on the stage in my time, and the most singularly original.

***Marie Wilton as Pippo in* The Maid and the Magpie**

Among the cast of *The Maid and the Magpie* was a young actress called Maria Ternan, one of the older sisters of Ellen 'Nelly' Ternan, with whom Marie had acted in *Atalanta and the Golden Apples.* It was around this time that Dickens first met and fell for Nelly and it is possible that he attended the Strand in her company to watch her sister, Maria, perform.

Another keen enthusiast for burlesque, particularly if Marie Wilton was in the cast, was Montagu Williams*, a barrister, magistrate and man about town. He wrote of visits to the Strand Theatre, 'then under the management of the beautiful Miss Swanborough,' to see the burlesques of 'that most popular author, my old friend Henry Byron .... The interpreter of his excellent lines was Marie Wilton, that perennial favourite, whose equal, in my humble opinion, we have never seen. I would travel any distance, or get up in the middle of the night, for the privilege of once more seeing her in *The Maid and the Magpie.*'

More breeches parts followed for Marie over the next few years at the Strand, in more and more burlesques, in which cross-dressing was the rule. The leading girls played the boys' parts and the male actors played the women. At the end of 1858 Ada Swanborough played the Earl of Leicester and Marie played Walter Raleigh in an extravaganza called

---

* Montagu Williams QC, 1835-92, tried a variety of careers before being called to the bar in 1862. He became a successful defence lawyer in criminal cases.

44

Kenilworth: 'very good and magnificently placed on the stage,' wrote E.L.Blanchard. However Marie did occasionally have girls' parts, as in 1859 when she played Juliet in what Blanchard considered a 'bad burlesque of *Romeo and Juliet*'. But it was mostly boys: she played Albert in *William Tell*, with her sister Ida also in the cast, and she was Gringoire in *Esmeralda*, a Byron burlesque of *The Hunchback of Notre Dame* – 'full of puns …. puns that are not very successful' wrote Blanchard. In 1861 she starred in the first pantomime production of *Aladdin*, also written by the prolific Henry James Byron. An actor called James Rogers, a backbone of the Strand, created the part of Widow Twankay[*] (the more familiar spelling came in later). The previous year Byron had also introduced the character of 'Buttoni' into *Cinderella*, who would later evolve into the familiar 'Buttons'. Montagu Williams enjoyed *Aladdin*: 'Who ever saw the equal of [Jimmy] Rogers as an impersonator of female characters? I remember laughing …. until my sides ached.'

In spite of her successes, Marie remained discontented, believing that authors and the public had come to think that she could only play boys. 'Why can't I be allowed to be a girl?' she complained bitterly to her mother. 'It's all very well to be a great favourite with the public, and to be told that I am so natural in a boy's dress. Well, if so, why was I not *born* a boy?' Her mother thought she should make the best of it. As she and Marie knew well, some very prominent actresses had made their names in burlesque, including, many years before, the famous Mrs Jordan[*], and, still well-remembered in the 1850s, Madame Vestris. By Marie's time, however, burlesque was already beginning to evolve into a more risqué form of show. Late in her life Marie commented that since those days, 'although [burlesque] may not have fallen off, certainly some of the dresses have, many of which might be described as beginning too late and ending too soon.' Montagu Williams also later regretted the passing of what he called 'true burlesque, not mere sketches, filled in with gags and pulled through by skirt-dancing and limelight.'

It was during her time at the Strand Theatre that Marie was twice forced, by major events in her domestic life, to take time out from her work. At the end of 1860 the Wilton family increased by one, when Marie gave birth to what was to be the first of two illegitimate children. Her baby girl, named Florence Ellen Blanche Baker Wilton, was born in Lambeth in December of that year. Marie, being the highest earner in the family, would undoubtedly have had to return to work as soon after the birth as

---

[*] 'Twankay' is an ancient kind of Chinese green tea.
[*] Dorothea Jordan, 1761-1816, a hugely popular actress, famed for her breeches roles. She became the long-term mistress of the Duke of Clarence, later King William IV, who was the father of ten of Dorothea's fourteen children.

possible, so it is interesting to speculate who might have taken care of her baby while she was at rehearsals most days and on the stage most nights. Maybe Georgiana Wilton cared for her first grandchild, but if this is the case then she and Robert failed to include the baby in their census return of 1861. It is also possible that the baby was fostered out. Little Florence did not live long, dying in 1862, before she was two years old. The address given for the child at the time of her interment at West Norwood Cemetery was Ashley Place, Westminster, the address of William Fletcher, who was some years later to become Ida Wilton's husband and where Ida herself may have already been living as 'Mrs Fletcher'. So it would appear likely that it was Marie's sister Ida who took care of the child, although she can have been no more than twenty herself.

Early in 1863 Marie was once again pregnant. At that time young actresses would work as long as they could through pregnancy, almost up to the time of the birth, and Marie would certainly have needed to keep working for as long as possible, although she would have had to wear looser costumes than usual. What is certain is that she could not have afforded to stop work as early as she might have wished and at a time when a 'confinement' meant literally that, with days of being confined to bed rest following the birth and some weeks of being treated as an invalid. Her second child, named Charles Edward Wilton, was born in St John's Wood in London on 20 October 1863, at the home of a Robert Faulkner, a portrait painter who lived there with his wife and their 15-year-old daughter. Faulkner must have been a relative of Marie's mother Georgiana, possibly the son of one of her two brothers, which would make him a cousin of Marie's. Soon after Charles's birth, *The Era*, an influential newspaper of the time that reported in depth on theatrical events and carried reviews of almost every production, London and provincial, ran a brief notice referring to 'the return of Miss Wilton' to the Adelphi, the reason for her absence being no more than hinted at.

Most of Charles Edward's early days are a mystery. Little is known of him until he was eight, when he was at a small boarding school in Marylebone. There is again the possibility that he was cared for by his grandmother, Georgiana, or possibly by one of Marie's sisters, or he might have been fostered out. What seems certain is that Marie herself could not have cared for him full-time.

Although Marie was now the highest earner in the Wilton family, her wages being more than she had ever earned before – up to nine guineas a week – she would not have been able to support so many of her family on her pay alone. Her father, Robert Wilton, was also finding work and it is known that the older girls were well established in their London stage careers. Emma married around the time that Charles Edward was born, near the end of 1863. She married well, becoming the wife of a young barrister with the surprising name of Francis Drake. The next sister, Ida, lived for some years as Mrs Fletcher, although she and William Fletcher did not actually marry until some years later, in 1874. Neither of these two sisters appear to have had any children of their own or, at any rate, none that survived infancy.

In her memoirs, written in her ultra-respectable late middle-age, Marie gives no hints as to who might have fathered either or both Florence or Charles; indeed she wrote not a word about either of them, of their births or their childhood, or indeed about their very existence. Any romantic involvements Marie had, she either doesn't mention, or she carefully relates them in parts of her story that would disguise any possible identity. It is possible that the children may have had different fathers – there is speculation on Charles's paternity in a later chapter – but the major challenge is to find even one man who was close to Marie at that time. Florence's fourth name, Baker, could be an indication as it would seem to be a surname, possibly that of the father, but no Baker can be identified as a possible candidate. There was an unidentifiable young man called Underwood who would occasionally call on her. A second cousin of Marie's, Charles William Wilton, kept a journal in which he mentions visiting his cousin at her home in July 1862. He wrote that 'poor little Marie Wilton had fallen down stairs and hurt her spine. The doctor's account is bad; poor girl.' Four days later Charles Wilton visited again, having heard that the doctor was unnecessarily pessimistic and that Marie was recovering well. 'Took Miss W. some small cigars one of which she smoked. Mr Underwood came in and had a pleasant evening.' In August cousin Charles wrote that he was 'sorry to learn that little MW has a bad cold and could not sing in a new piece brought out last Monday so the piece is put off for a week.' Five days later she was better and he was at last able to see her at the Strand, and again a couple of times in September, when he was able to write in his journal that he 'Went to Strand Theatre. Little Marie looks charming in her new piece of "Marriage at Any Price".'

It is possible, but unlikely, that this Charles Wilton was himself the father of one or both of the babies as he seems to have been very fond of his cousin Marie. He was just a couple of years older than Marie and the baby boy was named Charles – but this can be no more than speculation and Charles is not an unusual name. Also from his journal he is known to have been interested in another young woman at that time, also one of his cousins. Unfortunately only parts of his journal survive and there are large gaps in the vital months. Nothing more is known about who 'Mr Underwood' might have been. He must have been quite a close friend: for a pair of young men to visit a young woman alone in her rooms would indicate a degree of familiarity, and smoking was not something that any respectable young woman would do in public or in 'polite' company. A further name that has come to light, on a scrap – literally – of evidence, is

47

that of a Mr Alfred Shoolbred, a bachelor of around Marie Wilton's age, who was a member of a family of wealthy drapers who had a shop in the Tottenham Court Road. In the Harvard University Theatre Collection there is a photograph of Marie with a cryptic pencilled note on the back that reads: 'Marie Wilton. Kept by A.Shoolbred, who left her £30,000.' Shoolbred died in 1872, aged thirty-five, and there is no mention of Marie Wilton in his will, although it does confirm that he was extremely wealthy and left large sums to his family and servants. But Marie could have been his mistress at some stage, and he might well have supported her financially; he could have been the father of either or both of her illegitimate children. But if the astronomical sum of £30,000 – well over a million pounds in today's money – had ever come her way her financial worries would have been at an end.

Following her enforced break Marie returned to work as soon as she was able and eventually, after some more seasons at the Strand, and in a vain attempt to steer her career in another direction, she took the brave decision to turn down a part, no small thing in view of the terms of her agreement, under which a refusal to act any part that she should be offered meant that she forfeited her engagement. A burlesque called *The Miller and His Men* was to be revived; she had played in it before and she was offered a boy's part that she was familiar with. She declined to play the part – and she was duly sacked. Her entire income was instantly and totally cut off. This was a risk she must have considered worth taking as her father and young sisters were now working in London and bringing in some earnings for the family. Marie had refused the part in the hope and belief that she would soon be offered an engagement in comedy, but nothing was forthcoming and she soon had to give in and accept the offer of yet another burlesque boy in *The Heart of Midlothian*, based on Sir Walter Scott's novel, at the St James's Theatre in the spring of 1863. She was offered the part at ten guineas a week, a guinea more than she had ever been paid before. She bravely demanded fifteen pounds, a sum more than anyone else in the company was earning. The St James's must have really wanted her on board as eventually a compromise was reached: ten guineas would be written into her agreement, but there would be an extra five pounds in her pay packet. This was to avoid the arrangement coming to the attention of others in the company, whose wages were not so much.

Marie was delighted to find that her old friend Jimmy Rogers was also at the St James's and was also to be in *The Heart of Midlothian*. However, it was clear that Rogers was now a very sick man, dying of consumption – tuberculosis – a prevalent and much-dreaded disease at the time. Marie wrote that, 'I was shocked and pained when I held his poor, thin hand in mine, and gazed at his wan face and sunken eyes.' She watched him deteriorate and found each night's performance distressing. 'It was such a ghastly mockery to act in burlesque with a man who was dying before my eyes.' One night Marie found him coming down the stairs towards the stage with great difficulty, scarcely able to breathe. He put his hand on her shoulder and she helped him to a chair. He whispered to her, 'Marie dear, help me through it tonight …. I am not well – not at all well.' Somehow they made it through that night's performance, Marie, whenever possible, supporting him by holding his hand or by standing close to him so that he could lean on her. Towards the end 'his hands became cold …. and my heart was sick with fear.' Rogers's performance was as entertaining as ever, in spite of his illness. 'The audience little knew that they were laughing at a dying man. How I managed to get through it all I don't know …. I thought the end of the play would never come. He would allow no one but me to help him.' When the curtain finally fell he was taken home for the last time and his final words to his wife were, 'The farce is over – drop the curtain.' He was only forty-two. Very soon after his death Marie took part in a benefit held at Drury Lane on behalf of Rogers's widow. Her good friend John Lawrence Toole also took part, along with Benjamin Webster, the playwright Byron and Marie's young sister Augusta, who made her London stage debut on the occasion. The great theatre was packed with a fashionable audience. Half the pit was converted into stalls for the occasion, and the orchestra was moved to behind the scenes to allow still more seats to be installed. The mixed programme of entertainment continued until well after midnight and £350 was raised.

Following the engagement at the St James's, Marie returned for a while to the Adelphi, still under Webster's management, in a piece called *The Little Treasure*: she remarked that although she had finally managed to shake off the 'Cupid' label it was, greatly to her annoyance, to be replaced by 'Little'. She was cast as 'The *Little* Treasure,' 'The *Little* Savage,' 'The *Little* Devil,' '*Little* Don Giovanni.' She seemed doomed to be forever typecast. Then she was invited to rejoin the Strand company to play the hero in a Byron burlesque, *Orpheus and Eurydice*. As Marie put it herself, 'I was a beggar and could not choose.'

The Swanboroughs welcomed her back: it appears that although she had broken her previous contract they harboured no hard feelings. It was during her time back at the Strand that the tercentenary of Shakespeare's birth in 1564 was celebrated in theatres throughout the country. The Strand's additions to their regular fare of burlesque and farce were scenes from *A Midsummer Night's Dream* and the balcony scene from *Romeo and Juliet*, in which Marie appeared as Juliet – a girl at long last! Ada Swanborough herself played Romeo. Marie received many complimentary letters. One of these ironically, at the very moment when she hoped to be working herself free from the world of burlesque, came from W.S.Gilbert, himself an increasingly successful writer of the genre.

John Lawrence Toole at the Adelphi, 1850s; Marie Wilton, early 1860s

James Rogers in Esmeralda *at the Strand; Marie Wilton as Aladdin, 1861*

The Swanboroughs often sent their people on tour to different parts of the country. Early in 1862 Marie was at Cork, in Ireland, and by May she was at the Prince of Wales Theatre, Liverpool, where she again played 'Pippo' in *The Maid and the Magpie*, among other pieces. Her performance was eagerly anticipated and the theatre inserted an advertisement in the *Liverpool Mercury* advising the public that, 'In order to avoid the rush at the pay places during the engagement of Miss Marie Wilton' patrons were 'respectfully requested' to buy their tickets in advance at the box office. The theatregoers of Liverpool were not disappointed and the Prince of Wales Theatre had an unprecedented success on their hands.

PRINCE OF WALES THEATRE,
CLAYTON-SQUARE.

TRIUMPHANT SUCCESS
OF

MISS MARIE WILTON,

Who was received with the greatest enthusiasm, and her performance of her celebrated character of "PIPPO" excited the loudest Roars of Laughter ever heard within the walls of a Theatre.

from the **Liverpool Mercury,** *13 May, 1862*

On 20 May the *Mercury* reported that Marie's performances in Liverpool had been enthusiastically received: '... the production has been attended with much success, to which the introduction of the charming and really clever little actress Miss Marie Wilton has greatly contributed. This young lady is doubtless one of the best burlesque actresses of the day. There are a dash and a vivacity in her acting that cannot fail to please.' Towards the end of the Strand company's visit to Liverpool there was a benefit evening on Marie's behalf. 'Judging from the marks of favour with which she had been greeted nightly,' wrote the *Mercury*, 'there is sure to be a good house.' No doubt the benefit contributed a welcome sum to Marie's earnings.

It was on this visit to Liverpool that Marie Wilton, now twenty-three, first met a tall young actor who was by then part of the regular company at the Prince of Wales Theatre. He was Squire, then known as Sydney, Bancroft, who would one day become her husband.

3

BOYHOOD TO BANCROFT

On 14 May 1841 a boy who would one day become known as the actor Squire Bancroft was born in Rotherhithe, in the London docklands. The very first issue of *Punch* was published that same week – in years to come, he would say that 'the weeks of my age I can count every Wednesday by the number recorded on the cover of the most popular humorous journal in the world'. The boy was given the improbable names of Squire Bancroft White Butterfield, 'Squire' being the name of his paternal grandfather. Born in 1768, this earlier Squire Butterfield, a schoolmaster from Yorkshire, was at one time employed as a tutor at Chatsworth in Derbyshire to the heir of the Duke of Devonshire. He had three sons: he gave the first one the perfectly ordinary name of John, but being something of a Latin scholar he could not resist naming his second and third sons 'Secundus Bancroft' and 'Gulielmus Tertius'. Not surprisingly these two tended to use simpler names: Secundus was usually known by his middle name of Bancroft, and Gulielmus generally used his name's English translation – William.

Secundus Bancroft Butterfield and his wife, Julia, at first intended to name the first of their five children 'Julian', after his mother. However at the very last minute, when already in the church, they changed their minds and the baby was instead christened 'Squire' after his grandfather. His other two names were Bancroft, his father's middle name, and White, the maiden name of his paternal grandmother, Sarah Butterfield. Bancroft is a familiar Yorkshire surname, but there appear to be no Bancroft connections in the Butterfield family; maybe Secundus had a Bancroft as a godfather and he passed the name on to his own son. Two more sons followed, who also were also given curious names: Hastwell, born in 1843, and Lambeth, who was born in 1844 and died in the same year.

Although the Butterfields seemed to go in for strange names for their male children, the three girls who followed in 1845 and 1847 were, fortunately for them, blessed with the simpler names of Julia, Laura and Jane.

Bancroft Butterfield was an oil merchant, then as now a lucrative trade. He dealt chiefly in whale oil. Whale oil was used as a lubricant for locomotives and trains and for the many other mechanical needs of the industrial revolution. It was also used in lamps, but only by the more wealthy householders. Those who could not afford lamp oil generally used tallow candles, which gave off bad light – and they stank vilely. In contrast 'spermaceti', from the oil of the sperm whale, was clean and light. It didn't smell, but it was very expensive: in the early 1800s spermaceti oil was $2 a gallon, around $200 at today's prices. In 1880, a report in *The Era* described the lighting in the old Haymarket Theatre: 'Until 1843 [it] was illuminated only by oil and spermaceti candles, the former suspended in patent lamps round the upper circle, the latter fixed in cut glass chandeliers over the dress circle.' It was also used in cosmetics. The whaling industry then grew to meet the demand both for spermaceti oil and for the cheaper oils processed from the blubber which were used as lubricants for machinery. By the mid-1850s some five million gallons of spermaceti and ten million gallons of engine oil were produced annually. Oil was transported in barrels and was brought into the London docks for onward distribution – to this day the unit of measurement for oil supplies is a 'barrel'. The huge demand for their oil drove several species of whale to the brink of extinction, and had it not been for the development of petroleum products there would probably be even fewer whales left in the oceans today.

Butterfield appears to have been a successful oilman as he and his family were comfortably off, living in a house in Rotherhithe. This would have been an ideal location from which to conduct the oil trade: the docks and wharves of the Surrey side of the Thames were close at hand, with fanciful names such as Lavender Pond, Acorn Pond, Albion Dock, Quebec Pond, Canada Pond and the Great Surrey Dock. The Butterfields' house had an equally romantic name. It was called 'Crystal Cottage', which in spite of its name would have been a fairly substantial house – the word 'cottage' then was often applied to houses of some size, and even the Royal Family used it for their smaller houses. The household at Crystal Cottage was, in 1841, of a size to include, in addition to the family, two living-in servants – a general servant and a nursemaid for the baby, Squire – and there would certainly have been other non-resident servants as well. The Rotherhithe house was probably rented, although Butterfield owned some properties in London. In the memoirs he was to write many years later, Squire recalled a privileged early childhood. He had memories of his father on horseback, dressed in a fine blue coat with gilt buttons and a fancy cravat, and of an extensive garden, complete with greenhouses, where he remembered playing beneath a large mulberry tree. Indeed, the only disturbing memory he would recall of his very early years was of a strange fear he had of a large long-case clock that stood in the hallway: he would always hurry past it, fearful that someone was hidden inside waiting to leap out at him.

This privileged way of life was not to last: Secundus Bancroft Butterfield was stricken with a serious and painful illness, probably cancer, and he died in 1848, at the age of forty-nine, when his oldest son, Squire, was just seven years old. It was a bad year for the family, as within a few months both of Butterfield's parents died in Derbyshire.

There appears to have been no one to take over the Rotherhithe oil business following Secundus's death. In some trades, following the death of the breadwinner while in his prime, the wife would take over, often with considerable success. Julia Butterfield, however, was some twenty years younger than her husband and, accustomed to the life of a leisured lady, had taken no part in her husband's business during his lifetime. Neither of Butterfield's brothers came to Julia's help; anyway, they were hardly equipped to run an oil business. The eldest, John, had been ordained as a Church of England minister, while the younger brother, Gulielmus, was a rather dodgy, or maybe just unlucky, character, as in March 1848, the very year of his parents' and his brother's deaths, he was declared bankrupt; he may even have served a term in a debtors' prison. The hearing was at the Court of Bankruptcy in London, and records reveal that Gulielmus, who just a few years earlier had been living, along with his wife and their several children, in some style on Kew Green, eight miles south-west of London, was by then lodging at an inn in London's Oxford Street called 'The Victory'. His occupation was given to the court as a 'drug grinder and dealer in drugs, commercial traveller, victualler, dealer & chapman', a chapman being a travelling salesman of various kinds of goods. He appears to have recovered from his financial problems, as by 1851 he was back on the fringe of the oil business, as a commercial traveller in tallow and candles.

The widowed Julia had to make the best she could of the situation. The oil business was probably split up, or sold. However, a certain amount clearly remained from her late husband's fortunes, as the family appeared to remain comfortably provided for, if no longer wealthy: they never had to face real poverty, but they would have had to forego some of the luxuries they were accustomed to. Julia and her children left Rotherhithe and moved to Islington where she operated as an oil merchant herself for a time – probably on a much smaller scale. Julia remarried in 1858. Her new husband was Thomas Maltby, a widowed Islington grocer with several children of his own. Julia did not have long to enjoy her new life. Her health was poor and she died in 1861 at the age of only forty-two.

By then Julia had sent Squire and his brother Hastwell away from home to board at a private school in Wiltshire, in Stratton St Margaret, a village which is now part of Swindon. 'Private schools', as opposed to the great public schools, were small establishments, often run by clergymen, and the fees would have been considerably less than those for a public school. This school accommodated just seventeen little boys. There were three teachers, a Mr Large, the headmaster, assisted by his wife and his sister-in-law. Squire at the age of nine, was among the oldest boys, and Hastwell was eight. The youngest children at Mr Large's school were just six years old. Squire moved on to a school for older boys at about the age of twelve, and then attended a school in France for part of his teens, probably so that he would learn the language. In his memoirs, Squire recalled just one memory of this school: a frightful old woman would enter the boys' dormitory each morning at six o'clock and flinging the windows wide open, whatever the weather, and with a cry of 'Levez-vous, messieurs!' she would fill basins with icy water in which the boys had to wash. Shudder as he might at this memory, maybe he was lucky: if he had had the public school education that had been intended for him, there would have been full immersion in a cold bath, daily and in all weathers, along with the beatings and bullying described in Thomas Hughes's *Tom Brown's Schooldays*, published in 1857.

Squire recounted little of his schooldays, but he wrote descriptively of his impressions of the London streets of his boyhood:

The 'twopenny' and 'general' postmen, with their royal-blue or scarlet coats, looking, indeed, very like the guards of the stage-coaches, I remember quite clearly, as I do the policemen in their blue tail-coats, their hats with shiny tops and sides, their duck trousers, and white gloves. The foot-guards, clad in swallow-tails, with epaulettes and cross-belts, white trousers and giant bearskins (how often have their little effigies been bought for me in the Lowther Arcade!), I picture readily in Hyde Park, where then, at the keepers' lodges, Cockney boys and girls invested pennies in curds-and-whey or hardbake*. The Quakers in their quaint clothing I also recollect. I remember the boys who swarmed the chimneys and wore brass badges on their caps; the sweep's street-cry, the dustman's bell, the old-clothes man's husky call as he tramped along under the burden of his bag and pyramid of hats, the song of the buy-a-broom girls ('a large one for the lady and a small one for the baby') – all are treasured by me as part of the music of my childhood .... And I remember going to Blackwall by the Rope Railway, the Colonnade in Regent Street, the pens in Old Smithfield Market, the piling and strapping of luggage on the roofs of the railway carriages when travelling by train ....

---

* Curds and whey: a milk product like cottage cheese; hardbake: a sugary cake made with almonds.

The Rope Railway mentioned by Squire covered a distance of 3½ miles on two parallel lines between Blackwall and Minories in east London. It must have been an extraordinary construction. Completed in 1841, its coaches were operated by means of a total of 14 miles of hemp rope, 3½ miles each way on the two lines. A static engine at each end provided the power source for hauling the carriages. As these winding engines were continuously turning, the rearmost carriages were slipped off at the stops and picked up again on the way back. It was a short-lived operation: inevitably the ropes would frequently break, so they were replaced by metal cables, which in turn got twisted and bent. In 1849 the gauge of the line was changed to fit in with the rest of the railway system and the Rope Railway was dismantled, so Squire must have been very young indeed when he rode it.

He told of some of the most memorable events that took place during his young days. He was taken to see the Thames Tunnel between Wapping and Rotherhithe, which had been opened in 1843. This amazing structure was a remarkable piece of engineering. Designed and engineered by Marc Isambard Brunel, its construction was overseen by his twenty-year-old son, Isambard Kingdom Brunel, the first of his many famous projects. Started in 1825, it was the first tunnel to go under a river – anywhere in the world. Thousands of men worked on it in desperately dangerous conditions, excavating the earth entirely by hand. Six men were killed in 1828 when the tunnel flooded and Isambard Kingdom Brunel himself narrowly escaped with his life. There must have been many more casualties during the construction of the tunnel.

When completed the tunnel became a major tourist attraction for millions of visitors, including Queen Victoria, accompanied by Prince Albert. It was sometimes described as the eighth wonder of the world, There was a large entrance rotunda, with all kinds of stalls and shops selling refreshments and souvenirs, as well as street entertainers such as fire eaters and sword swallowers. Then for a penny you could go through the turnstile, and descend several flights of stairs to another circular chamber, 50 feet in diameter. Lined with marble walls and with ironwork for the railings, it was decorated with statues and pictures. Around this gaslit chamber there were alcoves where more entertainers performed. The tunnel itself stretched for 365 metres below the Thames and here still more traders set up their stalls between the supporting arches, creating a shopping arcade beneath the river. Originally the tunnel was intended for horse-drawn traffic, so that goods could be transported back and forth beneath the Thames, but this was never to happen as the cost of making ramps so that the entrances would be accessible to wheeled traffic was just too enormous and it remained a pedestrian tunnel until 1865, when it eventually became part of the London Underground system, linking Wapping and Rotherhithe stations. Closed at the end of 2007, it was reopened in 2010 as part of the London Overground network.

In 1851 Squire was taken to see the Great Exhibition in Paxton's Crystal Palace in Hyde Park, and in November 1852 he was allowed home from school to watch the magnificent state funeral procession of the Duke of Wellington. Among what was left of his father's London properties was a small house in Fleet Street, near Temple Bar. This house was rented out to a tailor who offered Julia and her children seats in his window from where they could watch the huge funeral procession that started out from the Iron Duke's London residence, Apsley House, at Hyde Park Corner, and wound its way through the streets of London to St. Paul's Cathedral. Temple Bar was draped in black and had urns of burning incense placed around it. Squire recalled that not many years later the little house in Fleet Street was demolished and the site became part of a large insurance office.

When he was quite young Squire Butterfield discovered that he was extremely short-sighted. His sisters had a governess who wore spectacles. One day Squire found these lying on a table: he picked them up and tried them. He was astonished to find that suddenly he could see things he had never seen properly before, such as pictures that he had only been able to look at by climbing upon a chair to see them from close up. From then on he wore spectacles; later, in adulthood, he adopted a monocle, a single eyeglass on a cord that was to become his trademark.

As a young boy Squire's favourite plaything was his toy theatre. Original examples of these exquisite miniature theatres can now only be seen in museums or in the hands of private collectors. They were produced by small printers or stationers such as Martin Skelt, who created some of the earliest ones in the 1840s. In later years Benjamin Pollock was to become the best-known producer of these theatres: Pollock's Toy Museum[*] was to be named after him, and facsimiles of 'Pollock's Toy Theatres' can still be bought today. Victorian children such as Squire Butterfield would spend their pocket money on the necessities for a 'production': sheets of scenery, complete with sets of little paper 'actors', recognisable portraits of such stars as Edmund Kean, William Charles Macready, Madame Vestris or the clown Joseph Grimaldi. These cost one penny for the plain ones, or twopence for a full colour version and were the origin of 'Penny Plain, Twopence Coloured', the title of a piece about these little theatres by Robert Louis Stevenson. Stevenson, who was born in 1850, had also loved these theatres as a boy and he claimed that in buying a coloured set you were denying yourself the real pleasure of painting the scenes and the figures for yourself. Young enthusiasts could

[*] Pollock's Toy Museum, Scala Street, London. Named after Benjamin Pollock, 1856-1937, it is a treasure house of old toys, including model theatres such as Squire Bancroft would have played with, all displayed in tiny rooms up winding wooden stairs, in a pair of houses virtually unchanged since Victorian times.

also buy scripts, adapted from London plays, and so direct their own performances in their own toy theatre: '*The Red Rover* and *The Miller and his Men* enjoyed very long runs,' wrote Squire of his productions of these two plays, both of which are mentioned by Stevenson in his essay.

a Pollock's toy theatre

Squire remembered being taken to the circus, and to pantomimes at the old Surrey Theatre in the Blackfriars Road, Lambeth. He was also taken to see Madame Tussaud's famous Waxwork Exhibition at its home which was then in Baker Street. Madame Tussaud[*] herself, by this time a very old lady, would sit each day on a chair just inside the entrance, so he was able to compare her waxwork self-portrait with the original. Madame Tussaud had been living in exile in London for over thirty years. She died in 1850, so Squire could have been not more than eight or nine when he saw the old lady.

He was taken to the theatre from an early age and could recall most of the plays he saw, featuring many of the well-known actors and actresses

---

[*] Anna Maria (Marie) Tussaud, 1761-1850, worked in Paris before and during the French Revolution. Her first model was of Voltaire, made in 1777. During the Revolution she made death masks of famous victims of the guillotine. Later she showed her large collection of waxworks all over Europe. While in London with her show, she was unable to return to France because of the outbreak of the Napoleonic War. She remained in London for the rest of her life. Today there are Tussaud waxwork museums in cities all over the world.

of the day, with one notable exception: 'Macready I never saw; but I do not forget as a very small boy reading and devouring, with a longing to be present, the bill of his farewell performance.' Most of the great names of the 1850s are now long-forgotten, names such as William Farren, described by Squire as 'that great actor', and 'the incomparable Madame Vestris'. Many of the famous actors of the time, and indeed some of the actresses, were also managers, leasing the great London theatres. Chief among these was Lucia Elizabetta Vestris, always known as Madame Vestris. Born Lucia Elizabeth Bartolozzi in 1797, she worked mostly in London and Paris. Her first husband, whom she married when she was only 16, was French and, although he abandoned her after just a few years of marriage, she retained his French name. She had a fine singing voice and in her youth she made a great impact, particularly in Italian opera, and she was especially popular in 'breeches roles', such as Cherubino in *The Marriage of Figaro*. Her first success in London, in a burlesque on *Don Giovanni*, called *Giovanni in London*, in 1817, led to considerable fame and fortune and in 1830 she took over the Olympic, a major London theatre which stood on the corner of Drury Lane until it was demolished in 1904. Madame Vestris made the Olympic famous with her burlesques and extravaganzas. Later, together with her second husband, the actor Charles James Mathews*, she managed both the Lyceum and Covent Garden. She introduced significant reforms in the theatre. She took more care of the welfare of her actors and theatre staff than was usual, paying them promptly and making sure they had proper breaks during rehearsals, which she supervised herself and controlled to an unusual extent. She was also responsible for important innovations in stage production, reforms that included ensemble playing, along with realistic scenery unlike anything that had been seen before. She was the first to introduce the 'box-set', complete with walls and ceiling, carpets, curtains and realistic furnishings. Her innovations and style of management were to prove a major influence on Marie Wilton and Squire Bancroft.

Squire attended the theatre at every opportunity, always in the cheapest seats as there was little money to spare for entertainment:

These were the days when young theatregoers had little ambition beyond a front seat in the pit: the days when one's toes were trodden on between the acts by horrible women who sold apples, oranges, and ginger-beer: the days when the bill of the play was little better than a greasy mass of printer's ink on paper nearly two feet long.

Squire tells in his memoirs of one memorable evening in 1856 when,

---

* Charles James Mathews, 1803-78, one of the best-known actors and theatre-managers of his time.

aged fifteen, he went with his mother to the Lyceum to see *Belphegor*: 'In the touching scene between the Mountebank and his son,' he was one day to write, 'we little thought that the pretty girl who made us cry by her pathetic acting as the boy Henri, in which she first appeared in London, would be my future wife.'

As a boy, Squire would always prefer to read a play, preferably a tragedy, rather than a novel, until his mother introduced him to Dickens, whose work he quickly grew to love. His favourite was, inevitably, *Nicholas Nickleby*, with its theatrical content, in which, as he said, 'the stage episodes naturally and fiercely fanned the dramatic flame'. Certainly by the time he was in his teens he was totally stagestruck and contemplating becoming an actor, although his family considered this idea an entirely unsuitable ambition for a young man of his respectable background.

Squire Butterfield had to leave school while quite young as what was left of the family money was dwindling fast and he needed to find some way of earning a living. How he set about this is unclear from his memoirs, apart from where he tells of a short visit to New York in a vain attempt to seek his fortune. He sailed in September 1858, aged seventeen, on the Cunard paddle steamer *Persia*. The Cunard fleet was at that time entirely composed of paddle steamers and the *Persia* was then the largest vessel in the world and had won the Blue Riband for the fastest transatlantic crossing just a few months after she was launched in 1855, coming to be known as 'the greyhound of the Atlantic'. Squire's crossing took thirteen days. It was fortunate that he chose the *Persia* for his passage to New York. An alternative option had been the *Austria*, a liner of the Hamburg-American Line, which left Hamburg on 1 September, picking up passengers in England en route for New York. She caught fire at sea, and 470 of her 546 passengers lost their lives.

In 1858 New York was growing rapidly, the heart of the city being in the area of Lower Manhattan. Central Park had been opened only the previous year, but the great skyscrapers, the Statue of Liberty and the Brooklyn Bridge had yet not appeared. It was a dangerous city, controlled by the infamous gangs of New York and a mostly corrupt police force; and in 1857 there had been a financial depression and riots. Most of the city's theatres, dance halls and brothels were clustered in the Bowery district of Lower Manhattan. Squire gave a colourful description of his first impressions of the city:

> My visit was in the fall, so I came in for the lovely Indian summer, a far more beautiful and much longer autumnal visitation than .... the short gleam we sometimes get in England .... The strange, palatial, gliding ferry-boats, the tall, rough telegraph-posts which then crossed and

recrossed the city, the many white houses with their green Venetian shutters, the brown-stone mansions of Fifth Avenue, are as vivid in my remembrance as the, then, terribly paved and dirty streets ....

Squire's fortune-seeking in America was conspicuously unsuccessful. He did not reveal what kind of work he was hoping he might find there, but at least his stay did not pass without visits to the theatre. Most notable of the productions he saw was the English playwright Tom Taylor's comedy, *Our American Cousin,* which had had its New York premiere at Laura Keene's Theatre a few months earlier, in May. Laura Keene herself, an English actress who became the first woman manager in America, played the leading female part and Edward Askew Sothern* created the part of 'Lord Dundreary', an imbecilic aristocrat with immense side whiskers which gave the name of 'Dundrearies' to this extraordinary style of facial adornment. Extravagant whiskers quickly became the height of fashion, a fashion that was fortunately short-lived. Sothern shot to fame as Lord Dundreary, although he had initially been reluctant to take the part, and he was to play it many times in future years, developing and exaggerating it further each time.

Edward Askew Sothern as Lord Dundreary

Our American Cousin became notorious more than six years later, when, on 14 April 1865, it was the play that Abraham Lincoln was

---

* Edward Askew Sothern, 1826-1881, a versatile English actor, popular on both sides of the Atlantic.

watching at Ford's Theatre in Washington when he was assassinated by John Wilkes Booth, an actor. So the familiar, if apocryphal, words in which the president's widow is asked, 'But what did you think of the play, Mrs Lincoln?' refers to *Our American Cousin*. Lincoln's assassin was from a well-known American theatrical family, his elder brother, Edwin Thomas Booth, being considered possibly the finest American classical actor of the nineteenth century.

Another play that Squire saw while he was in New York was a production of *The Merchant of Venice,* in which Shylock was played by the actor-manager James Wallack at his own Wallack's Theatre. The night Squire was in the audience someone offstage played a disruptive practical joke on Wallack: in the trial scene, when Shylock came to the words 'a harmless, necessary cat', a large tabby was let loose and shoved onto thestage. At first, not spotting the cat, Shylock carried on, unable to understand why the audience had burst into laughter during his speech. The unfortunate cat, alarmed by the other actors' attempts to shoo it off, and terrified by the roars from the audience, dashed around the stage in a panic. Eventually it ran past the Venetian noblemen seated in the courtroom, who were also helpless with laughter, and finally managed to escape. Needless to say, this ruined the most important scene in the play.

On his return from New York, Squire's visits to the London theatre were promptly resumed. In August 1859 he was at the Princess's the night Charles Kean retired from management, with Kean playing Cardinal Wolsey in Shakespeare's *Henry VIII*, and with his wife[*] as Katharine of Aragon. The 'after-piece' that rounded off that evening's bill included a performance from Ellen Terry, then only twelve years old. One evening he attended the Strand Theatre, to see a burlesque based on Bulwer Lytton's play *The Lady of Lyons,* and on the same bill there was a farce with Marie Wilton in the cast. He seems to have been less taken with her than when he saw her in *Belphegor* a few years earlier and he didn't remember much about the piece, save 'the ungallant [memory] that she was the thinnest girl I had ever seen'. He would not see her again until they met a few years later – on stage in Liverpool.

Squire never related how he made a living after his return from New York – possibly, like Bob Cratchit, he was a clerk in an office – but he had set his heart on the stage, despite a total ignorance of what the profession demanded: 'Often as I went to the play, dearly as I loved the theatre, until I was one I never knew an actor, and very rarely had even seen one off the stage.' In spite of opposition from his family he set about bombarding the lessees and managers of provincial theatres all over the

---

[*] Charles Kean's wife was Ellen Tree, 1805-80, one of the foremost actresses of the time.

country with letters asking to be taken on as an actor. From most of these he received no reply at all, and those who did reply, not surprisingly, had no interest in engaging a young man with no stage experience whatsoever. But eventually his luck changed, and on 1 January, 1861, he left home and travelled to Birmingham where he presented himself at the stage-door of the Theatre Royal, in New Street, which was managed by a Mr Mercer Simpson, the only manager to have sent him an encouraging response. 'I remember well my awe at finding myself, for the first time, "behind the scenes," and my impressions of the dimly-lighted theatre as I stood close to the footlights and talked my stage-struck project over. After kind advice, it was arranged that I might regard myself as a member of the company, with a commencing salary of one guinea a week.'

A few nights later, on 6 January 1861, the nineteen-year-old Squire Butterfield made his first appearance on stage, in a pantomime. He had no words to speak and his face was hidden under an enormous mask, but his career as an actor had begun. His first speaking part soon followed in a play by Bayle Bernard* called *St Mary's Eve*. He kept the playbill for the rest of his life, as it was the first on which his stage name, 'Squire Bancroft', ever appeared: he had dropped his family name of Butterfield as soon as Mercer Simpson had accepted him into his company, so that his family should not be embarrassed by its eldest son entering the acting profession. He used the name unofficially until 1867, when he adopted it formally by deed poll.

The mixed programme at the Theatre Royal was varied, changing several times per week, usually with 'blood-and-thunder' melodramas on Saturday nights, in many of which, during the first season of his acting career, Bancroft appeared 'as the perpetrator, or the victim, of a wide range of the vilest crimes'. As a 'walking gentleman' Squire would have had to supply all of his own props and most of his costumes. J.Palgrave Simpson*, writing in 1880 of earlier times, described a walking gentleman's responsibilities:

> The position of the walking gentleman is a pitiable one. His salary is feeble, to say the best of it – one-fourth, or perhaps less, of that received by the light comedian or juvenile tragedian; and yet he has far more parts to play .... three, or even four, in the same evening perhaps. For each part he has to find a change of dress; he is sometimes obliged to supply two or three changes in one piece. His wardrobe must be necessarily extensive, however limited his salary may be; and in how many shifty ways has he to pinch himself in order to meet the requirements of his position – how

---

* William Bayle Bernard, 1807-75, critic and prolific playwright, was one of the leading figures of the London 'Bohemian' scene in the mid-nineteenth century.
* John Palgrave Simpson, 1807-87, novelist and author of dozens of plays.

many devices to eke out his store of gloves, and give the due polish to his boots. He is expected to be fully up to the standard of the fashion of the day .... Although actors are expected to find their own modern clothes, the managements are obliged to supply all dresses in 'costume plays'. It must be a relief then, you may think, to the poor walking gentleman when he has a part in a costume piece .... Alas! no such thing .... He has probably only a small part to play; but still he has to find, out of his own scanty resources, all the requirements of his dress beyond the mere bare costume – his wigs, his shoes or boots, his tights, his lace, his buckles, his sword, his feathers, sometimes his cap, and a dozen other accessories to complete his attire.

Squire Bancroft in his early twenties

The life of a young actor in a provincial city was hard, although not as hard as it had been for actors on the circuits like the Wiltons. Squire's starting wage of one guinea (one pound, one shilling) per week was the equivalent of around £45 in today's money. He lived in cheap theatrical 'diggings', with simple meals included. His landlord registered Squire's occupation on the census the year that he arrived as a 'writing clerk' rather than as an actor. So it is likely that he had to supplement his meagre income with clerical work that fitted in with his hours at the theatre and also, maybe, with copying out, by hand, scripts for other, more senior actors. Several full-length copies of plays would have been needed for the stage-manager and the prompter. Individual players would be given scripts with just their own parts written out, along with their cues.

While in Birmingham, Mercer Simpson, an accomplished swordsman, introduced Squire to the art of fencing, an essential skill for a male actor. He would have regular lessons in the mornings with the manager and he quickly became a skilful fencer himself. This stood him in good stead in many of the parts he was to play over the next few years, although his poor eyesight must have presented problems, as he could hardly play a swashbuckling swordsman wearing spectacles.

In stock companies such as Mercer Simpson's most performances would be undertaken by the company's resident actors playing all the parts. However several times a year, as with the circuits, Britain's more important stock companies would be visited by a 'star' actor or actress who might be touring the provinces. The last 'star' to appear at the Theatre Royal during Squire's first season was a well-known and popular actor called T.C.King[*] who had taken a short lease on the theatre in Cork for the summer break – most theatres worked on seasonal cycles, breaking for the summer. King invited Squire and another young actor from Simpson's Birmingham stock company to join him there – at an increased salary. They accepted with enthusiasm. They took the train, third-class, from Birmingham to Bristol, from where they sailed to Cork.

At that time a first-class one-way passage from Bristol to Cork was about a guinea and second-class around 10s.6d. Unable to afford such luxuries, Squire and his unnamed friend bought the cheapest 'deck tickets' and travelled among the ship's cargo of cattle. Sitting on one of the paddle-boxes, they passed under Brunel's great suspension bridge across the Avon Gorge. Squire claimed to remember this bridge from his boyhood as the Hungerford Suspension Bridge in London. He believed that the earlier great bridge had been dismantled and moved to Bristol, but his memory was not quite accurate here: Brunel's Hungerford Bridge had indeed been dismantled, but only its chains had been used for the Clifton bridge. The great brick foundation buttresses of the original bridge can still be seen from the present Hungerford Bridge, as part of the bridge that carries the railway from Charing Cross Station. Soon after the ship passed into the Bristol Channel Squire began to feel very seasick. It was raining,

---

[*] Thomas Chiswell (T.C.) King, 1818-93, was with Mercer Simpson's company in Birmingham early in his career. Moving to London, he became well-known as a tragedian. For much of his career he toured extensively.

and he tried going below, but 'I got no further than the companion-ladder, where I was checked by clouds of bad tobacco-smoke and other fumes, the forbidding-looking hold being full of boisterous soldiers, so I returned to the wet deck.' He was then rescued by the generous ship's carpenter who was on duty during that night and kindly offered the two young actors his cabin, where they got a good night's sleep.

The small company played in Cork for thirty-six nights and Squire, who by now had turned twenty, played forty different characters. They opened with *Hamlet,* in which Squire played no fewer than five parts, Marcellus, Rosencrantz, Second Player, a Priest, and Osric, several of which would have involved at least wearing his sword, if not using it. There was little time for anything but work, rehearsing, studying and copying out parts from perhaps just one well-thumbed copy of a book which had to be passed on quickly as it was shared by several members of the company. The programme, or part of it, was changed practically every evening. He regarded this intensive work, hard though it was, as excellent practice – 'I felt already that I might some day be a fair actor – and so went back to Birmingham full of hope and high spirits.'

At the beginning of the new season at Birmingham a ballet was to be produced and Squire asked to be allowed to appear in this. How he could possibly have thought this suited his talents is a mystery, as he had little or no training in dance, was extremely tall, his full adult height being at least six feet two inches, and was never described as graceful. But then probably the 'ballet' concerned was far from the classical ballet we might think of today. In fact Squire himself admitted that he was pretty useless in it: 'I have not the smallest doubt I made a frightful hash of it, but I am equally certain it was as fine a month's training as I ever had.'

During his first full season at Birmingham, which started in September 1861 and ran through to the summer of 1862, Squire played sixty-four new parts. He was now beginning to be given better roles and his starting salary of one guinea per week was increased slightly. Another young actor who had arrived in Birmingham during that year was an eighteen-year-old called William Hunter Kendal. The two became good friends and in later years Kendal was to tell his biographer, T.Edgar Pemberton, how late one Saturday night, after they had finished at the theatre, he and Squire celebrated the small raise in their wages in a nearby tavern where they indulged in 'the almost unheard-of extravagance of a beefsteak dinner'.

That year Squire spent the summer season in Devonport, close to Plymouth. The lessee of the theatre there was an actor called James Doel, who was approaching sixty. (Decades later, Squire was to meet Doel again while on a visit to Plymouth, by which time he was in his nineties, and was believed to be the oldest living actor in the world, eventually living to be ninety-nine.) During a short break before the summer season began Squire went to London for a few days, where he once again saw

Edward Sothern playing Lord Dundreary in *Our American Cousin*, the play he had first seen in New York. Bancroft set about learning the part of Dundreary himself and would do a passable imitation of Sothern to show off among his friends. One night James Doel persuaded him to perform the piece at the theatre, which had been having poor attendances during the hot summer months. Squire's Dundreary was a great success, increasing the takings and filling the house nightly for as long as he played the part. The *Plymouth Telegraph* of 6 September 1862 said:

> The principal attraction of the week has been the appearance of Lord Dundreary .... the lessee could, indeed, hardly have done better if he had engaged the original impersonator of his lordship, Mr Sothern, for, by general consent, Mr Bancroft's Lord Dundreary is as much like the original in dress, manner, action, and appearance as it possibly could be, and has shown not only a wonderful amount of imitative talent, but an appreciation of character .... which stamps him as an able actor.

Bancroft as Lord Dundreary

Squire performed his 'Dundreary' again in Birmingham, before leaving Mercer Simpson's company for good as, while he was at Devonport, he had an offer to join the Theatre Royal in Dublin – once again at an increased salary. Simpson generously encouraged him to accept the offer, although this must have given him very short notice to find a replacement for his 'walking gentleman'. A change of company would, Simpson suggested, add usefully to his experience. It also bizarrely led to yet another change of name.

When he first arrived in Dublin playbills were prepared listing the names of the actors in the company and a printer misread the unusual name of 'Squire' as 'Sydney'. The name stuck, so for the duration of his time in Ireland he was billed as Sydney Bancroft, and for several years afterwards he used this name before reverting to the more bizarre 'Squire'.

The Theatre Royal, Dublin, was magnificent and attracted many star actors from London in spite of the distance and the sea crossing. Among the many celebrated players who visited the city during Bancroft's time there were Charles Kean and his wife, Ellen, whom he had seen on their last night at the Princess's Theatre in London. The Keans spent four weeks with the company.

Kean was at this time only fifty-two but already seemed like an old man. His memory was beginning to let him down and someone always had to be on standby in the wings ready to prompt him. Meanwhile his wife and the rest of the company fussed around him in their attempts to keep him happy and make certain there were no unscripted noises-off that might disturb his concentration.

Carpenters and stage-hands would dread Kean's arrival. The order for strict silence would go out: there must be no hammering or sawing, no creeping about with squeaky shoes, no coughing, sneezing or whispering while Mr Kean was rehearsing. A story went around of how once he had been playing in a town on the south coast where the occupants of the gallery were cracking nuts throughout the performance. Following the first night, a furious Kean sent someone to buy up all the nuts that were to be found in the town. Silence reigned through the next couple of performances, but soon the sound of nuts being cracked was once more heard from the gallery. The fruiterers of the town, puzzled by the unexpected run on their stock of nuts, had sent to every market for miles around and bought in vast supplies. The ensuing glut had been followed by reduced prices, with the result that more nuts than ever before were cracked in the theatre during the following nights' performances, each of which was torment for Kean.

Charles Kean

Although Charles Kean's acting never reached the heights that his great father, Edmund Kean, had achieved, it was always memorable, as Shylock, Othello, or Benedick, or in many non-Shakespearean parts, well-known at the time although unheard of today. Squire Bancroft was very proud that when they were in Dublin playing together in *Much Ado About Nothing* Kean complimented him on his performance of the part of Borachio, for Kean had been known to repeat Garrick's advice to young actors: 'You may humbug the town as a tragedian, but comedy is a serious thing, my boy, so don't try that just yet.'

It was while he was in Dublin that Squire received his first invitation to join a London theatre, the St James's Theatre, but after some consideration he decided to decline the flattering proposal as he felt he had not yet had enough experience to justify setting out for London. Instead he was to remain in Dublin for two happy and successful years, playing over sixty new parts as well as some old familiar ones. It was at this time he became very aware of the problems his poor eyesight could present: he was cast in a part in *Rob Roy* that involved a fierce, long sword duel. This gave Squire great anxiety as he was seriously afraid that he might injure his 'opponent' on stage. After many hours of rehearsal, all went well on the night, but later he more than once reluctantly declined some good parts rather than take the risk of 'killing a tyrant king in earnest, through not seeing his majesty'.

During that Dublin season of 1863-64 Bancroft met the actor Edward Sothern personally for the first time and gave him the playbill he had treasured since he first saw him act in New York in *Our American Cousin*. In spite of having achieved considerable fame as the ludicrous Lord Dundreary, Sothern believed that his true vocation was that of a serious actor and while in Dublin revived what Squire described as 'a powerful but gloomy drama called *Retribution*', casting Squire in one of the main supporting parts. *Retribution* was not a success but the pair of them worked together in several other productions and became good friends. Sothern gave Bancroft some good advice on his next career move, suggesting that he should consider trying for a move to the Prince of Wales Theatre in Liverpool, widely thought to be the best stepping-stone for London, Dublin being too far away for him to be noticed. So, when a few months later Squire heard that a vacancy might be coming up in Liverpool, he immediately wrote a letter of application to Alexander Henderson, the manager of the Prince of Wales, who, after a positive report about him from Sothern, invited Squire to join his company at Easter 1864. He was sorry to leave Ireland as he had been happy there and believed it had been invaluable experience for him: '…. to the two long seasons of hard work I passed there I owe a large share of my success as an actor, and my stay in Dublin has a foremost place in my happiest remembrances.'

Bancroft much enjoyed his year at the Prince of Wales, playing some interesting parts and making friends with many actors and actresses who were one day to become famous, most notably a young man called John Hare, who was embarking on his stage career under the tuition of a well-established actor, Leigh Murray[*]. Hare and Bancroft would often visit Murray and, in spite of suffering severely from asthma and rheumatism, the older actor would entertain the younger pair with anecdotes of his early days in the theatre. Squire looked back on these visits as unforgettable lessons in the art of acting.

The Prince of Wales, Liverpool, was quite a change from the Theatre Royal, Dublin, being a lot smaller, but it was a favourite theatre for visiting companies and star players. The time of his arrival, the spring of 1864, coincided with Shakespeare's tercentenary, so Shakespeare's plays were being performed all over the country. During his first months in Liverpool Squire played Gratiano in *The Merchant of Venice* and Laertes

---

[*] Leigh Murray, 1820-70, a highly-regarded actor whose ill-health severely affected his career. By the 1860s he had virtually retired from the stage and he died at the early age of fifty. His actress wife, Elizabeth, 1815-92, continued her own acting career for many years following the death of her husband.

in *Hamlet,* Alfred Wigan[*] and his wife being the visiting stars for these productions.

Often, at around midnight after the evening's performance in Liverpool, Bancroft, Hare and two or three other young actors would pile into a hired dog-cart and drive themselves to Chester, some twenty miles away. 'How we risked our young necks, and what a life we led the toll-keepers and the slumbering villagers!' What these reckless young men got up to in Chester in the early hours of the morning he does not relate; it is hard to imagine that city providing exciting nightlife for unattached young men at that time.

John Fairs, later John Hare, aged about 19

[*] Alfred Wigan, 1814-78, and his wife, Leonora, 1805-84, were a popular theatrical couple. Wigan's younger brother, Horace, 1815-85, was also a well-known actor and playwright.

John Hare, destined to be one of the best-known comic actors of his time, was to become Bancroft's closest lifelong friend. He was born John Joseph Fairs in 1844, in London, the youngest of four children. Both his parents were from farming families in rural Berkshire, but before John was born they had moved to London, where his father worked as a painter and decorator, eventually setting up his own business. His father died when John was only four years old, and his mother took over the running of the business.

When he was in his early teens John was sent up north to live with a maternal uncle in Knutsford, Cheshire. This uncle became his legal guardian, and he sent John to Giggleswick School, near Settle in Yorkshire, where it was intended that he should become an engineer, but clearly his talents did not lie in that direction. Instead he was already showing a talent for acting. The school records report that the Headmaster said to him, 'You become an engineer! You are fit for nothing but the stage!'

On leaving school, hoping to make the stage his profession, John Fairs was taken on at the Prince of Wales Theatre, Liverpool, and it was in Liverpool that he met an Irishman, John Hare Holmes from Dublin, and his young daughter, Mary. John Fairs adopted Holmes's middle name of Hare as his stage name – this seems to have been a none-too-subtle ploy to win Holmes's approval when John sought his daughter's hand in marriage. John Fairs and Mary Holmes were married in August 1865, when they were just twenty-one and nineteen respectively. Fairs was known professionally as John Hare for the rest of his life.

It was not long before Squire Bancroft was back in Ireland for a short visit when Alexander Henderson took his whole company over to Dublin for a month. He was met with an unexpectedly rapturous reception from the Dublin audiences who regarded him as one of their own. As soon as he stepped on to the stage there was so much applause that his Liverpool colleagues gathered in the wings to see who could be the object of such an ovation. The Liverpool company were performing a programme of familiar pieces needing little or no further rehearsal, so Squire could explore more of Dublin and the surrounding area than he had been able to during his two years hard work in the city. Near the end of his stay in Dublin he even had the cheek to attempt an Irish brogue in a play – as a character called 'Murphy Maguire'– and his Irish fans accepted this impertinence with enthusiasm.

Then it was back to Liverpool, and a meeting that was to change Bancroft's life. The celebrated burlesque company from London's Strand Theatre came to Liverpool for a short visit, part of their tour of the north. One of the stars of the company was their queen of burlesque, Marie Wilton. This was when Squire met her for the first time, previously only having seen her from afar years before in London, when she was on the stage and he was in the audience. This was the first of two visits by Marie, as she returned to Liverpool towards the end of the year when she and Bancroft appeared on a stage together for the very first time, in a comedy called *Court Favour* by James Robinson Planché[*].

Squire Bancroft in the early 1860s

Bancroft had by now completed more than four years of 'apprenticeship' in the provinces, and from his early start as a 'walking gentleman' he had played almost 350 different parts. 'He was in everything,' wrote one paper, many years later, summing up his early career. 'Marcellus, Rosencrantz and Osric in *Hamlet* were his, all at one

---

[*] James Robinson Planché, 1796-1880, was a leading figure in an extraordinary number of different fields. An actor, theatre manager, costume designer and prolific writer for the stage, he was also a drama critic, an antiquarian, and a founder member of the British Archaeological Association, and he was Somerset Herald. He was among the original members of the Garrick Club.

time. If *Richelieu**[*] required a captain of archers or *The Colleen Bawn**[*] a corporal, not even to be mentioned in the bills, Mr Bancroft was promptly to the fore ....' He might well have continued to spend many more years 'learning his trade' in this manner, in various parts of Britain, as Henry Irving would do, but it was now that he unexpectedly decided that the time had come for him to make the big move to London.

The clue for Bancroft's decision probably lies in a request he made soon after they met for a photograph of Marie Wilton. She did not keep his letter, but he kept her reply. It was a fairly conventional response, written in her almost illegible handwriting, but it was to be followed up with a far more significant letter, offering him an engagement with a new company she was in the process of forming. He accepted her offer without a moment's hesitation, astonishing his Liverpool friends, who, knowing he had turned down a couple of previous good offers to join established London companies, thought he must be mad to contemplate joining an untried new company in an obscure little theatre – and there could hardly be a more obscure theatre than the one that Marie Wilton was now planning to manage.

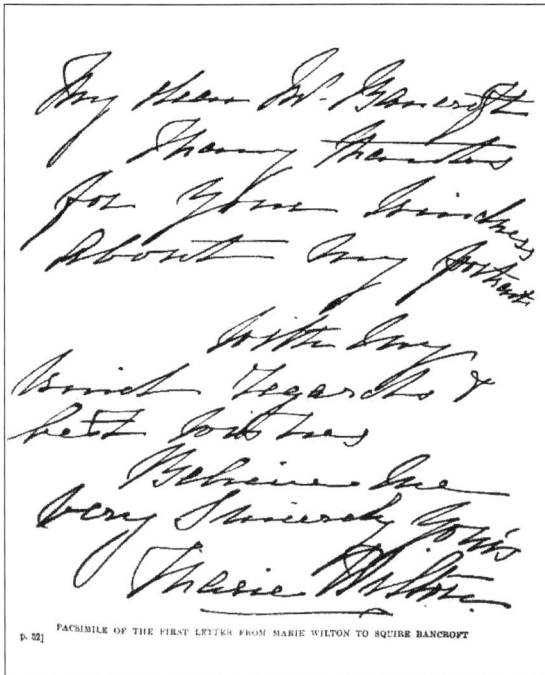

p. 52] FACSIMILE OF THE FIRST LETTER FROM MARIE WILTON TO SQUIRE BANCROFT

Marie Wilton's first letter to Squire Bancroft

---

[*] *Richelieu*, an 1839 play by Edward Bulwer Lytton.
[*] *The Colleen Bawn*, an 1860 play by Dion Boucicault.

Why should she have offered? Why should he have accepted? We know no more than that they had met and acted together in Liverpool. One thing is clear: it was for an entirely unprofessional reason that Squire Bancroft chose to risk his future at that moment. As he was one day to admit, he had fallen in love with Marie Wilton – it had been 'love at first sight' he declared in his memoirs – and very probably, she with him.

4

THE GOLD-DUST-HOLE

The end of the year 1864 was to be a major turning point in the life of Marie Wilton. Now aged twenty-five, she had long been discontented with the direction in which her career seemed to be set. She had given up her childhood ambition to play Lady Macbeth or indeed any other of Shakespeare's great female roles, accepting that her diminutive size and vivacious personality would not be seen as appropriate for most of Shakespeare's dramatic heroines. However, she was determined that she wanted to turn her back on burlesque and concentrate on comedy.

Among the many varieties of nineteenth-century stage production, Victorian comedy provided the nearest equivalent to what might today be called a 'straight' play. Although it usually had a humorous side, the word 'comedy' was still used as it was in Shakespeare's time as an indicator that the content of the play was less portentous than 'tragedy', and did not contain numerous deaths. An actor would often define himself either as a 'comedian' or a 'tragedian', as opposed to simply an actor: a biography of John Hare by T. Edgar Pemberton, written in 1895, was entitled *John Hare, Comedian*, and Squire Bancroft entered his occupation as 'comedian' in the census of 1871, although he did in later years describe himself as 'actor' or 'theatre manager'.

One day, while visiting her married sister Emma, now Mrs Francis Drake, Marie was bemoaning the fact that nothing had come of her countless letters to every theatre manager in London asking them to consider her for their comedy productions. Buckstone at the Haymarket had replied that if she would continue to perform in burlesque he would be happy to engage her immediately, as he could only associate her with 'the merry sauciness of that wicked little boy, Cupid'. She began to despair of ever escaping from burlesque.

Marie Wilton, c.1867

Then her brother-in-law, Francis Drake, a barrister, came up with a bombshell of a suggestion. 'I see no chance for you but management,' he said to Marie. 'How would it be if you had a theatre of your own?' Emma indicated that she was absolutely in agreement with her husband. Marie decided they must both be mad, or joking, and, 'after looking hard at them both to assure myself that they were not dangerous', and pointing out that she had not a penny in the world, she asked how they thought that she could possibly take the lease on her own theatre with no money. Drake suggested that she should come back in the morning, by which time he and Emma would have had time to discuss his idea. So the next day Marie returned to the Drakes' house, where Francis came up with a proposal: he was prepared to lend her a thousand pounds if she could find a theatre to lease. If the venture was successful she could pay him back with generous interest. This interest he would pass directly to his mother-in-law, Marie and Emma's mother Georgiana, as a gift. If she failed, then he accepted that he would lose his money: Marie would be in the clear financially and would not be expected to pay him back. It was an enormous gamble on Drake's part. Emma encouraged her sister to accept her husband's generous offer and, being a superstitious Wilton girl, she reminded her sister of the occasion way back in their childhood when the old woman had prophesied good fortune for Marie. 'Don't be nervous,' she said, 'you are sure to succeed.'

A thousand pounds was an enormous sum in 1864. For Marie, who had never possessed much more than ten pounds at any one time in her life, it was an unimaginable figure (in today's money, not far off £45,000). It would be interesting to know how Emma Wilton met Drake. As a lawyer, he might well have been a friend of Thomas Crispe, who had cast Emma in his educational institute's play during her early days in London. It is possible that Drake saw her acting when she first arrived in London, when she appeared at the Strand Theatre as the heroine in a dramatised version of Dickens's *Little Dorrit*, produced in November 1856, even though Dickens did not complete the serialisation of his novel until the following year. *The Era* was not impressed. Its review read:

> The slight drawback that Mr Dickens has not got more than halfway through his novel of *Little Dorrit* has not in the slightest degree proved a barrier to the work being dramatised .... With that easy recklessness of adapters generally, and with sublime indifference to the original author's design .... we have the plot capriciously twisted, turned and terminated to suit this stage and forestall the others, and the unfortunate victim is mutilated on the same principle as that adopted by the classical robber of antiquity and cut down Procrastes fashion to fit the place, the lopping off of a head or limb producing no remorse with the operator.

However, *The Era* did have a few kind words for the eighteen-year-old Emma: 'Miss Emma Wilton, who plays Little Dorrit, exhibits no inconsiderable amount of talent and her earnestness and pathos showed a power of delineation that induces a belief in a longer professional career than her apparent youthfulness would suggest.' The dramatisation only ran for seventeen performances, but that may have proved long enough for Emma to attract and hold the admiration of the generous Mr Drake.

Although it was not uncommon for upper-class, often wealthy, young men of the time to enter into relationships with pretty young actresses, only occasionally did they actually marry them. Emma Wilton was one of the fortunate ones, especially as Francis Drake, clearly an enlightened Victorian gentleman, was happy that she should continue with her career, in a somewhat amateurish way. In 1864, not long after their marriage, Emma performed Shakespeare readings billed as 'Miss Bouverie (Mrs

Francis Drake)'. This is an intriguing choice of name, considering her own first name: when Gustave Flaubert's famous novel *Madame Bovary* was first published in book form in 1857 it caused considerable controversy due to its scandalous story-line. Emma Bouverie – Emma Bovary: the name was surely no coincidence and had to have been deliberately chosen, although there was the excuse that she had a family connection with the name, there being Pleydell-Bouveries in Robert Pleydell Wilton's family. Later Emma also used the feminine version of her husband's name, calling herself 'Miss Frances Bouverie' when in 1868 she played Desdemona at the Haymarket, and the following year Portia at the Princess's.

Marie Wilton quickly accepted Drake's offer, in the belief that even if the enterprise failed she would at the very least have had the opportunity to show the theatre managers of London that she was capable of a wider range of talents than she had been permitted to demonstrate so far. She immediately set out to find a theatre to lease. Among the first of her theatrical friends to hear of her project was the writer H.J. (Henry James) Byron. Byron had also been closely connected to the Strand Theatre for some years, turning out dozens of burlesques and extravaganzas for the Swanboroughs, often with parts expressly written for Marie Wilton. He told Marie that she was embarking on a 'very dangerous experiment'. Nevertheless, when Marie proposed that they should enter into a partnership, with Byron writing exclusively for their theatre, he overcame his misgivings and accepted, agreeing that in their joint venture he would be prepared to write comedy plays for Marie rather than burlesques. It was also agreed that Byron, being unable to contribute financially towards the project, would be indemnified from sharing any of the losses they might incur.

H.J.Byron was only a few years older than his new partner. Born in Manchester in 1835, he had tried various careers in his youth, including a brief spell as a law student in the Middle Temple in 1858, no doubt at the insistence of his diplomat father. All the while he was turning out comic plays and burlesques. His legal career lasted for a very short time: either he failed in the law, or more probably it was not to his liking as he quickly changed direction, first becoming an unsuccessful actor in the provinces but soon finding far more success with his writing. In later years he still occasionally acted, in his own plays, as characters he had written for himself. Since 1857 dozens of his burlesques and extravaganzas, farces and pantomimes, had been produced, mostly at the Strand. He also wrote magazine articles and a novel.

Henry James Byron

Byron has been described as the most prolific playwright in mid-Victorian London, his work being among the most popular of its time, but of a type, full of outrageous puns, that would be considered very unfunny today. Indeed it was beginning to fade from fashion even in his own lifetime and it is little wonder that none of his plays has been seen for well over a century. Socially Byron was a hugely popular figure with many friends, by whom he was much loved for his wit, humour and general good nature. Squire Bancroft and others were to tell many stories about him. One that particularly amused Bancroft was some years later when, during a performance of one of his plays in which Henry Irving and John Lawrence Toole were acting, there was a long, unexplained delay between acts. Byron was anxiously pacing around at the back of the auditorium, wondering what was the cause of the hold up. Suddenly the rasping sound of a saw could be heard working away behind the scenes. Byron was heard to remark, 'I think they must be cutting out the last act.' Another example of his ready wit was when he complained to a lodging-house landlady about fleas in his room. The indignant woman exclaimed, 'Fleas sir! Not a single flea in my house, I'm sure of it!' Harry Byron's response was, 'I'm sure of it too; they are all married and have large families.'

The search for a theatre proved to be quite brief: Marie Wilton and Byron heard that the lease on the small, 600-seat Queen's Theatre – the theatre where Madame Celeste had made her debut on the London stage – was shortly to become available and enquiries were made with the then lessee, a Mr Charles James. Situated in Tottenham Street, just off the Tottenham Court Road, the Queen's Theatre had been through mixed fortunes under a variety of names since it first opened as 'The New Rooms in Tottenham Street' in 1772. It continued for many years under a succession of different names, among them 'The King's Concert Rooms', 'The Cognoscenti Theatre', 'The Regency Theatre', and 'The Tottenham Street Theatre', and many managements, with varying degrees of success, or for the most part lack of success.

the Regency Theatre in Tottenham Street in 1817

Mr Charles James, who had been leasing the theatre since 1843, agreed to sublet to Marie Wilton and Henry Byron. Over the years the Queen's had fallen more and more into decline, and had become popularly known as the Dust-Hole. It was mostly the home of the more lurid type of melodramas, with blood-curdling titles such as *The Demon Nun, The Spectre Bride* and *Footpad Joe, the Terror of Charing Cross*. These were performed to full melodramatic effect, complete with much exaggerated rolling of eyes, raising and lowering of brows, leering glances at the audience and long, significant pauses between words. It had the reputation of being 'the lowest theatre in London'. Many years later a contributor to *The Theatre* magazine recalled what it was like to be in the audience at the old Queen's Theatre, seated in 'the slimy fungosity of that "front circle"

81

.... the glutinous grime that made it literally impossible to tear oneself away from that performance.' A French visitor to London, Augustin Filon[*], recalled the 'squalid little playhouse in Tottenham Street .... where all sorts of things had been achieved, but bankruptcy oftenest of all .... and where the stalls, when they had dined well, were given to bombarding the boxes with orange peel.'

interior of the Regency Theatre in 1817, showing the pit benches, the boxes and the gallery. By 1864 it was called the Queen's.

Tottenham Street is in the district of London that is now the stylish Fitzrovia, named after the Fitzroy Tavern public house, once much frequented by 'Bohemian' patrons. It is close to the traffic and bustle of Tottenham Court Road; the Euston Road underpass is not very far to the north, and the BT Tower is just around the corner. Yet, even on a busy weekday, Tottenham Street, like many other narrow streets in Fitzrovia, today feels like a quiet backwater, with small restaurants, pubs and galleries tucked in amongst the office buildings. It is not far from the heart of London's theatreland, and today the distance appears negligible. In 1865, however, it was still deep in the heart of a very unfashionable

---

[*] Pierre Marie Augustin Filon, 1841-1916, an academic who was a tutor to the French Prince Imperial. In 1870 he accompanied the prince into exile in England. He wrote on English literature and theatre.

82

corner of the metropolis. This was one of the poorest parts of London, with the infamous district of St Giles close by, known for the desperate poverty and crime associated with its 'rookeries', streets of closely-packed, overcrowded slum dwellings. This was the area into which Marie Wilton proposed to throw all her hopes and her energies – and the whole of her borrowed thousand pounds. This is where she would either succeed in her ambitions – or where her career could sink without trace.

Almost everyone consulted regarded the venture as total madness and Marie's friends and colleagues begged her to reconsider. H.J.Byron began to show signs of cold feet and consulted a friend of his whose judgment he respected. This gentleman, the newspaper proprietor Joseph Moses Levy[*], discussed the matter in detail with Marie, and unexpectedly gave her some encouragement. He thought she might succeed, but only if, at least for their first productions, she stuck to what she and Byron were already famous for: she should not risk losing her considerable fan base who were accustomed to seeing her play in burlesque and might not support her if she changed direction too soon. Levy suggested that if Marie's current popularity attracted audiences for their early productions, Byron could write a few comedies for her, and not until then, if these went down well, should she contemplate abandoning burlesque for ever. Marie accepted Levy's advice and Byron was reassured.

It was agreed that for a period of two years, starting from Easter 1865, Charles James of the Queen's Theatre would receive £20 per week to cover both rental and his own services as 'acting-manager'. The acting-manager then was the equivalent of today's front-of-house manager, in charge of everything that goes on in front of the curtain, the word 'acting' in this context indicating that he would 'act' on behalf of the management. As well as being around to welcome the theatre's patrons, he was in charge of the box office and organized the production of programmes, playbills and other publicity. He was also responsible for organising the wages of the company and all the backstage staff.

Marie Wilton and H.J.Byron signed a financial agreement. It was agreed that they would each draw a salary of £10 per week. They would share equally all management and stage management duties and they would equally own all the publishing and acting rights of whatever Byron wrote during their partnership. The agreement recognised the need to repay the loan of £1000: £10 per week would go towards repayment, a sum that would ensure that the thousand pounds could be paid back by the end of the second year. After these deductions, along with all the other costs involved in running a theatre, Byron and Marie would share any profits that might be left over. Byron was indemnified from any financial

---

[*] Joseph Moses Levy, 1812-88, was the proprietor of the *Daily Telegraph*.

risk in the venture, with Marie agreeing that, 'At the end of our tenancy, should the thousand pounds be lost, or any portion thereof, I am not to have any claim on you for said sum, as the venturing of the money is voluntary on my part.' On 21 January, 1865, accompanied by her brother-in-law, Marie Wilton opened the first bank account she had ever held in her life, at the Westminster Bank in St James's Square, and the promised £1000 was deposited there.

The only source for the story that the loan came from Drake is Marie Wilton's own account: that account appears never to have been challenged. Francis Drake must have had access to considerable funds, in order to have so much ready cash to spare. He had certainly not had time to establish a successful legal career, having been called to the bar not long before, in 1863. There might well have been some family money: the Drakes seem to have been very comfortably off, Drake senior being a surgeon with the Horse Guards, and the family lived in a substantial house in South Kensington. It is nevertheless possible that the money came from Alfred Shoolbred, if he was, or had been Marie's lover, or 'protector'. The anonymous pencilled note on the photograph of Marie, with his name mentioned, is hardly evidence and £30,000 is a highly improbable sum – with that sort of money Marie could have leased any theatre in London rather than the insalubrious Dust-Hole. But Shoolbred could have provided the loan, or the gift, of a far more modest sum, with the Drakes agreeing to provide a cover story for the sake of respectability. And the Dust-Hole was just around the corner from the Shoolbred family emporium in the Tottenham Court Road.

Legal and financial formalities completed, the partners could now set about planning their venture in detail. Marie, with Byron and his wife, took a box at the old Queen's Theatre one night. Marie described it as 'a well-conducted, clean little house, but oh, the audience!'

> My heart sank! Some of the occupants of the stalls (the price of admission was, I think, a shilling) were engaged between the acts in devouring oranges .... and drinking ginger-beer. Babies were being rocked to sleep, or smacked to be quiet, which proceeding, in many cases, had an opposite effect! A woman looked up to our box, and seeing us staring aghast, with, I suppose an expression of horror on my face, shouted, 'Now then, you three stuck-up ones, come out o' that, or I'll send this 'ere orange at your 'eads.' Mr Byron went to the back of the box and laughed until we thought he would be ill. He said my face was a study. 'Oh, Byron!' I exclaimed, 'Do you think that people from the West End will ever come into those seats?' .... I think, if I could, I would have at that moment retired from my bargain, but there was no going back from it.

It was a small theatre, its stage measuring twenty-one feet across at the proscenium, and thirty-six feet deep. The seat prices were indeed low, even for 1865: Charles James had not long before reduced his prices to one shilling for the pit, and sixpence for the gallery. The pit, the ground floor of the auditorium, at the time consisted of rows of backless benches which, along with the gallery benches, were the cheapest seats in the house. Audiences could be rowdy and boisterous and occasionally fights would break out. Missiles such as orange peel would be hurled from the gallery onto the heads of those below in the pit. Loud barracking from the gallery would sometimes lead to the perpetrator being forcibly and noisily thrown out of the theatre by his neighbours.

In Thomas Wright's[*] *Some Habits and Customs of the Working Classes*, published in 1867, there is a chapter entitled *Among the Gods* in which he wrote descriptively of the theatre audiences of his time. Being of limited income, Wright was proud to be a 'god', a frequenter of the gallery seats. He acknowledged that the 'gods' were often noisy, and were 'sometimes given to discharging nutshells, peas, orange-peel, and other annoying, though harmless missiles, at the heads of the devoted occupants of the regions below'. However, he claimed that they would often earn the applause of the rest of the audience when, as sometimes happened, loud-mouthed, inebriated young men, sort of nineteenth-century hooray Henrys arriving at the theatre half-way through the evening's entertainment when entry prices were halved, set out to disrupt the performance.

> Stupid-looking and more than half-drunken 'swells' who have come into the boxes at half-price time, begin to annoy the audience by talking and laughing in a very loud tone, and making grimaces at and trying to interrupt the actresses, is it not the gods who bring them to order? Scornful looks and indignant hushes …. have no effect upon them, but when, at the end of the scene, the gods give loud utterance to their well-known war-cry 'Turn them out!' the effect is instantly apparent. The swells at once subside into silence, and suddenly become very much interested in the perusal of the playbill. And beside materially assisting to keep order during the performance, it is admitted by all who know anything of theatrical matters, that the gods are by far the most lively portion of a theatrical audience, and the witticisms and eccentricities of those in the gallery are sometimes quite as entertaining as any part of the legitimate performance.

Marie Wilton had about a month in which totally to refurbish the theatre, of necessity on the tightest budget. One thousand pounds may

---

[*] Thomas Wright, 1839-1909, was a largely self-educated blacksmith. Following the 1870 Education Act he was employed as a school board visitor, an official who kept track of children who should be attending school. He wrote extensively on social issues under the pseudonym of 'The Journeyman Engineer'.

have been a lot of money but a total refit was a costly business and the work had to be done economically but as stylishly as possible. The theatre was duly 'taken to pieces, cleaned, painted, re-seated, re-decorated, furnished, and it was not pleasant to see the money gradually getting less and less'. Most of the bills, such as those of the builders and decorators, carpenters, upholsterers, gasfitters, scene builders and others, had to be paid weekly. By the time the theatre was ready to open the thousand pounds had dwindled to around £150.

It was decided that the old theatre should be renamed yet again for its new incarnation. Marie chose the name of the Prince of Wales's, a name that had to have permission from Albert Edward, the Prince of Wales, himself. Henry Byron applied for this permission and the following letter was duly received:

Lord Chamberlain's Office,
St James's Palace, Feb 3 1865

Sir – I am desired by the Lord Chamberlain to acknowledge the receipt of your letter of 26th ult, requesting jointly with Miss Marie Wilton, as lessees of the Queen's Theatre, in Tottenham Street, that the name of that building may in future be the Prince of Wales's Theatre; and I am to inform you, in reply, that his lordship accedes with pleasure to your request, his Royal Highness the Prince of Wales having signified his consent to the proposed change.

A company of twelve actors was engaged, all at extremely modest salaries, even for 1865. Among them were two of Marie's five sisters, Blanche and Augusta, along with Fanny Josephs, a well-known, very pretty, young actress with whom Marie had worked at the Strand and who later went into management herself. One of the six male actors was Squire 'Sydney' Bancroft.

In keeping with the conventional form of an evening's entertainment at the theatre at the time, three pieces were offered for the opening bill and were in rehearsal for the short time leading up to the first night. Byron and Marie had been offered a new one-act play to consider as a curtain-raiser. It was sent to them by its author, the playwright J.P.Wooler. His play was entitled *All's Fair in Love and War*. Byron and Marie accepted it but, thinking that the title was too long, they persuaded Wooler to change it to *A Winning Hazard*. It only struck them later that this was a peculiarly appropriate title with which to embark on their venture. Wooler's piece was to be followed by 'a new and original operatic burlesque extravaganza' by Byron called *La! Sonnambula!* A farce called *Vandyke Brown* was to wind up the evening's fare.

For Marie, the last few weeks before opening were hectic. In addition to hurried rehearsals, there were decisions to be made daily, builders and decorators still to be supervised, costumes to be arranged; she had her own part to be studied. When rehearsals began, Marie noticed that the friends who now made up her company appeared to expect her to behave differently towards them as their manager. She insisted that they regard her always as their friend and colleague and that they should all work together as equals. She attempted, throughout all her future years in management, to retain this kind of relationship with her actors.

The new Prince of Wales's Royal Theatre, to give it its full name, was finally ready to open on schedule under its new management on the evening of 15 April 1865. That afternoon a strange incident only helped to confirm the superstitious Wilton women's belief in signs and omens. Their mother, Georgiana, far too nervous to contemplate attending her daughter's opening night, was in such an anxious state all day that to calm her down her eldest daughter, Emma Drake, took her for a drive to a place that was then no more than a village, way out in the countryside – Willesden. Georgiana often called her second daughter Mary, rather than using the French pronunciation of Marie by which she was generally known, so when she caught sight of a carved name stone on a row of cottages that read 'Mary's Place, Fortune Gate', she and Emma immediately took it to be a good omen for Marie's momentous first night. The story spread around the company and became part of the legend that was to grow around the Prince of Wales's. Many years later, when the little row of rural dwellings was demolished to make way for the ever-growing London suburbs, Marie was sent the stone as a gift by the developer of the land, who had read of its significance to the by then famous Marie Wilton.

The first night arrived and more cabs and carriages than had ever been seen there before were lined up in Tottenham Street. One newspaper described the opening of the Prince of Wales's as 'the most stirring event of the season', and went on to report that 'the doors were literally besieged', as crowds gathered to see what Marie Wilton, London's favourite burlesque queen, had done to transform the old Dust-Hole. They would find that the theatre had been almost totally gutted and elaborately redesigned using elegant materials. The auditorium was decorated in gold, white and blue and was fitted with carpets, an unheard of refinement at the time. The pit benches had been moved towards the back to make room for four rows of stalls with fifty-four comfortably upholstered, sprung seats in blue leather with white enamelled studs. These seats had white lace antimacassars to protect them from the sticky 'macassar oil' (palm or coconut) used by Victorian gentlemen as a hairdressing. This was the first time antimacassars had ever been used in a theatre although they had become essential in the home, as it would have been almost impossible to clean the oil off the heavy upholstery of the time. These antimacassars would have needed frequent laundering and the seats must have had quite high backs for them to serve any practical purpose. The boxes had looped-back lace curtains around them; they too had blue leather seats and there were vases of flowers attached to their sides. All the public areas of the theatre were freshly painted in blue and white. On either side of the stage were niches holding displays of fresh flowers. The ceiling was deep blue and dotted with gold stars. The refurbished theatre certainly met with the approval of the reporter from *The Era*:

The elegant appearance of the house .... seemed to excite no less admiration than surprise .... The decorations of ceiling, boxes and proscenium are in white, gold, and blue, and form a happy combination of the Italian and French styles. The area of the proscenium is framed with white enamelled scroll, the panels in blue, and the Prince of Wales's feathers in white relief forming the centre .... The whole of the box circle has been lined with rosebud chintz and brilliantly illuminated .... all the passages and lobbies have been covered with pink stripe. The draperies are of white lace and geranium silk. The new act-drop represents a garden landscape of the Louis Quatorze period, with Watteau-like groups of figures.

When the time finally came to prepare herself before the doors opened, Marie was exhausted and nervous: little did the queue waiting outside know that barely five minutes before they entered the theatre its new manager had been perched on a stool in one of the boxes tacking up the final lace curtain. Then gradually the excitement of the occasion began to rise and 'I went on to my own little stage without exhibiting any sign of fatigue. It would be affectation to pretend that I did not know I was already a great favourite with the public, although the warm welcome I received almost overpowered me, but soon added force to my acting.'

The Era described the evening's entertainment in detail: 'The first piece was a new original comedietta by Mr J.P.Wooler, entitled *A Winning Hazard* and, pleasantly written and ingeniously constructed, furnished an hour's very agreeable entertainment.' Of Bancroft's first appearance on the London stage it said: 'Mr Sydney Bancroft (from the Prince of Wales Theatre, Liverpool), who played Jack Crawley, seems a young comedian of promise ....'

Then followed the main attraction – a 'burlesque extravaganza', called *La! Sonnambula! or the Supper, the Sleeper and the Merry Swiss Boy*, written and directed by H.J.Byron. Burlesque invariably carried a double title, hinting at the parodies to come. Set in an Alpine village, it was a version of a famous and popular opera *La Sonnambula* (The Sleepwalker) that was currently on in London, by the Italian composer Vincenzo Bellini. The opera is still occasionally performed today. Byron had closely adhered to the plot and used much of the music from the original opera.

For Marie he had written up the 'trifling' role of Alessio into a much larger part as a burlesque boy, the kind of role for which she was already famous.

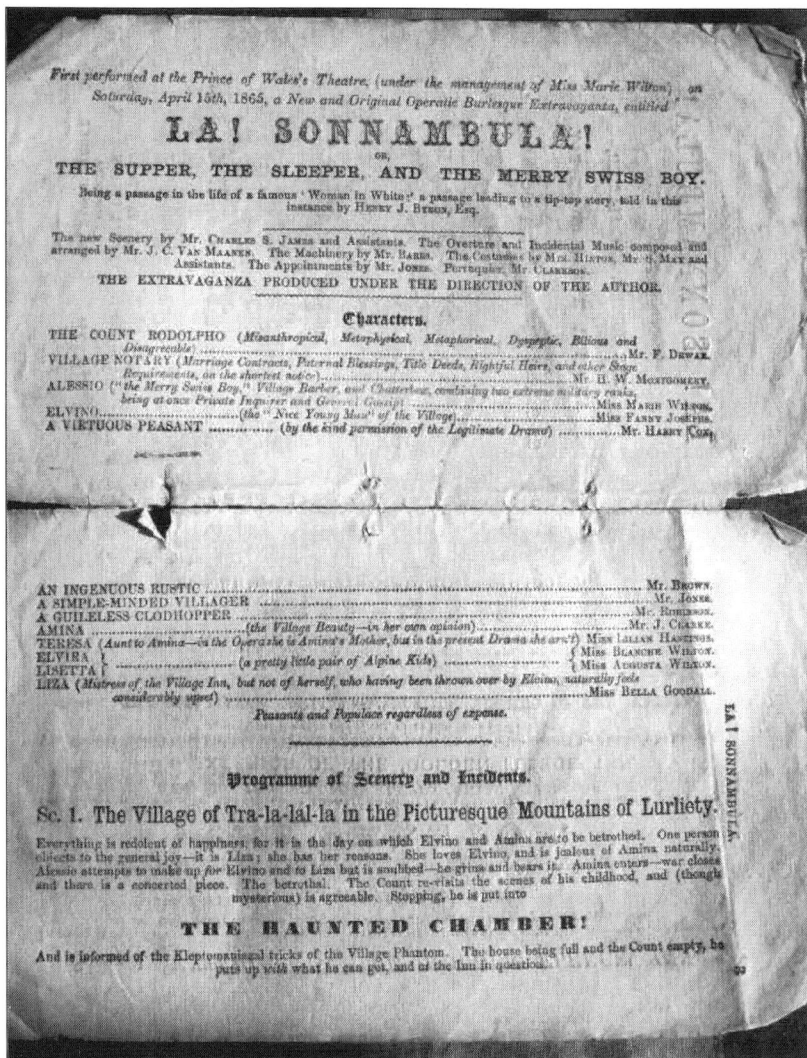

First performed at the Prince of Wales's Theatre, (under the management of Miss Marie Wilton) on Saturday, April 15th, 1865, a New and Original Operatic Burlesque Extravaganza, entitled

LA! SONNAMBULA!
or,
THE SUPPER, THE SLEEPER, AND THE MERRY SWISS BOY.

Being a passage in the life of a famous 'Woman in White,' a passage leading to a tip-top story, told in this instance by HENRY J. BYRON, Esq.

The new Scenery by Mr. CHARLES S. JAMES and Assistants. The Overture and Incidental Music composed and arranged by Mr. J. C. VAN MAANEN. The Machinery by Mr. BARRS. The Costumes by MRS. HILTON, MR. S. MAY and Assistants. The Appointments by Mr. JONES. Perruquier, Mr. CLARKSON.
THE EXTRAVAGANZA PRODUCED UNDER THE DIRECTION OF THE AUTHOR.

Characters.
THE COUNT RODOLPHO (*Misanthropical, Metaphysical, Metaphorical, Dyspeptic, Bilious and Disagreeable*)...Mr. F. DEWAR.
VILLAGE NOTARY (*Marriage Contracts, Paternal Blessings, Title Deeds, Rightful Heirs, and other Stage Requirements, on the shortest notice*)..Mr. H. W. MONTGOMERY.
ALESSIO ("*the Merry Swiss Boy*," *Village Barber, and Chatterbox, combining two extreme military ranks, being at once Private Inquirer and General Gossip*).....................................Miss MARIE WILTON.
ELVINO...(*the "Nice Young Man" of the Village*)......................Miss FANNY JOSEPHS.
A VIRTUOUS PEASANT ....(*by the kind permission of the Legitimate Drama*)..................Mr. HARRY COX.

AN INGENUOUS RUSTIC .... Mr. BROWN.
A SIMPLE-MINDED VILLAGER .... Mr. JONES.
A GUILELESS CLODHOPPER .... Mr. ROBINSON.
AMINA ....(the Village Beauty—in her own opinion)............................Mr. J. CLARKE.
TERESA (*Aunt to Amina—in the Opera she is Amina's Mother, but in the present Drama she arn't*) Miss LILIAN HASTINGS.
ELVIRA)   { Miss BLANCHE WILSON.
             } (*a pretty little pair of Alpine Kids*) ....{
LISETTA)   { Miss AUGUSTA WILSON.
LIZA (*Mistress of the Village Inn, but not of herself, who having been thrown over by Elvino, naturally feels considerably upset*) ....Miss BELLA GOODALL.

Peasants and Populace regardless of expense.

Programme of Scenery and Incidents.

Sc. 1. The Village of Tra-la-lal-la in the Picturesque Mountains of Lurliety.

Everything is redolent of happiness; for it is the day on which Elvino and Amina are to be betrothed. One person objects to the general joy—it is Liza; she has her reasons. She loves Elvino, and is jealous of Amina naturally. Alessio attempts to make up for Elvino and to Liza but is snubbed—he grins and bears it. Amina enters—war closes and there is a concerted piece. The betrothal. The Count re-visits the scenes of his childhood, and (though mysterious) is agreeable. Stopping, he is put into

THE HAUNTED CHAMBER!

And is informed of the Kleptomaniacal tricks of the Village Phantom. The house being full and the Count empty, he puts up with what he can get, and at the Inn in question.

***one of the first programmes from
the Prince of Wales's Theatre, April 1865***

The *Morning Post* reported that 'she was warmly received, and the applause was redoubled when she delivered her opening lines. She played in her accustomed vivacious and piquant style, looked the part to perfection, sang well, and danced with infinite spirit.' The *Post* went on to say that there was more genuine wit in Byron's puns than there was usually to be found in such pieces. Having no idea that Marie Wilton's long-term ambition was to abandon burlesque altogether, the reviewer remarked that 'burlesque is evidently to be the staple commodity at the Prince of Wales, with comedietta and farce to make up the bill'.

When the curtain fell many well-wishers came to offer their congratulations. 'Harry' Byron was delighted at the success of their opening night and headed home in high spirits. When the night's takings were given to Marie she had never before held so much money in her hand and had no idea what she should do with it. She did not dare take it home – a young woman carrying so much cash across London and keeping it overnight would have been at considerable risk. Fortunately a friend, Joseph Levy's son, Albert, came to her rescue. He took charge of the money overnight, taking it home with him, wrapped in his silk pocket handkerchief. On Monday morning Marie and Byron opened an account for the theatre at a nearby bank, so each night's takings could be securely placed in a deposit box.

Meanwhile, Marie's recruit from Liverpool was especially content. Squire Bancroft relished being in London and socializing with the many congenial people he met there. Before the opening night, following the final rehearsal, he was taken to a supper party by John Clarke*, one of the company, where they joined a gathering of theatre people, many of whom were to become friends. 'My introduction to these men filled me with happiness, and opened, as it were, the doors to a companionship with the lights which then illumined that happy world – Bohemia!'

It was not until some days after the opening night that Marie was informed of an alarming event that had taken place just as the curtain was about to rise: a pile of wood-shavings that had been left lying around beneath the pit area somehow caught fire. Fortunately this was discovered in time to avert what would have been a major catastrophe – the Prince of Wales's could have burnt down on its very first night. It was a narrow escape from a terrible disaster. Theatre fires were a constant hazard at that time of open flame gas lighting, and there were many fatal accidents, usually involving young girls. Just a couple of years before the opening of the Prince of Wales's, *The Era* conducted a campaign against the fashion for the crinoline dress. Although not quite as enormous as at the height of the fashion around the beginning of the decade, when they could measure as much as six feet in diameter, by the mid-1860s these huge skirts were still made with many yards of highly inflammable fabric and with several layers of petticoat, held out by a great wire 'cage' creating a large air pocket. Every year, while the crinoline remained in fashion, much tragic

---

* John Clarke, 1830-79, came with Marie Wilton from the Strand Theatre, where he was a popular burlesque actor.

90

loss of life was caused when the huge skirts caught fire. In homes, where naked flames burned everywhere, women were in particular danger while undressing: a skirt might brush against a candle and be alight within seconds. In theatres the girls were especially at risk. The critic E.L.Blanchard wrote in his diary of one of these theatre tragedies. 'Jan 23rd 1863: Fire at Princess's; poor little ballet girls burnt in pantomime .... [they] died from their hurts.' The flimsy dress of one girl had brushed against a gas footlight and caught fire, the flames catching hold of the other girl's dress. An editor's footnote read: 'The girls' names were Hunt and Smith. Robert Roxby, stage-manager, was seriously injured in endeavouring to put out the flames. It was fortunate, with such a number of people on the stage, that the accident did not result in more evil consequences.' *The Era*'s campaign led to many articles and much correspondence on the subject, but the dangerous fashion for crinolines prevailed and ran its course.

The Prince of Wales's Theatre immediately proved a huge success. Barely a month after its opening, according to *The Times* of 13 May 1865, it was 'nightly thronged by one of the most fashionable audiences in London.'

The disreputable area of Tottenham Street had never before seen such an invasion of upper and middle-class visitors from smart parts of town such as Belgravia, Mayfair and beyond. Before very long the theatre was to lose its old name of the Dust-Hole and was sometimes jokingly referred to as the 'Gold-Dust-Hole'. One night Wooler, the author of *A Winning Hazard,* wove his way into the green-room after an evening dining out rather too well, to offer his congratulations on the venture. His only criticism was that he felt that Marie and Byron should have accepted his own offering of *All's Fair in Love and War* as the opening piece rather than *A Winning Hazard,* which he condemned as 'rubbish'. He had totally forgotten that *Hazard* was his very own comedietta under a different title. When Marie passed this story on to Byron he was highly amused. 'Ah well,' said Marie, 'he was full of congratulations!' to which Byron replied, 'Full of congratulations! I thought it was liquor!'

The opening programme ran until the middle of June and then at long last Marie had the chance she had been waiting for: Byron completed a comedy for her. It was called *War to the Knife* and it was played for the first time on 10 June. E.L.Blanchard wrote that it was 'written with much smartness and goes off well.' This short opening season at the Prince of Wales's came to an end on 5 August. The whole company then went on a provincial tour, taking *War to the Knife* and *La! Sonnambula!* up north to Liverpool for three weeks, then for two weeks into the west country, to Bristol, Bath and Exeter, after which most of them managed to snatch a few days of relaxation by the sea together, at Dawlish.

Marie Wilton and Henry Byron's first full season at the Prince of Wales's Theatre began on 25 September, 1865. There were a few changes in the company. Some remained, including Marie's sisters Blanche and Augusta, as well as Squire Bancroft; a few moved on and some new faces joined, the most significant among them being John Hare, the young actor with whom Squire had worked in Liverpool. Hare had written to Marie around the time of the opening of the Prince of Wales's, asking her to consider including him in her company. They had first met in Liverpool when Marie was there on tour with the Strand, but by the time he contacted her she had already filled her small company. Now there was a vacancy and Squire recommended him; so Marie invited him to join her at the Prince of Wales's, an invitation that Hare was keen to accept. He was to become a key member, sharing a dressing room with Bancroft for many years.

War to the Knife, *1865, l-r Fanny Josephs, Marie Wilton,*
Frederick Dewar, 'Sydney' Bancroft

Marie and Byron opened the new season with the usual mixed-bill of comedy, burlesque and farce, the first programme including another new Byron burlesque, based on *Lucia di Lammermoor.* The opening comedy, in which Hare made his London debut, was called *Naval Engagements.*

Byron remarked one day during rehearsal that the diminutive Hare's part, a landlord called Short, was truly suitable for him: 'Short figure, short name, short part.....the critics will say, "Mr Hare, a clever young actor, made his first bow to a London audience, and was most excellent; in Short, perfect".' 'Yes,' replied Hare, 'but what will happen if they don't like me?' 'We'll just have to rechristen the piece *Short Engagements*.' Fortunately Hare was a success, then and later, and more than justified Marie's faith in him. Rounding off the bill was a farce called *A Lover by Proxy* by Dion Boucicault, the well-known Irish playwright, in which Bancroft had the main part.

In the early days the little theatre in Tottenham Street was still generally known by its old familiar name, as Marie discovered one evening when she asked the driver of a hansom cab to take her to the Prince of Wales's. Anxiously worrying about the evening's performances she paid little attention to the direction they were going. They turned into the Mall and drew to a halt. Puzzled, Marie asked the driver where they were. He replied, 'Didn't you want to be drove to the Prince of Wales's? Well, here you are.' He had taken her to Marlborough House, the London residence of the Prince of Wales, later King Edward VII.

Rides in London cabs could occasionally be perilous. One day Marie hired a cab to take her south of the river. The man was apparently drunk and he drove his unfortunate horse like a maniac. Setting off at an alarming speed, they tore through the streets, terrifying passers-by and passenger alike. Crossing the river at Vauxhall Bridge, then a toll-bridge, the cab flew through the toll without a pause, leaving the toll-keeper shouting after them in vain. Marie became 'resigned to the fact that the horse, man, cab, and myself would very soon be smashed' but somehow she was deposited at home in one piece: 'My thankfulness when I found myself not only safe, but sound, was indescribable!' She gave a distressing description of another cab horse. 'It could scarcely crawl. The cab was a wretched, broken-down thing and .... the horse was rickety too, but showed a desire to do his best, poor creature.' (This was twelve years before the publication of *Black Beauty*[*] which highlighted the plight of the unfortunate working horses of London with its heartrending story of the poor, broken Ginger, who after years as a cab horse on the London streets, ended her miserable, overworked life pulling a heavily-laden cart when she could no longer draw a cab.) The driver of the cab Marie described was a very old, very deaf man and the poor old horse plodded along a circuitous route through unfamiliar, narrow backstreets. Becoming anxious she hung out of the window and shouted to the driver, to no avail as he didn't hear a word. Eventually she stuck her umbrella out of the

---

[*] *Black Beauty*, by Anna Sewell, was first published in 1877.

window and prodded him with it, shouting that he was going the wrong way. He stopped, threw down his reins and turning around said, 'Look 'ere, Miss, I'll get inside and you can jump on the box.' Once again, she was greatly relieved to reach home in one piece.

Soon after the start of the new season a meeting occurred that Marie was to describe as the 'most important event in my career as a manager'. Harry Byron introduced her to an old friend of his, a struggling playwright called T.W.(Tom) Robertson, who brought with him a play he hoped Marie would consider.

Thomas William Robertson was born in Newark-on-Trent, Nottinghamshire, in 1829, the eldest of a very large theatrical family. It has been said that there were as many as twenty-two children but it is more probable that there were actually no more than fifteen or so; perhaps there were some who did not survive infancy. The youngest Robertson child was Margaret, who was one day to become famous as the actress Mrs (later Dame) Madge Kendal, who was born in 1848. Their father, William Robertson, was an actor who was also manager of the large Lincoln circuit, which covered several East Midlands towns during the declining years of the circuit system. The young Tom Robertson grew up doing virtually every job there was to be done in a provincial theatre, as stage carpenter, scene painter, scene builder and scene shifter, as prop maker, prompter and general dogsbody, even, occasionally as an actor, although never a good one. He also wrote plays and songs for his father's company. He had some formal education but left school at fourteen. He was described by his sister, Madge, as 'rather above middle height, with a full beard and moustache.' Marie Wilton said that he had 'piercing brown eyes that were ever restless,' and that 'personal appearance never seemed to enter much into his thoughts; I don't think the idea of being tidy or untidy occurred to him, for he was a Bohemian to the heart's core.'

Through the 1850s and early '60s Robertson accepted whatever theatre work he could find while desperately trying to find a taker for his early plays, often adaptations or translations from the French, but meeting with no success. In 1856 he married a young actress called Elizabeth Burton and they soon had children to support. Much of the time Robertson and his family were living close to real poverty and Elizabeth, in spite of ill health and against doctor's orders, had to continue taking what acting work came her way.

Eventually Robertson began to find some small success, if not fortune, with his journalism, contributing to many papers and magazines, notably the *Illustrated Times* for which he became theatre critic under the name of the 'Theatrical Lounger' and for which he wrote a series of humorous articles entitled 'Theatrical Types', about the various people concerned with the daily routine of the theatre, as well as the performers on the stage.

Although the pieces are exaggerated generalizations, they also contain some truths. Some of his portrayals must have been much resented by their subjects, particularly the Stage-Managers, for whom he seemed to have a special dislike. The Frenchman, Augustin Filon, described the pieces as 'observant, natural, alive, with here and there a gust of passion and a vent of spleen'. His 'Cruel Stage-Manager' surely must have been based on Marie's description of Barrett, her old adversary at the Lyceum when she first arrived in London:

> The Cruel Stage-Manager .... abuses his power in the largest spirit of the smallest tyranny, and, while he fawns on public favourites, is the bane of the actors of inferior parts and the terror of the ballet. If a poor girl be one minute late by the Cruel Stage-Manager's infallible chronometer (which, with the green room clock, he always keeps five minutes before the Horse Guards) he directs the Prompter to 'fine her' .... and the girl who walks twenty miles a day, and being a clever dancer, earns eighteen shillings a week, is mulcted of one shilling.

The 'Affectionate Stage-Manager', on the other hand, was clearly a proper 'luvvie':

> With him every male is his 'dear boy', every woman 'his darling child', every manager 'a splendid fellow', every actor 'a first-rate man', every actress 'a charming creature', every supernumerary 'a good chap'. 'Whatever is best' is his motto and his *bonhomie* is supposed by actors – an easily-persuaded and credulous race – to spring from a kind heart, whereas it is only pure, simple, unadulterated blarney.

At last, in 1864, Robertson found success with one of his plays. *David Garrick* was loosely adapted from a French play, and its leading character had little to do with the great eighteenth-century actor beyond his name and the fact that he was an actor. It was produced at the Haymarket with Edward Askew Sothern, of Dundreary fame, in the leading role and Robertson was paid the high – for him – sum of £50. But it was the meeting with Marie Wilton the following year that was to change the lives of both of them.

Although Marie Wilton implied that when Byron introduced them in 1865 it was the first time she and Robertson had met, they must surely have known each other some four years earlier: Robertson had written a farce that was produced early in 1861 at the Strand, when Marie was at the height of her burlesque fame at that theatre. Among the many other plays he wrote around that time that never saw the light of day, there was one that had Marie's name listed among the cast he had in mind. So it would seem he must have known her, if not well. As well as his 'Cruel Stage-Manager' being so close to her description of Barrett at the

Lyceum, it would also seem more than likely that he modelled his portrait of the 'Burlesque Actress' on Marie Wilton herself:

> [She] is young, elegant, and accomplished and handsome .... She can sing and she can dance, and as for acting, she must play farce, tragedy, opera, comedy, melodrama, pantomime, ballet, change her costume, fight a combat, make love, poison herself, die, and take one encore for a song and another for a dance, in the short space of ten minutes. The young actress in possession of all these abilities wakes up in the morning after her appearance in London to find herself famous. The men at the clubs go mad about her. She is almost pelted with bouquets and billet-doux; enthusiasts crowd round her cab to see her alight or waylay her in omnibuses; old gentlemen send her flowers, scent-bottles, ivory-backed hairbrushes, cambric pocket-handkerchiefs, and parasols; matter-of-fact barristers compose verses in her honour; and photographers lay their cameras at her feet. Half Aldershot comes nightly up by train. She is a power in London, and theatrical managers drive up to her door and bid against each other for her services. Fortunate folks who see her in the daytime complain 'that she dresses plainly' 'almost shabbily'; but, then, they are not aware that she has to keep half a dozen fatherless brothers and sisters and an invalid mother out of her salary which intelligence, when known to the two or three men who really care for her, sends them sleepless with admiration. Here is a household fairy who can polk, paint, make puddings, sew on buttons, turn heads and old bonnets, wear cleaned gloves, whistle, weep, laugh, and perhaps love.

If there had been paparazzi around in the middle of the nineteenth century, the burlesque actress as described by Tom Robertson would surely have found herself being pursued by them and their cameras pointed at her wherever she went.

The play Robertson offered to Marie Wilton was called *Society*. It had already been produced with some success in Liverpool, but every London manager had turned it down contemptuously. One returned it with 'bosh' scrawled across it and Buckstone at the Haymarket described it as 'rubbish'. Robertson himself was a popular member of the Arundel and the Savage clubs that were frequented by London's 'Bohemians' but many of the London managers feared that that the all too recognisable club and café crowd who are satirised in the play might be offended at their portrayal. Byron read the play through to Marie, even though he had his own doubts as to how his friend's work might be received in London, and shared his anxiety that their potential patrons might object. Marie, however, loved the play: she thought it clever and original and was keen to produce it at the Prince of Wales's. 'Danger is better than dullness,' she said and Byron was persuaded to agree. Without knowing it at the time, Tom Robertson and Marie Wilton were on the brink of bringing about a quiet revolution in the theatre of mid-Victorian London. The playwright Tom Taylor wrote of the work that they were to do together: 'The author and the theatre, the actors and the roles, all seem made for one another.'

Society was to be the first of several Robertson plays to be produced at The Prince of Wales's Theatre over the next few years. They were to prove a goldmine for all concerned and brought Robertson himself from a life of struggling obscurity to being recognised as one of the foremost playwrights of his day. At the Prince of Wales's he was paid one pound per performance for *Society*, a respectable sum at the time, and this was to increase over the years.

T.W. 'Tom' Robertson

The first night of *Society* was on Saturday, 11 November, 1865, and it was an immediate success. There was a good turnout of what the critic Clement Scott described as 'the light literary division' – London's Bohemian society – for many of whom, including Scott himself, it was standing room only in spite of the addition of more seats. A further row of stalls had been put in to accommodate the extra audiences who wished to see the play from comfortable seats and did not want to sit in the pit, and shortly after the first night the Prince of Wales himself, the future King Edward VII, came to see the play that had become the talk of the town. In the event, whether they recognised themselves or not, the 'Bohemians' of the clubs and the eating houses loved the play and relished the camaraderie of a scene set in the 'Owl's Roost' club, in which one member needed to borrow five shillings from a friend. He had no money either, so asked another member if *he* could borrow five shillings. And so it went on, until eventually it was the club waiter, the only man who had any cash on him, who produced the five shillings, which was then passed back from man to man until it reached the original borrower.

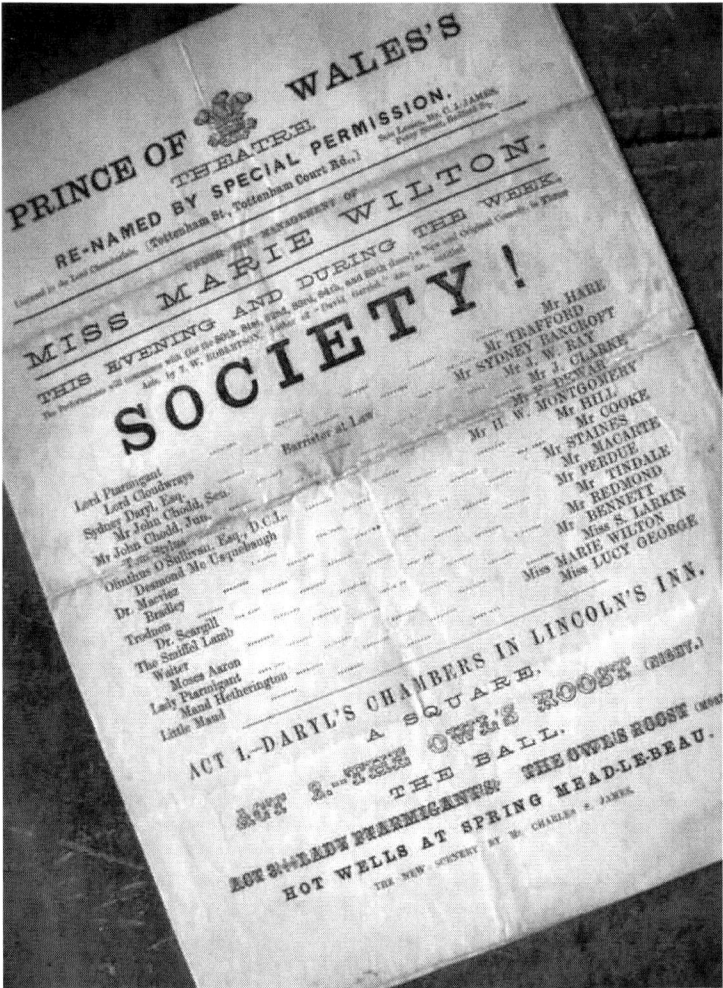

programme for Society, *featuring Mr 'Sydney' Bancroft*

98

Determined to break into this upper-class society came an obnoxious, nouveau-very-riche man and his even more obnoxious, social-climbing son who had ambitions to become an MP and who believed that money could buy him anything. 'I wish for the highest honours − I bring out my cheque-book,' he declares. 'I want to go into the House of Commons – cheque-book. I want the best legal opinion in the House of Lords – cheque-book. The best house – cheque-book. The best turn out – cheque-book. The best friends, the best wife, the best-trained children – cheque-book, cheque-book, and cheque-book.' When asked about such things as 'honour, love, obedience, troops of friends'*, he replies, 'Can buy 'em all, sir, in lots, as at an auction.' Needless to say, he gets his come-uppance. Marie's own *ingénue* part was insignificant, but Squire played the lead, a dilettante young barrister. It was, he wrote, 'a very important [role] to entrust to so young an actor as I then was, bearing, as it does, much of the burden of the play. I would like to note how much the success I was fortunate enough to achieve was due to the encouragement and support I received from the author, who spared no pains with me.' John Hare played a very elderly club member, who spent much of the time falling asleep, a portrayal that delighted critics and audiences alike. 'Few of us had ever heard of him,' wrote the critic Clement Scott in his memoirs, '…. but the little actor made the hit of the evening. When we were told that he was a "mere boy" we laughed; when we …. found that he was a boy indeed, we could scarcely believe our eyes.'

Robertson insisted on stage-managing, that is directing, his own plays, having definite ideas as to just how he wanted them presented, insisting on convincing realism, both in the acting and in the sets. Years later W.S.Gilbert was to say of him, 'I look upon stage-management, as now understood, as having been absolutely invented by him.' Also many years later, in 1898, Arthur Wing Pinero, who described Robertson as 'the first "modern" playwright', was to set his famous play *Trelawney of the Wells* in the 1860s, inspired by the early life of Robertson. It features as one of its characters a struggling young playwright called Tom Wrench, who aspires to write his plays in a more realistic style than was normal for the time. In case of any doubt, Pinero made the identity of his character very clear: first the name Tom; then the initial letter T together with the first two letters of Wrench spell out the initials TWR. In the play, Pinero even has as one of his characters a young actress who is loaned the money to set up in management of her own theatre: he can only have had Marie Wilton in mind. (By the time the play was written, she was a close personal friend of Pinero's.) *Trelawney* reminded turn-of-the-century theatregoers of how revolutionary it had been back in the mid-'60s to see

---

* 'Honour, love, obedience, troops of friends' ('that which should accompany old age'): a quote from *Macbeth*, Act 5, Scene 3.

actors portraying realistic characters on a stage set with realistic fittings to match. 'I tell you, I won't have doors stuck here, there and everywhere,' says Tom Wrench. 'No, nor windows in all sorts of impossible places! Windows on one side, doors on the other – just where they should be architecturally. And locks on the doors, real locks, to work; and handles to turn ....'

For his actors, the fictional Tom Wrench spoke the words that could have been spoken by Tom Robertson himself: 'I strive to make my people talk and behave like live people, don't I? .... Naturally, the managers won't stand that.' In *Society* Robertson's characters were performed by actors who portrayed the characters they were playing as recognizable, believable people. One of those who had to stand that night was the critic, Clement Scott, who was captivated by the play and its actors, particularly Bancroft as the young lover and Hare, in his London debut, as the old aristocrat. Years later he recollected:

> Think what it was to see a bright, cheery, pleasant young fellow playing the lover to a pretty girl at a time when stage lovers were nearly all sixty and dressed like waiters .... What astonished us even more than the success of young Bancroft was .... [when] a little delightful old gentleman came upon the stage dressed in a long, beautifully-cut frock coat, bright-eyed, intelligent, with white hair that seemed to grow naturally on the head – no clumsy wig with a black forehead-line – and with a voice so refined, so aristocratic, that it was music to our ears. The part played by Mr Hare was, as we all know, insignificant. All he had to do was to say nothing, and to go perpetually to sleep. But how well he did nothing! How naturally he went to sleep! .... We knew instinctively that John Hare was an artist .... Tom Robertson's lucky star was in the ascendant when *Society* was refused by the Haymarket management .... The refusal of [his play] by Buckstone and the keen and penetrating intelligence of Marie Wilton .... were the turning points in the career of a broken-hearted and disappointed man.

The sets for *Society* at the Prince of Wales's were, in 1865, regarded as ground-breaking. Many years earlier, in around 1830, Madame Vestris had first introduced what was known as the box-set at her Olympic Theatre, complete with four walls and a ceiling, carpets on the floor and windows and doors that opened. In 1854, Robertson had for a while been employed as a prompter at the Lyceum, then under the management of Madame Vestris and Charles James Mathews. Inspired by Madame Vestris's innovations, he carried them still further in *Society*, introducing realism to an extent that had not been seen before. Rooms were furnished in a way they would be arranged in a home of the time, for instance a dining-room scene would include chairs set around a table as you might expect to see them, not just those that were needed for the number of characters in the scene, arranged in a straight line facing the audience. Other furnishings and decor were such as one would expect to see in such a room – and in the cluttered rooms of mid-Victorian England these were numerous.

Squire Bancroft in the 1860s

Society ran until Christmas, after which the company returned to some more seasonal fare – yet another Byron burlesque, *Little Don Giovanni*. This was the last burlesque part that Byron was to write specially for Marie Wilton and it was also to be the last time that she was ever to play a boy. The time had finally come when, to her delight, she was to cast off burlesque for ever, less than a year after taking over the unprepossessing old Dust-Hole. 'The success of our management made me firmly determined to insist on my original intention to give up acting that kind of part.' *Don Giovanni* ran for a few weeks, then *Society* was resumed in the early spring. In total it played for one hundred and fifty nights, 'in those days an extraordinary and seemingly, to us, never-ending run.' Then the season was rounded off with a short run of an original Byron comedy, *A Hundred Thousand Pounds*, which opened in May.

For some while Marie had been anxious about the health of her mother, and she now appeared to be getting worse. Not wanting to worry her daughter at a time when she was so preoccupied with her work, Georgiana had tried to disguise her condition from her, but it was clear that she was suffering severe abdominal pain. The Prince of Wales's company had been engaged to go for a summer season to Liverpool and Manchester and Marie was contemplating sending the company off without her, but Georgiana's doctor assured her that her mother's condition was not as alarming as it appeared and that she was in no immediate danger. Reassured in the knowledge that several of her many sisters were around to take care of their mother, Marie headed north near the beginning of August as planned and she and the rest of the company enjoyed a pleasant summer season there. As there was some kind of an epidemic in Liverpool that summer (there had been outbreaks of both cholera and typhus in the city in that year) they decided to stay outside the city centre and several of them travelled each night to where they had all found lodgings in a row of villas overlooking the sea. These included Henry Byron and his wife, as well as John Hare and his wife Mary, Squire Bancroft, and Marie's sister, Augusta Wilton. Tom Robertson was also there, on his own. Sadly, during the run of *Society*, his wife, Elizabeth, had died at the age of just twenty-nine, leaving him to bring up two young children, Tom and Maud, on his own. He was now working on a new play, to be called *Ours*. Hare and Bancroft were delighted to be back in the city where they had spent such a happy time not long before and enjoyed showing their friends around the city they knew so well and its surrounding area.

The assizes were on in Liverpool during the six weeks they were there. Assizes were held periodically in large towns and would run for a few weeks. Long lists of trials were waiting to be heard that were too important for the local magistrates' courts and had to wait for the arrival of the assize judges and their entourages. The arrival in a town of the assizes would produce a large influx of visitors, mostly lawyers and their staffs but also many others. It could prove a profitable time for theatres and other places of entertainment, not to mention hotel and lodging-house keepers, shops, inns and taverns.

Although they were working every evening, six days a week, their time in Liverpool was almost like a holiday for the Prince of Wales's company. The visitors knew some of the junior barristers who had travelled up from London and they all socialised together in what little spare time they had. Among the lawyers in Liverpool for the assizes was W.S.Gilbert, who was still trying to pursue his career as a barrister while writing plays in his spare time. The actors and the barristers enjoyed performing mock trials, with John Hare nearly always taking on the character of the criminal in the dock and Marie usually playing the part of the judge, wrapped in a pink shawl which was the best she could come up with as a judge's robe and with a wig made of cotton-wool; one evening they staged a mock opera, with Marie as the *prima donna* and Gilbert as her lover. Hare was his rival in love, arrayed in a cloak and a large hat, and armed to the teeth with knives and daggers. This 'opera' was sung throughout in mock Italian gibberish and provided everyone with a great evening's entertainment. This may have been Gilbert's first attempt at a comic opera. There must have been many late nights for all concerned, as, apart from Sundays, the actors would not have been free until midnight or even later.

Marie Wilton and her friends also enjoyed sitting in on some of their friends' cases in court. They could spare the time for this as, knowing their plays so well, they did not need to spend too much time rehearsing. On one of these occasions Gilbert made his maiden appearance as a barrister, and his friends from the Prince of Wales's were in court to support him. The case quickly turned to farce when he attempted to examine his client, an elderly Irish woman, charged with theft. She would not allow Gilbert to get a word in edgeways, constantly interrupting him with such remarks as 'It's a lie, yer honour!' 'Shut up, yer spalpeen!' and 'Ah, if ye love me, sit down!' every time Gilbert attempted to question her. Gilbert himself recounted this story in later years in a piece he called *My Maiden Brief*. He also described her 'torrent of invective against my abilities as a counsel'. The judge found the prisoner guilty, sentenced her, and ordered her to be returned to the cells. As she was being taken from the dock, she bent down and removing one of her boots she hurled it at the head of the far-from-learned counsel. With the court in an uproar of laughter, she was removed from the dock, and the unfortunate Gilbert's first case ended in disarray.

The easy summer weeks in the north had to come to an end and at the beginning of September the time came for the Prince of Wales's company to return to London and prepare for the start of the new season.

5

THE ROBERTSON YEARS

While she was in the north, Marie received regular letters from her mother. Georgiana was too ill to write herself: her letters were usually written for her by one of her daughters, and Georgiana was just able to sign them. Although these letters always seemed cheerful and reassuring, Marie was worried that her mother was unable to write them herself, and she was dismayed on her return to find that Georgiana's health had deteriorated far more seriously than she had been prepared to let Marie know. She was in fact suffering from terminal cancer of the womb and her doctors could do no more for her. It seems that the exact diagnosis of her condition was kept from Georgiana, and quite possibly from her family. At that time, indeed until well into the twentieth century, cancer was spoken of in hushed tones if at all. Georgiana must have been in continuous pain and it was clear that she only had a short time to live. With the new season at the Prince of Wales's soon to start, and with the shadow of her mother's illness hanging over her, it was a worrying time for Marie. On top of her anxieties about her mother, she now had more of the responsibilities of management on her shoulders than before, as while they were all in Liverpool Henry Byron had entered into a business arrangement with a couple of theatres in that city, requiring his frequent presence there on top of his responsibilities at the Prince of Wales's in London.

During their stay in Liverpool, Tom Robertson had completed his new play, *Ours*, and the Prince of Wales's company duly read, rehearsed and immediately produced it in Liverpool in August 1866. This was an invaluable way of trying out the new play before its London opening, giving Robertson the opportunity to make any alterations he considered necessary in time for the start of the new season in London, on Saturday, 15 September.

Ours was set during the Crimean War which, having ended just ten years earlier, was still fresh in people's memories. It opens in the elegant drawing-room at the country estate of the aristocratic Sir Alexander Shendryn, commander of his regiment, the 'Ours' of the title, and his formidable wife, who is convinced he is deceiving her. Their ward is a sweet young heiress, Blanche Haye, and Lady Shendryn's 'companion' is the impoverished but high-spirited and not-at-all-sweet Mary Netley, played by Marie Wilton. Blanche's hand is sought by a courtly, middle-aged but immensely rich Russian diplomat, Prince Perovsky (John Hare) but she is in love with a poor but noble officer, Angus Macalister (Squire Bancroft). Meanwhile a Beatrice and Benedick relationship develops between Mary Netley and the rich but far from noble Hugh Chalcot (John Clarke), heir to a brewing fortune.

When Shendryn's regiment, 'Ours', is ordered to the Crimea, the realism Robertson had introduced in the production of *Society* was taken to even greater lengths. In a scene at the end of the second act the regiment's off-stage departure is watched from a window by several of the characters, while the officers' commands and the tramp of marching feet can be heard from the street 'outside', to the accompaniment of a military band playing 'The Girl I Left Behind Me'. The stage direction for the close of the act reads, '*Music forte. Band plays "God Save the Queen". Cheers. Tramp of soldiers. Excitement .... Chalcot and Mary waving handkerchiefs and cheering at window .... Blanche totters down and falls fainting.*' (Robertson's sweet young things had a true Victorian inclination to flutter and faint, unlike the feistier characters usually played by Marie Wilton, who were made of tougher stuff.) The women then follow their men to the Crimea, arriving while the war is at its height. Improbable as this may seem today, the Crimean war did indeed attract 'battlefield-tourists'. It was the last time that women, both wives and other less respectable camp-followers, were to be permitted to accompany their men to war, or to watch the battles from supposedly safe vantage points, clad in crinolines and armed with parasols and picnic baskets, ready to offer 'home comforts' of every kind.

The final act of *Ours* shows an icy, dilapidated hut near Balaclava, in the depths of winter. There is a howling wind outside and every time the door opens flurries of snow are blown in through the door. Robertson's lengthy stage directions at the opening of this act detail precisely the props that were to ornament this sparsely-furnished shack, where a roly-poly pudding is prepared by Mary Netley in full view of the audience, using real ingredients, an improbable episode which was much remarked upon at the time. (It is also highly unlikely that Marie Wilton knew how to make one: she probably produced an inedible lump of dough.)

105

John Clarke and Marie Wilton in Ours

a hut in the Crimea, in Ours

Ours proved to be a success with audiences and critics alike and, as Marie Wilton put it, 'did much to decide the ultimate fortunes of the theatre and the fame of its author'. The *Daily News* reviewer wrote that 'the acting of the comedy was very near perfection': Louisa Moore, as Blanche, 'looked as well as she played and the fair manageress, whose reception was overwhelming, played as well as she looked.'

Robertson's plays were considered quite revolutionary in their time, with their credible dialogue, realistic sets, costumes and props, and plots that explored, if timidly, issues of the day, such as class, wealth and social position in a rigid society that had not yet begun to look forward to the changes that were to come later in the century.

Today his plays are almost unknown. However, in 2007, a production of *Ours*, directed by Phoebe Barran, ran for a month at the Finborough Theatre, an award-winning fringe venue in London's Earl's Court, as part of their 'Rediscoveries' season. This was the first time the play had been staged for almost a century and the production attracted favourable reviews, the critics concurring that the play stood up well in the 21st century in spite of being far less ground-breaking in retrospect than Robertson's plays appeared in their own time.

With Byron as her business partner, Marie Wilton had still not found the courage to demand that they should abandon his beloved form of popular entertainment completely, and yet another new burlesque of his was to follow *Ours* as an afterpiece. But this time, although Robertson's new play was pulling in the audiences, Byron's new burlesque was not a success. The 'king of burlesque' appeared to be losing his touch, maybe because his business ventures in Liverpool were occupying much of his time and energies. Marie had decided she would not act in it herself which had upset Byron considerably, even though she had secured the services of another celebrated star of the London burlesque scene for the main role. Lydia Thompson was just a year older than Marie and they had often worked together. Just a couple of years later Thompson was to take New York by storm when she took a troupe of 'British Blondes' – not all of whom were necessarily either British or blonde, but had what really mattered, shapely legs to display – to tour America. Transatlantic audiences were entranced, and at the same time scandalized, by them; and what was originally intended as a tour of a few months ran to several years. However, even this star could not save Byron's latest work.

Meanwhile Marie's mother was fading, and one evening at the end of November, during a scene in *Ours* when someone spoke the words, 'What a charming girl! How interesting! No father, no mother,' referring to Mary Netley, the character played by the ever-superstitious Marie, she had a premonition that this time the words were telling her that her dying mother's end was near and as soon as the curtain fell she hurried to her bedside. There she was met by her sister Ida, who said that their mother's life was indeed slipping away. Georgiana Wilton died on 30 November, 1866, at three o'clock in the morning, surrounded by her six daughters and her husband, Robert. She was only forty-six years old. She was laid to rest in a catacomb at West Norwood Cemetery, in south London, alongside her baby granddaughter, Florence Wilton.

These catacombs, or burial vaults, were constructed beneath a chapel, which would take a direct hit from a bomb early in the Second World War. Fortunately the cemetery records survived and these records reveal that several spaces in the vault were originally purchased by Robert Wilton in 1862, and that the first member of the family to buried there was Marie's baby, Florence, in September 1862. This appears to be the only surviving record of Florence, apart from a birth certificate which confirms her as Marie's child, and her death certificate, as Marie never mentions her child in her memoirs. She did however write that she herself paid for her mother's burial in the cemetery in 1866 'although I could as yet but ill afford the cost', but the records show that the vault had actually been paid for five years earlier at the time of baby Florence's death. As Robert was even less likely than his daughter to have been able to afford a vault, it is possible that, being the highest earner in the family as well as the mother of the child, it was Marie who actually paid for it back in 1862, although the purchase was in Robert's name, possibly to preserve Marie's anonymity.

The last burlesque to be produced at the Prince of Wales's Theatre was put on over Christmas 1866. Once again it was a poor affair of Byron's and was not well-received, as was reflected in the box-office takings. Byron was now spending most of his time in Liverpool and the partners rarely saw each other. The inevitable break came early in the New Year. In a letter dated 6 February, 1867, Byron wrote from Liverpool suggesting that they should terminate their partnership:

> It will be better for us both to cease our joint management at the end of our two years, and I shall willingly dissolve partnership, if you wish it, on the 15th April. I consider that by refusing to play in burlesque you have done me an irreparable wrong, and yourself harm; however, I have met your views always, and it is no doubt too late for me to repeat what I have so often said, and what is the general opinion of the public.

Marie replied immediately:

> You tell me that 'by refusing to play in burlesque' I have done you an 'irreparable wrong.' I don't acknowledge anything of the kind. All my acting in the last two burlesques would have done very little good for

them, beyond saving my substitute's salary. I can't help it if my candour wounds you, my dear Byron, but neither of the pieces has been worthy of you ....

You have often upbraided me with the sacrifices you have made in writing for only one theatre; I admit that your literary reputation would naturally suffer, but it has been a very great commercial gain. You have written five burlesques and two comedies, for which you will have received, by April next, a thousand pounds in salary and half of the entire profits. You must also remember that when we started you risked nothing – I risked all. You even made me sign a paper to indemnify you from any share in whatever loss I might suffer; and for the money I borrowed I have been paying a high interest, not a penny of which have I claimed from the treasury.

You must remember, too, Byron, that when you took the Liverpool theatres I never murmured .... although I felt it must prove a fatal blow to my interests; now tell me, frankly, if any other partner would have done this? It is impossible for me not to see that all your energies are now in Liverpool, and if we dissolve partnership at Easter, and I carry on the theatre without you, I don't think my conduct during our two years' business connection will cause you to entertain a single unfriendly feeling towards me.

The eventual outcome of this exchange of formal, very chilly letters was, as Marie put it, that 'our partnership – I rejoice to add, not our friendship – ended on April 15th, two years after its commencement.' Byron's final letter on the matter read:

Our letter of agreement is in my desk in London. It settled you were to receive ten pounds weekly until the end of the second year, thus making the thousand pounds you advanced. This you have done with the exception of one week. If you will draw all the money banked in our joint names out of the bank, after paying yourself the extra ten pounds, you can send me my share of it. I waive all right to half the value of the property in the theatre in consideration of your taking any outstanding debts on your own shoulders. Mrs Byron sends you her kind love. God bless you.

To the credit of both, Marie and Byron remained friends. Now, with the formal ending of the Byron-Wilton partnership, Marie found herself relying more and more on the advice and help of Squire Bancroft, who was turning out to be dependable and efficient and blessed with a good head for business. Even before the break with Byron they were beginning to work as a team and now that Marie was in sole charge of the Prince of Wales's, Bancroft's support became crucial to her, especially in management decisions.

A close personal relationship had also developed between them, a relationship that very likely commenced as soon as he accepted Marie

Wilton's offer to join her company in London. Bancroft repeated several times in his memoirs that he had fallen in love with her when they met in Liverpool and it seems probable that his feelings had been reciprocated, resulting in Marie's invitation to him to join her company as soon as she began to form it. From now on she began to show total confidence in his judgment, not only in business matters – at which he excelled – but also when it came to the choice of plays. Should there be any disagreement between them in such matters, she would from now on appear to accept his way of thinking, while probably subtly bringing him around to hers, particularly in matters directly connected with what plays they should produce and how they should be staged.

She was more than happy to let Bancroft take care of the business side of things. From being the strong, independent manager, she seems to have been happy to begin conforming to the accepted role of the submissive Victorian woman, although he never appears to have attempted to dominate her, and they invariably worked as equals over the years of success that were to follow.

Ours had run for 150 nights, and Marie had no hesitation in accepting as her next production Tom Robertson's new play, *Caste,* which was to become the best-known of all his plays. It is one that has occasionally been staged during the twentieth century and also sometimes features in university syllabuses on Victorian theatre. It was considered at the time to have brought about a complete reform of drama. Robertson demonstrated his growing affection for Marie and his gratitude to her for believing in him when he dedicated the play to her with the words 'To Miss Marie Wilton, this comedy is dedicated by her grateful friend and fellow labourer, the Author.' *Caste* opened at the Prince of Wales's on 6 April 1867, and it was an immediate and acclaimed success.

The theme of *Caste* is marriage across the class divide and the love between an aristocratic young officer, George D'Alroy, and Esther Eccles, a pretty young ballet girl. Esther's lively younger sister, Polly, is a burlesque actress, a part Robertson had written specifically for Marie Wilton, the character being drawn around her sparkling personality and her earlier days as a star of burlesque. All the parts that Robertson wrote for her from this time on drew directly on her boyishness and playfulness. Augustin Filon considered that, 'whether he was conscious of it or not, Robertson made her play Pippo all her life.'

Esther was played by a new addition to the company, Lydia Foote, a niece of the distinguished actress, Mary Ann Keeley. A fine actor called George Honey had the part of the girls' drunken layabout father and Sam Gerridge, a good-natured, salt-of-the-earth gasfitter and devoted 'follower' of Polly Eccles, was played by John Hare. The gallant hero, D'Alroy, was played by Frederick Younge and his snobbish, autocratic mother, the Marquise de Saint-Maur, was played by Sophie Larkin, who

110

had been the formidable Lady Shendryn in *Ours*. Squire Bancroft played D'Alroy's languid, foppish friend, Captain Hawtree.

The scenes move between the Marquise's elegant Mayfair drawing-room and the Eccles's modest home in Stangate, a working-class riverside district just south of Westminster Bridge, near Lambeth Palace. (All that remains of the district today is a short road that bears its name near St Thomas' Hospital.) Soon after Esther and D'Alroy have married in secret, D'Alroy's regiment is ordered overseas to serve in the Indian Mutiny and he leaves his bride behind, unaware that she is carrying his child. Word soon arrives that he has been killed in action. There is a wonderful scene when Esther defies her daunting mother-in-law, who has discovered, to her horror, about her son's secret marriage to the socially inferior Esther and that Esther is struggling to bring up his child on her own. The Marquise descends on Stangate, demanding that her grandson should be handed over to her immediately, to be raised by herself in a style appropriate to the infant aristocrat. Esther flatly refuses to hand over her child and shows the Marquise the door.

Polly is now the only breadwinner in the Eccles household, supporting her sister and the baby as well as her drunken father. In one of the most celebrated comic theatrical scenes of the day she is serving tea – real tea, of course, with real bread-and-butter (this *was* a Tom Robertson play) – to Sam Gerridge and Captain Hawtree, whose haw-haw, upper-class exterior hides a kind heart. He has been secretly providing some financial support for his best friend's penniless wife and her baby. Suddenly Captain D'Alroy walks in, alive and well, and the horrified Polly and Sam, believing they are seeing a ghost, slowly sink beneath the table.

One night there was a near fiasco when it came to the scene of D'Alroy's return from the dead. A member of the back-stage staff decided to play a practical joke on Frederick Younge, the actor playing the gallant Captain, by hiding the wig he wore for his part. Younge, unable to find his wig, was forced to make his entrance and return from the dead without it. With no wig beneath it, the hat he wore was now much too big for him and came way down over his eyes. The result was that instead of appearing to be suitably terrified when the 'ghost' walks in, Polly and Sam were barely able to stifle their laughter. Marie drew back to hide herself completely under the tablecloth and poor Hare, with a mouth full of bread and butter, almost choked with mirth. The blond wig was in itself a break from tradition. Convention dictated that the sentimental hero should be tall, dark and handsome, while the dandy or fop, in this case Bancroft in the part of Hawtree, should have long, floppy, fair hair – much as Sir Andrew Aguecheek has often been portrayed in *Twelfth Night*. Robertson reversed these conventions. So Younge, presumably a dark-haired man, and Bancroft, a fair-haired man, must both have worn wigs. The foppish, often idiotic, haw-haw swell had been for years a stock

111

character and was almost invariably exaggerated, overplayed and unbelievable – a figure of fun. Bancroft played Hawtree as languid indeed, but as a laid-back, humorous, somewhat cynical character and the part thoroughly established him in what became known as a 'Bancroft part'.

Marie Wilton and John Hare as Polly Eccles and
Sam Gerridge in Caste

The reviews were mostly glowing, enthusing in particular about the performances of George Honey, John Hare and Marie Wilton. The *Daily News* said that *Caste* was 'a play with a purpose …. brilliantly written.' Honey had 'never acted better' as Eccles, the feckless, drunken father of the girls, who constantly holds forth on the rights of the labouring man but has never been known to do a stroke of work in his life. The reviewer wrote that as Sam Gerridge, Hare performed 'the most exquisite and unforced bit of comedy we have seen in years'. *The Times* had concerns that the portrayal of working-class characters, particularly Eccles and Gerridge, might be regarded as offensive by the occupants of the gallery, '.... many of those working men who patronized [the Prince of Wales's] when it was the humble Queen's.' However, the gallery regarded Eccles as 'a proper object of derision and Sam as a person to be respected.' The *Illustrated London News* considered that *Caste* was 'most conscientiously acted' and that it would 'command the success that it deserves, for there is a truth and vitality in it which will preserve it in its freshness for many a month to come.' Interestingly, all the reviews of the time, of this and of other plays on the London stage, gave lengthy and detailed outlines of the entire plot, far more than would be considered either necessary or desirable today.

Caste ran to great acclaim until July 1867, when the production was taken north to play for a four-week summer season, first in one of Henry Byron's theatres in Liverpool, and then in Manchester. It was enthusiastically received in both cities. When the company returned to London the new season opened with *Caste*, which was finally withdrawn near Christmas after 156 performances.

Many years later the cartoonist Linley Sambourne[*] presented Squire Bancroft with the first drawing he ever did for *Punch*, which had appeared in the issue of 20 July, 1867. His caricature, of John Hare, Squire Bancroft and George Honey in the original production, showed Sam Gerridge, Captain Hawtree and 'Papa' Eccles enclosed in a large letter C. 'I went to the pit to delight in *Caste*,' Sambourne wrote, 'and drew the sketch from memory.'

1867 was a year of marriages. In June, just seven months after the death of his wife, Georgiana, Robert Wilton remarried. His new wife was Susan Heal, with whom he had probably been living for part of the previous few years in Bristol. In the census of 1861 Robert is registered in two different places – with Georgiana and their daughters in Lambeth, and also near Bristol, with a 'housekeeper', Susan Heal. (He must have been registered for census purposes by both women, although he could only have actually been with one of them on census night.) Robert was probably still finding work in Bristol and renting lodgings in the area. It cannot necessarily be

---

[*] Edward Linley Sambourne, 1844-1910, was for many years a leading cartoonist for *Punch*. The house in Kensington, London, where he and his family lived from 1874, is today open to the public, complete with many of its original decorations and furnishings. It is a fine example of a late Victorian upper-class domestic residence.

assumed that Susan was his mistress, but it seems probable in the light of their marriage so soon after Georgiana's death.

caricature by Linley Sambourne of
Hare, Bancroft and Honey in **Caste,** *1867*

Next, Tom Robertson remarried. He and his new wife, a young German woman called Rosetta Feist, had met in London the previous year but she had to return to her family in Germany, where Robertson went for their wedding, which took place in Frankfurt in October.

Then three days after Christmas, on Saturday, 28 December 1867, Squire Bancroft and Marie Wilton were married at the Church of St Stephen the Martyr in St John's Wood. The ceremony was conducted by Squire's uncle, the Rev John Butterfield, MA, who was then curate of a church in Hampshire. (This clergyman uncle is the only one of Squire Bancroft's family about whom anything much is known – and that is very little. Squire's only sibling who appears to have survived to adulthood, his sister Julia, is never mentioned in his memoirs.) The marriage certificate gives Marie's address as 8 Circus Road, St John's Wood, close to Lord's cricket ground and Squire's as 3 Eaton Terrace.

Marie Wilton and Squire Bancroft, around the time of their marriage

Just a fortnight earlier, Squire had legally changed his name from Butterfield to Bancroft by deed-poll. From then on his name was officially Squire Bancroft Bancroft. (It seems decidedly odd that he chose to keep Bancroft as his middle name, repeating it as his new surname.)

I, the undersigned, SQUIRE BANCROFT BUTTERFIELD, of No. 3, Eaton-terrace, St. John's Wood, in the parish of Saint Marylebone, in the county of Middlesex, gentleman, having ever since the year 1861 used for all purposes and on all occasions the surname of "Bancroft" only, DO HEREBY GIVE NOTICE that I intend from the date hereof to USE for all purposes and on all occasions the SURNAME of "BANCROFT" only, in lieu of and in substitution for that of "Butterfield." And I hereby declare that my signature "S. BANCROFT BANCROFT" is and shall be as effectual and binding as my heretofore signature. And I further give notice that I have by deed-poll under my hand and seal, dated this day, and duly acknowledged by me, and intended to be forthwith inrolled in her Majesty's High Court of Chancery, declared my intention as above expressed. As witness my hand this 13th day of December, 1867.
S. BANCROFT BUTTERFIELD.
Witness, ALFRED GROOM, 3, Raymond-buildings, Gray's-inn, London, Solicitor.
JOSEPH GROOM, same place.

notice of Bancroft's deed-poll, 1867

Marie and Squire started their married life together in Circus Road. In the 1860s St John's Wood was way out in the suburbs, although already quite fashionable. In their joint memoirs the Bancrofts do not give their marriage so much as a mention in passing. There was certainly no time for a honeymoon. Probably they went back to work immediately after their wedding, partners now in every sense of the word.

Just before Christmas *Caste* was succeeded by Dion Boucicault's comedy, *How She Loves Him*. This had originally been produced in America, and the Prince of Wales's production was to be the play's first showing in England. The remarkably-named Irish dramatist Dionysius Lardner Boucicault was a prolific writer: during his long career he produced some 200 plays. Born in Dublin in 1820, he began writing plays while still in his teens, and several had been produced in the provinces by the time he arrived in London. Here he began bombarding Madame Vestris and Charles James Mathews with his work. Eventually they succumbed and what was to become his best-known play, *London Assurance*, was first produced at the Theatre Royal, Covent Garden in 1841 when he was just twenty years old.

Dion Boucicault had a colourful private life. Invariably hard up, in his early twenties he married a wealthy French widow, some years older than himself. After only a year or so the unfortunate lady died in mysterious circumstances and there were rumours in circulation that Boucicault might have had a hand in her demise. This is highly unlikely and, although he undoubtedly benefited from his wife's death, he rapidly spent the fortune he inherited from her and was soon bankrupt. In 1850 he was taken on by Charles Kean at the Princess's Theatre to write popular melodramas to accompany Kean's productions of Shakespeare. Among his work for the Princess's was a play that was hugely popular for many years, *The Corsican Brothers,* adapted from a Dumas novel.

Boucicault then became romantically involved with Kean's ward, the 19-year-old actress Agnes Robertson, described by the *Daily Telegraph* as 'the embodiment of charming Irish beauty'. In 1853, the lovers ran away to America, where they married. The Boucicaults were a successful partnership during their years in America, with Dion writing many plays and both Agnes and himself acting in them. While in America Boucicault's work included plays that addressed contemporary issues in melodramatic form, including *The Poor of New York* of 1857, which over the years was adapted by its author as *The Poor of London* or *The Poor of Liverpool*, or wherever, to suit whichever city it was being played in. In 1860 came one of his most acclaimed plays, *The Colleen Bawn*, a melodrama based on a true story of the murder of a lovely young girl in the west of Ireland. The Boucicaults returned to London and *The Colleen Bawn* went on to have a long run at the Adelphi with Boucicault and

Agnes in the leading roles. It ran for almost 300 performances, a record for that time, Queen Victoria seeing it three times.

Dion Boucicault is one of the very few playwrights of the mid-Victorian era whose work has survived to the present day There was a dazzling production of *London Assurance* at the National Theatre in London in 2010, starring Simon Russell Beale, Fiona Shaw and the late Richard Briers. *The Colleen Bawn* and another of his important Irish dramas, *The Shaughraun,* have also both been seen at the National.

How She Loves Him has seldom been revived and it appears in only a few of the more extensive lists of Boucicault's works. It had first been produced in New York in 1863 and Marie Wilton had been considering the comedy for some time but had reservations about it. A letter from Boucicault dated 10 November 1867 indicates that he was quite prepared to accept alterations to his work: 'My dear Marie.......show me how good you think me by saying outright what you think, and don't offend me by "doing the nice," and by imagining that you can ever wound my vanity.'

Dion Boucicault

Boucicault was a gifted stage-manager and Marie Bancroft was more than happy to leave the direction of *How She Loves Him* to its author, aware that she herself could learn much from him. She wrote, 'Boucicault's accomplished power as a stage-manager is too well known

117

to need our praise.' Even so, during rehearsals further small alterations appeared to be necessary which she was hesitant to suggest outright: 'We hardly, in those days, liked to interfere with such an autocrat, kind as we had always found him.' Somehow she tactfully managed to get alterations incorporated in such a way that Boucicault believed the change in the script had been his own idea all along. The comedy revolved around the differences of opinion between various types of alternative therapists that were fashionable at the time. The first couple of acts went well, in particular 'an immensely amusing scene .... between a patient and doctors of every opposite belief – allopathic, homoeopathic, hydropathic, and galvanic – was received with hearty laughter.'

Unfortunately the rest of *How She Loves Him* did not go so well and it failed to attract the full houses that the Prince of Wales's had become accustomed to with its Robertson plays. This was a particular disappointment for Squire Bancroft as he had mostly received favourable attention for his part in the play, 'a character in which I built up some eccentricities founded on the peculiarities of two friends, neither of whom detected me, and both of whom were among the warmest in their praise.' Bancroft's reviews for previous performances had been mixed. Almost invariably playing the part of an upper-class swell ('Bancroft parts'), such as Captain Hawtree in *Caste,* but never acting in the usual exaggerated style of the time, he had clearly met with some adverse notices from traditionalists. However, a popular playwright, journalist, critic and gossip columnist of the time, Edmund Yates[*], came out firmly in support of his performance:

> It is the fashion with some journals to find fault with Mr Bancroft. I am bound to state that the parts I have seen him fill in *Ours, Caste,* and the comedy now under notice, could not possibly have been better played. All the characters are of the *genus* 'dandy.' In former years, the actor personating them would have worn spurs, carried a riding-whip everywhere, and would have simply substituted the letter 'w' for the letter 'r' throughout his part – the whole personation representing a creature such as had never been seen by mortal man off the stage. But I maintain that in voice, costume, bearing, and manner, Mr Bancroft is an exact type of the class he is intended to represent, with a very slight exaggeration, which is as necessary for stage purposes as rouge itself.

[*] Remarkably, it is still possible to hear the voice of Edmund Yates: it was captured on a wax cylinder by Thomas Edison's European agent. This cylinder, along with six others recorded one evening in 1888, also includes the voice of Sir Arthur Sullivan, who describes Yates's contribution as 'a little incoherent' – it was clearly an excellent dinner. The cylinder still exists in America at the Edison National Historic Site in New Jersey.

How She Loves Him ran for only forty-seven nights. Dion Boucicault accepted his disappointment with a good grace. It might have been even fewer nights if Robertson's new play had been ready, but he finished it hastily and its first night was on Saturday, 15 February, 1868. Another of Robertson's one-word-titled works, *Play* was set in Germany, where he had spent part of the previous summer, before his marriage to Rosetta. The set for *Play* was elaborate, featuring scenery complete with a ruined castle and a river – quite a change from Robertson's previous cosy interiors. The Bancrofts had misgivings about *Play*, feeling it was not up to the standards set by *Caste* and the other Robertson plays. However, it was quite well-received, and on the fourth night the Prince and Princess of Wales attended the play. They visited the green-room after the show. 'It was,' wrote Bancroft, 'the first time we had either of us ever been in conversation with the Prince, whose well-known love of exactitude in such matters enabled us to correct a slight error in [a German] uniform.'

It was around this time that Squire Bancroft met the man who was to become the leading figure of the Victorian stage, Henry Irving. Squire had seen Irving act in Manchester, but they had never been properly introduced – a matter of some importance in those formal times, even among the sector of society that considered itself Bohemian. Bancroft described the occasion: he was walking arm-in-arm one morning through the fashionable Burlington Arcade off Piccadilly with his friend H.J. (Harry) Montague*, one of the other actors of the Prince of Wales's company, when they ran into Irving. Hats were politely lifted and Montague, who knew Irving well, greeted him and introduced his two friends to each other. This meeting was the beginning of what was to become a close friendship between Bancroft and Irving that was to last for the rest of their lives, although they were not to work together for many years, and then only in one production.

Three years older than Bancroft, Irving was before long to make a name for himself in London, having spent many years working in the provinces. The scene conjures up an attractive picture – three young men, who all thought of themselves as artistic 'Bohemians', were most probably attired in formal frock coats and top hats and carrying canes, Bancroft complete with his eyeglass and Irving with his pince-nez, strolling, deep in conversation, through the elegant Burlington Arcade.

In May of 1868 a great heatwave began and for five consecutive months temperatures often soared to more than 30° Celsius. With their gas

---

* H.J.Montague, 1844-78, a much-loved actor in England and in America, where he died of tuberculosis at the age of only thirty-four.

lighting and packed human bodies, the interiors of theatres must have been unbearable during this very hot weather, and the takings of all London's theatres suffered accordingly. *Play* was taken off and *Caste* revived for a few weeks in June, running through to the end of July when the season ended.

A couple of days following the end of the season at the Prince of Wales's the Bancrofts took part in a 'benefit' evening given at Covent Garden for a well-known singer. Benefits could be an essential way for entertainers to supplement their meagre incomes at a time of very poor pay. The Bancrofts thoroughly disliked the system of benefits, describing it as 'obnoxious', although they often took part in them to help raise funds for their colleagues. They believed that actors should be paid enough for such supplements to be unnecessary. Benefits were usually a mixed bill made up of short offerings from different companies, as it was on this occasion in the hot summer of 1868, the Prince of Wales's contribution being the first act of *Caste.* On a stiflingly hot evening, while waiting for their turn in the lengthy programme, Squire Bancroft and John Hare, along with a friend from another theatre, decided they were in need of some liquid refreshment. In full costume, the three of them sauntered to a nearby hotel where they ordered brandy-and-sodas at the bar. Squire Bancroft was dressed as the 'swell', Captain Hawtree, their friend was in full evening dress of white tie and tails ready for his part in the show, and John Hare was dressed and made up ready to play Sam Gerridge, the Lambeth gasfitter. The other occupants of the bar looked shocked, unable to comprehend how a rough member of the labouring classes could be on such familiar terms with two obviously upper-crust 'toffs'. In the shadowy, gaslit bar they could not spot that the three were all in stage makeup.

By the end of the season Marie was six months pregnant, and the Bancrofts rented a house in Broadstairs, Kent, for the hottest weeks of July and August, when temperatures soared to near record levels. The sea air must have been a great relief from the heatwave that continued until September. They broke their seaside holiday with a trip to Paris, where they spent the best part of a week, in the intense heat of the city. This was Marie's first ever trip abroad, although in her youth she had worked in Ireland, which was then, although technically 'overseas', not considered to be 'abroad'. She had a lifelong terror of the sea, and the Irish Sea or the English Channel presented the most challenging voyages she was prepared to undertake.

Following their few days in Paris, the return to cooler Broadstairs and the seaside was a welcome relief. Friends and family members came and stayed with them there, including Ida Wilton and Edmund Yates. Though best known for his journalistic work, Yates also wrote plays. He had already sent the Bancrofts the first act of a new comedy he had written, hoping they might take it and he brought the second act down to Kent with him. They were at this stage not entirely happy with Yates's play but, assuming that he would improve it by the third act, they accepted it, agreeing to put it on in the new season.

Yates's comedy being unfinished, the Prince of Wales's re-opened on 21 September with a revival of Tom Robertson's *Society*. For the first time, the cast did not include 'Miss Marie Wilton', Marie's pregnancy by then being well advanced. The part of Maud Hetherington that she had created was taken by a young actress called Carlotta Addison[*].

There was another new recruit to the cast of *Society*. A persistent young man had called several times at the Bancrofts' home in Circus Road, St John's Wood when they were out. Eventually he turned up at a time when Squire was at home and, pushing past the maid who opened the front door, marched unannounced into the Bancrofts' drawing-room. At first annoyed at this intrusion, Squire was quickly won over by the personable and handsome twenty-one-year-year-old, who declared that he was determined to become an actor. He told Squire that he had actually been born in Circus Road, in the house directly opposite where they were standing. He insisted that he would not leave until Squire agreed to take him on at the Prince of Wales's. Recalling the time when he himself had been rejected by theatre managers all over the country, Squire relented and offered the pushy but charming young man, whose name was William Terriss (born William Lewin in 1847), a small part in the revival of *Society*.

When the play opened, in September 1868, many of Terriss's friends were in the theatre. At his entrance he was greeted with enthusiastic cheers and prolonged applause, which they kept up whenever he was on the stage. One of his brothers was also there and after the play Terriss asked what he had thought of his performance. 'Chuck it up, dear boy. You'll never do!' was the reply. Terriss must have taken his brother at his word, as he did not settle in his newly acquired profession for long. In 1870 he married and, with his new young wife in tow, set off to try his hand at sheep-farming in the Falkland Islands, where their daughter, Ellaline, was born in 1871. He then tried horse-breeding in America. Back in London he returned to the stage, eventually establishing himself in Irving's company at the Lyceum, as a glamorous, dashing matinée idol, much loved by his colleagues and swooned over by his female fans. For his easygoing manner and carefree charm, he was nicknamed 'Breezy Bill'. His daughter, Ellaline Terriss, who married the actor Seymour

---

[*] Carlotta Addison, 1849-1914. Born in Liverpool to theatrical parents, like Marie Wilton, she was a child actress from an early age.

Hicks[*], became a star of Edwardian musical comedy. She lived to the great age of ninety-nine.

William Terriss

Terriss's career thrived. He became one of the best-known figures on the London stage and by December 1897 he was managing the old Adelphi Theatre in the Strand. Sadly this career was brutally cut short when he became the victim of a sensational murder. He had befriended an unsuccessful actor called Richard Prince, and had often helped him out in various ways. Nevertheless the mentally unstable Prince developed a grudge against Terriss. On the night of 16 December he lay in wait in the dark back street outside Terriss's private door into the Adelphi and, when Terriss arrived to prepare for the evening's performance, the deranged Prince stabbed him to death. He was found guilty of murder but insane

---

[*] Seymour Hicks, 1871-1949, was one of the best-known stage actors of his generation, later appearing in many films. He received a knighthood in 1934.

and was committed to Broadmoor for life. Terriss's horrifying death shocked London, and his ghost is said to haunt the present Adelphi Theatre, which is built on the site of its predecessor. At the back of the Adelphi, near the stage door, there is a plaque commemorating William Terriss. He is buried in Brompton Cemetery.

The Bancrofts' son, George Louis Pleydell Bancroft, was born on 1 November 1868. True to form, his parents made no direct reference to the birth of the child in their memoirs, not so much as a mention of his name. The only reference to the happy event is contained in a brief letter from Marie's old partner, Harry Byron. Squire quoted it almost apologetically, writing that, as it referred to 'a domestic matter', it had no real place in the memoirs. The letter read:

> My dear Bancroft.
> Accept our united congratulations. May the infant grow as clever as its mamma, and as tall as its papa, and as good as both!
>> With all good wishes, believe me, my dear Bancroft,
>>> Yours very sincerely, H.J.Byron

Many years later, in 1939, when he was over seventy, George Bancroft wrote his own memoirs, in which he told that his first outing as a very young baby was when he was taken along to the Prince of Wales's: 'My mother being a terribly superstitious woman, I was rubbed against the wings of the stage for luck and formally introduced to the company.'

Edmund Yates's play, *Tame Cats*, opened on 12 December. Throughout rehearsals, the Bancrofts had been uneasy about the piece. 'Scenes which had read well acted tamely (no pun intended),' wrote Squire Bancroft. Marie was back in the cast, even though her baby, George, was only about six weeks old, an age that was then considered rather early for a new mother to return to work. Also in the cast was Augusta Wilton, and a newcomer to the company, a young man of twenty-six called Charles Collette. This was his first appearance as an actor, having previously served in the army in India. On his return to England in 1868 he sold his commission and was taken on by the Bancrofts. On the first night of *Tame Cats* there was a large group of rowdy young officers, friends of Collette's, in the audience, who behaved even more disruptively than had William Terriss's friends not long before. W.S.Gilbert, in his review of *Tame Cats* for the *Illustrated Times*, wrote that 'he was so hampered by the preposterous enthusiasm of foolish friends (who appeared to occupy at least two thirds of the stalls and half the private boxes) that his success was greatly imperilled more than once.' Collette somehow survived this embarrassing baptism to enjoy a long career as a comic actor. In 1870 he married Marie Bancroft's youngest sister, Blanche Wilton, and they had one daughter, Mary Effie Collette, who herself became an actress.

In an attempt to brighten up the first act of *Tame Cats*, Marie had come up with a bizarre idea: 'While considering how best to make the scene of the first act, the garden of a pretty villa on the Thames, as effective and natural as possible, it occurred to us that a macaw with his gay plumage would be a beautiful bit of colour on the well-kept lawn. We purchased one of the handsomest birds I ever saw, and had a large stand made for him, which the bird seemed to appreciate immensely, especially when its bright tin dishes were well filled.'

How she could have imagined that a brightly-coloured parrot could be considered 'natural' in a Thames-side villa is a mystery, though it oddly foreshadowed a time, 140 years later, when Thames-side gardens are now regularly invaded by flocks of rapacious green parakeets. 'Mac' the macaw was clearly a stroppy bird. He would allow no one near him apart from Marie, to whom he was devoted. Whenever she was out of his sight he would squawk furiously until she returned. Then he would become 'languid with affection' and behave beautifully. His acting career was short. On the first night the scene was all set with Mac on his perch, but no sooner did the curtain rise than the unfortunate bird was so alarmed by the glare of the gaslight and the sound of applause from the audience that he spread his wings and jumped off his perch. He rushed around the stage, squawking loudly and dragging the perch behind him, which only terrified the poor creature all the more. The more the audience laughed the more he screeched with fright as he staggered around trying to escape. He had a savage beak and only Marie dared approach him. She managed to grab him and remove him. After this first and last appearance on stage, Mac was presented to the London Zoo, where Marie visited him regularly for many years afterwards and where it is to be hoped he led a happier life.

John Hare's part in *Tame Cats* was that of a disreputable released convict. As always he relished a part that involved an inventive costume. On this occasion his part demanded a truly ragged outfit. He scoured second-hand clothes shops in the shabbier parts of London in search of suitably scruffy, worn-out garments, which needed to be carefully fumigated before their new owner could wear them; then one day he spotted a filthy, battered hat on the head of a complete stranger in the street. To this man's astonishment he was offered a good price for his hat. Totally bewildered, he happily accepted this offer from the 'madman' who had approached him.

Quite apart from its chaotic opening, *Tame Cats* was not a success. The *Athenaeum* reviewer wrote that the play 'failed to please or interest the audience and was hissed', and W.S.Gilbert observed of Bancroft's part that it 'seemed scarcely fitted to this gentleman's unmistakable talents'. Bancroft himself wrote that his performance as a 'mock poet' was 'resented by the audience and critics, some of whom mistook it for a caricature of the genius of one far above such ridicule, Algernon Charles Swinburne, the poet and associate of the Pre-Raphaelites, no such idea having entered the head of either author or actor.'

The play was withdrawn after just eleven performances. Some years later, Edmund Yates asked if the prompt copy of the play was still around. Squire found it stored away somewhere and sent it to its author, who read it and returned it with the comment: 'My dear B, it's poor stuff, and well deserved its fate.' *Society* was hastily brought back to fill the gap until Robertson's new play was ready.

Marie had not intended to act in this production, but the actress who was to play the elderly Lady Ptarmigant was ill, so Marie had to replace her. Squire described her in her new part: 'I have rarely seen anything more ludicrous than she looked. Every impromptu effort to produce the semblance of age only added to her then girlish appearance.'

Society ran for about three weeks after Christmas and then Tom Robertson's new play, *School,* was ready to open on 16 January 1869. In spite of being rehearsed in a hurry, everyone was confident that this time they had a success on their hands. Squire Bancroft wrote to a friend, saying, 'We are on the eve of the greatest success we have yet had.' Sure enough, *School* proved to be a record-breaker and ran for longer than any other of their productions. The part of the schoolgirl Naomi Tighe, was to become Marie's favourite of all her Robertson parts.

School was inspired by a German play called *Aschenbrödel* – Cinderella, from the fairy tale, originally by Perrault, later by the brothers Grimm. Robertson had come across the play during his visit to Germany at the time of his marriage. It consisted of recognisable elements of the fairy tale, with Cinderella in this case an impoverished young girl employed as a pupil-teacher in a school for young ladies. As usual, Robertson's plot centred around the fate of a sweet-natured young girl, the pupil-teacher Bella, and her spirited schoolgirl friend, Naomi. Of course, 'love conquers all' and Bella marries her 'handsome prince'.

Naomi Tighe seems a strange choice of favourite part for Marie, as the character is less memorable than either Polly Eccles in *Caste* or Mary Netley in *Ours*. However, many years later, Marie and Squire's son, George Bancroft, was to name his youngest daughter Naomi, no doubt because the family retained fond memories of the play and of his mother's role in it.

School also occasioned the first use of Marie's pet name for Squire, which she would use for the rest of their lives. According to their friend

Alice Comyns Carr[*], at some point during rehearsals Marie swathed herself in a sheet and leaped out at Squire in an attempt to give him a fright. From then on she called him 'Bogey'. Among his friends he was always known as 'B'.

programme for School, *1869*

Victorian audiences loved the romantic sentimentality of *School*, with its cast of several pretty young 'schoolgirls', and the play met with unanimous critical approval. *The Times* review read: 'The fact is not to be denied, that the production of a new comedy by Mr T.W.Robertson at the theatre which, once obscure, has become, under the direction of Miss Marie Wilton, the most fashionable in London, is now to be regarded as one of the most important events of the dramatic year.'

The demand for tickets was unprecedented. Extra seats were somehow fitted in and box office takings soared, helped by the fact that the prices had been increased a few months previously, at the start of the new

[*] Alice Comyns Carr, 1850-1927, designed many of Ellen Terry's stage dresses, including the remarkable gown Ellen wore as Lady Macbeth, which was decked with thousands of iridescent green beetle wings, in which she was painted by John Singer Sargent: the portrait is in the Tate Gallery. Alice's husband was Joe Comyns Carr, 1849-1916, critic, playwright and art gallery director. Mrs Comyns Carr's *Reminiscences* were published in 1926.

season. The stalls went up from six to seven shillings, the dress-circle from four to five shillings, and the pittites, behind the stalls, now had to pay two shillings, up from one and sixpence. This sudden increase in the Bancrofts' fortunes opened, as Squire wrote, 'a vista of prosperity such as we had not dreamed of'. So great was the demand for seats that they tried an experiment, morning performances of *School*, the first of these being on 6 March. This proved not to be a popular venture. As Squire put it, 'It only attracted a moderate house in the daytime, and it was not for some years that *matinées* became popular.'

John Hare as 'Beau Farintosh' in School

It is only John Hare's character in *School*, that of an ageing and decrepit, once-fashionable relic of a bygone era, striving with the aid of cosmetics to retain his lost youth, that appears relevant and sympathetic today, moving smoothly from a comic caricature to a sad old man who comes to recognise his own foolishness. Of his performance the *Daily Telegraph* said:

127

Whatever part Mr Hare undertakes we may be quite assured the utmost amount of pains will be bestowed on every detail; this most creditable characteristic of the actor is especially to be noticed in his latest assumption. Beau Farintosh, who might have been a young 'buck' in the days of the Regency, but who is now only a padded old man striving to repair the ravages of nature by the appliances of art, must be ranked the very best of Mr Hare's impersonations. The carefully made-up face .... the affected jaunty air of youth contrasting with the unavoidable feeble gait, and the blundering short-sightedness of which he seems to be so amusingly unconscious, are admirably exhibited. An effective contrast is also produced when he no longer affects to conceal the years he has attained; and when, clasping his long-sought grandchild to his arms with emotions which overpower his utterance, the old beau reappears as a grey-headed old gentleman, inspiring reverence instead of ridicule. The burst of pathos which accompanies this wholesome change favourably displays the power of the actor in a strong situation.

A few months after George Bancroft's birth, in the spring of 1869, growing prosperity enabled his family to move from the small house they had been renting in Circus Road in St John's Wood to a larger house not far away. 'In the spring of the year, when the apple-blossoms made its big old-fashioned garden look beautiful, we saw a house in the Grove-End Road, near our little villa, which we felt justified in taking on a lease, and soon after occupied,' wrote Squire. The household at No 11, Grove End Road included a nursemaid, Caroline Lambkin, who was responsible for the day-to-day care of the baby, George, who adored her, and Marie's son, Charles, now six years old, who, since his mother's marriage to Squire Bancroft, had been known as Charles Edward Bancroft. In addition to Caroline, there were two other living-in servants. This might sound like a rather lavish life-style, but servants came cheap in those days, and despite her famous roly-poly pudding in *Ours* Marie was not known for domesticity.

Marie and Squire Bancroft were now joint managers of the Prince of Wales's. On the playbills Marie still used the maiden name under which she had become famous, and continued to do so for some years following her marriage, although by 1870 she had the name 'Mrs Bancroft' in brackets following 'Miss Marie Wilton'. From this time too, in spite of the fact that it had been Marie who had brought the Prince of Wales's Theatre from obscurity into the full glare of the popular limelight, it was Squire who began to receive the greater attention in the male-oriented society of the time. However, Squire was always the first to acknowledge that Marie was his inspiration and that of their company and that the recognition that now began to come his way was almost entirely due to her efforts.

One instance of this recognition was Bancroft's election to the Garrick Club, in April 1869, when he was twenty-eight. He was to become a devoted member and in the memoirs gave this eloquent description of the club that he grew to love and some of its members, nearly all now forgotten names:

> Let me light a cigar in the smoking-room, and, at peace in one of its big armchairs .... I see the forms of Wyndham Smith and Andrew Arcedeckne [sic: this remarkable name is apparently pronounced 'Archdeacon'] seated together by the fire and hear their interchange of stories .... Over an early dinner I hear Phelps[*] telling of 'a splendid day's fishing' whilst Charles [James] Mathews whispers to me that the only time in his life he began to get fat was when he took to riding. I picture in the card-room the ever-kindly presence of Lord Anglesey, the merry eye and musical brogue of Charles Lever (home on leave from his consulate, and keenly interested in the Tichborne trial); the gruff exterior which hid the soft and tender heart of Anthony Trollope. I see kindly 'Joe' Langford and dear old 'Bunsby' (Merewether Q.C.) arrive for their rubber; 'cutting-in' with gentle, pipe-loving Edward Breedon, the novelist, and Dr Duplex, who once prescribed for Edmund Kean, who complete the table.
>
> Higher still the smoke of my now half-burnt cigar ascends, and in its fumes I picture again delightful visits to the billiard-room. Over a crowded contest I see the portly form and hear the jovial laugh of General Napier; by his side is the handsome face of Palgrave Simpson.... As I go downstairs again I linger for a chat with my kind proposer, Shirley Brooks, fresh from a Wednesday *Punch* dinner or to listen to a keen and caustic criticism from Tom Taylor, so soon to be his successor in the editorial chair. In the hall I interrupt two serjeants[*] 'learned in the law', who are talking out the points of that day's conflict in the Common Pleas; and, as I leave, am awakened by my surprise at meeting Henry Byron, whose rare visits to the club, he laughingly said, made his annual subscription mean 'five guineas a wash'!

Founded in 1831, the Garrick Club appropriately moved to Garrick Street in London's Covent Garden in 1864 – both the street and the club were named after the famous actor, David Garrick. The club's aim when it was founded was that it 'was to be a place where actors and men of refinement and education might meet on equal terms, where patrons of the drama and its professors were to be brought together and where easy intercourse was to be promoted between artists and patrons.' Distinguished members included Charles Dickens and the playwright Arthur Wing Pinero, as well as the artists Dante Gabriel Rossetti and Sir John Millais, and the composer Sir Edward Elgar. To be elected a member

---

[*] Samuel Phelps, 1804-78, one of the most distinguished theatrical figures of his generation. For many years he managed Sadler's Wells Theatre and was responsible for many celebrated productions of Shakespeare and other plays.
[*] Serjeant-at-law: an ancient but now obsolete rank of senior barrister.

was an indication that an actor had indeed 'arrived'. Bancroft seems to have been elected at a very young age, as was John Hare who, although younger than Bancroft, had been elected a year earlier. When someone is proposed for membership, his name – it is always 'his' name: to this day the Garrick Club does not admit women members – is entered in a book where other members can sign their names in support of the candidate. However, in Bancroft's day, it seems to have been a question of luck as to who was sitting on the election committee when a name came up for consideration. The membership included many die-hard traditionalists with prejudices against younger arrivals on the theatrical scene. Bancroft and Hare must have been lucky with the make-up of their selection committees. The greatest actor of all, Henry Irving, was not so lucky. He was proposed as a member of the club early in 1873 and the page with his proposal was filled with signatures of support for his membership, including those of Bancroft and Hare. However, Irving was not elected. This led to fury among many of the members, including the novelist Anthony Trollope and the painter, Frederick Sandys, who expressed his 'entire disgust', and there were many threats of resignation. Irving was persuaded to let his name be put forward again in 1874, and this time he was duly elected by an overwhelming majority.

School ran and ran. Even the Bancrofts were somewhat bewildered by its success. As Squire Bancroft said, 'although it grew to be the greatest favourite of all Robertson's works, it cannot be compared in a dramatic sense with *Caste*, nor does it contain a scene to equal the second act of *Ours*. The public however chose to raise it to the position we have indicated, and it was not for us to quarrel with so pleasant a verdict.' *School* appealed to the middle-class Victorian audiences' liking for unchallenging but well-acted plays with characters they felt able to identify with and that challenged, but not too seriously, the social order of the time.

In the spring the Bancrofts had embarked on some refurbishment of the theatre, breaking the run of *School* while these decorations were completed. Their team of craftsmen worked in relays to complete the work in just eleven days and nights. The new decorations were even more lavish than when the Prince of Wales's originally opened, with much use of pale blue satin; and for the first time the positioning of the orchestra – plays at that time always featured an overture and other incidental music and the musical director was an important figure in a company – was moved from a prominent position in full view of the audience to a position where it was almost out of sight, partly below the stage. Marie described the change: 'The space formerly occupied by the musicians was filled by rockwork, with running water, and a fernery.' Lavish décor and furnishings were at their mid-Victorian height. The alterations were popular with the public and prompted a letter of congratulation from no less a person than the President of the Royal Academy:

Holland Park Road

Dear Mrs Bancroft,

A line to say that I think your theatre quite the dandiest thing I ever saw. I should have gone round to tell you so after the play, but that I had a complete extinction of voice, and could therefore not have made myself audible. How well it went off last night, and how dead tired of it you must be! Not so we. – Believe me, with kind remembrance to Bancroft, yours very truly,

Fred. Leighton

School resumed after its brief closure and ran right through until the season ended very late, on 28 August, with its 192nd performance. The summer break was short and on 11 September 1869 *School* was once more resumed. A couple of months later, on 17 November, the Prince and Princess of Wales attended the 250th performance of the play. It was a miserably cold evening, with a fog so dense that homeward journeys were dangerous for all. Film representations of Victorian London, with fog swirling around its dimly-lit streets, are no exaggeration. Each winter those 'peasoupers' made the late-night journeys of theatre-workers and audiences alike long and hazardous. That evening the Bancrofts did not reach St John's Wood until the early hours of the next morning and even the royal carriage got lost on its way home.

6

FROM SCHOOL TO SCANDAL

Early in the new year of 1870 Marie Bancroft had once more to take an enforced break as she was again pregnant. Her sister Augusta took over her part of Naomi Tighe in *School*, and another baby boy, Arthur Hamilton Bancroft, was born on 20 January. Sadly this child lived for only four weeks. There must have been concerns as to his chances of survival as he was hurriedly baptized on 16 February and he died of convulsions three days later. It is likely that he did not go to full term, as only three weeks before his birth Marie had taken part in a benefit for the actor Charles James Mathews who was off on tour to Australia.

Grief at the death of their child led the Bancrofts to break their intention of keeping 'matters of home life' entirely out of their joint memoirs, and exceptionally to 'raise the veil that shrouds such things, and allude to a wretchedness that befell us'. Describing how he was urgently sent for one night, even before the curtain fell, Squire wrote: 'I was summoned home, a child-illness having quickly grown alarming. In a few hours the little being died, and, while we lived there, saddened the house in which he slept away his thirty days of life. The thoughts of those days that followed can be ever raised, and the ghosts of them can be never laid.' If the baby was indeed premature, he was born at a time when such children had little hope of survival. In the mid-nineteenth century there were many illnesses, now almost totally eradicated in Britain, that could be contracted quite easily and could rapidly prove fatal, especially to infants or small children, including polio, diphtheria, scarlet fever, measles and whooping cough. The Bancroft baby's death certificate merely states that the cause of his death was 'convulsions', the reason for which must remain a mystery.

scene from *M.P.*, Prince of Wales's Theatre, 1870

At around the same time that the Bancrofts lost their child, the playwright, Tom Robertson, who had been suffering from a heart condition, became seriously ill. He had been working on a new play, called *M.P.,* which was to succeed *School.* Robertson was far too unwell to attend the theatre, so groups of the actors would go to his home at Haverstock Hill in north London to rehearse so that he could direct them as usual. The Bancrofts felt that *M.P.* was not up to Robertson's usual standards and that his condition had affected his work, but they were determined that he should not know of their unease about the play.

School was finally withdrawn after a record 381 performances and *M.P.* had its first night on Shakespeare's birthday, 23 April, 1870. With its author too ill to be present, messengers hurried to his home at the end of each act to keep him informed with news of how the play was being received. Happily the Bancrofts' fears were not realized and the play was another success. Such was the demand for seats that the elaborate rockery-and-water feature in front of the orchestra was removed to make room for more stalls. A rapturous review in *The Times* read: 'Mr Robertson has added another leaf to the garland he has so honestly and honourably won at this theatre .... Author, actors, and theatre seem perfectly fitted for each other .... Light as [these comedies] are, there is in them an under-current of close observation and half-mocking seriousness which lifts them above triviality.'

During that summer of 1870 the nation was shocked by the sudden death early in June of the giant of English literature, Charles Dickens, at the age of only fifty-eight. Just a week or two before, knowing that he was suffering from neuralgia, Marie Bancroft had written to the great novelist recommending some remedy she believed might help his condition and offering to order it for him. The reply she received read:

> Gad's Hill Place, Higham by Rochester, Kent
> Thursday, May 31, 1870

My dear Mrs Bancroft,

  I am most heartily obliged to you for your kind note, which I received here only last night, having come here from town circuitously to get a little change of air on the road. My sense of your interest cannot be better proved than by my trying the remedy you recommend, and that I will do immediately. As I shall be in town on Thursday, my troubling you to order it would be quite unjustifiable.

  I will use your name in applying for it, and will report the result after a fair trial. Whether this remedy succeeds or fails as to the neuralgia, I shall always consider myself under an obligation to it, for having indirectly procured me the great pleasure of receiving a communication from you; for I hope I may lay claim to being one of the most earnest and delighted of your many artistic admirers.

> Believe me, most faithfully yours,
> Charles Dickens

Unfortunately his death came before Dickens was able to try Marie's recommended cure. In writing of his death, the Bancrofts described how Dickens was responsible for the 'abolition of the dreadful paraphernalia' attached to funerals, by caricaturing characters like the undertaker, Mr Sowerberry in *Oliver Twist*, complete with 'long black cloaks, scarves, and enormous hatbands which once so commonly formed part of the trappings and the suits of woe'. These had all been swept away along with the 'dreadful mutes who used to stand as sentinels outside the house of mourning'. Nevertheless, the Victorian way of death, even if less elaborate than earlier in the century, was still a matter of much formality, with drawn curtains, black-edged writing paper, the wearing of mourning for months, followed by half-mourning, and funerals that remained deeply solemn and traditional occasions. This particular Victorian obsession is not surprising as deaths were frequent and often unexpected. Funerals were attended by large crowds, who would gather both inside and outside the church for the service and then follow in procession to the cemetery afterwards. For people of any note the occasion would be reported in the press, complete with lists of the mourners present and of their floral tributes and messages of condolence. In contrast, in accordance with his wishes, Dickens, though buried in Westminster Abbey, had a strictly private funeral with only a handful of mourners.

In spite of its successful start, the Bancrofts' early misgivings about *M.P.* were justified. The play's fortunes quickly took a downward turn and it did not continue to attract the audiences it had during the spring and early summer. It ran for four months, at the end of which the Bancrofts took themselves and their family off to Scarborough for a month's holiday and, although *M.P.* resumed at the start of the new season in September, it was clearly essential to find something with which to replace it as soon as possible. Robertson was still very ill and although he had started on a new play it seemed highly unlikely that he would ever complete it. The Bancrofts decided to replace *M.P.* with a revival of *Ours*, even though it was only four years since Marie's original production in 1866. There were changes in the cast as some members of the company had left and newcomers had arrived since the first production, and Squire Bancroft, who had previously played the part of the young hero, Angus Macalister, this time took the part of his friend, the cynical Hugh Chalcot.

There was a poignant reminder one day of how recent was the history that *Ours* portrayed. A rehearsal was interrupted by the sound of a woman weeping in the stalls. While she was at work brushing down the seats, one of the cleaners at the Prince of Wales's was overcome when she heard the troops departing for the Crimea. She had lost a son at the Battle of the Alma.

The play was even more elaborately staged than before, with particular attention paid to accuracy in the military costumes and props. The Bancrofts even acquired a genuine Russian drum that had been captured in battle in the Crimea. This was lent to them by their next door neighbour in St John's Wood, Admiral Inglefield[*], a retired veteran of the Crimean campaign. The friendship with their neighbours had become particularly close at the time of the loss of their baby, Arthur, as the Inglefields had themselves lost a child at around the same time. A man of many talents, Inglefield was a gifted artist (he exhibited at the Royal Academy) and an inventor. Bancroft admired him and wrote of his DIY skills with admiration: 'If his watch stopped, he could mend it; if he broke a window, he could replace it; if a chimney smoked, he could cure it.' On Sunday evenings Squire and the Admiral would often greet each other over the

---

[*] Rear-Admiral Sir Edward Augustus Inglefield, 1820-94. In 1852 he led the search for the missing Arctic explorer, John Franklin. He later served in the Crimea. A WW2 destroyer, *HMS Inglefield*, was named after him.

garden wall with the Admiral enquiring, 'What time do you splice the mainbrace?' Drinks would follow.

During rehearsals one freezing day in November, when London was enveloped in a fog so thick that it had even penetrated deep inside the theatre, to everyone's astonishment word came that Tom Robertson himself had arrived at the stage-door. He was helped inside and stayed watching the rehearsal of his play for about half an hour, but he was soon overcome with coughing and was persuaded to go home. *Ours* opened on 26 November and its author insisted on being present for the first night. He watched the performance from his usual box. It was to be the last night he ever visited the Prince of Wales's, or any other theatre. The following day he wrote:

My dear Marie

You know that I am not given to flattery [but] I was really charmed and the remark of everyone I heard was, 'What wonderfully good acting!' I was pleased to find Boucicault descanting on it to a chosen few. He said that not only was the general acting of the piece equally admirable, but that he had never seen such refinement and effect combined as in the performance of the second act. He said, too, that the actors who had played in the piece before acted better than ever. I mention this, because the same thing struck me. Bancroft was most excellent, and I have never seen him succeed in sinking his own identity so much as in the last act.

He went on to remark that he now felt his play was perhaps a bit too long, making it very late for audiences to return home:

.... could not the first and third acts be relieved of some ten minutes' talk? Cut wherever you like, I shan't wince .... If they had been less perfectly acted they would have missed fire, and deservedly.

Yours very sincerely,

T.W.Robertson

During this run of *Ours* the Bancrofts tried to increase the fees they were paying Tom Robertson for the production of the play. Robertson wrote back to Squire immediately:

Don't be offended that I return your cheque. I recognise your kindness and intention to the full; but having thought the matter over, I cannot reconcile it to my sense of justice and probity to take more than I bargained for. An arrangement is an arrangement, and cannot be played fast and loose with. If a man – say an author – goes in for a certain sum, he must be content with it, and 'seek no new;' if he goes in for a share, he must take good and bad luck too. So please let *Ours* be paid for at the sum originally agreed on. With kind love to Marie, and many thanks ....

136

Since his connection with the Prince of Wales's Theatre, Robertson had been paid increasing sums with each play, enabling him and his family to live comfortably. For *Society*, the first of his plays to be produced there, his fee in 1865 had been a pound for each performance. For the 1870 revival of *Ours* he received five pounds a time. However, Robertson, along with other successful playwrights, suffered from the lack of copyright laws at the time. Expert shorthand writers would sit in the audience at London theatres, surreptitiously taking down every word of the scripts, which would then be transcribed and sold to the United States, where plays would be performed without their authors seeing a single penny for their work.

Following his successful connection with the Prince of Wales's, interest in Robertson's reputation had grown, and he had during those years written plays for other managements. The last play he ever wrote, *War*, was produced at the St James's Theatre in January 1871. His spirits were particularly low as it failed badly and had been withdrawn after very few performances.

The winter of 1870-71 was another severe one, so Robertson's family took him to Torquay in the hope that the milder climate of the south west might improve his health, but the visit was no help. At the beginning of February Marie and Squire visited Robertson at his home in Haverstock Hill, where they found their favourite playwright propped up in a large chair, fighting for breath. They talked together for a while and he told them about his ideas for a new play. They left him, fearing that this new play would almost certainly never be written, and just two days after their visit, following the evening's performance on 3 February, 1871, they found Dion Boucicault waiting for them, with the news that Tom Robertson had died. He was just forty-two.

With Robertson's death the Bancrofts had lost a dear friend and colleague. They had worked closely together for five years to their mutual advantage. They made his name as a playwright and he made their names as managers, his plays being the foundation upon which they established their own success. Today his plays seem insignificant and frivolous but in their time they were hailed as groundbreaking. The Frenchman, Augustin Filon, wrote of them: 'It would be but an ill service to Robertson to give an outline of his plays. A mere outline would give the impression that they were childish and absurd, and they were neither the one nor the other ....' Marie Bancroft wrote, 'There is no doubt that when he wrote for us, his whole heart was in his work, for his best plays were written for that theatre where he never knew failure. As we perfectly understood one another, there was not a single contretemps between us, during a friendship which was broken only by his death .... He and I never once during the whole of our acquaintance knew what it was to have an angry word.'

For too few years had Robertson managed to enjoy the prosperity that his alliance with the Bancrofts had brought to them all. Marie believed that he had never really overcome his resentment over the hardships he had suffered in his earlier years before recognition and he often spoke to her about the years before they met. He was a deeply sensitive man and she felt that 'his early troubles soured his nature'. He told her about his years of struggling to support his family 'with such bitterness that it often made me feel sorry that he would not take a less jaundiced view of the world, which he said he should like to have "as a ball at his feet, that he might kick it."' In spite of this deep-seated bitterness, he remained a kindly, ever encouraging figure to all the actors who performed in his plays.

The funeral of the much-loved playwright was attended by a huge crowd of actors, actresses and literary people from all over London. Every single person from the Prince of Wales's – actors, stage-hands, door-keepers – was there and Marie Bancroft was visibly distressed. That night the Prince of Wales's Theatre stayed dark as the Bancrofts took the unprecedented decision to close their theatre as a mark of their love and respect.

It was rumoured that the Prince of Wales's Theatre might not survive the death of Tom Robertson. Expressions such as 'the bubble has burst' reached the Bancrofts' ears, but *Ours* continued to run smoothly and in March they received a reassuring letter from no less a person than John Ruskin* saying how much he had enjoyed the play and the Bancrofts' parts in it. He sent his regards to John Hare, expressing disappointment, 'not with his doing of it, but with his having so little to do'. He had expected the Russian prince that Hare was playing to 'wear a lovely costume of blue and silver, with ostrich feathers, and when he was refused, to order all the company to be knouted, and send the heroine to Siberia.'

Early in that summer of 1871 the entire company of the *Théâtre Français* came over from Paris. Their city had been devastated by the terrible Siege of Paris, and was then living under the brief reign of the Commune. The Bancrofts attended many of their Saturday matinées, often in the company of the Hares who were now close neighbours in St John's Wood. At the end of the visit there was a great luncheon given for the French company at the Crystal Palace, which was now at its new home in south London, having been dismantled and moved there from Hyde Park in 1854. The occasion was 'attended by all our leading literary and artistic people of the day' (that is, it would appear, the leading *male* literary and artistic

---

* John Ruskin, 1819-1900, a friend and patron of the Pre-Raphaelite painters, was the foremost art critic of the day.

people). Unfortunately no one had thought to inform the guests of honour from Paris that the dress for a midday event in England, however grand, would be less formal than for an evening event, and the Frenchmen all turned up resplendent in full evening dress.

The run of *Ours,* and the 1870-71 season, came to an end in the middle of August when the Bancroft family again spent a holiday in Scarborough, a popular spa resort for summer vacations in Victorian times. Many visitors came to take the waters and to enjoy the town's pleasure gardens, its fine beach, and its bracing bathing in the North Sea. Well-known entertainers would perform at the Spa Saloon; that year they included John Lawrence Toole, by now probably the most popular actor in the country, who was on a summer tour with his company. The Bancroft family spent much time with friends who were also holidaying in Scarborough, including the Hares, the Yateses and the Boucicaults. *The Era* reported that one evening they, along with other 'dramatic celebrities' vacationing in the resort, took part in an entertainment that was staged in aid of a local charity. There were drives out into the country for picnics as well as bathing parties, when Squire, who was a keen swimmer, started to teach the seven-year-old Charles Bancroft to swim and young Dion 'Dot' Boucicault, aged about twelve, to dive.

As nothing new and suitable had appeared, after 'wading through reams of rubbish' the Bancrofts decided to play safe and opened the new season in September 1871 with a revival of *Caste*. It was enthusiastically received and played to full houses night after night. Most of the original cast were still with the company, the only major change being that this time a young actor called Charles Coghlan joined the company and played the aristocratic George D'Alroy. Early in the winter that followed, the thirty-year-old Prince of Wales became dangerously ill with typhoid fever, the deadly disease that had killed his father ten years earlier. Nightly bulletins from Sandringham were read out in the theatres of London between acts, and reports regarding the Prince's health were posted up in the foyers. For about a week in December he was not expected to survive and each night theatre orchestras played the National Anthem and 'God Bless the Prince of Wales', until his recovery, when the whole country rejoiced. In February the Bancrofts were invited to attend a great service of thanksgiving in St Paul's Cathedral.

Early in 1872 the Bancrofts had received a flattering, and lucrative, proposal that they should take *Caste* on a tour of the USA. Squire was keen to take up this offer but had first to overcome Marie's terror of crossing the ocean. Realising that this was an offer they could not afford to refuse, she was eventually persuaded that they should go and negotiations were entered into. Arrangements were well underway regarding pay and other details until, during a meeting at a dramatic agent's office in Garrick Street, 'our conversation was interrupted by the whistle of the speaking-tube which communicated with the room of his partner'. The partner had with him Craven Robertson, one of Tom Robertson's many brothers, who was keen to take a production of *Caste* to America himself. As Craven Robertson controlled the rights to the play, the Bancrofts' proposed tour had to be cancelled.

Without Robertson, the Prince of Wales's really did need to find some new work. They could not continue indefinitely staging revivals of just six plays. It was decided that the next production would be Edward Bulwer Lytton's *Money*, a play that had been the final production in which Squire Bancroft had acted in Liverpool, before coming to London. The comedy was first produced in 1840 by Macready, with the great man himself appearing in one of the main roles. Among Lytton's other plays was *The Lady of Lyons,* in which the teenage Marie Wilton so memorably played Claude's elderly mother at Bristol.

Bulwer Lytton[*] was equally famed in the nineteenth century as a prolific novelist, and even today his mainly historical-romantic novels can be spotted on the shelves of second-hand bookshops. He seems to have had a particular affection for 'last of....' stories, telling of great moments in history: among his best-known works were *The Last Days of Pompeii,* published in 1834, *Harold, the Last of the Saxon Kings* and *The Last of the Barons,* his version of the story of Warwick the Kingmaker. He was also responsible for penning several classic literary clichés: his long-forgotten novel, *Paul Clifford,* opened with the immortal words, 'It was a dark and stormy night .... ' which has given rise to the annual 'Bulwer Lytton Fiction Contest', which to this day awards a prize for the best worst opening words to an imaginary novel. Other deathless clichés for which Lytton was responsible include 'the pen is mightier than the sword', 'the almighty dollar', and 'the great unwashed'. For a time he lived in the house called Craven Cottage, that then stood on the site that is now Fulham Football Club.

Money's plot revolves around Alfred Evelyn, a much-despised 'poor relation' employed at a pittance as secretary and general dogsbody by his cousin, Sir John Vesey. When Evelyn unexpectedly inherits a fortune he finds that the very same people that sneered at him or simply disregarded him, while he was poor and unimportant, are suddenly fawning all over him – until he tricks them into believing he has gambled away the lot. Many of the Bancrofts' friends and connections advised them against attempting such a 'standard' work but, with a dearth of anything new and worthwhile on the horizon, they felt the need, after several years of almost uninterrupted 'Robertsons', to stage a play that was by the 1870s already

[*] Edward Bulwer, 1st Baron Lytton, 1803-73. Playwright, novelist and politician.

considered something of a minor classic. A few alterations were needed to suit the play to the time and to their theatre, and the Bancrofts wrote to Bulwer Lytton asking for his permission. He wrote back, agreeing to 'a few verbal cuts here and there', adding that he doubted he would have any argument with 'a management so accomplished and so skilled as yours'. The production was the most elaborate that had yet been attempted at the Prince of Wales's. One scene was set in the card-room of a West End gentlemen's club and called for several walk-on parts representing members of the club. For these the Bancrofts hired some inexperienced but stage-struck young men who were hoping for a career in the theatre. No doubt they came cheap, but it worked well for some of them, who, as they had hoped, went on to make their names as actors.

The first night of *Money* was at the beginning of May. The main members of the cast included all the stalwarts of the company, the Bancrofts themselves, as well as John Hare, George Honey and Charles Collette. Charles Coghlan, now a rising star of the company, played Alfred Evelyn. Fanny Brough[*] played the sweet young ingénue who of course won her hero in the end, with his fortune intact, while Marie Bancroft played Sir John Vesey's young daughter, Georgina, a scheming gold-digger, after the once-despised Evelyn for his money. Bancroft played a toff whose speech was entirely lacking the letter r, the part being 'witten thwoughout' to indicate this defect. The author, Bulwer Lytton, was himself present on the opening night and expressed his delight at the production, particularly at John Hare's performance as the cynical and devious Vesey, declaring that Hare had played the part better than the great Macready, for whom it had been written. The reviews were good and such was the demand for seats that the play could have run on throughout the summer, but some months earlier they had agreed to take *Caste* and *School* to Manchester and Liverpool for three weeks at the end of July. So they made the break, trusting that *Money* would not suffer by having its run broken as, having nothing else ready for September, they intended to continue with Lytton's play after the summer break.

There was just time at the beginning of September 1872 for a short holiday. Marie went to stay with one of her sisters while Squire Bancroft and Charles Coghlan, who had become good friends, went off together on a hurried 'bachelor' trip around Europe. This was to be quite an adventure for Squire as he had never been further than Paris, when he had been at school there. Coghlan however was well-travelled. He had been born in Canada in the same year, 1841, as Bancroft. Their journey began when

---

[*] Frances 'Fanny' Brough, 1852-1914, was well-known for her many successful roles in a career that spanned some four decades. In 1902 she created the title role in G.B.Shaw's *Mrs Warren's Profession*.

they crossed the North Sea, sailing from London docks to Belgium. As always, Bancroft's writings on his travels were descriptive:

> I stood at daybreak on the deck, gazing at the lace-like tower of Antwerp's beautiful cathedral, when suddenly the biggest of its bells quite startled me by powerfully telling out the hour of six, which was followed by such a merry peal from its smaller brethren that it almost sounded like laughter at the solemnity of their companion. We only stayed a few hours in the quaint old city .... I remember especially how strange the little milk-carts looked as they were drawn about the streets by dogs.

They continued on to Brussels for a hasty visit that Bancroft described as 'doing the city *à l'Americaine'*. (It would appear that the Americans were already known as enthusiastic travellers, keen to cover as many sights as they could fit into a short time.) They ended their single day in Brussels at the theatre, although they were so tired they almost fell asleep in their seats. The next day they took the train to Cologne and after seeing the sights, and following an early-morning swim in the Rhine, they set off up the river by steamer, admiring 'its castles, its legends, and its villages dotted about among the vineyards on the hills, each looking, in the distance, very like a box of eighteen-penny German toys, and sixpence extra for the church.'

Leaving the Rhine, the travellers made their way to the casino town of Wiesbaden. The main object of their journey had been to visit the German spa and gambling towns, as the casinos were about to be closed down by the government and they wanted to see them before they disappeared. They were not to reopen until some sixty years later in the 1930s. After Wiesbaden they went on to visit casinos at Homburg and Baden-Baden. Coghlan might well have had a flutter at the tables, but Bancroft had never been a gambler and in spite of being a keen racegoer in England, never missing a Derby Day since 1865, he claimed that he never bet. So, the visit to the gaming tables of Germany was out of sheer curiosity. They were fascinated watching the gamblers at play – or at work, for it was a serious business for them and they could be found at the tables from morning till night. Bancroft and Coghlan concluded they were not missing much: 'Several remarkable "punters", who had spent not only their money but their lives at the [tables], were pointed out to us, some of whom had strange and awful faces, looking akin to hungry birds of prey.'

After a week or so on the Continent, with another full week to spare, after a 'fearful combat with Baedeker', they decided to visit Switzerland, where Squire Bancroft was to begin a lifelong love affair with the Alps. They took the train to Basel and then on to Lucerne where they boarded a boat from which they could admire the spectacular scenery as it took them in leisurely style along the length of the lake. They then drove up the St

Gotthard Pass, where they paused to watch the construction work that had just begun on the great 16-kilometre tunnel that is still in use today. They covered huge distances, mostly by road, either on foot or 'driving', presumably in some kind of small horse-drawn vehicle. At one point they walked many miles towards Chamonix, their luggage following in a little mule cart, the two men removing more and more of their clothing as the day grew hotter. Bancroft wrote: 'In all my life I think I can safely say I have never felt so tired as on that night. I almost feel the pain when I think of what I suffered as we went up never-ending stairs at Chamonix to the double-bedded room which was all the accommodation a crowded hotel could give us.' They finally arrived home on 17 September, Baden-Baden and Paris being the only places where they had spent more than one night. Squire's only regret was that Marie had not been with him on this exhilarating journey and he was determined that she should accompany him on his next European visit.

Following Squire's return to England, *Money* was immediately resumed and continued to attract audiences throughout the autumn and into the new year. It was early in that new year, 1873, that the author of *Money*, Lord Lytton, died. Bookings for the play increased noticeably for the weeks immediately following his death. However, at last something new had turned up. For some months the novelist Wilkie Collins had been working on a play based on his novel, *Man and Wife*, hoping that it would be produced at the Prince of Wales's. John Hare had met Collins and taken him to meet the Bancrofts, and it had been agreed that they would put his play on in 1873, following a revival of *Caste*.

Wilkie Collins attended most of the rehearsals and made adjustments to his script as they went along. In one scene – a storm – electricity was used for the first time, to create effects such as lightning and moving clouds. *Man and Wife* opened towards the end of February 1873 and its author spent most of the first night cowering with anxiety in Squire Bancroft's dressing room 'in a state of nervous terror painful to behold'. From there he could just hear the muffled applause and when the curtain fell for the final time he was loudly called for by the audience to take a bow. *Man and Wife* ran until August, and Collins was very happy with how his play had been received. In a letter to Squire Bancroft he wrote:

> My play has been magnificently acted, everybody concerned in it has treated me with the greatest kindness, and you and Mrs Bancroft have laid me under obligations to your sympathy and friendship for which I cannot sufficiently thank you. The least I can do, if all goes well, is to write for the Prince of Wales's Theatre again, and next time to give you and Mrs Bancroft parts that will be a little more worthy of you.
>
> Ever yours, Wilkie Collins

The final sentence was a reference to the relatively minor roles that the Bancrofts had taken for themselves in the play. Unlike many managers, if there was not an appropriate large part for either or both of them in a play, they were content to play minor roles. This was to happen quite often as each of the couple had distinctive personalities and physiques that did not invariably fit the leading parts in many of the plays they were to produce.

Man and Wife became a great favourite with the royal family, the Prince of Wales seeing it twice and the Princess three times. On one of these occasions the royal couple was accompanied by their relative, the heir to the throne of Russia, and his wife. This royal patronage led one night to what Squire Bancroft described as 'a little domestic drama'. Having no 'Royal' Box at the Prince of Wales's, two ordinary private boxes were hastily knocked together to create a spacious enough area for the party of royals and their attendants. Both these boxes had already been reserved for the night in question, so great efforts had to be taken to track down their purchasers. One was easily found, as he had come into the theatre in person to buy his seats. He was offered alternative seating and, no doubt, some complimentary seats for the future to compensate for the inconvenience.

The other patron was harder to trace. As well as being sold at their own box-offices, tickets for London theatres were sold at other outlets, such as booksellers and libraries; one of the Prince of Wales's agents was at a librarian's in Bond Street. A messenger was urgently dispatched from the theatre to locate the man who had reserved the box. This patron was, he was told, a very agreeable gentleman, a stockbroker. So the messenger was directed to this gentleman's office in the City, only to find that he had already left for his home in the suburbs. His private address was a lot harder to extract from his office, but the messenger managed to persuade them that his errand was of the utmost urgency involving members of the Royal Family. He was eventually given the address and immediately set off for the stockbroker's home. The door was opened by a maidservant who informed him that her master was in Liverpool on business. 'But he's going to the Prince of Wales's Theatre this evening,' insisted the messenger. 'I've been sent to see if it's possible to exchange the box the gentleman has taken, through some of the royal family coming and wanting it.' As he was speaking, an inner door opened and a middle-aged lady emerged and asked what the problem was. The messenger repeated his story and the lady smilingly assured him that her husband would, she was sure, be quite happy to accept the alternative seating that was being offered. The messenger departed, much relieved that his mission had been accomplished.

That evening the stockbroker's arrival was watched for anxiously so he could be welcomed and escorted to the alternative box that had been

144

reserved for him. He duly arrived, accompanied by a handsome young lady. He turned out to be agreeable and good-natured, just as the librarian had said, and was happy, indeed honoured, to make way for the royal party. However, no sooner had he and his companion settled into their seats than Mrs Stockbroker swept into the theatre, and insisted on being shown to her husband's box. No one ever discovered what the outcome of this domestic drama was or how the gentleman explained his 'business-trip to Liverpool' to his wife.

It was in April 1873, during the run of *Man and Wife,* that the great William Charles Macready died, at the age of eighty, having lived in retirement for more than twenty years. In spite of his being out of the public eye for so long, his funeral attracted an enormous crowd, including many old actors whom people had thought long-since dead. Squire Bancroft recalled a favourite anecdote told of Macready of when he had been playing *Hamlet* in a provincial theatre, his starring role supported by the stock company. During rehearsals he had constantly found fault with the actor playing the king. On the first night this actor took his revenge: on being run through by Hamlet's sword, he fell and expired on the very spot that had been intended for Hamlet's own death in Horatio's arms. A furious Macready muttered to the dying king, 'Die further up the stage, sir. Get up and die elsewhere.' At which, to the astonishment of the audience, the corpse sat up and said 'Look here, Mr Macready, you had your way at rehearsal, but I'm King now, and I shall die where I please!'

As well as being a member of the Garrick Club, and later of the Athenaeum, Squire Bancroft also belonged to several much smaller, more intimate clubs. The memberships of these were, of course, invariably made up entirely of men. One of these was called the Lambs Club, a small dining club consisting of no more than a dozen members plus a rotating chairman, known as the Shepherd, inevitably leading to there always being an unlucky thirteen at table, which Squire insisted did not appear to have ever led to any dire consequences. About half the members appear to have been actors, among them several from the Prince of Wales's company, including John Hare, Charles Collette and Harry Montague. Each June the Lambs held a special Sunday dinner out of town at the fashionable riverside hotel, Skindles*, beside the Thames at Maidenhead. The non-theatrical members of the Lambs would arrive there on the Saturday, while the actor members would follow them after their Saturday night commitments, usually not arriving until the Sunday morning.

---

* Skindles Hotel remained a fashionable, somewhat raffish, watering-hole beside Maidenhead bridge, patronised by royalty and celebrities. It flourished well into the mid-20th century but in later years it began to decline and at the time of writing is a sad sight, derelict and boarded up.

One year Squire Bancroft and John Hare decided to set off for Maidenhead late one very dark and stormy Saturday night, after the theatre. They took the midnight train, which stopped at Slough, where there was much banging and shunting of the carriages. On enquiring about what was going on, they were told that part of the train was going on to Windsor, and the rest was to remain in Slough. It would not be going to Maidenhead. Stepping out into the pouring rain with their bags, the pair hoped to find a cab to take them on to Maidenhead, but the station was dark and deserted. They were assured by a sleepy porter that there was no chance of transport of any kind. There was nowhere they could stay for the rest of the night and they realised that they would have to walk the seven miles to Maidenhead. The rain was tipping down as they set off in what they hoped was the right direction. There was no lighting at all on what is now the A4, but was then a quiet country road. Hungry and thirsty, they had been looking forward to a good late supper at Skindles and it was impossible for them even to light their pipes or cigars in the rain. After a mile or so they reached what looked like an inn and banged at the door hoping that they might be able to get a room. It must by now have been around 1.30 am and, instead of a welcome, they got a mouthful of abuse and threats from an upstairs window from the landlord who assumed they must be tramps on their way to the races at nearby Ascot. So they had to carry on, not certain they were even going in the right direction. Eventually, and with a glimmer of dawn beginning to show in the sky, they reached a crossroads with a fingerpost indicating directions. This presented them with a quandary. It was pitch dark: Squire was too shortsighted to read the signpost and Hare was too short in stature to see it properly. So Hare clambered up onto Squire's shoulders and just managed to get a damp match to light so he could see which way they should go.

Finally they reached their destination but they still had to gain admittance to the darkened hotel which was locked up for the night. So they used the time-honoured method of throwing handfuls of gravel at a randomly-selected upstairs window, which with great good luck turned out to be the bedroom of the proprietor, Mr Skindle himself, who let them in. They were, Squire recalled, 'like water-rats, ravenously hungry, and horribly tired, and heartily glad to get rid of the weight of our luggage'. The kind landlord found them some food and a much-needed brandy and soda each and showed them to a room where they could at last sleep – beyond caring that the room only had a double bed.

During the summer break in 1873 the Bancrofts accepted an invitation to take their production of *Caste* to the enormous Standard Theatre in Shoreditch for a four-week run. They were anxious about how Robertson's delicate comedy would be received in the vast East End theatre and were delighted when it was received with enthusiasm. It played to full houses every night, remarkable for an intimate play in a theatre that could seat 3000. A press report read: 'From basement to ceiling within its vast area gathered night after night an interested, intelligent, enthusiastic audience; the cold though confirmed approval of the Prince of Wales's audience was replaced by storms of impulsive applause. It made one think Mr and Mrs Bancroft, wise as they are, err but in one respect – that of playing ordinarily in too small a theatre for the attractions they offer and the amazing popularity they command.' The programme included helpful information as to transport to and from the Standard Theatre.

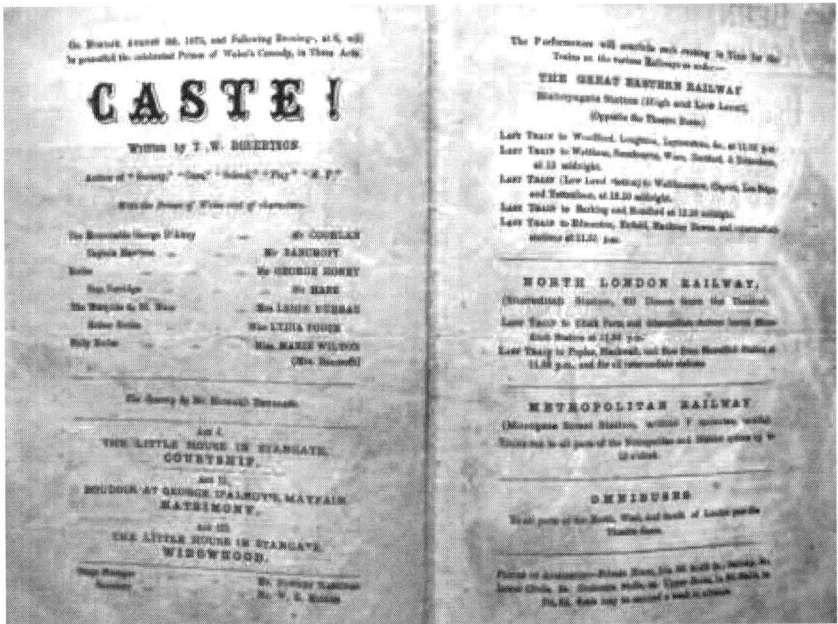

programme for **Caste** *at the Standard Theatre, Shoreditch, 1873*

After the first couple of weeks at the Standard, the Bancrofts handed their parts over to other actors, with Augusta Wilton taking over her sister's part of Polly Eccles. Marie and Squire headed for Europe. They visited many of the places that Squire had seen the previous year, exploring churches and art galleries in Belgium and Germany and marvelling at the Alpine scenery of Switzerland. Squire took every opportunity to indulge his love of swimming by taking dips in the icy lakes and glacier-fed rivers. They spent a night in a 'simple but clean' room in the monastery of St Bernard near Martigny, where they were woken early in the morning by the bell for matins. They then had 'a lovely walk round the lake at the top of the pass, being accompanied by some of the famous dogs .... hearing stories of their rescues of many a poor

147

traveller from a shroud of snow.' There was no charge for their stay at the monastery: there was simply an alms box where travellers could leave what they pleased in return for the food and lodging they had so generously received.

Back in London, early in September 1873 the Bancrofts acquired the lease on a building adjacent to the Prince of Wales's Theatre. This they incorporated into the theatre, creating much-needed extra space, with more dressing-rooms and a larger, more comfortable green room as well as a new props store. They also managed to create a proper new royal box in anticipation of more royal visits. They opened the new season in the newly refurbished theatre with a revival of Tom Robertson's most popular and most frivolous play, *School.*

On 26 November, Marie's father, Robert Pleydell Wilton, died at the age of seventy. The one-time travelling actor was buried alongside his wife, Georgiana, in the vault in Norwood Cemetery. Robert Wilton was survived by his much younger third wife, Susan.

While the revival of *School* continued to play to full houses, the Bancrofts were as ever on the lookout for fresh material for the Prince of Wales's. There was still very little new work around that appealed to them. Mid-Victorian England was a bleak time for creative drama. The plays of Ibsen were still in the future and even when the great Norwegian's work did begin to attract notice – *A Doll's House* was published in 1879 and did not appear on the English stage until ten years later – the Bancrofts would surely have found it too avant-garde for the distinctly lightweight and conservative mid-Victorian tastes. So once again they chose to revive a much-loved classic, this time a major work, Richard Brinsley Sheridan's famous comedy, *The School for Scandal*. It was not far short of a hundred years since Sheridan's masterpiece was originally performed at Drury Lane in 1777, since when it had been revived many times. An ambitious production was planned which was months in preparation. The Bancrofts wanted every detail of the set and costumes to be in authentic eighteenth-century style, exactly as it would have looked in the high society of a hundred years earlier. Squire Bancroft spent many hours researching what he described as the 'patch and powder period' and along with his set designer he visited stately homes to study furnishings and décor of the time.

The School for Scandal was a lavish and expensive production, so it was not without some trepidation that Squire Bancroft, who was by now entirely responsible for the business side of the Prince of Wales's affairs, decided to raise the price of admission to ten shillings (50p) for the stalls, with proportionate increases in other parts of the theatre. This bold decision, although something of a gamble, was essential if the costs of staging the production were to be met. The new prices were expensive for the time and the ticket sellers of Bond Street were sceptical, declaring that these new, outrageous charges must surely be for the first night only. On discovering that they would be permanent, they tutted their disapproval, certain that London's theatregoers would never pay so much. They assured their customers that the Prince of Wales's management would soon be forced to revert to their earlier rates. However, the new charges stayed and not long afterwards other theatres in London began to follow suit and raise their own prices. Soon the 'ten-shilling stalls' were the norm.

Among the many elaborate touches of the production, regrettable from today's perspective, was that in the Bancrofts' quest for authenticity at any price, Marie was determined that her Lady Teazle should be attended by a small black pageboy, who would wait upon her and hold her train. Marie was convinced that a woman of Lady Teazle's social aspirations at the time would have had such an attendant. In 1874 this would have been seen as an exotic theatrical touch rather than being regarded as exploitation of a vulnerable child. Indeed, by the 1870s hundreds of children regularly worked long hours in the theatre, to an extent that would certainly be considered exploitation, even child labour, today.

Finding a boy of no more than ten years old to play the part proved difficult. It would not have been hard to find an adult black man in London, as although slavery had long been illegal in England, there had been a steady trickle of people of African origins into England, as freed slaves and black sailors made their way into the country. Even so in 1870s London there were few black families with young children.

Eventually, after scouring London Marie Bancroft was contacted by a man who brought with him a small boy with what she described as 'the true type of African beauty'. In photographs he appears to have been about nine years old. He was called Biafra, after the name of the ship in which he had arrived in England, which would suggest that he was from the Igbo people of Biafra in Nigeria. The man who committed the child into the Bancrofts' care insisted that he should live with them; so they took him home to St John's Wood where he lived with the servants when he was not at the theatre. In *On and Off the Stage* Marie does not say why he had been brought to London, nor does she give any indication of whether or not he was paid. Almost certainly the man who loaned him to her received a handsome sum of money for procuring the child and it is highly unlikely that the boy himself ever saw any of it.

In the event, Biafra was an instant hit on stage but rather less so among the Bancroft household. Initially the servants thought he was sweet and were delighted with him, but he was a spirited, mischievous child and was soon running riot around the house tormenting them with his antics. He would throw vegetables around the kitchen, hide the housemaid's boots in the oven, and eat anything sweet he could get his hands on. Only Marie could exert any control over him. If anyone else told him to do something he would look towards Marie until she indicated that he should indeed do as he was asked.

One afternoon, to give the servants a break, the Bancrofts took Biafra out with them in their carriage, riding on the box with the coachman. Heads turned as they passed, and street boys shouted taunts at Biafra – almost certainly racist in nature. Leaving him in the care of the coachman, the Bancrofts went into a shop, only to find mayhem outside when they emerged. Three or four urchins had been jeering at Biafra, who had leapt down from his perch to tackle them. A furious fight was taking place in the street, with Biafra sorely outnumbered but giving a good account of himself. After the fracas was broken up he was hurriedly taken home, this time *inside* the carriage.

At the theatre it was much the same story: Biafra played havoc behind the scenes but as soon as Marie indicated that he should pick up her train and follow her on stage he played his part to perfection. 'He looked,' she wrote, 'a perfect picture in his laced scarlet coat and knee-breeches, his white turban and gilt dog-collar.'

In *On and Off the Stage*, Marie told the story of her involvement with Biafra in considerable detail over several pages. Curiously, twenty years later, when *Recollections of Sixty Years* was published, Biafra's story was told in one short paragraph: perhaps by this time the Bancrofts had come to feel less comfortable about their exploitation of the African boy. Indeed, one can only speculate on Biafra's life before and after his brief spell as a child actor. He 'belonged to' – the Bancrofts used that term – the owner of a sugar plantation in West Africa. Undoubtedly this plantation owner would have spent only a small part of his life actually in Africa and probably had a large house in London as well as a country residence, and he might have brought Africans over to England to work as his servants. As slavery was illegal they would have had to be paid, but this wage would have been a pittance – as all servants' wages were – and a young child would be unlikely to have seen a penny himself. He would have been clothed and fed but he would still have been essentially the 'property' of his master.

At the end of the season, following the run of *The School for Scandal* poor Biafra was returned to the man who had procured him. It can only be hoped that he went on to lead a happy life, either in England or back home in West Africa. From the little we know of his few weeks as an actor, it is possible to tell that he certainly had the personality and spirit to make a good life for himself. His final farewell was to stuff the cook's cap up the chimney.

The first night of *The School for Scandal* was on 4 April 1874, and was received with great acclaim. Although the play was well-known and frequently revived, London audiences appeared ready for what was a

150

lavish production of the familiar story in which the elderly Sir Peter Teazle's attractive young bride, an unsophisticated country girl, discovers the delights of decadent London Town. Dismayed at her extravagant behaviour, Sir Peter, played by John Hare, protests that she spent 'as much to furnish [her] dressing-room with flowers in winter as would suffice to …. give a *fête champêtre* at Christmas'. Lady Teazle's reply is: 'Am I to blame, Sir Peter, because flowers are dear in cold weather? You should find fault with the climate, and not with me!'

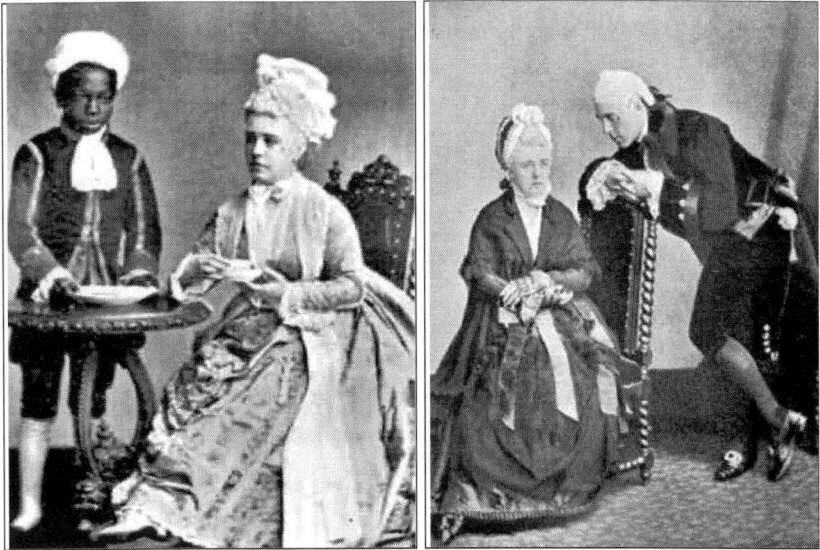

The School for Scandal, 1874: *(l) Marie Bancroft as Lady Teazle with Biafra and (r) with Squire Bancroft as Joseph Surface*

Sir Peter is guardian to a sweet young heiress, Maria, who is in love with a charming, spendthrift young man-about-town, Charles Surface, whose scheming older brother Joseph appears by contrast to be a model of sobriety and good sense. In reality Joseph Surface wants Maria for himself for the fortune she is to inherit, so he sets about convincing Sir Peter that he would be a far finer match for his ward than his improvident brother. With the connivance of a spiteful widow, Lady Sneerwell, who is after Charles for herself, he hatches a plot to destroy Maria's regard for his brother by spreading a rumour that Charles is having a clandestine affair with Lady Teazle, who herself meanwhile embarks on a flirtation with Joseph – knowing it to be the height of fashionable behaviour for wives to indulge in extra-marital dalliances. Eventually, after many farcical shenanigans, Joseph is revealed as the devious hypocrite he truly is and his machinations are foiled. Harmony is finally restored with Maria and

151

Charles united and with the long-suffering Sir Peter reconciled with his young wife.

Sir Peter and Lady Teazle (John Hare and Marie Bancroft) dance the minuet in **The School for Scandal**

In the Prince of Wales's production no expense was spared. The gentlemen were resplendent in embroidered velvet frock coats, with lace frothing at their throats and wrists, and the ladies wore exotic gowns of silks and satins, with elaborately dressed and powdered hair. It is interesting to see from photographs that both Bancrofts sported the 'beauty spots' or 'patches' that were once regarded as a highly fashionable way to enhance facial beauty, at the same time possibly helping to disguise an unsightly blemish, such as a smallpox scar. Such a small black spot on the face was also in the eighteenth century, as indicated by Hogarth, an early indication of syphilis – maybe the Bancrofts were unaware of this. An ecstatic review in the *Daily Telegraph* by Clement Scott described its impact on the audience:

All eyes are attracted by [Lady Teazle's] diamonds while all tongues are wagging about the young wife who has married an old bachelor. The music gives out the first bars of a glorious minuet .... we know not which most to admire, the refined orchestration or the studied courtesy of the polished dance. [In Sir Peter Teazle's house] a rare chandelier, suspended

by a crimson silken cord, contrasts well with the carved oak ceiling ....
The whole apartment is rich, heavy, and luxurious – the favourite
apartment of a wealthy man of taste [and in Joseph Surface's library] ....
The furniture is massive, heavy, and important. The fireplace is carved and
pillared. The bindings of the books are of Russia leather. The carpet is of
thick pile, and from Turkey .... Oriental blue vases on the mantel-shelf ....
blue Delft dishes on the walls .... the gleam of the Venetian mirror ....

Dutton Cook, the influential critic of the *Pall Mall Gazette*, concurred,
slightly grudgingly: 'On the whole, the rearrangement of the play to suit it
for performance at the Prince of Wales's Theatre inflicts no real injury
upon the author's design.'

Cook's various judgments on the cast were of special interest. Of
Marie Bancroft, still billed as 'Miss Marie Wilton (Mrs Bancroft)' in the
cast list, he wrote that as Lady Teazle she played the role as 'more of the
country hoyden .... less of the consummate woman of fashion, than she is
usually represented to be'. He compared her style to that of the famed Mrs
Jordan.

Of Squire Bancroft, as the odious Joseph Surface, Frederic Whyte, in
his book *Actors of the Century*, written more than twenty years later,
remembered his Joseph Surface as a 'polished, handsome, insinuating
rascal .... It was a performance, from all accounts, that Sheridan would
have rejoiced in.' Critics generally admired Squire's interpretation of the
part, more subtly played than in previous productions when Joseph was
invariably portrayed as a stereotypical stage villain.

However, the highest praise was reserved for the newcomer to the
company, the handsome Charles Coghlan, Squire Bancroft's travelling
companion of a few months earlier, who played the charming, extravagant
Charles Surface. Years later H.Barton Baker wrote in his *History of the
London Stage* that 'no actor within my memory has equalled him in
Sheridan's gay hero. He was the full-blooded, port-wine drinking,
boisterous young gentleman of the 18th century.' *The Times* also admired
Coghlan's Charles: 'He is easy, elegant, buoyant, gentleman-like, without
any of the coarseness which frequently disfigures him.'

In addition to the critics' praise heaped on the performances of the
cast, the Bancrofts received many letters of appreciation, including one
from the Royal Academician, William Powell Frith, famous for, among
other paintings, *The Derby Day*. He wrote, 'You and all your people gave
to me and mine very great pleasure last night .... Mrs. Bancroft was, as
she always is, perfect .... the minuet was one of the most delightful bits of
grace and exquisite taste ever seen.'

The minuet Frith referred to was performed during the scene
representing a ball at Lady Sneerwell's. In 1874 this was an innovation
that attracted much attention, as it was the first time the stately dance had

been introduced into *The School for Scandal*. It was to become a standard part of subsequent nineteenth-century productions. The artist Val Prinsep, a contemporary and follower of the Pre-Raphaelites, who was later to become an RA, did a small painting of the minuet scene which he gave to Marie Bancroft.

By the time *The School for Scandal* finished in August 1874 the Bancrofts knew that they were about to lose the most talented and long-standing member of their company, John Hare. Squire Bancroft was later to describe the years that Hare had spent at the Prince of Wales's as 'perhaps the ten happiest years of my life'. Hare was leaving to set up in management on his own account, taking over the lease of the little Court Theatre, in what had once been a nonconformist chapel just off Sloane Square. It was soon renamed the Royal Court. Towards the end of the 1880s it moved to Sloane Square itself, where it is now one of the most innovative theatres in London.

the minuet in **The School for Scandal,** *by Val Prinsep*

Meanwhile, the Bancrofts themselves were on the move. Feeling the need to live nearer the centre of town, they had been house-hunting. They were happy in St John's Wood, with their spacious, tree-filled garden and proximity to Lord's Cricket Ground, a favourite haunt of Squire's, where he loved to watch the MCC play. But they were travelling between home

154

and the theatre often twice a day; the journey, through streets jammed with horse-drawn traffic, was taking up a great deal of time and they were arriving home very late at night. Eventually, after much searching, they found a more conveniently situated house that suited them, a tall, red-brick house in Cavendish Square, just north of Oxford Street, with plenty of trees in the centre of the square, if not in the garden. They were now about a mile and a half from the theatre: it was a much shorter cab ride and was even walkable.

7

THE MERCHANT AND MASKS

The Bancrofts received several lucrative offers to take their production of *The School for Scandal* to various provincial cities in the summer, but they declined, as over recent years Marie had begun to suffer severely from hay-fever each summer, which would have made a provincial tour very difficult. They also had enticing proposals from America: this time they decided they would not even contemplate facing Marie's dread of the Atlantic crossing. Instead, at the end of the 1874 season they took themselves off to the continent and the clean Alpine air. They also planned to combine their holiday with research for their next ambitious project. They had decided that the time was right to go for a production of Shakespeare. It was to be *The Merchant of Venice*, planned for the spring of the following year.

First they headed for Switzerland where they spent a few days by Lake Lucerne. Then they crossed the Alps over the St Gotthard Pass in a carriage, to Lugano and into Italy, where for the first time they visited Lake Como, staying at Cadennabbia, on the western shore. Marie fell in love with this lakeside village to which she was to return many times over the years. After a couple of weeks in 'this earthly paradise' they headed for Venice, arriving in the intense heat of early September.

Together with George Gordon, whom they had engaged as set designer and scene-painter for *The Merchant of Venice*, they explored the magical city together and marvelled at the sights. They decided to base the set for the courtroom scene on one of the great rooms of the Doge's Palace. They bought reproductions of Titian and Veronese, whose paintings were to be the inspiration for costumes for the planned production. While Gordon worked at his sketches, Marie and Squire found time for some relaxation, feeding the pigeons in St Mark's Square, and escaping to the Lido to bathe and escape from the mosquitoes that plagued the city in the high summer.

When the Bancrofts reluctantly returned home, leaving Gordon to continue seeking inspiration for the lavish sets he would design for the tiny stage of the Prince of Wales's Theatre, the early stages of the planning for *The Merchant of Venice* were already underway. Wishing to avoid too many changes of scene, Squire Bancroft had made some rearrangements to the text. However 'no syllable of Shakespeare's text was altered, transpositions of the dialogue alone being necessary for an arrangement of the play ....' The Bancrofts had invited a comparatively unknown young actress called Ellen Terry to be their Portia and she had accepted, 'content with the modest sum of twenty pounds a week – which ranked as a high salary in those days'. The choice of Ellen Terry as Portia was to prove an inspired one. She had not long returned to the London stage after an absence of several years caring for her two young children and she had yet to reach the stellar heights she would one day achieve as the most renowned actress of her time. That was all in the future.

The beautiful Ellen Terry was born in 1847 into a large theatrical family, many of whom went into the family profession. Three of Ellen's sisters, Kate, Marion and Florence, and two of her brothers, Charles and Fred, were all on the stage from an early age, as were many of the later generations of the family. Ellen's childhood career had its similarities to Marie Wilton's as her young days were spent as a child actress travelling around provincial theatres with her theatrical parents. In 1861, the Terry girls were in Bristol, as members of J.H.Chute's stock company, only a few years after Marie Wilton. A year later Ellen was in London, with Buckstone's company at the Theatre Royal, Haymarket. In 1864, just before her seventeenth birthday, she married the distinguished painter George Frederic Watts[*], who was then in his late forties. Watts's painting of his enchantingly beautiful young wife, entitled 'Choosing', hangs in the National Portrait Gallery in London. However, the marriage lasted less than a year and Ellen returned to the London stage for a time, during which, in 1867, she acted with Henry Irving for the first time, in *Katherine and Petruchio*, a play that Ellen herself described as '[David] Garrick's boiled-down version' of *The Taming of the Shrew*. She and Irving were neither of them impressed with each other at the time. 'He played badly, nearly as badly as I did,' wrote Ellen, years later.

---

[*] George Frederic Watts, OM, RA, 1817-1904, widely considered the finest English painter and sculptor of the Victorian era. The beautiful, purpose-built Watts Gallery in Compton, Surrey, devoted to his work, opened shortly before his death. It fell into disrepair and was reopened in 2011 following a major restoration project.

Ellen Terry as a young girl

In 1868 Ellen entered into a relationship with the architect and designer Edward William Godwin*. She left the London stage and lived with Godwin in Hertfordshire. They had two children, both of whom grew up to have long careers in the theatrical, artistic and literary world. Born in 1869, Edith, known as 'Edy', Craig was an actress, director and costume designer. She became a prominent campaigner for women's suffrage and in 1932 she edited her mother's memoirs. Ellen's son, born in 1872 and known as 'Teddy' in his childhood, grew up to become the artistically gifted Edward Gordon Craig. Not wholly appreciated in his own day, in time the maverick Craig was recognized as an immensely influential stage designer, moving the art forward from what came to be regarded as the over-realistic sets pioneered by the Bancrofts into abstract, avant-garde designs that are still regarded as ground-breaking today. For

---

* Edward William Godwin, 1833-86. Hugely influential. In addition to his architectural work, he designed furniture, textiles, wallpaper and ceramics, as well as sets and costumes for the stage.

six years Ellen Terry stayed at home caring for her children then in 1874, when her relationship with Godwin was beginning to deteriorate, she was persuaded to return to the stage by Charles Reade, a well-known playwright. During that year she acted in several of Reade's plays. Then came the unexpected offer from the Bancrofts. In her memoirs, Ellen told of the day that Marie Bancroft turned up at her home in London and invited her to be their Portia.

> The smart little figure – Mrs Bancroft was, above all things, petite – dressed in elegant Parisian black – came into a room which had been almost completely stripped of furniture. The floor was covered with Japanese matting, and at one end was a cast of the Venus of Milo, almost the same colossal size as the original. Mrs Bancroft's wonderful gray eyes examined it curiously. The room, the statue, and I myself must all have seemed very strange to her. I wore a dress .... that had not a trace of the fashion of the time. [She] however did not look at me less kindly because I wore aesthetic clothes and was painfully thin. She explained that they were going to put on *The Merchant of Venice* .... and had thought of me for Portia .... 'Well, what do you say?' said Mrs. Bancroft. 'Will you put your shoulder to the wheel with us?' Portia! It seemed too good to be true .... I answered incoherently and joyfully that of all things I had been wanting most to play in Shakespeare; that in Shakespeare I had always felt I would play for half the salary; that – oh! I don't know what I said! Probably it was all very foolish and unbusinesslike, but the engagement was practically settled before Mrs Bancroft left the house. She told me that the production would be as beautiful as money and thought could make it.

Ellen Terry wrote of the Bancrofts' determination to make a complete change from Robertson: 'It was not only because [they] were ambitious that they determined on a Shakespearean revival in 1875: they felt that you can give the public too much even of a good thing, and thought that a complete change might bring their theatre new popularity as well as new honour.'

The Merchant of Venice would not be ready for some months; so for the first half of the new season of 1874-75 Tom Robertson's *Society* was revived on a double bill with a brand new production, *Sweethearts*, a short, two-act romantic comedy by W.S.Gilbert, which he had written specially for the Prince of Wales's. *Sweethearts* opened in November. Squire described it as 'one of the most charming and successful plays we ever produced', and it was to remain an often-revived favourite of the London stage for some fifty years. At the Prince of Wales's Gilbert directed *Sweethearts* himself. He was much influenced by Robertson's work and had often sat in on rehearsals of his plays to learn from his style of directing. He subsequently developed strong ideas of his own on the directing of his plays, and later of his operas, insisting on exactly how his

159

characters should be played: this was unusual as actors had often been left more or less to decide for themselves how their characters should be interpreted.

Each of the two acts is set in the garden of a large country house, with a gap of thirty years between them. By the second act the garden has matured and new houses and a railway can be seen in the distance. Marie Bancroft played eighteen-year-old Jenny Northcott, who is in love with Henry Spreadbrow (Charles Coghlan). He comes to take his leave of Jenny, on the eve of departing for India, where he is to become a colonial administrator. He declares his love for her but, upset at his departure, she pretends she no longer cares for him. Nevertheless, they plant a tree together and exchange flowers as mementos of their affection for each other. Jenny nonchalantly puts hers on one side, but when Henry leaves, she weeps alone. Returning to England after thirty years in India, Henry, who had put Jenny – and the flower she gave him – out of his mind, goes to visit her. He finds that the tree they planted has grown tall – and that Jenny has remained single. She has kept his long-faded flower safe through all the intervening years, while his has long been lost and forgotten. Henry says, 'How like a woman! You threw it away as something utterly insignificant; and when I leave, you pick it up, and keep it for thirty years!' She replies 'How like a man! You seized the flower I gave you, pressed it to your lips, and swore that …. you would never part with it – and you quite forgot what became of it!' The play closes with the possibility that even in late middle age it is not too late and their youthful love could be rekindled.

Marie Bancroft and Charles Coghlan in a scene from **Sweethearts**

Sweethearts, and in particular Marie's portrayal of the same character at the ages of eighteen and nearing fifty, an age considered almost elderly in the 1870s, was well received. Ellen Terry later wrote of Marie that '.... the best thing I ever saw her do was the farewell to the boy in *Sweethearts*. It was exquisite!' Marie received an appreciative letter from Charles Kean's widow, the fine actress born Ellen Tree. Mrs Kean wrote: 'Allow me now to thank you for the enjoyment you afforded me by your charming acting as Jenny Northcott. Perhaps it may not be unpleasing to know that a very old actress thought it perfection. Your style is all your own, and touchingly true to nature.'

The first night of *The Merchant of Venice* was on 17 April 1875. George Gordon's sets were stunning. The costumes, designed by Ellen Terry's lover, Edward William Godwin, were exquisite and Ellen herself created a sensation as Portia. In *On and Off the Stage*, Bancroft wrote that her Portia 'was, without doubt, the foundation stone' of the brilliant career that now opened up in front of her. Overnight she became the talk of London. The critics were unanimous in their praise of her. In the *Pall Mall Gazette*, the influential Dutton Cook wrote that, 'Miss Terry's Portia leaves little to be desired .... the passion with which she watches Bassanio's choice of the leaden casket, while the confession of her love which follows .... is delivered with a depth of feeling such as only a mistress of her art could accomplish.'

Yet sadly, in spite of the months of preparation, the massive expense on the widely-acclaimed sets and Ellen Terry's personal triumph, the Prince of Wales's *Merchant of Venice* was a miserable failure. 'The gallery jeered and the press condemned,' wrote Bancroft. The failure was almost entirely attributed to the miscasting of Shylock. Charles Coghlan, the handsome leading man who had been with the company since 1870, had been chosen for the most important male part in the play and it was his interpretation of the role that condemned the production to a spectacular disaster. Ellen Terry wrote that although her triumph as Portia made her very happy, nonetheless 'it made me miserable because I foresaw, as plainly as my own success, another's failure.' Dutton Cook wrote of Coghlan's interpretation:

> The result of his performance is to reduce Shylock to quite a subordinate position in the drama. The early actors of the 18th century were apt to treat the character as one pertaining to comedy if not to farce; Shylock was to them a ludicrous Jew, wearing a red beard and otherwise of very grotesque appearance .... By accident or by intention, Mr Coghlan makes Shylock a man of indistinct character, weak and irresolute of mind, assuming at times a certain hard vehemence of action under which no genuine passion lies, but generally mild of demeanour and slow of speech, much addicted

161

to muttering, and incapable of investing his utterances with anything like incisiveness of tone or pungency of sarcasm .... Such a Shylock could scarcely stir or impress and he left his audience at last more apathetic than he found them.

Coghlan cannot be blamed entirely. With no living author to direct how he would like his play acted, it was Squire Bancroft's responsibility to ensure that Coghlan's interpretation of the part harmonised with the production as a whole. Squire accepted that the fault lay with him. 'I alone was responsible for the mistake, if, in truth, it was a mistake, in casting Mr Coghlan for the part of Shylock,' he wrote. 'My error [was] in asking a tenor to sing a bass song. Had I been less ambitious, and had chosen either *As You Like It* or *Much Ado About Nothing*, I think success would have rewarded the attempt. With what charm Ellen Terry plays Beatrice all the world now knows, and how beautiful she would have been as Rosalind, all the world may guess; while Coghlan, either as Benedick or as Orlando, would have been a perfect companion picture. We missed, therefore, an opportunity by my first choice of a Shakespearian play being unfortunate.'

Charles Coghlan

In fact, Coghlan's Shylock did not meet with universal disapproval: a now defunct weekly paper, the *Examiner*, came out firmly in favour of Coghlan, saying that, 'His rendering of Shylock has the merit of keeping nearer to the just artistic proportion of the character in the drama than when Shylock is so acted as to engross the whole attention of the audience and dwarf the other personages. [He] plays the part throughout with subdued force, and the prominence of the character is not increased by any of the artificial means by which the other parts are commonly reduced to insignificance when Shylock is played by a "star".'

It would seem that Coghlan's interpretation was ahead of its time. Just four years later, in 1879, when Henry Irving produced *The Merchant of Venice* at the Lyceum, Irving himself portrayed Shylock as a sympathetic character and the production was a brilliant success, with Ellen Terry once again playing Portia. Irving himself wrote of the character: 'Shylock is a bloody-minded monster − but you mustn't play him so, if you wish to succeed; you must get some sympathy for him.' But Irving was an actor of genius and Coghlan, although a competent actor, was far from being a great one.

The Merchant of Venice was withdrawn after just three weeks. Ironically, as soon as its withdrawal was announced audiences improved and by the last few performances it was playing to houses that were three-quarters full. The Prince of Wales came to see it and expressed his enjoyment of the production and his regret that it had failed to please the critics, and Bancroft received a petition, signed by many leading lights in the world of the arts, a group of them even offering to raise subscriptions to keep it going, as it must surely soon attract full houses. Bancroft rejected this plea, insisting that if a production could not survive on its own merits then it must be withdrawn immediately. In spite of the critical failure of *The Merchant,* it did just about break even, although the cost of the production had been, 'some three thousand pounds − a large sum to spend upon a play in such a little theatre.'

The Bancrofts decided to play safe and replace *The Merchant* with yet another revival, so a production of Lord Lytton's *Money* was hastily rehearsed. It opened at the end of May, with Charles Coghlan once again playing Alfred Evelyn, the young hero, in the hopes of restoring his shattered morale; Squire Bancroft 'wesumed', his r-less Captain Dudley Smooth. Marie, now thirty-six and becoming distinctly plump, returned in spite of the hay-fever that was plaguing her, knowing that her presence in the cast would pull the audiences in. This time she played the older woman, Lady Franklin. Ellen Terry was the young Clara: 'I found Clara Douglas difficult, but I enjoyed playing her,' she wrote. Maybe Clara was too 'sweet' after the challenge and triumph of her Portia.

The fortunes of the Prince of Wales's were immediately restored with the revival of *Money*, which ran to full houses until the end of the season, when the Bancrofts set off for Europe, travelling to Zurich and Lucerne and on into the mountains. Most of their belongings travelled in the guard's compartment of the train in an enormous leather portmanteau, while they kept enough necessities for immediate use in smaller bags in their own quarters. (With women's full-length, many-layered dresses and men's heavy three-piece suits, until the arrival of lightweight, wash-and-wear clothing, well on in the twentieth century, travel necessitated the accompaniment of large and weighty items of luggage – and plenty of employment for porters.) As there were frequent changes of train, this great double-compartmented trunk kept going astray and Marie and Squire would arrive at their next hotel to find it missing. Telegrams would be sent to locate it and eventually it would catch up with them. Marie described how at one of their stops she had virtually run out of clothes from her hand-baggage. One evening she was in her room when from the corridor outside she heard the sound of voices. She opened her door to find a procession, headed by an old friend, the playwright Palgrave Simpson, followed by several other guests and two porters bearing the great trunk, decorated with flowers and ribbons. The wretched portmanteau was to end up back at the Prince of Wales's, where it spent the rest of its days as an occasional stage prop, and for future travels the Bancrofts used smaller trunks.

While taking a day-trip on a steamer on Lake Lucerne they met the Duke of Connaught, one of Queen Victoria's sons, who was also staying by the lake. Several of the other passengers seemed to be surreptitiously pointing and staring at the Bancrofts. The Duke laughed at this, saying, 'You see, Mrs Bancroft, I have the advantage of you here; they all know you, but they don't know me.' One day, at their hotel they were suddenly aware that the staff were scuttling around anxiously, securing windows and doors and urging people inside. A huge black cloud was to be seen over the mountains and the worst storm that Marie had ever seen was soon upon them. 'The wind howled as if all the wild animals in the world had been lashed into a fury. The thunder was terrible, and filled one with a religious awe, as if it meant the end of all things. The lightning came like knives cutting the clouds into shreds; then the hailstones, which fell with such force that they seemed to split the air as they descended. It was a terrible but grand experience. Presently a change, as sudden as the storm, restored to us the giant sun, and all was calm and beautiful again.' But the storm had taken a tragic toll: earlier in the day a young Frenchman and his bride, on their honeymoon, had, in spite of being warned of the imminent severe weather, taken a small boat out on Lake Lucerne. When the storm broke they were far from the shore and the boat capsized. The young woman was drowned.

Back in London, the revival of *Money* continued when the new season opened in September 1875, while the next production, *Masks and Faces*, was in preparation. This was a play written in collaboration between Charles Reade (the playwright who had brought Ellen Terry back to

London) and Tom Taylor in 1852. Both Reade and Taylor are now almost entirely forgotten. Taylor's best-known works were a melodrama called *The Ticket of Leave Man* and, of course, *Our American Cousin*, with Lord Dundreary of the extravagant whiskers. Reade wrote several plays, but was best known for his novel *The Cloister and the Hearth*.

The main character in *Masks and Faces* was the celebrated eighteenth-century actress Margaret 'Peg' Woffington. Born in Ireland in around 1720, as a child Peg Woffington sang on the streets of Dublin. She came to London in 1740, where she was employed by John Rich, the famous manager of Covent Garden. It was Rich who first produced Gay's *Beggar's Opera* in 1728, making 'Gay rich and Rich gay'. Woffington went on to become the most famous actress of her day. Determined to retain her independence, she never married, although she had many lovers, among them the great actor, David Garrick, with whom she lived openly for some time. The writing of *Masks and Faces* had been divided fairly equally between Tom Taylor and Charles Reade, who had been inspired by a portrait of Peg Woffington in the Garrick Club, but by 1875 Reade had bought out Taylor's share in the rights to the play, so it was with Reade that the Bancrofts had to negotiate over various alterations they wished to make to the original script. Reade proved difficult and took some persuading. Eventually, wrote Marie, 'after many a tough fight, we won the day …. afterwards having the great satisfaction of Charles Reade's approval of every change.'

The play included what was to become Squire Bancroft's favourite role, quite unlike the foppish, stereotyped 'Bancroft part' he had played so often. This was James Triplet, an impoverished artist and playwright, desperately trying to earn enough to support his starving family. Triplet believes his fortunes would be restored if he were to paint a portrait of the celebrated Peg Woffington and if she were to persuade John Rich of Covent Garden to produce his plays. Ernest Vane, a handsome young man from Huntingdonshire, and a dissolute roué, Sir Charles Pomander, are both seeking the famous actress's favours. Pomander offers her everything she could possibly want if she would become his mistress – house, money, dresses – but she rejects him scornfully. However, attracted by the charming and good-looking Vane, she indicates that she might consider his advances, unaware that he is married, with a pretty young wife, Mabel, languishing neglected at his country estate. Mabel Vane, played by Ellen Terry, turns up at her husband's London home unexpectedly to find him entertaining fashionable guests, including Peg Woffington and Pomander, along with a duo of critics, Soaper and Snarl, the former a cringing flatterer, and the latter a spiteful cynic.

The next act is set in the Triplet family's attic home, where Peg visits unexpectedly. The playwright's hungry children are enchanted with the lovely lady who brings gifts of food for the family and plays with them, and who produces red wine for their sick mother to encourage her recovery to health. Triplet shows Peg his unfinished portrait of her, but despairingly cuts out the face as it could never match up to its original. A farcical scene follows when the other hangers-on turn up to view the portrait and Peg, behind the easel, puts her own face into the space in the picture, 'end-of-the-pier' style. The visitors all declare scornfully that the painting is totally unlike its subject until they realise that in the dim light their eyes had been deceived and that it is the face of Peg herself that they are looking at.

Poor Mabel is devastated to discover that her husband's neglect of her is due to his pursuit of another woman. However Peg, discovering that Vane is married, is won over by Mabel's sweetness and sends Vane packing back to his wife. Vane returns grovelling to Mabel, who forgives him for his faithlessness. Meanwhile, with Peg's support, Triplet's future as a playwright, if not as a portrait painter, is assured.

Marie Wilton as Peg Woffington in **Masks and Faces**

The sets for *Masks and Faces* were, as usual with the Bancrofts' productions, meticulously and authentically designed. The first act was set in the green-room of Covent Garden Theatre, in sharp contrast to the sparsely furnished garret where Triplet lived in poverty with his family. The green-room walls were hung with copies of works from the renowned collection of the Garrick Club, including a famous portrait of David Garrick. Other portraits shown were of the actor, playwright and Poet Laureate, Colley Cibber, and the actress Kitty Clive, another celebrated figure on the mid-eighteenth-century stage, who both featured as characters in the play. On 11 November 1875, Dutton Cook, commenting on the scenery, spotted a historical inconsistency: there was a Chippendale chair in the green room and he gleefully pointed out in the *Pall Mall Gazette* that the '…. immortal carpenter could only, we fancy, have been an apprentice when Mrs Woffington was the talk of the town.' This slip-up in his attention to detail must have mortified the meticulous Bancroft.

***Squire Bancroft as Triplet in* Masks and Faces**

Marie Bancroft played the part of Peg in a deeper and more thoughtful way than it had been performed in its original production. Hers are the final lines in the play and, where Reade's original version ended with a comic rhyme after which Peg goes off in a peal of laughter, Marie chose to bring the curtain down with some more rueful words referring to her profession that come earlier than the original ending: 'When hereafter, in your home of peace, you hear harsh sentence passed on us, whose lot is admiration, rarely love – triumph, but never tranquillity – think sometimes of Margaret Woffington, and say stage-masks may cover honest faces, and hearts beat true beneath a tinselled robe.' Charles Reade initially insisted

167

on his original ending, but at an early rehearsal Marie found the playwright in tears as she delivered her preferred lines to close the play. 'He took my hands in his, and said, "You are right, you have made me cry; your instincts are right; it shall be so."'

Squire Bancroft approached the part of the impoverished Triplet with some trepidation: 'I felt that unless I made some effort that I should be doomed to …. ringing the changes on what had for some time grown to be called "Bancroft parts".' His lack of confidence in the part apparently showed and his interpretation of it was not met with universal approval, although the *Dramatic Review* of 7 March said of his Triplet that 'it can no longer be said that this excellent actor is merely a "haw haw" swell'.

The same reviewer described Ellen Terry's Mabel as 'an exquisite performance,' although Ellen herself found the part hardly challenging. Later, in her memoirs, she told how the fans – not a word that would have been used at the time – of the two leading ladies led to some embarrassment between them. Ellen's 'Portia' had won her a considerable following of admirers who would attend *Masks and Faces* every night and applaud their goddess loudly and vigorously and 'it got about that I had hired a claque to clap me! Now, it seems funny, but at the time I was deeply hurt at the insinuation, and it cast a shadow over what would otherwise have been a very happy time …. I don't say for a minute that Mrs Bancroft's Peg Woffington …. was not appreciated and applauded, but I know that my Mabel Vane was received with a warmth out of all proportion to the merits of my performance, and that this angered some of Mrs Bancroft's admirers, and made them the bearers of ill-natured stories.' There may well have been some tension between the pair for a while, but Ellen went on to say: 'Any unpleasantness that it caused between us personally was of the briefest duration.'

Following *Masks and Faces* the Bancrofts reluctantly staged a production of a new comedy by H.J.Byron. They had earlier rejected one of his plays but had promised that they would produce one that he planned to write expressly for them, agreeing that it would immediately follow *Masks and Faces.* This proved to be an unwise agreement and the Bancrofts resolved never again to accept an unseen, unwritten play from anyone. Byron's play, entitled *Wrinkles*, was dreadful. He dug his heels in and flatly refused to incorporate any suggested changes. They were not prepared so much as to suggest to Ellen Terry that she might appear in it, and even Charles Coghlan refused to play the part intended for him. But they were in honour bound to go ahead with the production, so *Wrinkles* opened on 13 April 1876, with Marie and Squire Bancroft both in it. In fact their parts were 'so amusing, and provoked such roars of laughter that at times they almost threatened to save the play [but] the story was so poor …. that our fears were prophetic.' The play was doomed. A mortified Byron made the requested alterations too late and he also offered to forego his fees, an offer that the Bancrofts declined.

Wrinkles ran for just eighteen performances before being withdrawn, to be replaced by a hastily-prepared revival of Tom Robertson's *Ours*, with Ellen Terry as Blanche Haye and with Squire and Marie in their earlier parts of Hugh Chalcot and Mary Netley. There is an incident during the Crimea scene in *Ours* which involves the young women, Blanche and Mary, mock-fighting with the men's weapons. Ellen Terry wrote of an unfortunate incident that occurred during one performance: 'When I was playing Blanche Haye in *Ours* I nearly killed Mrs Bancroft with the bayonet which it was part of the business of the play for me to "fool" with. I charged as usual; either she made a mistake and moved to the right instead of to the left, or I made a mistake. Anyhow, I wounded her in the arm. She had to wear it in a sling, and I felt very badly about it, all the more because of the ill-natured stories of its being no accident.'

Meanwhile there was nothing ready for the following season. The Bancrofts had for a while been considering looking to the French stage for inspiration and for new material. They had hoped to produce a fresh English version of Victorien Sardou's comedy, *Les Pattes de Mouches,* a play that had been around for many years as *A Scrap of Paper*. Soon after Tom Taylor had begun work on a completely new adaptation, word came from John Hare that he was himself preparing a production of the same play, in its existing English version. Not wanting to conflict with Hare's plans, the Bancrofts stopped Taylor's work. Next they looked to Wilkie Collins's own stage version of *The Moonstone* that the novelist was working on, but decided that it would not suit the Prince of Wales's. Then misfortune fell upon the production of *Ours*: it was playing to full houses when Marie Bancroft and Ellen Terry both fell ill in June. The season was forced to end early and, once Marie had recovered, she and Squire set off once more for Switzerland.

On their return they announced significant changes in the Prince of Wales's company for the new season of 1876. Ellen Terry left, to join John Hare's company at the Court Theatre. She played in several productions there, and it was while she was with Hare at the Court that, at last divorced from Watts, she married a fellow actor, an ex-soldier called Charles Wardell, who used the stage name of Kelly. This marriage was also short-lived, and they separated less than three years later. (Her third marriage, to American actor James Carew in 1907, lasted for three years.) Ellen was at the Court until 1878, when she joined Henry Irving who had taken over at the Lyceum for the start of his long reign there. Irving and Terry were to work together for more than twenty years, becoming the most celebrated theatrical duo in the history of British theatre.

Charles Coghlan also moved on. Despite his general success both as an actor and a playwright, he had never entirely got over his failure as

169

Shylock. After starring in several other roles elsewhere in London, he then moved to America, where he achieved considerable success. He joined the company of Augustin Daly, a famous theatrical manager and impresario, who had been searching for 'a leading man of distinction and personal charm'. Coghlan fitted the bill. He returned to England briefly in 1879, but was soon back in the United States, where he became the leading man at Wallack's Theatre, working alongside his younger sister Rose Coghlan who was a leading actress there, having first gone to America in 1871 as one of Lydia Thompson's 'British Blondes'. The actor Fred Kerr, in his memoirs[*], considered that Coghlan was 'a brilliant actor .... but he invariably kicked away the ladder just as he was mounting its highest step.' Coghlan would die while on tour in Galveston, Texas, in 1899.

The Prince of Wales's compensated for these departures with some valuable additions to the company, among them Henry Kemble[*]. A member of the great theatrical family that had included Sarah Siddons and John Philip Kemble, Henry Kemble was to work with the Bancrofts for many years, becoming a close personal friend as well as a colleague. He was nicknamed 'the Beetle', because in bad weather his short, rather stout figure would be seen scuttling around in a long brown cloak, with an astrakhan collar, which he would pull up right over his head. George Bancroft had fond memories of him, and wrote that he was a very amusing man who had 'the most melancholy way of saying the funniest things'. The Beetle never married, but George wrote that he was devoted to Marie. Once, when the two of them were waiting for their 'call' in the green-room at the Haymarket, he was heard to say to her, 'Oh, Mrs B. *All* the nice women are married.'

The most distinguished of the new recruits were the Kendals, who were already well established in their careers and invariably worked together. It was a considerable coup for the Bancrofts to have signed them up. Margaret Kendal, always known as Madge, was a handsome woman, who excelled in playing Shakespeare's heroines. Born in 1848, she was the youngest of the numerous siblings of the large Robertson family of whom Tom, the playwright, was the oldest. Like Marie Wilton and Ellen Terry, and many other actresses of that time, Madge Robertson had embarked on her stage career as a young child. Also like Marie, Madge had joined Chute's company in Bristol, and then later was with Buckstone at the Haymarket in London where she met William Hunter Kendal.

Kendal was born William Hunter Grimston in 1843. Male actors were less often from a theatrical background, coming into the profession as

---

[*] Frederick 'Fred' Kerr, 1858-1933, a successful actor-manager whose memoirs, *Recollections of a Defective Memory*, were published in 1930.
[*] Henry Kemble, 1848-1907, was a grandson of Charles Kemble.

adults, often having set out in a different career. Kendal's father was an artist and William himself was a talented self-taught artist who as a young man enjoyed hanging around theatres where he would sketch the actors; throughout his life he was to remain a keen amateur. Originally intended for a career in medicine, instead he joined the theatrical profession while in his late teens, soon adopting the name of Kendal: it had been suggested to him that the potential for confusion with the great theatrical name of Kemble might do his career no harm. It was in Birmingham, in around 1861, that he first met Squire Bancroft, who described him as 'a fair, handsome young fellow'. He then worked in Glasgow for four years before going to London, where he met Madge Robertson. Following their marriage in 1869, the Kendals retained the name Grimston in their private life. Madge was to become one of the most distinguished actresses of her day and was also known for her often alarmingly high moral standards: she was 'Victorian values' personified. William Kendal was to die in 1917. Madge lived on to 1935, having been awarded the DBE in 1926.

When she first arrived at the Prince of Wales's Madge Kendal – still billed as 'Miss Madge Robertson' – expressed her concern about the dressing-room arrangements. It was a very small theatre, and most of the actors and actresses had to share dressing-room space. Mrs Kendal insisted that she was accustomed to having a dressing-room to herself and could not contemplate sharing. Marie Bancroft, without hesitation, said that her own dressing-room was fairly spacious and could easily be divided into two with a couple of screens. The newly-created small dressing-room was fitted out with every comfort and Mrs Kendal appeared satisfied with the arrangement.

The Prince of Wales's Theatre itself had undergone another complete makeover during the summer break and was totally refurbished with new seating throughout, this time upholstered in deep red and amber. The décor was more elaborate than ever, with allegorical paintings on the box fronts, a peacock frieze over the proscenium and fans made of real peacock feathers adorning each of the private boxes. Peacocks' feathers were a surprising choice of decoration, in view of Marie Bancroft's superstitious nature, as it was widely believed that they brought bad luck. Sure enough, on the first night of the new season, two ladies in the audience were suddenly taken ill during the performance. The peacock feathers were hastily removed, never to be reinstated.

Squire Bancroft, who was now almost entirely responsible for the choice of new productions at the Prince of Wales's, was depressed by what he described as 'a wilderness of manuscripts' in the English language, and decided to turn to the thriving French drama scene. He chose an adaptation of Victorien Sardou's play *Nos Intimes*. Sardou was, along with Alexandre Dumas and Victor Hugo, one of the best-known and most prolific playwrights in France. Following in the footsteps of the slightly earlier Frenchman, Eugene Scribe*, Sardou perfected what had become known as the '*pièce bien faite*' (the 'well-made play'). This typically had a complex plot, which would develop logically, with a build-up of suspense, leading to a happy ending that would tidily resolve all loose ends. Bernard Shaw despised the format, coining the term 'Sardoodledom' to describe it, but nevertheless was not entirely uninfluenced by it. Born in 1831, Sardou wrote literally dozens of plays. Many of his later ones starred the great Sarah Bernhardt. He was awarded the Légion d'Honneur in 1863. Today his work is best remembered by Puccini's opera, *Tosca*, which was adapted from his play *La Tosca*.

Two people collaborated in the translation and adaptation of *Nos Intimes*, each using a *nom de plume*. Benjamin Charles Stephenson wrote under the name of 'Bolton Rowe' – he actually lived in a street off Piccadilly called Bolton Row. His collaborator on *Nos Intimes* was the critic, Clement Scott, who chose the improbable pseudonym of 'Saville Rowe'. The intended implication was that the two were brothers, but no one was fooled.

Nos Intimes was renamed *Peril* and it opened in September 1876. It met with a mixed reception from the critics, the theme of the play being adultery, a topic that raised English eyebrows, even though the adultery did not actually take place, as all attempts to seduce the impressionable young wife of a middle-aged baronet failed. Squire wrote: 'There was much division of opinion in the press as to the merits of *Peril*, some repining that we had not been able to find a new English comedy to our liking.' However, despite mixed reviews, the play was a box-office success, raising near record profits and almost matching the financial success of *School*. As always, the set was elaborate and costly, comprising the interior of a great Elizabethan hall, complete with a massive oak staircase and gallery, all constructed on the tiny stage of the Prince of Wales's. This great hall was adorned with outsized furnishings, as well as portraits, suits of armour and other trappings. The actors must have found it difficult to move around the stage. It was impossible to make scene changes, so smaller sets were placed within the walls of the main structure for intimate scenes such as a boudoir. During the run of *Peril* the Prince of Wales's embarked on a series of matinées on alternate Saturdays – an experiment which now proved popular.

That autumn, in October 1876, the Lord Mayor of London hosted a banquet at the Mansion House for almost 150 members of the dramatic profession. For once the guest list included women. The Bancrofts attended, as did the Kendals and Ellen Terry along with several other

---

* Eugene Scribe, 1791-1861, a prolific and highly respected French dramatist.

members of the theatrical Terry family. There were also John Baldwin Buckstone from the Haymarket, Ada Swanborough from the Strand, several actors and actresses from the Prince of Wales's company, and many of the other celebrated stage names of the day, apart from Henry Irving, who was touring Ireland and the provinces that autumn. Others present included Jenny Lind, 'the Swedish Nightingale', W.S.Gilbert, the critic and playwright Clement Scott and Charles Dickens (junior), the son of the novelist. There were numerous after-dinner speeches – at least fifteen, including one from Squire Bancroft who replied to the toast to the drama. This was a recognition that the Prince of Wales's was unquestionably now one of London's leading theatres. Although many women were present as guests, it was nevertheless a man, Arthur Cecil, of the Prince of Wales's company, who replied to the toast to 'the ladies'.

Squire and Marie Bancroft in the 1870s

As there was no appropriate part for Marie Bancroft in *Peril*, she was free to take part in a charity event in February of 1877, in aid of the organ fund of a church in Bayswater. The mixed programme included songs and

173

recitations and the star of the occasion was Marie reading from *Bleak House*. *The Era* reported:

> This was Mrs Bancroft's first attempt as a reader, but her success was unequivocal. Naturally enough, she started somewhat nervously, but presently in her own arranged sketch of the life of Poor Jo from Dickens's *Bleak House*, had her audience completely under her control, touched all hearts and caused tears to flow copiously from all eyes .... Later in the evening Mrs Bancroft opened a brighter page, and proved that laughter as well as tears are at her command, the audience fairly screaming with hilarity .... Mrs Bancroft is accustomed to applause, but she has seldom, if ever, been the object of any more genuine and hearty that that which attended her efforts on this occasion.

8

END OF ACT ONE

Following the success of *Peril* Squire Bancroft again looked to France and Victorien Sardou in his search for a new production. The prolific French dramatist's newest play, *Dora*, was about to open in Paris, and Bancroft was keen to see it. Unable to get away from London during the early days of *Peril*, he sent the probable future adapter of the play, 'Charlie' Stephenson, across to Paris to see it soon after its opening. As a result of Stephenson's report, along with the glowing French reviews, Squire telegraphed the agent for the English rights and persuaded him to let him have first refusal on the play. Determined to see *Dora* for himself, Bancroft managed a rushed trip to Paris early in February, leaving on a Sunday morning, accompanied by William Kendal. They saw the play that evening at the Théâtre du Vaudeville (theatres in Paris, unlike those in Britain, were open on a Sunday) and by the end of the first act, were excited by what they had seen so far. They met up with the agent during the first interval and Bancroft made an offer then and there for the rights. Immediately after the final curtain he handed over a cheque for fifteen hundred pounds, the largest sum ever paid for the rights in a foreign work. He was convinced he had a bargain and he and Kendal returned home in high spirits in time for the Monday evening performance of *Peril*.

While Bancroft and Kendal were in Paris, Marie Bancroft spent the Sunday with Madge Kendal at her home. After Madge had bathed her children and put them to bed – undertaking these tasks herself, much to the undomesticated Marie's astonishment – they went downstairs to dinner. Marie suddenly wondered out loud, 'What do you think the men are doing now?' Mrs Kendal suggested they were probably either dining together, or getting ready to go to see *Dora*. Madge Kendal wrote that, 'It was then I discovered that this vivacious little lady was in love with her husband, as he was with her.' She went on to remark that Marie seemed surprised that she, Madge, was never jealous of her own husband. Perhaps Marie was more worldly and was wondering what their men might be getting up to on their own in Paris.

Peril was extended until March, a run of six months. In the 1870s this was unusually long. A hundred performances, or around four months, was considered to be a long run and six months was rare. The English version of *Dora* was not scheduled to open until January of 1878, so the next production at the Prince of Wales's was a double bill of Dion Boucicault's famous comedy *London Assurance*, along with a short, one-act play called *The Vicarage*, another adaptation from the French by Clement Scott, writing as 'Saville Rowe'.

London Assurance has been described as a kind of bridge between Restoration comedy and the work of Oscar Wilde. A marriage has been arranged between Sir Harcourt Courtly, an ageing, foppish roué, and the young niece of his old friend, a country squire. With the help of corsets and lavishly applied cosmetics, Sir Harcourt is convinced he looks twenty years younger than he is. Eighteen-year-old Grace appears content with the match to so much older a man on the grounds that 'a young husband might expect affection and nonsense'. Her maid, Pert, worries that 'she doesn't seem to care whether he is sixty or sixteen; jokes at love; prepares for matrimony as she would for dinner; says it is a necessary evil and what can't be cured must be endured'. Sir Harcourt's handsome playboy son, Charles, who his father believes is a virtuous, studious young man, turns up, accompanied by a crafty hanger-on called Dazzle, who has picked a worse-for-wear Charles up from a gutter at the start of the play. Charles and the lovely Grace fall in love. When the magnificently-named, hunting-mad Lady Gay Spanker strides onto the scene, followed by her meek and submissive husband, Adolphus, Sir Harcourt is smitten with her. Farcical shenanigans ensue that lead to 'Dolly' Spanker being encouraged to challenge Sir Harcourt to a duel: neither is at all enthusiastic about this idea and of course they survive unscathed. Eventually all is sorted out, with Sir Harcourt finally coming to realise how foolish he has been and Grace and Charles happily united.

Back in June 1870, while he was still with the Prince of Wales's, a benefit had been held at the Princess's Theatre on behalf of John Hare. The main part of the bill was a performance of *London Assurance*. A remarkable cast was gathered together, which included Hare himself as Sir Harcourt, John Baldwin Buckstone as Dolly Spanker and John Lawrence Toole as a lawyer. Marie Bancroft played Lady Gay Spanker. She was photographed in a riding habit and top hat by Adolphe Beau, a well-known French portrait photographer who had settled in London where his career flourished. SquireBancroft played Dazzle, the con-artist who manages to trick each character into believing that he is either a friend or a relative of one of the others. When, near the end of the play, he is eventually asked, 'Who the deuce are you?' he replies, 'I have not the remotest idea! Nature made me a gentleman – that is, I live on the best that can be procured for credit. I never spend my own money when I can oblige a friend …. I'm an epidemic on the trade of tailor. For further particulars inquire of any sitting magistrate.'

Marie Bancroft as Lady Gay Spanker in Boucicault's
London Assurance, *1870, photograph by Adolphe Beau*

In the 1877 production Sir Harcourt Courtly was played by Arthur Cecil and the splendid part of the crop-wielding Lady Gay Spanker by Madge Kendal. Squire Bancroft again was the manipulative Dazzle and Marie played the small part of Grace's witty maid, Pert. For the first time the name 'Marie Wilton' was left off the playbills, her name appearing as simply 'Mrs Bancroft'.

Enter COOL, ~~with a letter~~, R

COOL. (R) Mr. Charles, I have been watching to find you alone. Sir Harcourt has written to town for you.

COURTLY. (*c.*) The devil he has.

COOL. He expects you down to-morrow evening. *Xis up to window*

DAZZLE. (c.) Oh! he'll be punctual. A thought strikes me!

COURTLY. Pooh! Confound your thoughts! I can think of nothing but the idea of leaving Grace, at the very moment when I had established the most——

DAZZLE. What, if I can prevent her marriage with your governor?

COURTLY. Impossible!

DAZZLE. He's pluming himself for the conquest of Lady Gay Spanker. It will not be difficult to make him believe she accedes to his suit. And if she would but join in the plan——

COURTLY. I see it all. And do you think she would?

DAZZLE. I mistake my game if she would not.

COOL. Here comes Sir Harcourt! *In –*

DAZZLE. I'll begin with him. Retire, and watch how I'll open the campaign for you.

COURTLY *and* COOL *retire through window*, R. U. E.

Enter SIR HARCOURT *by window*, R.

2 SIR H. Here is that cursed fellow again. *3 Day*   *Sir Harcourt!*

1 DAZZLE. Ah, my dear *old* friend!

4 SIR H. Mr. Dazzle.

DAZZLE. ~~There a secret of importance to disclose to you.~~ Are you a man of honour? Hush! don't speak; you are. It is with the greatest pain I am compelled to request you, as a gentleman, ~~that you will~~ *to* shun studiously the society of Lady Gay Spanker!

SIR H. Good gracious! By what right do you make such a demand?

DAZZLE. ~~Why~~, I am distantly related to the Spankers.

SIR H. Why, hang it, sir, if you don't appear to be related to every family in Great Britain?

DAZZLE. A good many of the nobility claim me as a connexion. But, to return—she is much struck with your address; evidently, she laid herself out for display.

SIR H. Ha! you surprise me!

DAZZLE. To entangle you.

SIR H. Ha! ha! why, it did appear like it.

DAZZLE. You will spare her for my sake; give her no encouragement; if disgrace come upon my relatives, the Spankers, I should never hold up my head again. *sinks on Ottoman C.*

SIR H. (*aside*) I shall achieve an easy conquest, ~~and a glorious~~. Ha! ha! I ~~traced~~ remark*ed* it before; but this is a gentleman.

DAZZLE. May I rely on your generosity? *sit LC*

SIR H. Faithfully. (*shakes his hand*) Sir, I honour and esteem you; but, might I ask, how you came to meet our friend Max Harkaway, in my house in Belgrave Square.

Cool Exit by Door L U E. when Sir H. enter down finished

57 . 10.36

5

a page from Squire Bancroft's prompt book for London Assurance, *1877*
(reproduced by kind permission of Brenda Bancroft)

178

Marie made the most of her small part: she almost doubled Pert's main scene in the second act with the additional 'business' that she incorporated. Boucicault was in America and Marie was to write: 'I don't know what [the author] would have said to the liberties taken with the text. The audience, however, laughed immoderately and seemed to thoroughly enjoy it .... I well remember one night Mrs Boucicault looking with amazement from a private box at my audacity, but at the same time laughing heartily.'

Squire Bancroft's prompt book for *London Assurance* is filled with directions. The prompt book of a play is far more than just a script in case an actor forgets his or her lines. Marked up by the stage-manager/director, it is annotated with the full directions for the play, along with sketches of the sets and positions of the actors. It notes all lighting, props, costumes, business and everything else connected with the production. Early prompt books are now rare and valuable.

Arthur Cecil and Marie Bancroft
in **The Vicarage**, *1877*

London Assurance was preceded by Clement Scott's short play, *The Vicarage*. It was consequently a very late night for audiences and actors alike. Adapted from an obscure French play, it told of a country vicar, well in his late middle years, whose worldly friend from his past

179

encourages him to believe that life in his rural backwater is dull and uneventful. The vicar was played by Arthur Cecil and his friend by William Kendal. Marie Bancroft played the vicar's wife, a sweet old lady who has to persuade him that all he could possibly wish for in life is to be found in his own home. The vicar and his wife had lost a baby who had died in infancy and Marie's part included lines that she found a painful reminder of the baby boy she herself had lost seven years before: 'God gave me a little child; but then, when all was bright and beautiful, God took His gift away.' She wrote that, 'The remembrance of the death of my own child was revived in these words. My mind was full of his image, and my tears came in tribute to his memory. I could not have stopped them if I had tried. The effect upon my audience was that not a heart amongst them did not feel with me …. Their tears told me of their sympathy.'

The reviews of both plays generally were not good. Although E.L.Blanchard reported that on the first night the 'house [was] crowded; all the notabilities were present,' nevertheless he considered *The Vicarage* a 'pretty adaptation' – a kinder verdict than that of the *New York Times* critic, who described it as a 'mutilation' of the French original. Another London reviewer wrote: 'That overrated comedy, *London Assurance*, was revived, with a notable cast, but the effect has been somewhat disappointing. There is a pretentiousness about the doings of the Prince of Wales's just now which is a little irritating.' Dutton Cook gave it a mixed review, approving of Arthur Cecil's Sir Harcourt Courtly. He also wrote that Marie played Pert 'with charming brightness and sauciness,' and that Bancroft's Dazzle showed 'good humour and good intentions'. However he thought William Kendal was 'inclined to overact' as Charles Courtly, that Madge Kendal was 'scarcely seen to advantage', as Lady Gay, and that Henry Kemble was 'rather dull than droll as Dolly Spanker'. He also said the play displayed 'Tom-and-Jerryism', a term originated in 1821 by the journalist Pierce Egan[*] to refer to drunken, loutish behaviour on the streets of London and later used by Jerome K. Jerome in *Three Men on the Bummel*. So the twentieth-century cartoon cat-and-mouse cartoon had early nineteenth-century origins.

It was during the spring of 1877, while *London Assurance* was on, that the Bancrofts first met a woman who was to become one of the most celebrated beauties of her time. From across the room at a party Squire spotted an extraordinarily beautiful woman, in a simple black dress and with hardly any jewellery. Turning to a friend he asked, 'Who is that

---

[*] Pierce Egan, 1772-1849, a well-known journalist. He was the author of *Life in London*, a series that first appeared in 1821 featuring his hugely popular characters, London men-about-town, Tom and Jerry.

lovely woman?' 'I am told she is a Mrs Langworthy, or Lang-something – her father is the Dean of Jersey,' was the reply. It was one of the first occasions that Mrs Lillie Langtry had been seen in London society. They were introduced and Squire wrote, 'I found the manner of this since celebrated woman as full of charm as were her looks.' Of future meetings with Mrs Langtry, he wrote that 'this charm of manner never changed – a charm, it always seemed to me, as potent as her beauty .... I don't remember much stir about her on that occasion although she looked graceful and gracious.' It was not long after this that the Prince of Wales began a notorious liaison with 'the Jersey Lily' which was to last for three years.

If the critics were beginning to tire of the Prince of Wales's productions, the theatre-loving public were not: once again the box office returns were more than satisfactory and the double bill ran to full houses until the end of the season, when the Bancrofts took their regular holiday in Europe. For the first time they stayed at Pontresina, an alpine village in the beautiful Engadine valley, near St Moritz in the southeast of Switzerland. They fell in love with the place and were to return many times in future years. Pontresina was popular with English holidaymakers and the Bancrofts were regularly to meet up with old friends there, including Arthur Cecil and the composer Arthur Sullivan.

After a couple of weeks in Pontresina they travelled on into Austria, to the Tyrol, where they walked to the top of the Stelvio Pass, the highest pass in the eastern part of the Alps. In the nearby town then called Botzen (now Bolzano, in Italy) they made a visit to the local gaol, where Henri de Tourville, a notorious Englishman who claimed aristocratic French origins, was awaiting sentence for the murder of his wife. The Bancrofts and other visitors were allowed to watch the prisoner walking up and down in an exercise yard. De Tourville was a famous swindler whom the Bancrofts might well have come across during the days when he posed as a fashionable Londoner. He took his wealthy second wife to Austria where he did away with her by pushing her off a cliff into a ravine. This was at first declared an accident and he returned to London, but the investigation was reopened and he was extradited back to Austria where he was charged with his wife's murder. De Tourville was eventually sentenced to twenty years in the nearby salt-mines, where he died before his twenty years were up. Undisturbed by this rather ghoulish visit the Bancrofts 'bought grapes as big as walnuts, and melons fit for prizes, at a cost of very small coins, in the pretty market-place.'

They then set off by train over the Brenner Pass towards Innsbruck. Here they ran into trouble. Flooding over the past year had caused landslips and the line was blocked. Their train came to a halt at a small mountain village where they were held up for many hours, with more and more trains queueing up behind them. The village shops soon ran out of food, and the despairing and helpless stationmaster, unable to cope with the desperate queries from the hungry, stranded passengers, removed his uniform coat and cap so he could no longer be identified. The Bancrofts were resigned to their discomfort: 'After all, we were travelling for our pleasure, and the inconveniences we put up with were small indeed compared with the anguish we saw endured by a traveller who had been summoned by telegraph from Vienna to a sick-bed; the despair of a commercial person at some important difference the delay would cause in his affairs; and the moans and cries of starving animals and fowls, packed in trucks or cooped up in pens .... without food, or drink, or standing space, crowded in on each other, and fighting in the heat for every inch of breathing-room.'

The train was stuck for more than seven hours. Night fell and it began to pour with rain. Finally word came that the line had been cleared enough for the first of the trains to pass. Passengers from the other trains were transferred forward to the front train, clambering over debris by the light of lanterns in the thunderstorm that was raging. Luggage was hauled along by 'gangs of labourers, who looked like devils by the torchlight, grimed as they were with dirt, having been throughout the day and the past night at work to clear the way.' Eventually, 'wet, tired-out, and almost past hunger', they reached Innsbruck at one o'clock in the morning. Alas, 'the fate of the wretched cattle in the trucks and the cooped-up fowls we never knew.'

After recovering from this horrendous journey the Bancrofts enjoyed the sights of Innsbruck for a couple of days, and then visited Salzburg. From there they went on to the underground salt-mines of Berchtesgaden, just across the border in Germany. Berchtesgaden was to become notorious many years later when it became a Nazi headquarters, with Adolf Hitler's mountain residence, the 'Eagle's Nest', nearby. This visit to the salt-mines was a strange experience. First the visitors were given protective clothing: the men wore white linen overalls and the ladies were issued with white jackets and enormous baggy trousers into which their own voluminous dresses could be stuffed. These must have emerged very crumpled. Both men and women wore felt hats like saucepans and large leather aprons. All this was to protect the visitors' clothes from the salt, not the visitors themselves from injury – there were no hard hats issued in the 1870s. They were then led into a mine-shaft that led deep below ground to where they were taken in a boat across 'a black, silent, subterranean lake .... feebly-lit by faint, glimmering oil-lamps .... just revealing the forms of shadowy-looking creatures who rowed the boat, and calling up mental pictures of the Styx.' The salt-mines at Berchtesgaden are still functioning and are a popular tourist attraction today, although nowadays visitors are issued with miners' outfits rather than baggy white suits.

It was decided that the English version of *Dora* would open after Christmas, as the Kendals were not available during the autumn months; so the new season opened towards the end of September with a pot-boiler programme, a double bill of two one-act Tom Taylor comedies in which the Bancrofts had unchallenging parts, allowing them to spend plenty of time with the 'Brothers Rowe' as Scott and Stephenson had become generally known, polishing their adaptation of Sardou's play for English audiences. Clement Scott ('Saville Rowe') was to write that, 'No actress of my time has so helped authors and clever men who wrote for the stage as Marie Bancroft. For she was as bright in conversation, in suggestion, in the art of description, and in humour off the stage as on it.' Squire too had considerable input. Scott wrote that he 'deserved to share fairly in any credit that fell to the adaptation of a very difficult work. He did not actually write the dialogue, but his judgment and suggestions were invaluable. I have never met so careful, experienced, and diplomatic an editor of dramatic work as Bancroft .... he had such consummate tact, such patience, such knowledge of men and things.'

Sardou's storyline remained the same, but the final result was definitely more an adaptation than a translation, with many of the characters having their nationalities changed from French to English. In Sardou's original a young Frenchwoman is charged with spying for the Germans, the recent Franco-Prussian war being still fresh in French memories. In the new adaptation a young English naval attaché is tricked into believing that his beautiful young bride, Dora, is a spy, who has been sending plans of the fortifications of the city of Constantinople (Istanbul) to the Russians. She has actually been framed by a vengeful Russian, Countess Zicka, who wanted the young man for herself. Dora's innocence is established when Zicka is trapped into revealing her guilt. The international intrigue that formed the subject matter of the play was topical at a time when Britain, Russia and other powers were embroiled in plots and counter-plots throughout Asia and the Middle East, and when diplomats and spies were plotting with and against each other throughout Europe's capital cities.

A new title had to be chosen for Sardou's play as *Dora* was already the title of a play by Lord Tennyson. Many other titles were considered, including *The Mousetrap*, but that title had also been used not too long before – for a work that was soon to be entirely forgotten, leaving the title free to be used again so famously – and for so long – almost eighty years later. Finally *Diplomacy* was chosen, an entirely appropriate title.

The forthcoming production of *Diplomacy* was eagerly anticipated and attracted much speculation in the papers. Just a few days before the first night Squire Bancroft was approached by a leading Bond Street librarian, a Mr Ollier, who ran one of the many outlets that acted as ticket agents for London theatres. Ollier had a proposal: he offered a cheque then and there

183

for £9000, in exchange for buying up all the stalls for every night until the middle of July. When an astonished Squire asked why he had come up with this proposal, Ollier replied that he knew that the play had been a huge success in Paris and he could not remember when a production had aroused such interest among the press and public. To Ollier's amazement, and no doubt to his annoyance, Squire declined his flattering offer. 'If the play should succeed, as you expect,' he explained, 'you would have a monopoly of the stalls, and could put them at any price you like, leaving Mrs Bancroft and myself to bear the natural anger of the public.'

Diplomacy opened on 12 January 1878 and was, in Bancroft's words, 'from start to finish a triumph.' As well as both Bancrofts, the cast included the Kendals, with Madge Kendal in the leading female role of Dora, Arthur Cecil and John Clayton. Marie Bancroft played the part of Countess Zicka, a wicked Russian spy, and Squire Bancroft was a Russian diplomat, Count Orloff.

the Kendals in **Diplomacy,** *1878*

184

At the final curtain there was an extraordinary ovation, with countless curtain calls and when the audience began to call for the author of the play to come before the curtain, as often happened in those days, Squire stepped forward to announce that the 'Rowe Brothers', the English adapters of the play, insisted that all the credit should go to Monsieur Victorien Sardou, author of the French original, and that the news of his play's reception was being telegraphed to him. In response, a letter arrived from France the very next day, with Sardou expressing his delight at how his play had been received in London.

The reviews, when they came out, were mostly good. Dutton Cook wrote that it 'left little to be desired and was entirely free from that air of genteel torpor which sometimes oppresses the stage of the Prince of Wales's theatre'. He went on to say of Marie's performance that she 'strengthens the cast by the spirit with which she sustains the incredible character of Countess Zicka,' who he believed 'would not have fallen into the trap laid for her'. He was less impressed by the Kendals, suggesting that the character of Dora hardly suited Mrs Kendal. 'She plays with grace and skill,' he wrote, 'but .... her lack of youthful impulsiveness and genuine spontaneity is seriously felt.' Of William Kendal, Cook wrote that he 'seems over-anxious to be impassioned and declines somewhat into the conventions of French melodrama.'

The queues outside each day were huge. The theatre could have been filled several times over, even if, as Bancroft said, it had been double the size. Seats were booked up for months ahead. Extra afternoon matinées, now customary, as well as some morning performances, were fitted in. The Prime Minister, Benjamin Disraeli, by then Lord Beaconsfield, rarely attended the theatre – but he went to see *Diplomacy*. Even the most distinguished theatregoers were not always able to get a box and had to make do with the stalls or the circle. When the exiled French 'Prince Imperial', son of the Emperor Napoleon III and the Empress Eugenie, came to see the play there was no box available for him, but he was content to sit in the dress-circle.

Perhaps the greatest compliment to be paid to *Diplomacy* was when a burlesque of it was produced at the Strand Theatre under the title of *Dora and Diplunacy*. It was written by Frank Burnand*, who was later to become the editor of *Punch*. While *Diplunacy* was in rehearsal, actors from the Strand attended the Prince of Wales's matinées to study the actors they were going to caricature. *Diplunacy* was also a great and deserved success, and ran for months. Many years later Madge Kendal

---

* Francis Cowley Burnand, 1836-1917, prolific dramatist and humorist. He was a frequent contributor to *Punch*, becoming its editor in 1880, a position he held for more than twenty years. He collaborated with Arthur Sullivan on the comic opera *Cox and Box* in 1867. Burnand was knighted in 1902.

was to write that the 'extraordinarily fine burlesque of Mrs Bancroft ....
made her very angry.' However, Madge Kendal was known to have very
little sense of humour. Marie was famed for hers, and she and Squire
actually saw *Diplunacy* more than once, attending matinées at the Strand
on days when there was none at the Prince of Wales's and were greatly
amused by the parody of their hit. 'Not only was the travesty immensely
funny, but it was remarkably well played .... and we laughed heartily at
the good-natured caricatures of our peculiarities.' One result of the
success of both versions of the play was that the Prince of Wales's was
often sold out, so that people who were unable to get tickets decided to
see the parodied version instead. Many years later, in 1926, a film was
made of *Diplomacy*.

Squire Bancroft as director triumphed in *Diplomacy*. He also enjoyed
his part in the play: 'Count Orloff perhaps gave me greater pleasure to act
than any character I have ever played,' he was to write, 'although it is
confined entirely to the one great scene – hardly appearing in the first act
of the play, and not appearing after the second.' He was referring to an
important dramatic scene in the second act that featured Bancroft with the
two leading male actors in the play, William Kendal and John Clayton, as
the naval attaché and his diplomat brother. Among the many letters of
congratulation he received was one from Wilkie Collins, who wrote, 'I
have never seen you do anything on the stage in such a thoroughly
masterly manner as the performance of your part .... Your Triplet was an
admirable piece of acting, most pathetic and true .... but the Russian (a far
more difficult part to play) has beaten the Triplet. There was no mistaking
the applause that broke out when you left the scene. You had seized the
sympathies of the audience. Of the great success of the English *Dora* there
is no manner of doubt, and I heartily rejoice in it.'

Such was the demand for seats for *Diplomacy*, it was decided to keep it
on throughout the hot months in London at the end of July and into
August, but with a total cast change as the Bancrofts were headed for the
Alps, and the Kendals went on tour to the provinces. A good replacement
cast was found, which included a young actress called Amy Roselle as
Dora and the twenty-five–year-old Johnston Forbes-Robertson in
Bancroft's part of Count Orloff. The promising young Amy Roselle was
to have a tragic life. Born in 1854, she played Lady Teazle at the
Haymarket at the age of sixteen. This was followed by many other
successes. Then, in 1881, she married an actor called Arthur Dacre. Amy
was in greater demand than her husband but, as they insisted on always
working together, they were often out of work. Soon they were heavily in
debt, and decided to try their luck in Australia. There things only got
worse for them and tragically they committed joint suicide in a Melbourne
hotel room in 1895.

Bancroft, Kendal and Clayton in Diplomacy

Marie and Squire Bancroft set off in August to spend a few weeks travelling in the Alps, finishing up, inevitably, at Pontresina. There they met another regular visitor to the village, a Mrs Otto Goldschmidt, better known as the famous soprano, Jenny Lind[*], who had retired some years earlier and was living in England.

The 'Swedish Nightingale' had a habit of rising very early, before anyone else was up. She would go downstairs to the hotel drawing-room where she would sit at the piano to sing before anyone was around. One morning the local doctor was passing by on an early morning call and heard the music. He slipped in and stood quietly just inside the room without her noticing and 'feasted upon this accidental banquet of sweet voice-notes .... a pleasure,' he said, 'that he would never forget.' The Bancrofts offered the Goldschmidts the use of a box at the Prince of Wales's whenever they might want it. Marie repeated her readings from Dickens's *Bleak House* in Pontresina that summer, as part of an entertainment that was put on to raise funds for the building of an English church in the village, a cause in which the Bancrofts became deeply involved for several years.

---

[*] Jenny Lind, 1820-87, was the most famous soprano of her generation. Her husband, Otto Goldschmidt, 1829-1907, was a distinguished German composer, conductor and pianist who founded the Bach Choir in London.

187

On the way home from Switzerland Marie and Squire stopped off briefly in Paris where they visited the great Exhibition that was being held to celebrate France's recovery from the devastations of the Franco-Prussian War of 1870-71. This was a vast show of exhibits from all over the world. The huge head of the uncompleted Statue of Liberty was on display. The great statue, by the French sculptor Frédéric Bartholdi, was not finished until 1884, when it finally made its long journey to New York, where it was dedicated in 1886. Other exhibits included a monoplane built in 1874, Alexander Graham Bell's telephone and Thomas Edison's early phonograph. The Bancrofts were especially impressed by a realistic 'panorama' depicting the Siege of Paris. This was a huge painting that ran all around a circular room so that visitors in the middle were surrounded by the events depicted. They also visited the Comédie Française, where they were 'enraptured' at seeing the great Sarah Bernhardt perform and where they were fortunate enough to be invited to visit the green-room of 'this most complete of theatres'.

It was during this short stay in Paris that Squire Bancroft met the Victorien Sardou in person. He visited the playwright at his home in Marly-le-Roi, to the west of Paris, where he lived in an old house in a forest, behind massive, cast-iron gates guarded by sphinxes, not far from the small château belonging to Alexandre Dumas. Sardou, then forty-seven years of age, appeared much older than his actual age. Bancroft described him as 'a small, nervous, lean and wiry man, shabbily dressed, wearing an old smoking-cap, his throat enveloped in a white silk muffler .... he being a martyr to neuralgia.' They had a long talk, Bancroft's fluency in French, learned during his schooldays in France, standing him in good stead, as Sardou had never set foot outside of France and spoke no English. When they parted he presented Bancroft with a photograph of himself, inscribed 'Souvenir bien cordial au Directeur et aux Artistes du Théatre du Prince de Galles. Septembre 1878. V.Sardou.' It was taken back to London to hang proudly in the green room of the Prince of Wales's.

On returning to London the Bancrofts found that *Diplomacy*'s audiences had initially dropped off, maybe because of the hot summer weather, when London theatres could become unbearable, but they picked up when the worst of the heat was over and did well enough to run through until the following January – a full year.

The Bancrofts themselves decided not to return to the cast for the rest of that year. Instead they indulged in what they described as 'a short round of autumn enjoyment in town,' and they spent most of November in Brighton, deciding to travel slowly, taking two days to get there by road, rather than taking the train which would have got them there in not much more time than it would take today.

They had a pleasant month by the sea, with various friends from their company coming down by train for the day on Sundays, including Arthur Cecil, Harry Conway, Henry Kemble and Johnston Forbes-Robertson. Other friends were often in Brighton as well, including John Toole and John Hare, whose production of *Olivia** was playing at the Theatre Royal in the town, as was another of Hare's popular productions, Coghlan's *A Quiet Rubber**, in which he appeared in one of his most famous roles, elderly, bridge-playing Lord Kilclare.

Then in January 1879 *Caste* was revived at the Prince of Wales's, seven years after the previous revival of Tom Robertson's play and almost twelve since the original production in 1867. Only George Honey and the Bancrofts themselves were still around from the original cast. Times had changed. Honey had been paid eighteen pounds a week for his part of old Eccles in the 1867 production. Now, less than twelve years on, his salary, for a guaranteed six months' engagement, was sixty pounds a week. Honey and Bancroft were in their original parts of Eccles and Captain Hawtree and Marie once again played Polly Eccles, with Amy Roselle as her sister Esther. Arthur Cecil took on John Hare's old part of Sam Gerridge.

The production was well received, and provided a useful riposte in a lengthy correspondence in *The Times* regarding the neglect of English work by London managers. Squire Bancroft contributed to this correspondence, pointing out that at the Prince of Wales's they had produced twenty-two pieces since Marie Wilton had set up her company there in 1865. He listed them all. Of the twenty-two, thirteen were new works by English authors. However, Squire went on to argue that London playgoers did not much care about the source of their entertainment so long as it was well acted and enjoyable, and that 'managers would be indeed to blame were they to deny the English public the pleasure of witnessing adaptations to our stage of the many great dramatic works which are written by eminent Frenchmen'. He pointed out that if this were so, then there should be objections to Shakespeare being played in Germany or France.

Notwithstanding this hostility to work from non-English playwrights and still failing to find any new British material that they wanted to take on, the Bancrofts decided to go ahead and accept yet another Sardou play, *Les Bourgeois de Pont-Arcy*, which they had already rejected twice fearing it would not adapt well into English. They invited a popular

---

* *Olivia* was a dramatisation by William Gorman Wills of Oliver Goldsmith's novel *The Vicar of Wakefield*. Ellen Terry was such a huge success in the title role that many little girls at the time were named 'Olivia'.

* *A Quiet Rubber*: one of several plays written by the actor Charles Coghlan.

dramatist, James Albery[*], to undertake what they thought would be a difficult adaptation. He set to work early in 1879 and sent the Bancrofts the first instalment in the spring.

The high Victorian era was a time of countless magazines and periodicals that were published regularly, covering every imaginable topic. Over the years the Bancrofts' friend, the journalist Edmund Yates, had written for and later edited many publications. In 1874 he had started a weekly magazine called *The World*, subtitled 'a Journal for Men and Women'. *The World* published 'candid reviews of good books, good plays, good pictures, and discoveries in science', as well as 'the latest intelligence from the Turf, the Hunting-field, and the Stock Exchange'. Yates proudly claimed that *The World* would acknowledge women as a 'class of the community whose interests should be equitably considered.' For the first time women's issues were not confined to childcare, cookery, needlework and other such household matters.

The World became a very successful and widely-read publication. A regular feature was a series of profiles entitled 'Celebrities at Home'. These 'celebrities' included royalty (the Prince of Wales) and people from every imaginable profession and calling. Gladstone and Disraeli, Charles Darwin, Cardinal Manning, John Ruskin, Victor Hugo, Frederic Leighton RA, Henry Irving and W.G.Grace are just a few of the many names featured in the series that are still known today. Describing the homes and lives of their subjects, the articles were written by people who knew them personally. The interviews would be submitted in proof before publication – essential, particularly in view of the fact that Yates had more than once been involved in 'scraps' with people he had written about without authorisation in the past, notably with the novelist Thackeray, back in the 1850s, an episode that had led to Yates being expelled from the Garrick Club.

In the autumn of 1878 the Bancrofts featured in the series. The piece was probably written by Edmund Yates himself, being a close friend of theirs. It was far longer than such a piece would be today, running to several pages of text. It is interesting to note that the concept of 'celebrity' was already in current use. The article described a typical Sunday evening in the Bancroft household in Cavendish Square, Sunday being the only day when an actor is free to entertain dinner guests. 'As the dinner-hour

---

[*] James Albery, 1838-89, became so seriously alcoholic that his much younger wife, Mary Moore, 1861-1931, had to support their family. She went into partnership with Charles Wyndham, whom she eventually married, after the deaths of Albery and Wyndham's first wife.

approaches, Mrs Bancroft's pretty drawing-room is occupied by men and women celebrated in the world of politics, law, literature and art.' After dinner, following a short 'withdrawal' of the ladies, when the gentlemen sat around the table over their port, the Bancrofts and their guests, male and female, would gather together in the upstairs smoking-room to chat into the early hours. Here the air would be thick with smoke (or, as the article put it, 'fragrant with Cabanas'). Squire smoked large cigars and Marie also smoked – unusually for a woman at that time, at least in company. Squire possessed a silver cigar lighter that had been Marie's present to him on his thirty-first birthday, inscribed with his initials and the words 'To B, from Marie, May 14th, 1872'. Its centre is a double-sided silver disc, about two inches in diameter, with two sets of small spikes on its side. Around this runs a tube with a short, hinged opening section and ribbed parts on which a match can be struck. Through the tube runs an oil-soaked wick, secured by the spikes on the disc. The wick is exposed by rotating the disc until a small length emerges: it is then lit with a match from a silver 'vesta' case. The flame would be extinguished by drawing the wick back inside the tube and closing the lid – it has to be hoped that the flame was entirely snuffed out before the lighter was returned to a pocket.

Squire Bancroft's silver cigar lighter

Yates's article went on to describe the décor of the Bancrofts' home: crammed with furnishings and ornaments in true Victorian style, it contained 'many souvenirs of artist-life and artist-friends', with paintings, photographs of their fellow actors and friends, and with mementoes of their travels. The article ended with a description of the Bancrofts' current dog, a huge St Bernard called Monk, which they had brought back with them from Switzerland one year: 'This splendid animal is the pet of the house and the delight of all visitors.' However, there is no mention in *The World* article of the Bancroft children: the two boys by now would have

191

been sixteen and eleven, and were away at boarding school during term time. Once again, it seems, the Bancrofts were determined to maintain the privacy of their children from the curious press so far as they could, although this was not always possible: on Boxing Day of that same year, 1878, one newspaper – oddly, a Yorkshire one – reported spotting Mrs Bancroft and her two sons at the Drury Lane pantomime, where they were all seen to be 'laughing heartily' at a version of *Cinderella*, written by E.L.Blanchard, the production of which was enhanced by performing dogs, pigeons and monkeys as well as clowns, and a 'bicycle troupe'.

On the subject of 'celebrity' in general, Yates wrote, 'What names, except those of half a dozen leading politicians, were and are the best known even in this serious England of ours? Those of actors and singers.' In those days, many decades before film, television and the tabloid press, live stage performers were household names just as the stars of film, TV and sport are today: newspapers and magazines such as *The World* wrote countless columns about them and their lives. In 1945 Max Beerbohm made a broadcast entitled 'Playgoing', in which he said that when he was young, 'Actors and actresses were certainly regarded with far greater interest than they are nowadays …. It was with excitement, with wonder and with reverence, with something akin even to hysteria, that they were gazed upon.' The modern obsession with 'celebrity' was already flourishing.

The revival of *Caste* ran through until May. The production suffered a sad loss when George Honey, playing Eccles, was taken ill in the middle of a performance. He had been suffering from rheumatism for some time but, in spite of often appearing unwell, had never taken time off sick. Suddenly, towards the end of the first act, the call-boy rushed into the green room to fetch Squire Bancroft. 'Come down, sir, please: Mr Honey's in a fit, and can't go on!' He had suffered a stroke. Honey's understudy was Henry Kemble, who, complaining that he never had anything to do, had taken himself off that evening to the Olympic Theatre, near Drury Lane. Someone rushed out to fetch him back and a doctor was urgently summoned. Meanwhile Eccles's entrance was due. It was a scene in which he had to knock on the door and stagger on stage, fortunately wordlessly. This entrance was achieved by Squire who, holding up the unfortunate, desperately ill, Honey in his arms, knocked on the door, calling out for admission in his best imitation of the voice of George Honey's Eccles. He propped the barely conscious Honey upright in the opened doorway, managing to keep himself out of sight until, fortunately, the curtain fell, when he carried Honey back to his dressing- room. The audience, unaware that anything was amiss, shouted with laughter at the sight of the old drunk swaying helplessly in the doorway. 'To find our old comrade, who was a favourite with everyone, inarticulate, with one side of his body helpless, was a painful shock to us all,' wrote Squire. Henry

Kemble was found and rushed back just in time to take over in the next act; he played Eccles until the end of the run in May. At home Honey recovered enough to return a few weeks later, but this was for one night only as it was entirely against the doctor's orders and he was strictly forbidden to do so again. George Honey rarely worked again after his stroke, taking a few minor roles in benefits, and died the following year, 1880, of an aortic aneurism, aged fifty-seven.

The season of 1878-79 ended with a lightweight programme consisting of three short pieces, starting with Palgrave Simpson's *Heads or Tails* and followed by a revival of W.S.Gilbert's *Sweethearts*, this time with Squire Bancroft as Henry Spreadbrow, the part created by Charles Coghlan almost five years before, and with Marie in her old part of Jenny Northcott. To everyone's surprise, not least the Bancrofts, this insubstantial programme filled the theatre until August, when there was extremely hot weather and London theatres became intolerable. The final piece of this programme was an old Buckstone comedy, *Good For Nothing*, in which Marie Bancroft played a hoydenish young girl, Nan, a part she had first played back in her young days at the Strand.

Marie Bancroft as Nan in **Good for Nothing**

All three pieces were short, with intervals between, so that audiences could come and go and see one, or two, or all three pieces as they wished. *The Times* said it was 'so timed in commencement and duration that one of them must fit in with any dinner-hour and any train from town.' Marie had not lost her touch as Jenny Northcott. *The Times* reviewer wrote that: 'The emotions of Mrs. Bancroft are magnetic, and draw laughter and tears from some to whom these are rare luxuries.' Her versatility was finely demonstrated as she was transformed each evening from the dignified, softly-spoken Jenny Northcott to the grubby Cockney ragamuffin, Nan.

The time was about to arrive for the most significant event in the Bancrofts' joint professional lives. For a long time they had been feeling the need for a larger theatre. Their much-loved Prince of Wales's was small and inconvenient, and although regulations were minimal by today's standards, nevertheless the annual Lord Chamberlain's inspections invariably pointed out problems and demanded that they be sorted. London theatres in those days were squalid, insanitary places with cramped backstage areas. They were freezing cold in winter and stifling in summer, and infested with rats and mice. Dressing rooms were dark and cramped, and washing and toilet facilities were inadequate and leaky. The back-stage and below-stage areas could be draughty and damp or hot and airless, and often stank indescribably. The Bancrofts had been contemplating the possibility of building their own, brand new, up-to-date theatre and had been negotiating for months in connection with a site just off Regent Street. Ambitious plans had been drawn up for a large theatre with a hydraulically operated revolving stage but the plan came to nothing and was abandoned. If it had gone ahead, there might to this day be a 'Bancrofts Theatre' in London.

The theatre world had been aware for some time that the Bancrofts were contemplating a move and Squire was to write that over the years, 'nearly every theatre in London, at one time or another, had been offered to us'. They had always, half in jest, replied that only the Haymarket would tempt them. Most recently they had been offered the St James's at a very attractive price but had declined – maybe its reputation as an unlucky house had deterred the superstitious Marie. Shortly after this offer the Bancrofts heard that John Hare, in partnership with the Kendals, had taken on the lease of the St James's. Spurred on by this news and perhaps with a sense of friendly rivalry at their old friend taking over such a prestigious West End theatre, Squire felt the urge to 'checkmate' him. He approached John Sleeper Clarke[*], who had been the lessee of the Haymarket for the

---

[*] John Sleeper Clarke, 1833-99, an American born actor, married to a sister of Edwin Booth and John Wilkes Booth, Abraham Lincoln's assassin. Not long after the momentous event in Washington, Clarke moved to London.

past year. Confident that the time was right to face the challenge of a move to a large theatre and encouraged by the ease with which they had always managed to fill the little Prince of Wales's, Bancroft proposed to Clarke that he and Marie should take over his lease of the Haymarket.

Endless discussions ensued and for a time it looked as though negotiations were leading nowhere and eventually they came to a complete standstill. The Bancrofts had more or less decided that the move was not to be and that they would stay at the Prince of Wales's, when all of a sudden Clarke reopened negotiations. This time things moved fast. Squire Bancroft described the sudden conclusion of the business: 'In a few days all was settled. I agreed to buy the remnant of his tenancy; the trustees promised me a fresh lease of the property, and I undertook to rebuild the interior.' Then matters went in a rush: the season at the Prince of Wales's ended on 1 August 1879, on 2 August Squire Bancroft signed the lease for the Haymarket, and on the next day he and Marie left for Switzerland.

Back in their beloved Pontresina, another entertainment was staged to raise funds to build an English church. The programme included a piano duet performed by Arthur Sullivan and Otto Goldschmidt; Mrs Goldschmidt – Jenny Lind – sang. *Cox and Box*, Sullivan's one-act comic opera version of Burnand's farce *Box and Cox,* was performed, and Marie read Tennyson's *The May Queen*. She suggested that Otto Goldschmidt contribute some music to accompany the poem, and in a letter to a friend Marie wrote: 'He was so pleased with the idea that in the kindest manner he consented, and worked as hard as though he had been going to conduct the Bach Choir.' Once they were back home, the Bancrofts began their final few months at the Prince of Wales's Theatre with mixed feelings. They had enjoyed so many happy years there, and Marie in particular was only too aware of how much she was going to miss it. In the fourteen years since she had taken over the disreputable Dust-Hole in 1865, she had turned the little theatre into one of the most fashionable in London.

Duty, James Albery's adaptation of Sardou's *Les Bourgeois de Pont-Arcy*, opened on 27 September, with a cast that included Johnston Forbes-Robertson, Arthur Cecil and Henry Kemble, as well as Marion Terry and Augusta Wilton, the younger sisters of Ellen Terry and Marie Bancroft. Neither Marie nor Squire were in *Duty* as they needed to devote all their time to working on their plans for the Haymarket. Demolition of the interior of the great theatre began. It was to be totally redesigned at the immense cost of ten thousand pounds. Work went on in shifts around the clock and Squire Bancroft could not resist looking in daily to watch the work in progress. He would often drop by on his way home from a late evening at one of his clubs, and peering through gaps in the hoarding he could see 'falling masses of timber which were being hurled from the upper parts into the once classic pit by the night workmen, in hideous dust and uproar: the effect being rather that of demons joyfully engaged in some destructive orgie [sic]. While this work of demolition was in progress, I remember one of the men describing the fleas they disturbed as being "more like ponies"! .... The stage was a yawning cellar, the auditorium was a forest of scaffold-poles, supporting planks on which I walked many a dangerous distance. Everything was chaos.'

On 31 October, at the very time the interior of the old Haymarket was being gutted, its legendary manager John Baldwin Buckstone died at the age of seventy-seven. One of the most colourful characters of the London theatre world for the whole of the middle part of the century, Buckstone had managed the Haymarket for over twenty years, from 1853 to 1876. Born in 1802, he had gone to sea at the age of eleven. He tried the legal profession but gave that up to become a travelling actor on the circuits. He first appeared in London at the Adelphi when he was about twenty-one. He started to write and became a prolific playwright, performing in many of his own comedies: these included *The Green Bushes*, that old favourite that Marie Wilton had played in during her childhood, and *Good For Nothing*, in which she had been only the year before. He was undoubtedly London's favourite comic actor. Squire Bancroft wrote: 'What enjoyment his mere name recalls! How one began to laugh directly he spoke the simplest sentence .... He was the best comedian I ever saw.'

John Baldwin Buckstone

196

The Haymarket Theatre has long been famed for having its very own ghost: this ghost is reputed to be that of John Baldwin Buckstone returning to the theatre he loved. As recently as 2009 the actor Patrick Stewart reported coming across a phantom figure standing in the wings during a performance of Samuel Becket's *Waiting for Godot*. Maybe he brought Stewart luck, as he received a knighthood a few weeks later, in the New Year's Honours.

Meanwhile the Bancrofts were anxiously trying to decide with which play they should launch their management of the Haymarket after Christmas. They considered revivals of one of their successes of the past, maybe *The School for Scandal* or *Masks and Faces*; they even contemplated another attempt at Shakespeare, possibly *As You Like It*. Finally they settled on Bulwer Lytton's *Money* and rehearsals began at the Prince of Wales's. Meanwhile, *Duty* was not going well and was taken off after just eight 'languid' weeks and they decided that the last play they would produce at the Prince of Wales's should be one of Tom Robertson's, in honour of the playwright to whom they owed so much of their success. An announcement was made in the press that a 'Farewell Revival' of *Ours* would be the Bancrofts' final play at the Prince of Wales's. Marie, now forty, once again played her original part of Mary Netley and Squire played Hugh Chalcot, her suitor. Among the rest of the cast were Arthur Cecil, Marion Terry and Johnston Forbes-Robertson.

A hectic December followed, particularly for Squire Bancroft, who spent every spare moment at the Haymarket preparing for the opening in January. He was 'at the beck and call of architect, scene-painters, decorators, clerk of the works, stage-carpenters, costumiers, upholsterers, and the host of folk employed in and about a theatre'. Then every evening he was on stage at the Prince of Wales's. Being quite a workaholic, he admitted to 'a mania for doing much of other people's work in addition to my own'. Outwardly he would seem calm and in control but underneath he was feeling seriously stressed. Fortunately Marie's temperament was more relaxed, believing that everything would surely be all right on the night. The time grew rapidly closer and a team of Italian craftsmen worked throughout the Christmas holidays to ensure the mosaic flooring they were laying would be finished on time. Eventually the stage area was almost complete and the rehearsals of *Money* were able to transfer to the Haymarket stage after Christmas.

At last, on 29 January 1880, it was the Bancrofts' final night at the Prince of Wales's Theatre. It was bitterly cold and the frost outside was mirrored on stage by the final scene of *Ours*, with its Crimean winter set. As the final curtain fell both Bancrofts were called for over and over again, and from the front of the stage Squire thanked the audience for their years of support and encouragement. He expressed his own and Marie's appreciation of so many old friends who had come, in spite of the dreadful weather outside, to be present on their last night, and they wished Edgar Bruce, who was taking over the Prince of Wales's, good fortune in their beloved old theatre.

Marie was deeply distressed to be leaving. 'The prospect of having to say farewell to the dear little house, every brick of which I loved, was a sad one for me. I went there day after day, and wandered from room to room quite alone …. The silent walls seemed to look reproachfully at me and to say, "After all these years of service, are you going to leave us?"' She had even tried to persuade Squire that surely they could somehow keep the Prince of Wales's going at the same time as running the Haymarket and manage the two theatres simultaneously, but eventually she conceded that this was not a practical option, nor was it financially viable. After taking her final bow she wrote that, 'I left the little stage for ever, rushed up to my dressing-room, and cried bitterly.' For many years afterwards, if she was in the area, she would go to Tottenham Street and stand looking at her theatre, which was eventually to become abandoned and to fall into a state of disrepair.

*the derelict Prince of Wales's Theatre, with a portrait of
the Bancrofts in the top right-hand corner*

Edgar Bruce, the actor who took over the lease of the Prince of Wales's from the Bancrofts in 1880, only managed the little theatre for a couple of years. Then some kind of dispute arose between Bruce and Squire Bancroft and Charles James, who was still the freeholder. Bruce

198

moved on and built a new Prince of Wales's, the theatre of that name that stands today, itself rebuilt, in Coventry Street. The little theatre on Tottenham Street went dark until 1886, when it became a Salvation Army hostel. Then in 1903 it was bought by a Dr Edmund Distin-Maddock, along with several surrounding properties, so that he could build an entirely new theatre, on a much larger scale, to seat over 1000 people. The front of his handsome new Scala Theatre, built at immense cost, faced in the opposite direction, onto the road now called Scala Street. All that remained of the old Prince of Wales's was in the rear of the new theatre, with the Tottenham Street entrance portico becoming the stage door at the rear of the Scala.

'The last of the old Prince of Wales's Theatre – Squire Bancroft 1903'

Dr Distin-Maddock invited Marie Bancroft to perform the opening ceremony of his fine new Scala Theatre, saying that she should be the first to tread its boards publicly. The Scala was launched on 19 December, 1904. First Marie opened the new main entrance, with a golden key. Then she stepped onto the large new stage and attempted to address the audience who filled the auditorium and that included many old friends. Among those friends were many who had connections with the old Prince of Wales's, including John Hare, Johnston Forbes-Robertson and W.S.Gilbert. She tried to speak her opening words, but was so overcome with emotion that she could not hold back tears. Recovering her composure, she eventually managed to make her speech. *The Times* reported that she closed by saying that, 'With all her heart she wished that the new theatre might inherit the success and honour which were so freely bestowed upon its ancestor.'

A few years earlier, during the period that the Prince of Wales's was standing derelict, Marie happened to remark to a friend, who happened to be an assistant commissioner of the Metropolitan Police, how she wished she had just one brick to remind her of the old theatre she had loved so much. Jokingly he said that he would get one of his constables to steal one for her. A few days later a brick arrived, enclosed in a wooden case. It was inscribed 'A Souvenir of the old Prince of Wales's Theatre, the brick from its walls, the wood from its stage.' Marie and Squire Bancroft treasured their souvenir for the rest of their lives.

Sadly the fine new Scala did not thrive. It had mixed fortunes, becoming a cinema for a while; then for many years it housed amateur productions and the occasional pantomime. After World War Two it became the home of the annual Christmas production of *Peter Pan*, but was eventually demolished in 1969 and the site redeveloped as a faceless block of offices. Today, on the site of the old Prince of Wales's in Tottenham Street, there is no trace of either of the theatres that once stood there.

9

TO THE HAYMARKET

The Theatre Royal, Haymarket, was, and still is, one of the most beautiful and historic theatres in London. The first Haymarket was built in 1720 when it was known as the 'Little Theatre by the Haymarket'. In 1821 it was rebuilt to John Nash's design in a prime position slightly to the south of the original theatre, from where it faces directly down Charles II Street. Nash's theatre, now a Grade I listed building, included the great portico of six Corinthian columns that form its frontage. In 1879, just before the Bancrofts took it over, a useful guide to London was published – *Dickens's Dictionary of London*, compiled by Charles Dickens junior, son of the great novelist. In his guide, he helpfully told his readers how to get to the Haymarket by public transport: '*Railway Stations,* Charing-cross (Dist, and S.E.); *Omnibus Routes,* Piccadilly, Regent-street, Haymarket, and Strand' – not so very different from today.

In 1837 the legendary actor-manager Benjamin Webster took over the Haymarket and ran it for sixteen years, making many alterations, notably introducing gaslight. At the Haymarket Webster created the part of Triplet in *Masks and Faces* in 1852. Webster was followed in 1853 by the equally legendary John Baldwin Buckstone who reigned there for twenty-four years. It was under Buckstone's management at the Haymarket that Sothern first played Lord Dundreary in *Our American Cousin*, and in 1861 Edwin Booth, reckoned to be the finest American actor of his generation, appeared there on his first visit to London.

By Christmas 1879 the Bancrofts' refurbishment of the interior of the Haymarket was almost complete, at what *The Era* described as 'enormous outlay'. The entrance vestibule, decorated in olive green and gold, featured the fine marble mosaic floor laid by the hard-working Italians, in an elaborate design featuring an imperial crown, with roses, shamrocks and thistles. Doors and fanlights were fitted with stained glass.

THE LITTLE THEATRE BY THE HAYMARKET ABOUT 1821

Nash's Haymarket Theatre in 1821

The costly new décor in the auditorium was opulent: in true Victorian style it was resplendent with crimson carpets and velvet upholstery, ivory-coloured satin curtains to the boxes and gold-leaf on the mouldings. There were refreshment rooms on all levels as well as 'retiring rooms' for ladies and gentlemen. Backstage, the actors could prepare in comfortable dressing rooms, unlike the cramped, insanitary quarters that they were accustomed to elsewhere. The *New York Times* reported that the Haymarket had been transformed into 'the most elegant and luxuriously comfortable playhouse in London'.

The most spectacular innovation was a great gilded 'picture-frame' proscenium that totally surrounded the stage area on all four sides, giving the illusion of a framed picture, especially when the new act-drop was lowered between scenes: this featured a design based on the painting by Val Prinsep of the minuet as seen in the Bancrofts' production of *The School for Scandal* at the Prince of Wales's in 1874. This style of proscenium was soon to be copied by other theatres, in Britain and elsewhere. However, the installation of the surrounding frame and the act-drop presented problems with the gas footlights, which were set exactly where the drop would descend. Squire Bancroft instructed his construction team to contrive a means whereby the footlights could be lowered as the curtain fell, and raised back into position as it ascended.

The experts who had been called in to install the proscenium and the act-drop were dubious, their leader scornfully demanding how Bancroft thought such a thing might be achieved. 'I haven't the faintest idea,' was the reply. 'I can only tell you what I want done, not how to do it.' The next objection was that there would be a fire risk involved. 'Eliminate it,' demanded Bancroft. 'That's your job.' A final plea was that such a thing had never been done before. 'All the more reason for it to be done for the first time,' was the reply. It was done.

Another major innovation at the Haymarket was to prove far more controversial. This was the total abolition of the pit. At the Prince of Wales's the pit benches had gradually been squeezed further and further towards the back as ever-increasing rows of stalls seats were set in front of them. The pre-Bancroft Haymarket had a large traditional pit, with rows of benches immediately in front of the stage. Marie was concerned about her husband's proposal to abolish the pit entirely and pleaded for 'just a little tiny pit' to be retained, but Squire firmly overruled her, insisting that it would be impossible to run the theatre economically with the pit taking up the best space in front of the stage. The pit went.

Stalls had been rare in most old London theatres until they were introduced a few years earlier at the Prince of Wales's. The pit was a direct descendant of the central open area of Shakespeare's time, familiar once more today to audiences at Shakespeare's Globe on London's South Bank, where the 'groundlings' stand to watch the performance, or the new Rose Theatre in Kingston upon Thames, which includes an area known as 'the pit' in front of the stage where the audience sits on the floor.

The early nineteenth-century pit often occupied the whole floor space of the auditorium. As other theatres followed the lead of the Prince of Wales's, introducing more and more rows of comfortable stalls at ground-floor level, the pit was gradually pushed further and further towards the back of the house into what Squire described as a 'dark, low-ceilinged cavern hidden away under the dress circle'. But the theatre-going public loved their pit. The pit was traditional and the pit was cheap. Anyone and everyone could sit on the pit benches, eat oranges, and loudly cheer or hiss the performance on stage. The cost of a pit seat in most theatres in 1879 was three shillings and sixpence. Cyril Maude, a future manager of the Haymarket, was one day to write of its pre-Bancroft days that 'there was no better pit in all London than that of the Haymarket Theatre. Roomy it was, and comfortable, while it afforded a better view of the stage than that of any other theatre.'

the Haymarket: 1821 Nash interior, with pit benches and orchestra

the Haymarket in 1880 after redesigning, with framed proscenium

As the opening night drew near, rumours were flying around London that there might be some kind of a disturbance following the loss of the most popular pit in town. Squire Bancroft had an announcement put out in the press outlining the thinking behind his decision and explaining that in the running of a first-class theatre it was no longer financially viable for the lowest-priced seats to be in the most desirable part of the house.

To make up for their loss, the 'pittites' were being offered the whole of the second circle, an area previously occupied by upper boxes. They were assured that this area had been redesigned with their comfort in mind: its ceiling had been raised, patrons would have a clear view of the stage, they would have their own refreshment room for the intervals, the seats would be far more comfortable and they would be reasonably priced – if no longer the 'three-and-six' the pit had been.

At last the opening night of the Bancrofts' reign at the glorious Haymarket arrived. On Saturday 31 January 1880 the weather was filthy with a 'London Particular' fog, described by Clement Scott as 'about the thickest, strongest, and nastiest I had ever tasted'. Bancroft was in his dressing-room, preparing for his performance as Sir Frederick Blount in *Money*, when an unexpected visitor was announced. It was Henry Irving. The country's finest actor had made his way through the fog on his way to his own theatre, the Lyceum, to wish Squire and Marie good fortune in their venture. Squire showed him over the newly-designed Haymarket and, before leaving, Irving shook Bancroft's hand to wish him the best of luck, before vanishing into the freezing fog.

However, it was clear, even before the curtain rose on *Money*, that there was trouble ahead: the displaced pittites were not prepared to accept quietly their relegation into the gods. The *Daily News* reported: 'The mere sight of the luxurious crimson velvet armchairs which now occupy the entire floor of the theatre appeared to arouse feelings of jealousy and ill will; and from the opening of the doors until the somewhat tardy rising of the curtain murmurs and discordant noises, breaking at frequent intervals into manifestations of a stormy character, gave ominous token of impending trouble.'

As the curtain rose to reveal the characters of Sir John Vesey and his daughter, Georgina, there was a loud chorus of hooting and booing from the upper circle, accompanied by cries of 'Where's the pit?' The unfortunate actor playing Vesey studied his newspaper with far greater concentration than he might have intended to do and the girl playing Georgina, with her head well bent over her needlework, stitched away furiously. The uproar grew louder and it was clear to Squire Bancroft that he had to take action.

He walked out to the front of the stage to face the anger of the displaced pittites. He was at a considerable disadvantage, being in costume for his part of the foppish Sir Frederick Blount, and he had not even thought to remove his wig before facing the crowd. The vociferous boos and hisses and verbal abuse that greeted him from above quite drowned out the applause from the comfortable seats below. Totally unprepared for such a hostile reception, Bancroft hesitantly began to speak, struggling to make himself heard above the uproar: this would be hard enough today with the help of a microphone, but without it was almost impossible. Over and over again he attempted to make his voice heard as he spoke to the angry crowd in the upper circle. Clement Scott was in the audience. 'Poor Squire Bancroft was for twenty minutes in a very "tight corner",' he wrote, 'but he "faced the music" with remarkable pluck and confidence. He was naturally nervous and apprehensive, but he did not quail or flinch.' The *Daily News* reporter attempted to quote what he managed to hear of Bancroft's words to the audience:

Ladies and Gentlemen – allow me to express my regret at this disturbance of which I fear I alone am the innocent cause. (A voice: 'Where is the Pit?') If you will allow me one moment I will speak to you. (Renewed interruption. Cries of 'Where are the police?') Gentlemen! ('Order for the manager! Let us hear what he has got to say.') Let me frankly admit that I am the cause of this interruption .... ('We are not to be bullied!') I am quite unprepared to address you. You must take the words from me in my agitated state as they come. You ask me, gentlemen, 'Where is the pit?' I am a business man, talking I dare say to many other business men. I can only tell you, as I have already told you in the newspapers .... (Prolonged disturbance, which rendered the conclusion of the sentence inaudible.) Remember, I don't take you by surprise. You have all known that there would not be a pit in the reconstructed Haymarket Theatre. I will tell you in three or four words why there is no pit. I cannot afford it. However desirous I may be of following the example of my predecessors, there is one result in which I am certainly not anxious to maintain the traditions of this House. (Cheers from stalls and balcony, this being understood to refer to the losses sustained by previous managers.) .... A theatre, gentlemen, is after all a place of business. However inadequately I may be expressing myself, I will give you reasons if you will only let me .... (At this point there was a call, apparently from the gallery, for 'Three cheers for Mr Bancroft' which were given, while a well-known actress, under the excitement of the occasion, rose in the stalls and called aloud to the more peaceful spectators in the immediate neighbourhood of the disturbers to 'Turn them out!' This friendly intervention only provoked more noise from the gallery, and after waiting in vain for silence, Mr Bancroft asked by way of last appeal, 'Will you listen to the play,' and finally retired.)

While Bancroft was standing at the front of the stage, attempting to make himself heard over the uproar, the son of the previous lessee of the Haymarket, John Sleeper Clarke, was in the foyer waiting anxiously for his father who was delayed by the fog. Clarke junior went to their box and peered through the door, from where he could see Bancroft and could hear the noise. Not realising what was actually going on, he hurried back to find his father, who just then arrived. 'Come quickly,' he urged. 'Bancroft has been on stage for almost twenty minutes. He's getting such an ovation as you have never heard before.' It was not until they entered their box that the Clarkes realised what was really happening.

Listening anxiously offstage, an agitated Marie Bancroft could hear the uproar. At one point, feeling that she could bear it no longer, she hurried to the wings, intending to join Squire on stage, hoping that the affection the public held for her might give her more success than her husband in calming the protest. She was frightened at the prospect of being greeted by boos and hisses but fortunately her intervention proved unnecessary as at last the tumult subsided and the first night of *Money* was able to proceed. The *Daily News* reported that the disturbance 'had produced a visible effect upon the composure of the performers', which was hardly surprising, but that Marie, when she appeared on stage, received a tumultuous welcome, with prolonged applause. In this production she was playing the part of the middle-aged Lady Franklin rather than that of Georgina, the mercenary daughter out to get herself a rich husband. Squire Bancroft was once again the r-less Sir 'Fwedewick' Blount and this time, when he went on stage, he received a warmer welcome from many in the audience.

Returning home after that eventful first night in the thickest fog London had ever seen was adventurous for everyone. Squire and Marie Bancroft had to walk the mile or so to their home in Cavendish Square through the impenetrable 'pea-souper', as there were no cabs around and their own carriage could not be brought to fetch them. Indeed, it was probably a lot safer to walk. Marie had been showered with bouquets following the performance but these could not possibly be carried home, except for one bunch of white flowers, which was held aloft like a beacon by a servant, who had bravely come from their house to escort them home. It was barely visible.

The critics had a hard time of it too. It was vital that they should return to their Fleet Street offices that night to write up the evening's events. They had come expecting a regular first night, prepared to write their reviews of *Money*, maybe along with something on the reconstruction of the Haymarket. They found they had the story of a near-riot to tell. Clement Scott told of how he and a group of his colleagues struggled back to write their reports:

With brother drama critics .... I led the way, groping by the houses, railings and shops, and the rest followed hanging onto one another's coat tails. But we arrived at our workshops somehow, and, what is more, got safely home to bed afterwards.

The fog was so thick that a doctor friend of the Bancrofts, trying to grope his way home after the play, could not work out where he was, Harley Street, Wigmore Street, or Welbeck Street, where his home was. In this district of doctors, he held a lighted match close to a brass plaque, hoping to recognise a colleague's name and from that work out where he might be. He found he had reached his own front door, which he had been unable to recognise. A family of four from Putney had set out in their carriage in mid-afternoon in daylight and clear weather for the first night at the Haymarket. The fog didn't extend so far as the still semi-rural suburbs outside London and, with Putney being some five miles from the West End, they had no knowledge of what lay ahead. Before long they found themselves enveloped in thick, black fog. After the play, rather than attempt the journey back in the middle of the night, they were invited to stop over with friends in Bayswater. It took them several hours to cover the couple of miles in almost zero visibility. Arriving at their host's house they found the nearby mews stabling already full up with the horses and carriages of other stranded victims of the weather. Their dilemma was solved by leaving their carriage parked outside in the street, while their horse and its driver spent the night in the hallway. Fortunately the entrance halls of large Victorian houses were usually floored with handsome tiles, so any fine rugs could easily have been removed and straw laid down for the convenience of the horse.

That fog of 1879-80 was the densest, cruellest fog that London ever knew. It descended in November and lasted for weeks, not lifting until the end of February. It even made international news. A year later, in January 1881, by which time the results of the fog had been analysed, the *New York Times* ran a headline: 'London Fog and the Death Rate'. The report said that thousands of Londoners had died from the terrible pollution, peaking at 3376 deaths in one week from respiratory diseases such as bronchitis, pneumonia and pleurisy; asthma sufferers in particular were severely affected. During the worst week the mortality rate from bronchitis was 331 percent above its average. The terrible 'pea-soupers' that London so frequently suffered following the Industrial Revolution were caused by the combination of burning coal in hundreds of thousands of chimneys, both domestic and industrial, with cold, damp, windless weather conditions. Many decades later, following the 'Great Smog' which struck London in 1952 and again led to thousands of deaths, the Clean Air Act of 1956 finally enforced the reduction of smoke pollution in Britain's cities, and happily the fearful smog is now a thing of the distant past, although we have replaced it with other, less visible, forms of serious air pollution.

208

Soon after the events of 31 January, *The Theatre* ran a debate on what became known as 'The Pit Question'. Critics, dramatists and other correspondents contributed to the debate expressing their opinions on the hot topic of the moment. There was an anti-elitist attitude in some of the pro-pit arguments. The Bancrofts had been prominent in the move to turn theatregoing into a form of respectable entertainment that the fashionable middle classes could happily attend, and now it seemed to many that they were in the process of marginalising working-class theatre lovers, of whom there were thousands in London and elsewhere. Historically, theatregoers of all classes would frequent the pit. Indeed, Squire Bancroft himself had been a habitual pittite in his stagestruck youth, and Charles Dickens had been a regular in the pit at the Strand Theatre, where he saw the young Marie Wilton in burlesque. As theatregoing became a more respectable form of recreation, the middle-classes began to monopolise the comfortable seats in the stalls, the boxes or the dress circle. The majority of pittites were working-class enthusiasts, whose seats were not bookable in advance and who would often queue for hours in order to obtain their seats. The new middle-class audiences tended to be more reserved, considering it bad form to express their appreciation beyond polite clapping at the end of an act, in contrast to the pittites, who were loud and enthusiastic in expressing their appreciation or their disapproval of the performance on stage. One contributor to the debate made this last point forcefully:

> I hold it to be absolutely necessary for the actor's art that he should have in front of him an audience able and willing to express audibly their approbation or disapprobation .... I think most persons, who have observed carefully the behaviour of those who occupy the ten-shilling stalls and those who occupy the two-shilling pit, will admit that the latter have the decided advantage. If those who fill the stalls in the new Haymarket Theatre will condescend to be as attentive to the play, and as open in the expression of their applause or censure, as their humble predecessors, they will do more to justify Mr Bancroft's oligarchical revolution than any amount of argument founded on the basis of £.s.d.

Others were quite content with things the way they had been, and regular pittites did not see the alternative arrangements as being in any way in their interest. An old friend, Marie's first partner in management at the Prince of Wales's, Henry James Byron, reluctantly argued against the Bancrofts' policy, while at the same time admitting that the ousted pittites were being adequately catered for at the new Haymarket:

> Whether or not it is wise from a pecuniary point of view to abolish a pit is a question which can only be answered by results; at present it can only be a matter of surmise .... I for one imagine it will prove a mistake. The

Haymarket has always been a theatre where laughter has held its sway ....
As a rule, the occupants of the stalls – where the stalls greatly predominate
– do not laugh .... Whatever opinion one may entertain of the alteration
Mr Bancroft has effected – there can be no doubt that the malcontents, on
the opening night, forgot or ignored two facts. The one was that Mr
Bancroft had provided the ousted pittites with comfortable places in a
portion of the house always more expensive than the pit, whilst other
managers have been .... shoving them farther and farther back under a low
stuffy roof, in order to devote the best portion of the area to the swells, and
this without remonstrance.

However, the influential John Hollingshead[*] was clearly of the opinion
that *hoi polloi* should no longer be permitted to disrupt the enjoyment of
those whom he considered their 'superiors'. He wrote:

It has been assumed in many quarters that a theatre manager .... is bound
to carry on his business on sentimental principles, thinking more of some
mysterious duty which he is supposed to owe to the public, and of another
mysterious duty which he undoubtedly owes to his creditors and his
breeches' pocket .... Mr Bancroft takes the Haymarket at a very heavy
rental, on a not very long lease, and thoroughly rebuilds it at a 'cost which
will probably represent a charge of ten pounds a night as long as he
remains in possession.' He finds that the levels will not allow him to
excavate a pit under the dress circle, and .... for this he was exposed to
something like a riot on the first night by a number of people in a very
comfortable 'upper circle' who were assumed to be the old and
discontented pit frequenters of the Haymarket Theatre .... The only
shadow of an excuse for this outbreak of theatrical protectionism was the
comfortable character of the lost pit. In one of the worst-constructed
houses ever built it was the one place where all those who were fortunate
enough to get seats could sit, see, hear, and breathe. The pit visitors
enjoyed this place for fifty years at a too modest price, while their
wretched superiors were ricking their necks in the dress circle, or
cramping their legs in the private boxes ....

The editor of *The Theatre*, Clement Scott, decided to find out for
himself just what the new quarters for the pittites were like. He watched
the first night from the stalls, but returned two weeks later to try out the
controversial upper circle, alongside the displaced pittites. Usually a
devoted supporter of the Bancrofts and all their doings, Scott came down
firmly against their abolition of the pit in his summing up of the debate,
writing that the theatre should remain 'acceptable to the public at large

---

[*] John Hollingshead, 1827-1904, a journalist and theatre manager. In 1871 he
produced Gilbert and Sullivan's first collaboration, *Thespis*, and in 1880 was the
first manager to stage an Ibsen play in England.

and not only to the upholders of a fashionable and fastidious exclusiveness':

> The place was crammed .... In front of me was a lady with an enormous hat and a stupendous feather .... I could see nothing of the first act of *Money* except by standing up, and then I was howled down. But no one compelled the lady to take off her hat .... I represented my case to the attendant, who was extremely courteous .... and I was politely transferred to the 'side slips' .... It was better here, for I could see exactly one half of the stage but no more. All the action on the prompt side was lost to me entirely .... There was no seat in the old Haymarket pit where the whole of the stage was not seen.
>
> It is natural, is it not, that those who have spent the happiest days of play-going in the pit and who there inherited their first and earliest love for the drama, should strive their utmost to procure the same privilege for those who follow them? In the pit I saw my first pantomime at Drury Lane in 1851 .... here, at Sadler's Wells, I saw my first Shakespeare play .... here, at the Strand, the best burlesque company London has ever seen .... here, at the Haymarket, I first saw scores of classical comedies .... I believe that from no other part of the house is it possible so attentively and closely to study art. In the gallery the perspective is altered altogether. You seem to look down on the heads of the artists, the picture is dwarfed, and a great part of the pleasure of the spectator is taken away.

The Times, reporting the events that had taken place on the first night of *Money* at the Haymarket, conceded that a new manager, who had spent thousands of pounds in redesigning his theatre, could hardly be expected to give the best area in the entire house over to that portion of the audience that was going to contribute the least profit. The report concluded that 'the translated playgoers [found] that they were quite as well cared for under the new as under the old management; that they were more comfortably seated, and had as clear and comprehensive a view of the actions of the stage. We do not suppose that there will be any repetition of such a scene.' Happily *The Times* was right and there was no repetition of the events of the opening night. All the proceeds from the first night of *Money* at the Haymarket were donated to John Baldwin Buckstone's widow.

Once the killer fog had lifted *Money* ran for three months, to full houses. The reviews were generally favourable, particularly for Marie Bancroft in her part of Lady Franklin, the cheerful older woman, but Clement Scott's review was lukewarm. He considered that Bancroft had gone too far in his attempts to achieve naturalism. Of the club-room scene, where Alfred Evelyn plays cards and pretends to be losing his entire newly-inherited fortune, Scott wrote that, 'Mr Bancroft's idea is evidently to suggest the buzz and general conversation of a club-room .... attention is distracted by minor detail that has no bearing whatever on the dramatic position .... The stage-management is at fault .... the object of the scene is to have the attention fixed on the card table .... exactly the opposite result is obtained: minor frivolities are preferred to the major point.'

However, always a fan of Marie Bancroft, his praise for her was almost gushing. He especially enjoyed a scene where she, as Lady Franklin, flirts with a middle-aged and morose widower, played by the 'clever and perceptive' Arthur Cecil:

> I never remember to have heard applause more general and spontaneous at the close of the celebrated dancing scene by Mr Arthur Cecil and Mrs Bancroft as Graves and Lady Franklin .... The Lady Franklin of Mrs Bancroft stands out clear, sharp and defined, like a star of comedy that nothing can touch. It is exhilarating, refreshing, buoyant and altogether captivating. Good as it was at the Prince of Wales's, it is a thousand times better now. No stage or house is too large for the free and admirable style of this inimitable artist. Her laugh rings and echoes through the house ... She is so good that occasionally one is apt to complain that such cleverness cannot be learned .... Cleverness do I call it? No, it is something more than that, it is genius .... If anyone wants to know what we mean by comedy, let them study Mrs Bancroft as Lady Franklin.

Arthur Cecil and Marie Bancroft in **Money**

Despite the continuing pit debate, receipts at the Haymarket were soon showing a healthy profit, quickly exceeding the amounts that the Bancrofts had been accustomed to taking at the much smaller Prince of Wales's. This was partly due to a rush for seats from those unable to get to the Haymarket during the first few weeks because of the fog. A series of matinées was started to accommodate this surge in demand.

Among those who had missed the Bancrofts' first night at the Haymarket were the Prince and Princess of Wales. Maybe it was just as well that they were still at Sandringham following Christmas, with the 'pit riot' taking place, but they were back in London by the third night, by which time the dreadful fog had lifted slightly. Keen to see the changes that had taken place in one of his favourite theatres, the prince asked to be shown around after the performance. During this tour, at one point Squire Bancroft turned to his master-carpenter, whose name was Oliver Wales, to assist in explaining the details of the back-stage structures, and asked, 'Which way, Wales?' At his side, Prince Albert Edward was highly amused at the coincidence of the carpenter's name and his own title.

In May *Money* was replaced by a revival of *School*. The Bancrofts were unsure if Robertson's plays would translate comfortably from the tiny stage at the Prince of Wales's to the much larger Haymarket, but *School* proved as popular as ever. 'The reception it received was worthy of any new play, and the demand for seats as vigorous, leaving no doubt that this delicate little comedy, fragile in plot, would maintain the position .... of being the most successful of all our plays.'

a scene from **School** *at the Haymarket.*
The Theatre *magazine, 1 June, 1880*

The demand for seats was high throughout the run, in spite of some cool reviews. '*Money* was originally written for the old Haymarket,' wrote *The Theatre*'s reviewer, 'and there was therefore much fitness in selecting it for the inaugural performance at the new house; but another kind of interest was awakened by the transplanting of *School* from the little theatre in Tottenham Street to the larger stage.' The review went on to say that the light, slight play just about held its own on the large stage, with the possible exception of Arthur Cecil in John Hare's old part of Beau Farintosh. 'The silly old dandy could be admirably performed on the little stage of a little theatre. At the Haymarket it is lost .... and it is hardly possible to comprehend what he is about without employing an opera-glass oneself .... The fine microscopic work brought into fashion by Mr Hare and Mr Cecil should not be risked in a large theatre.' Oscar Wilde, then aged twenty-six, saw *School* at the Haymarket and wrote to Marie Bancroft requesting a signed photograph. She sent him one, and received a letter of thanks:

Dear Mrs. Bancroft,
    I am charmed with the photograph and with your kindness in sending it to me; it has given me more pleasure than any quill can possibly express, and will be a delightful souvenir of one whose brilliant genius I have always admired. Dramatic art in England owes you and your husband a great debt. Since Tuesday I have had a feeling that I have never rightly appreciated the treasures hidden in a girls' school. I don't know what I shall do, but I think I must hold you responsible.
                                            Believe me, sincerely yours,
                                                            Oscar Wilde

Marie Bancroft was now over forty, but her versatility allowed her to play, one immediately following the other, the middle-aged Lady Franklin and the teenage schoolgirl, Naomi Tighe. In *School* Squire played his old part of Jack Poyntz and the ingénue, Bella, was played by Marion Terry. To have any member of the Terry family on board at that time was an undoubted coup. Marion had joined the Bancrofts in their last year at the Prince of Wales's, where she had appeared in *Duty* and then in *Ours*, the final production at the old theatre, playing leading parts in both, and had remained with the company when it transferred to the Haymarket. The eldest Terry sister, Kate[*], who had left the stage when she married, wrote: 'I saw Marion play Bella in Tom Robertson's *School* .... Here were no wonderful dresses, no magnificence, no big thrills and no declaiming –

[*] Kate Terry, 1844-1924, was the eldest of the Terry girls and, like her sisters, on the stage from an early age. Considered potentially the finest actress of all the sisters, she left the stage early following her marriage in 1867. She was the grandmother of one the 20th century's greatest actors, Sir John Gielgud.

just ordinary folk in simple surroundings presented with great fidelity and infinite detail of setting.'

Although somewhat eclipsed by her supremely talented elder sister, Ellen, Marion Terry was a fine actress in her own right and a lovely young woman. Ellen described her sister: 'Oh, what a pretty young girl she was! Her golden-brown eyes exactly matched her hair, and she was the winsomest thing imaginable! From the first she showed talent.' During a long career that spanned more than fifty years and lasted well into the twentieth century Marion played many leading parts, at the Lyceum, at the Haymarket, at Stratford, and elsewhere. In 1887, when Marion was staying in the Lake District, Ellen was playing Viola in *Twelfth Night*. She was taken ill and Henry Irving sent an urgent message to Marion, begging her to come to the Lyceum and take over from her sister. This she did at very short notice, learning the entire part in the couple of days it took her to get back to London. (Their brother, Fred Terry, was playing Viola's twin brother, Sebastian.)

Marion Terry

215

Marion Terry was far more 'proper' and straight-laced than her sister. This seemed to irritate Ellen, who would on occasion make up stories that Marion had been involved in love affairs, upsetting her deeply. Nina Auerbach, in her 1987 biography of Ellen Terry, said that 'Ellen enjoyed spreading lurid stories about her untouchable sister, inventing a love affair between Marion and strutting old Squire Bancroft that was intended to scandalise London.' This suggests that Ellen had made the story up, as she had made up others. However, the eminent biographer, Sir Michael Holroyd, while researching for *A Strange Eventful History*, his fine 2008 biography of the Irving and Terry families, came across a letter indicating that there was some truth in the story, that Marion had indeed fallen in love with Squire Bancroft, and that they had had an affair. This was ended when Marie Bancroft had 'caught them on the sofa in his study'. Marion seems never to have got over this affair, and she never married. The relationship, whether entirely platonic or not, was likely to have taken place during the two years that Marion was at the Prince of Wales's and the Haymarket, when Marion was in her mid-twenties and Bancroft twelve years older. 'Strutting', he may have been, but 'old' he was not, certainly not at that time. Word of the affair never spread, London was not scandalised, and the reputations of both Marion Terry and Squire Bancroft survived unharmed.

Squire Bancroft's thirty-ninth birthday fell on 14 May, shortly after *School* opened. Henry Irving sent a note wishing him many happy returns and promising to join him for 'just *one* cigar' late that evening after they had both finished at their theatres. Irving ended by writing, 'No more, by heaven, for tomorrow is a busy day with both of us.' This was a reference to the fact that they were both due to appear in morning performances the following day, a Saturday, so could not afford to make a late night of it. Morning performances were becoming popular all over London, and by now were a key element in the Haymarket's business. That business was now going very well, and when the curtain fell on the final performance of the Bancrofts' first season there, the occupants of the upper circle, the once disgruntled pittites, cheered them loudly, with cries of 'Come back soon!'

Squire and Marie Bancroft immediately left for Pontresina, where they were by now well-known regulars. Over the years many old friends had gathered there, and the visitors all enjoyed each other's company at the long, communal dinner table of their favourite hotel. On many evenings the hotel guests would enjoy performances by travelling entertainers such as conjurers, Tyrolean singers, or, one year, a Hungarian band, which played alternate evenings at hotels in Pontresina and nearby St Moritz.

Clement Scott described how Marie would often organise the other guests into playing childish games: 'Never shall I forget one wet day up in the Alpine clouds .... when she made learned professors and head-schoolmasters and divines and doctors leave their books, their philosophical treatises, their Greek roots .... to play "dumb crambo" at her laughing command, or to turn themselves, these learned, spectacled gentlemen ..... into a sham orchestra, with make-believe instruments, which she conducted.'

Among the guests at the hotel that summer were some royal visitors, Princess Helena, the third daughter of Queen Victoria, with her husband, Prince Christian of Schleswig-Holstein, and their family. While at Pontresina their young son fell ill with a throat infection and Marie Bancroft volunteered to help care for him – this probably amounted to little more than sitting and reading to him, along with maybe a little brow-mopping, Marie being an unlikely sick-nurse. However children always found her fun to be with and responded to her. The boy became very fond of her, referring to her from then on as 'Dr Bancroft'. He was close in age to George Bancroft, who with his brother, Charles was almost certainly with their parents in Switzerland, and there were probably other children there as well. Although the Bancrofts never refer to them in their memoirs, George, in his own autobiography, written many years later, said that he first accompanied his parents to the Alps when he was nine, some two years before this holiday.

Once again the visitors to Pontresina were involved in raising funds for the small church that was being built. Arthur Sullivan took charge of the musical parts of the programme, while the dramatic side included the Graves and Lady Franklin scene from Lytton's *Money*, and the one-act *The Vicarage*, with Arthur Cecil and Marie and Squire Bancroft in the three leading parts: they all knew it so well that it needed very little rehearsal. Marie added to the play by writing up the small part of a manservant, so that a gentleman guest who was persuaded to play him had more to do. Without a proper stage, there was, of course, no curtain, so all the scene-changing took place in full view of the audience – a situation that would seem quite normal today, but then was most unusual. Tickets were sold at ten francs each, raising a large sum towards the church fund. Prince and Princess Christian attended, along with all the other summer visitors, and every available horse-drawn vehicle in nearby St Moritz was chartered to bring people to Pontresina to see the show.

Both Bancrofts were fond of long walks in the mountains of the Engadine. Although Marie never attempted anything beyond what could be accomplished with a pair of stout boots and a stick, Squire had ventured on a few rather more challenging climbs, including one to the 11,322-foot summit of the Piz Corvatsch mountain. Marie described one of their day-long outings: 'We started at an early hour, carrying a simple luncheon with us, consisting of substantial sandwiches and wine. On reaching the summit we sat down on a bench and gazed on the lovely

217

panorama before us.' There were always guides on hand to accompany visitors on their hikes in the mountains, where they would often cook meals for them in strategically-placed Alpine huts. One year at Pontresina the guests at the hotel entertained the local guides to a dinner. One of the visitors addressed a speech to the guides in fluent German and the guides presented all of the ladies with baskets of edelweiss. The gathering caroused late into the night and ended when the rowdy Swiss guests spilled out into the street 'where their parting cheers awoke the slumbering villagers and the visitors who had sought an early bed!'

When they returned to the Haymarket, *School* and *The Vicarage* were resumed. During the summer Francis Burnand, the author of *Diplunacy*, the burlesque on *Diplomacy*, had been working on *The Colonel*, a comedy that satirised the aesthetic movement. He had read the first and second acts of his new play to the Bancrofts in July, before they went away. They had found these two acts entertaining and amusing but when, on their return, Burnand read them the rest of the play, they were disappointed by the final act. However, they went ahead and rehearsals began, but the play would not work out, in spite of the author cheerfully making alterations as requested. Regretfully the Bancrofts decided that the play was not for them and suggested it would be more suited to a smaller theatre. Burnand's play was eventually produced by Edgar Bruce at their old home in Tottenham Street, starring Charles Coghlan, where it turned out to be a huge success and ran for a long time, coming to be regarded as Burnand's best comedy and making a fortune for Bruce at the Prince of Wales's.

At Christmas the Bancrofts were together involved in a nasty street accident one morning on their way to the Haymarket, the kind of mishap that was commonplace in the horsedrawn traffic that thronged the congested London streets. Their coachman was having trouble controlling the pair of young and rather nervous horses drawing their brougham, a type of four-wheeled carriage. Snow was falling heavily but, deeply absorbed in conversation, Squire and Marie had not noticed that they were travelling at an alarming speed. One of the horses somehow got a leg entangled in its harness and panicked, along with its partner. Squire held Marie tightly as the two terrified horses struggled to free themselves and the driver fought to control them. They collided with a passing coal-cart, severely injuring the horse that was drawing it, and the brougham's entangled horses staggered across the road, mounted the slippery, wet wooden pavement, and crashed into the railings in front of a house. The railings broke and they were only saved from falling right down into the 'area' – the narrow front yard that admitted light into the basement – by an iron grating that covered it. The brougham turned over and Marie and Squire had to be pulled out through a window. Fortunately neither they nor the coachman, nor the driver of the coal-cart, were badly hurt, but all three horses were injured; so although there were no doctors' bills to pay, the vets' bills were huge. Marie, in describing the accident, wrote, 'I was dragged through the carriage-window by a kindly navvy [and] Mr Bancroft, whose hat resembled a concertina, took me into the chemist's close by, where they were most kind, and gave me a restorative.' But 'the show must go on', and Marie ended her account: 'With difficulty I got through my work that night, for my nerves were completely unstrung.'

Meanwhile, the Bancrofts still had no ideas as to what might replace *School*. So they decided to fall back yet again on a revival of a success from the past, *Masks and Faces*. The winter of 1880-81 was another hard one: this time heavy snow almost brought London to a standstill in the New Year and it was difficult for the company to get to the Haymarket each day. Squire recalled a day in January when the pavement on one side of Regent Street was clear of snow, while on the other side the shops were unable to open as there were drifts reaching half way up their shutters. Horse-drawn vehicles had real trouble moving around the deserted streets and theatre audiences were sparse. Marie described the conditions in a letter to a friend:

It seemed as if Siberia and all the Russias had sent their snow to London .... The anxiety was 'how shall we manage to struggle to the theatre at night?' But where there's a will there's a way and we turned up at the stage-door in appearance like Father and Mother Christmas. Every member of the company reached the theatre safely, several having to come long distances; it was funny to see the various effects the weather had on us: some faces were white, others red, others blue – I was all three! .... The auditorium presented the strangest picture. There were seven people in the stalls with topcoats, mufflers, fur cloaks, and large hoods, hardly anyone in the balcony, and the people in the rest of the theatre swathed in shawls, leaving nothing but a row of noses to be seen .... I should have much liked to have invited them to tea in the green-room and have had no performance at all! It was like playing to a dead wall, not a sound of applause or laughter throughout the evening. When at last we arrived home, we found the coachman with a spade shovelling away the miniature mountains from the front of the house; he nearly shovelled us into the road too.

Fortunately the thaw came and *Masks and Faces* opened on schedule on 5 February 1881. Marie Bancroft again played Peg Woffington, while Squire Bancroft and Arthur Cecil alternated in the parts of the impoverished Triplet, and the Poet Laureate and theatre manager Colley Cibber. Marion Terry was the young wife, Mabel Vane, the part that her sister Ellen, now Irving's celebrated leading lady at the Lyceum, had played back in 1875. The alternating of the parts of Triplet and Cibber did

219

not entirely work as the short, rather plump figure of Arthur Cecil could not be entirely convincing as the half-starved artist. Squire Bancroft was given an amusing caricature, entitled 'The Two Triplets', depicting the two actors, their portfolios under their arms, 'one lean and hungry, the other in better feather, as both dressed for the part by mistake on the same evening'. It was drawn by an actor called Charles Brookfield, a member of the company who was playing the part of the obsequious critic, Soaper, with Henry Kemble, the 'Beetle', as his colleague, the disagreeable Snarl.

The new production of *Masks and Faces* was even better received than it had been at the Prince of Wales's in 1875. Squire Bancroft's performance was noted by the critic Clare Lincoln in the *Dramatic Review*:

> What he conveys so admirably is the idea of a man who has been crushed by misfortune .... He does not cringe or whine .... If you want to see a bit of delicate and suggestive art, watch how Triplet, ravenous with hunger, slips some of the biscuits into his pocket, and, looking into vacancy, says: 'For the little ones.' If this were flung at the heads of the audience, the idea would fail. But Mr Bancroft, by the way he does it, touches every sympathetic chord in the whole house.

'The Two Triplets' by Charles Brookfield

Among the illustrious visitors who came to see *Masks and Faces* was William Gladstone, then in his second term as Prime Minister. Tickets were sold out and the only seats that Mr Gladstone, by then in his seventies, had managed to get were right at the back of the stalls. He sent a message to the Bancrofts asking whether there was any possibility of finding him seats closer to the stage as he was becoming rather hard of hearing. The only vacant seats in the house were in the Royal Box, which was immediately offered to the Prime Minister. A day or two later Squire Bancroft received a letter of thanks from Downing Street:

Dear Sir,
    Let me thank you very much for your courtesy in allowing me with my party to occupy a most advantageous post in your theatre on Saturday night. By so doing you secured to me the fullness of a great treat, which otherwise declining powers of sight and hearing would somewhat have impaired. For the capital acting of the chief parts I was prepared; but the whole cast, likewise, seemed to me excellent.
                                    I remain, dear sir, your very faithful and obliged,
                                                                    W.E.Gladstone.

Charles Reade, the co-author of *Masks and Faces*, came to see the revival of his play, on what was to be the last time he saw it and was probably one of his last visits to any theatre. In failing health, having suffered for some years from asthma and bronchitis, he first tried a warmer climate, moving for a while to the south of France, but returned home and died three years later, in 1884, aged seventy.

After the Bancrofts returned from their usual continental holiday, Squire departed on a long Mediterranean voyage to Constantinople in the company of a friend, Joseph Charles Parkinson[*], a writer who had travelled extensively in the Far East. Marie came to see them off at Southampton on 28 September, coming on board to look over the P&O steamship, the *Deccan*, in which they were to sail. This visit to a large ship only served to confirm her terror of the sea, even though the three of them were entertained to lunch on board by the ship's captain and officers.

    The *Deccan* was a fine steamer, with one funnel and three masts for her sails. She had accommodation for around two hundred passengers, most of whom were soldiers and civil servants on their way to India, many of them accompanied by their families. The ship was packed, so Bancroft and Parkinson were offered officers' quarters, the obliging officers

---

[*] Joseph Charles Parkinson, 1833-1908, journalist and travel writer, involved in the early development of telegraphy.

doubling up with their colleagues. Parkinson was given the chief officer's cabin and Squire had the one normally occupied by the ship's doctor. He soon found that his cabin had its drawbacks – right outside was the pen where chickens were kept. Its occupants, undeterred by being at sea, would wake him very early each morning; he was also uncomfortably close by when, as he put it, 'their short span of life was noisily shortened for table purposes', as the slaughter-house and the area where the ship's butcher went about his business were also nearby.

The first leg of the voyage was uneventful with 'the dreaded Bay [of Biscay] almost pond like' and their fellow-passengers good company. The ship's crew was an exotic mixture of seamen from all over the world. Lascars, Chinese, Africans and many others stoked the boilers, manned the sails and looked after the passengers' needs. Daily life on board the *Deccan* provided Squire with all the background detail he could possibly want for a revival that he had in mind of a play by Tom Taylor, *The Overland Route*, much of which takes place on board a passenger ship. He took notes and made drawings of ship-board life.

They took on coal in Gibraltar, where passengers were able to go ashore and briefly explore the Rock. While there many of them telegraphed home to reassure their families that all was well, and there were visits to the English Club, where they could catch up on the news of the past few days. Back on board, Squire discovered a further drawback to his cabin's position: it was situated on the side of the ship where the coal was loaded. He had left his porthole open while he went ashore, and on his return he found everything inside the cabin covered with a thick, black layer of coal dust. The weather became very hot as they entered the Mediterranean, heading for their next stop, Malta. The ship's piano was hauled up on deck, so the ladies could play and sing in the cool of the evenings and impromptu dances could take place under the Mediterranean stars.

Parkinson and Bancroft had two days and nights in Malta, where they bought trinkets in a market and did some sightseeing. They visited the Church of the Knights of St John, but the event that remained most strongly in Squire's memory was a guided tour around a Capuchin monastery. In the crypt below the chapel were the mummified remains of monks who had gone before, still dressed in their brown Franciscan habits and propped upright in niches. Several niches were empty and the young monk who escorted them around this macabre vault proudly pointed to one of these. It was, he cheerfully informed the visitors, the space reserved for him when his time came.

At Malta, Bancroft and Parkinson left the *Deccan*, as the next part of their journey was on board the *Cherbourg*, a much smaller vessel, bound for Constantinople. The weather had taken a turn for the worse and a strong sirocco wind blowing from the Sahara made the sea choppy. For the first time Squire began to feel seasick and spent the first day on board the *Cherbourg* in his berth, reminding himself that the only other time in his life that he had ever taken to his bed was for the same reason – seasickness – in 1858, when he had crossed the Atlantic at the age of seventeen. On many occasions over the years when he had felt unwell and should probably have stayed at home in bed, he had struggled up to appear on stage however ill he was feeling. He had never missed a 'call'. Fortunately his queasiness did not last long, and Parkinson dragged him up on deck to recover 'in a condition of eccentric dishabille'.

Life on board the *Cherbourg* was very different from that on the *Deccan*. There were not many passengers and they often had the deck almost to themselves. The ship was carrying a heavy cargo and there were several stops en route, including Ermoupolis, the capital of Syros, the main island of the Cyclades group, and at the once great city of Smyrna, now Izmir, on the Aegean coast, the area then usually referred to as Asia Minor. Here they found 'types of every race and nation', reminding the travellers of the *Arabian Nights*. Bancroft wrote of 'caravans with their troops of camels, merchants and pilgrims, and many countenances whose owners looked like murderers or thieves'. They were guided deep into the bazaars, much further than they would have dared venture on their own, by a 'handsome, petticoated Greek, with his sash and girdle one mass of pistols, swords, and daggers, somewhat interfered with by a prosaic umbrella.' Forty years later, during the devastating conflict of the Greek-Turkish war of 1919-1922, the Greek population of Smyrna was expelled or massacred, and in 1922 much of the great city was devastated by the Great Fire of Smyrna.

As the *Cherbourg* was due to spend some days loading and unloading cargo at Smyrna, Bancroft and Parkinson found a Russian steamer, the *Nahimoff*, that was shortly leaving for Constantinople, on which they shared a large cabin complete with two comfortable iron bedsteads. Their fellow passengers were mostly either Russians or people from Turkey and Greece travelling on the cheap. 'Your Easterns,' wrote Squire, 'spend but little on transit – most of the travellers, in fact, carried their own bedding, or were contented with the hospitality of a prayer-carpet.' Only the very few first-class western travellers frequented the saloon or spent any money at all on food and drink, the others having brought their own food, such as bread, cheese and olives, as well as their own bedding. Each day, at the proper hour, the Muslim passengers would spread their mats to pray. The *Nahimoff* passed through the Dardanelles and on to their final destination, Constantinople, now Istanbul: 'We steamed down the Bosphorus at an early hour. The morning mists fortunately dispersed in time to show us the wonderful view as we approached Constantinople …. its mosques and minarets, its towers and temples, glittering in the Eastern sun.'

They hired a guide, 'an amusing rascal with a strong belief in the powers of "baksheesh",' who showed them the sights of the great city where Europe meets Asia. 'We ascended the Galata Tower, from which the sight well repays the toil; we "did" Santa Sophia and other mosques until we were tired of taking off our boots and shambling in ill-fitting slippers on the marble floors; we saw and marvelled at both the dancing and the howling dervishes; we rowed in a *caique* on the Golden Horn; we bought bad cigarettes. We thought the bazaars .... very inferior to those we had visited in Smyrna; we saw crowds of scarred street-dogs, and heard their howls too often in the night; we were jolted to death in the vilest vehicles over the worst-paved roads I have ever seen; in a word we rushed about from place to place and saw much that lies between Stamboul and Therapia, including a sweet and peaceful reminder of home in the green and well-kept cemetery on the heights of Scutari*, where lie the graves of many of our Crimean heroes.'

After these hurried few days in Constantinople the friends parted company. Bancroft needed to head for home and back to his work. Parkinson, who wrote books on his travels, had more time at his disposal and had plans to carry on, further east. Squire boarded the *Provence*, a French steamer bound for Marseilles, a voyage of six days, with brief stops at Piraeus and in the Bay of Naples, both late at night when it was not possible to go ashore, although street-vendors swarmed on board the ship with trays of 'mock coral and doubtful tortoiseshell'. On reaching Marseilles he headed for home by night express train via Paris, where it was now distinctly autumnal – far chillier than the Mediterranean heat to which he had become accustomed. Squire scarcely noticed the change in climate: his time was spent studying his part for the next Haymarket production, which was to be *Plot and Passion*, a play of 1853 by Tom Taylor.

---

* Scutari, town on the Asian side of the Bosphorus, where Florence Nightingale established a hospital to care for British soldiers wounded in the Crimean War of 1854-56. Now called Üsküdar, it is part of modern Istanbul.

10

HAYMARKET DAYS

Bancroft's journey had taken him away for about a month and he arrived home eager to start the new season. *Plot and Passion* was to run as a double-bill alongside a one-act play by Francis Burnand called *A Lesson*. As the Haymarket had been let out for the summer and early autumn months, these plays were rehearsed on familiar boards as Edgar Bruce at the Prince of Wales's offered them the stage at their old home for rehearsals. While these were ongoing, Bancroft snatched a few days in which to make another dash across to Paris to see the *première* of the latest Sardou play, *Odette*. He was impressed, describing it as 'one of the most powerful [Sardou] ever wrote.' He immediately bought the rights for an English version, and its production was planned for later in the new season.

Once again a first night was disrupted by the weather conditions outside: this time a ferocious gale was raging over south-east England and a ventilator high above the theatre rattled throughout the performance. Because of the weather conditions, Burnand, the author of *A Lesson*, was unable to come to the first night of his play. He wrote to Marie to congratulate her as he had read a reasonable review in the *Observer* and he went on to describe the storm on the Kent coast: 'Such a gale! The centre part of the veranda blown right down; wrecks, alas, everywhere. Tugs and lifeboats in full employ .... We thought of you at 10.30 last night ....' Most reviews were less kindly than the *Observer*'s lukewarm one. The double-bill of *Plot and Passion* and *A Lesson* was not a success and was clearly not going to last.

During November the Bancrofts were approached by Lillie Langtry, who had decided that she would like to become an actress. Since becoming the mistress of Albert Edward, the Prince of Wales and future King Edward VII, the beautiful 'Jersey Lily', now aged twenty-eight, was the most famous celebrity of her time, recognised and fêted wherever she went. Ellen Terry wrote that 'Mrs. Langtry could not go out anywhere, at the dawn of the 'eighties, without a crowd collecting to look at her! .... [She was] not a showy beauty. Her hair was the colour that it had pleased God to make it; her complexion was her own; in evening dress she did not display nearly as much of her neck and arms as was the vogue, yet they outshone all other necks and arms through their own perfection.'

Lillie Langtry, the 'Jersey Lily'

Her affair with the Prince of Wales had ended the previous year and now the resilient Mrs Langtry was proposing that she play the leading role of Kate Hardcastle in an afternoon amateur performance of Oliver Goldsmith's *She Stoops to Conquer* in aid of a theatrical charity. She

226

asked if she could use the Haymarket for the occasion. The Bancrofts quickly agreed, realising that if they did not take up Mrs Langtry's proposal, then some other theatre certainly would. They were convinced that her popularity would ensure a full house and certain that, even if the lady turned out to have no talent as an actress, she was so accustomed to being the centre of attention that at least she would be unlikely to suffer from stage-fright.

The date was fixed for 15 December and higher-than-usual prices were charged so that the charity, The Royal General Theatrical Fund[*], would benefit substantially from the sale of tickets. 'Never,' wrote Squire Bancroft, 'was a theatre more besieged for seats. All sections of society fought for places, and loud were the lamentations in many a high quarter where non-success had followed every effort to procure them.' When the day arrived the Prince – and the Princess – of Wales were in the Royal Box, and the rest of the theatre was filled with everyone who was anyone in London society, all wanting to see the theatrical début of the most celebrated woman in London. In the event, Mrs Langtry showed considerable talent and promise, and the large sum of £430 was handed over to the Theatrical Fund – worth well over £20,000 today.

So taken were the Bancrofts with Lillie Langtry's performance in *She Stoops to Conquer* that they immediately offered her the leading role of the ingénue, Blanche Haye, in yet another revival of the ever-popular Robertson play, *Ours*. Mrs Langtry accepted eagerly, declining many other flattering offers with which she had been deluged. *Ours* opened on 19 January 1882, with the Bancrofts taking the parts they had now played so many times before, those of Hugh Chalcot and Mary Netley. Arthur Wing Pinero, who had been with Irving at the Lyceum for five years, had also joined the company and had the part of Sir Alexander Shendryn. The playbill announced that the Bancrofts' rights in T.W.Robertson's plays were about to expire, which explained their eagerness to produce revivals while they still could.

Some years later, now a successful, established actress, Mrs Langtry was heading to the United States and preparing to act in a production there of *Peril*. Squire Bancroft presented her with his prompt book for *Ours* and in her letter of thanks she ended with the words, 'I shall never forget your and Mrs B's kindness in giving me my first engagement, for I feel that my subsequent success was owing in a very great degree to the position you gave me …. I must tell you again how grateful I am to you for the prompt-book, and if the piece succeeds, I shall attribute it to you.'

---

[*] The Royal General Theatrical Fund, established in 1839 to provide support for actors who were aged or infirm or otherwise in need, and for their dependants. Renamed the Royal Theatrical Fund, it is still active today.

Haymarket programme for Ours, *starring Mrs Langtry*

Meanwhile Clement Scott was working on the English version of Sardou's *Odette*, and preparations for the production were well underway. It was a tricky play, dealing as it did with the then sensitive subject of divorce. Suspected of infidelity, Odette is thrown out by her husband, and their daughter grows up believing her mother is dead. So when Odette returns in the third act her daughter does not recognise her and eventually Odette takes her own life. For the play, the Bancrofts had engaged the celebrated Polish actress, Helena Modjeska – always known as Madame Modjeska, or by her surname alone – to play the leading role for three months. The main drawback of the play was that a powerful first act rather eclipsed the rest of the play. A further problem was that after that first act the female lead did not reappear until half way through the third, and final, act. With an expensive international star in the part this would seem a considerable extravagance.

Rehearsals began in March and the play opened on 25 April 1882. Modjeska's performance was a triumph and on the first night she took many curtain calls following the first act and at the end of the play. In general, though, *Odette* had a disappointing reception from the critics and the public. This led to anxiety as advance bookings were slight. In the end it paid its way so far as the more expensive stalls and circle seats went, although it never proved popular with the cheaper seats in the gallery, which was rarely full. Fortunately Madame Modjeska's engagement was guaranteed only for a fixed, though expensive, term of three months from the play's opening near the end of April until the end of the season at the beginning of August.

Born Helena Modrzejewska in 1840, in Poland, then under repressive Imperial Russian rule, Modjeska became the leading actress in her own country. In 1876 she and her husband emigrated to the United States where she made her name – in a rather more pronounceable form – as a Shakespearean actress. In 1879 she came to London for three years and it was towards the end of this stay that she was engaged by the Bancrofts as their *Odette*. Although Clement Scott's English adaptation anglicized most of the characters, Scott kept Odette herself as a French woman, to allow for Modjeska's strong Polish accent. Squire and Marie Bancroft were among her greatest admirers.

The Bancrofts allotted themselves minor parts in *Odette*. Their decision to play insignificant roles prompted a letter from their old friend, Dion Boucicault, who wrote to Squire, regretting that he and Marie did not take the leading parts in their productions more often. 'Why are Mr and Mrs Bancroft taking a back seat in their own theatre?' he wrote. 'Tell Marie, with my love, that there is nothing so destructive as *rest*, if persisted in …. it becomes *rust*, and it eats into life. Hers is too precious to let her fool it away; she is looking splendid, and as fresh as a pat of butter …. I dare say you will ask me to mind my own business …. Well, if you do, I shall say that the leading interests of the Drama, which you and she now represent, *are* my business; that the regard and affection I have personally entertained for your wife since she was a child, and the friendship I have felt for you, induced me to repeat what I have heard from more than one person on both sides of the Atlantic.'

Boucicault's advice was not heeded. The Bancrofts' policy had always been not to take the leading parts in a play for themselves unless those parts were clearly suited to them. Neither did they choose a play on the basis of there being leading parts for themselves in it, as was usually the case with Irving's productions. Sometimes they would have no part at all, if there were no roles to suit them, although at times they might elaborate on their own smaller parts, either by inserting some extra dialogue or some business to give themselves a little more prominence. In most of the Robertson plays they produced after *Society* they had leading roles, as Robertson wrote parts specifically for them. Squire Bancroft wrote that he and Marie had 'been contented to sometimes …. merely aid a good *ensemble* rather than thrust ourselves into all the leading parts'. This policy undoubtedly contributed to the success of many of their productions, which might well have failed had they cast themselves in parts to which they were totally unsuited, even though there were times when the public were disappointed that they, Marie in particular, were not appearing.

In the event, in spite of its slow start, *Odette* played to reasonable houses until the end of the season. Then there were to be some significant changes in the company. Arthur Cecil, who after six years with the Bancrofts, both at the Prince of Wales's and then at the Haymarket, moved on to the Royal Court, later taking on its management, together with John Clayton, who had also been in the Bancrofts' company several years earlier. Cecil wrote to Marie from the Garrick Club referring to 'my happy association with you for six years – a longer period than I have ever passed under any other management, and a pleasanter one by far than I can ever expect to pass elsewhere.' They remained close friends until Cecil's death in 1896. At this time too Arthur Wing Pinero gave up acting regularly, in order to devote himself to writing. He also wrote to the Bancrofts expressing his appreciation of his time at the Haymarket, saying: 'The actor's willingness to do as much as he can for his manager is outmatched by his manager's anxiety to do more for the actor. I carry away with me a regard for you both which I am glad to acknowledge always and everywhere.'

The Bancrofts again spent that summer at Pontresina. The church for which they and others had spent so many years raising funds was almost finished and Bishop William Walsham How, the Bishop of Bedford, came from England to consecrate it. The bishop had many friends in the theatrical profession. His diocese was then responsible for the East End of London and, appalled by the conditions of the poor there, he succeeded in enlisting the sympathies and help of the rich West End to help support the impoverished East End. The bishop was especially famed for his work among the poor children of east London and was known as 'The Children's Bishop', and he later became Bishop of Wakefield. Bishop How wrote many popular hymns, including the rousing 'For All the Saints, who from their Labours Rest'.

The Schleswig-Holstein royals were again at Pontresina. It is probable that it was Princess Helena who invited the bishop to perform the consecration as she was deeply committed to his work in the East End of London. The princess was involved in many charitable causes and her involvement was more than purely token: she attended meetings and took an active part in many of the projects she supported, including the Red Cross, of which she was a founder member and the Society for the Prevention of Cruelty to Children. She donated a fine altar-cloth to the church and among other gifts were many from the theatrical visitors. Arthur Cecil donated complete sets of hymn-books and prayer-books, Squire Bancroft gave the church bell, and Marie Bancroft had a stained-glass window installed above the altar, as a memorial to her mother, Georgiana Wilton.

The Bancrofts were happy at last to be able to enjoy their stay in the Alps without the effort of fund-raising. Instead of countless rehearsals, they could now enjoy more walks and climbs and the company of friends. This year one of those friends was another prominent figure of the London stage, the actor-manager Charles Wyndham, who was staying at nearby St Moritz. Squire had first met Wyndham back in 1864 when they were both working in Liverpool and they had remained good friends. Born Charles Culverwell in 1837, Wyndham had started out in the medical profession, and when he and Bancroft first met he had not long returned from America where he had served as a surgeon on the Union side in the Civil War. He was something of a workaholic. Squire Bancroft wrote of him that 'unlike ourselves [he] allows his business affairs to follow him when he takes a holiday, and is consequently often a martyr to telegrams and letters.' To remind himself of work that needed doing, even when he was away, he sometimes went so far as to post letters or send telegrams to himself as reminders of essential 'must-dos'. Wyndham would surely have been one of those people who can never bear to be out of reach of his smart phone and his emails. The Bancrofts on the other hand left their work firmly behind them when on holiday, with the inevitable drawback that on their return home they would be met by a mountain of correspondence to be dealt with. In 1876 Wyndham took over the Criterion Theatre, in Piccadilly Circus, where he became one of the most successful actor-managers of the latter part of the century. In 1899, he opened his own Wyndham's Theatre, in Charing Cross Road, still one of London's major theatres, where almost every leading actor of today has performed. Charles Wyndham was much admired both by Shaw and by Wilde, who based the character of Jack Worthing in *The Importance of Being Earnest* on Wyndham.

On their return from holiday the Bancrofts were greeted with sad news: 'Joe' had died. Joe was a black cat who for many years would often appear at the stage door of the Prince of Wales's the night before the opening of a new production. His arrival usually seemed to predict success with any new venture, so it was eagerly looked forward to by all, and greatly appealed to Marie's superstitious nature. Each time the cat would be renamed for a leading character from the play about to open. On arriving at the theatre the night preceding a first night, Marie always hoped to be greeted by the porter with the news that the black cat had arrived. The night before *The School for Scandal* was due to open no cat appeared. Full of gloom and fearing for the fortunes of the play, Marie and Squire were leaving the theatre late after the final rehearsal when the black cat dashed past them and in through the stage door. He was duly named 'Joseph Surface'. The name stuck, as this time the cat took up permanent residence at the theatre, and when they left the Prince of

Wales's he was taken to the Haymarket, where he lived out his days and was finally buried beneath the stage.

The new season opened in October 1882 with Tom Taylor's comedy, *The Overland Route*, which was set partly on a P&O steamer on its way home from India and partly on a desert island where the ship was wrecked. It was full of farcical incidents, such as a handcuffed man trying to light a cigar and drink brandy-and-soda at the same time, problems with mislaid false teeth, and someone trying to steal the red wine that had been reserved for sick castaways. It had a large cast of seventeen, not counting many extras representing passengers, crew, lascars, ayahs, etc. It was preceded by a curtain-raiser, a practice that still survived with many productions at the time, even where fairly lengthy plays were concerned. Maybe it was felt that audiences would think they were not getting their money's worth unless there was more than just the one play each evening. This tradition persisted well into the film era, when a 'B-movie' was usually shown in addition to the main feature, not to mention the newsreel between the two, until at least the 1950s. *The Overland Route* was not a great success and ran for just a few weeks.

Over in France Sardou had been working on his latest play, *Fédora*, the plot of which had been kept a strict secret. All that was known was that it contained an important role for the great Sarah Bernhardt and that the plot involved nihilism, a topic that Squire Bancroft described as a 'modern terror': it was identified with Russian revolutionary plots and international terrorism. In December Bancroft went to Paris for the dress rehearsal. He had no great expectations of the play, in spite of its celebrated star, fearing it was going be no more than a bloodthirsty melodrama, but Paris was 'in a fever of expectation' and on the night the theatre was packed with Parisian celebrities – writers, artists, actors and actresses, and society figures: Alexandre Dumas was in a box, as were Alphonse Daudet and many other figures of literary and artistic Paris, such as the then famous actors Benôit-Constant Coquelin, Blanche Pierson and François Got. The critics were also there, among them Auguste Vitu of *Le Figaro,* and the dreaded Francesque Sarcey, a critic said to be so powerful that he could make or break a play single-handedly.

The long-awaited moment arrived when the play was to start – and nothing happened. Then someone stepped before the curtain to announce that there would unfortunately be an hour's delay as Mme Bernhardt's gowns had arrived late. The audience trooped out of the theatre, to hang around on the boulevard outside or to wait in nearby cafés, smoking and drinking until the hour had passed, when they all shuffled back into their seats. Then the author of *Fédora*, Victorien Sardou himself, was spotted being shown to his seat and the play at last began. Bancroft wrote that 'In five minutes the audience was under a spell which did not once abate throughout the whole four acts. Never was treatment of a strange and dangerous subject more masterly; never was acting more superb than Sarah showed that day to those privileged to witness it.' Without hesitation, he bought the English rights to the play.

Sardou's melodramatic story tells of a Russian Princess, Fédora, whose lover, Vladimir, has been brutally murdered. The handsome but sinister Count Loris Ipanoff, who is suspected of being a nihilist, falls in love with the princess. Fédora is beginning to return his love but comes to suspect that it was Ipanoff who was her Vladimir's killer. He eventually admits that he was indeed the murderer – but he will not reveal his reason for the killing. Then Fédora sees some passionate letters from Vladimir to Ipanoff's wife – he had been her lover as well as Fédora's and this was the reason for the murder. Fédora has already denounced Ipanoff to the secret police and, too late, she tries to save him by warning him that they are on their way. Discovering that it was Fédora herself who has betrayed him, in fury Ipanoff grabs her around the throat; but she has already taken poison and collapses unconscious in his arms – and dies, leaving Ipanoff to face arrest and certain death.

Born in 1844, by 1882 the legendary Sarah Bernhardt was the most famous actress in the world, and even today she is considered to have been one of the greatest the world has ever seen. She performed in works by all the great French writers, including Racine, Molière, George Sand and Victor Hugo. In 1880 she had famously played the part of Marguerite Gautier in Alexandre Dumas's *La Dame aux Camélias*. *Fédora* was the first of several Sardou plays in which she appeared, followed notably in 1887 by *La Tosca*, the play on which Puccini based his opera. She also acted in Shakespeare, memorably playing the title role in *Hamlet* more than once. Later she appeared in several silent films and in 1914 she became the first woman ever to receive the Légion d'Honneur. Bernhardt continued working almost up to the time of her death in 1923, at the age of seventy-eight.

The Bancrofts had first met Bernhardt in 1879, when the Comédie Française produced Racine's *Phèdre*. While the 'Française' were in London the Lord Mayor gave a luncheon at the Mansion House, at which Squire Bancroft was seated next to 'the Divine Sarah'. Unusually, but entirely appropriately considering who the guest of honour was, for once women were invited, so Marie was also present – but then it *was* a luncheon; dinners were almost invariably men-only occasions. Her hosts felt obliged to apologise to Bernhardt and her fellow members of the Comédie Française, who were annoyed to see busts of Wellington and Nelson prominently displayed. They were assured that no offence was intended and that it was due to an oversight that the busts had not been covered up or moved for the occasion. Many years later Marie Bancroft was chosen by her colleagues of the London stage to present Bernhardt with a testimonial honouring the fiftieth anniversary of her stage debut in 1862.

Squire Bancroft's admiration for the great French actress was, however, not entirely unqualified. He wrote, 'great as she was, unequalled in technique, wonderful in the range of her art, perfect in her command of every tone in her beautiful language, Sarah Bernhardt was never to my mind quite free from blemish – it may be thought heresy to say so – of being something of a show-woman. The drum was too big in her orchestra, while I always considered her to be surpassed …. by one other woman I have seen upon the stage – Aimée Desclée.' Unfortunately Desclée's career had been cut short: she died in 1874, at the age of thirty-eight. 'Had Desclée been spared …. her name would have lived among the immortals,' wrote Squire.

Theatre attendances all over London were badly affected around Christmas of 1882 when early in December a catastrophic fire broke out at the enormous Alhambra Theatre and Music Hall in Leicester Square. This fantastical theatre had been built only two years earlier to suggest the Moorish palace at Granada, complete with elaborate embellishments such as towers, domes and minarets. Famed for its musical extravaganzas enhanced by lines of dancing girls, the Alhambra was the nightly haunt of hundreds of prostitutes who gathered in the numerous bars in the intervals and after the shows to entertain the men who congregated there – single men, or married men whose unsuspecting wives had been left at home. A police officer once said that of the fifteen hundred girls in the building on any night, you could guarantee that at least twelve hundred of them were prostitutes. The most popular of the Alhambra bars, known as the 'Canteen', was right beneath the stage, a dark, mysterious area where patrons were encouraged to believe they were being entertained in some privileged inner sanctum: the thud of the dancing and the throb of the music could be heard from above and as soon as their performance was over the young, poorly-paid 'ballet girls', the likes of Esther and Polly Eccles in *Caste*, would come tripping down the stairs to the Canteen and the other bars, hoping to find a gentleman to buy them drinks, and maybe to supplement their meagre wages by accompanying them to some quieter place. The goings-on at the Alhambra of the 1880s might well have astonished the frequenters of twenty-first century lap-dancing clubs which are probably quite tame by comparison.

The fire at the Alhambra blazed for hours: more than twenty fire engines fought the blaze and two firemen died. The Prince of Wales came from Marlborough House to observe the conflagration and was nearly killed when a wall collapsed close to where he stood watching. All the scenery, costumes and properties for the Alhambra's Christmas production were destroyed in the flames. Disregarding the two unfortunate firemen, the press reported the disaster as having 'no victims'. The well-known journalist George Augustus Sala[*], responded angrily:

> No victims! But many scores of 'victims' must necessarily be made through the burning down of the great theatre in Leicester Square. It is towards Christmas-time that 'the ants behind the baize' are most laboriously busy. Scene-painters and scene-shifters, stage carpenters and property men, supernumeraries, ballet-girls, and 'extras' are all toiling and moiling night and day, with the intent of diverting you and your children at Christmas-time; and all for a little bit of bread. The burning down of a great theatre means not only the throwing out of employment of a great tribe of industrious and harmless folk, but the destruction of workmen's tools and the dresses of poor young women, and the spreading far and wide of misery and destitution.

the Alhambra, Leicester Square, before the fire of 1882

The fire at the Alhambra (the site of today's Odeon cinema) caused consternation among the public, and the consequent nervousness about

---

[*] George Augustus Sala, 1828–95, a prolific and widely-read journalist. A flamboyant character, he was specially known for his colourful contributions to the *Daily Telegraph* and many other journals and magazines.

fires in theatres meant that audiences were well down everywhere that Christmas, especially as London's fire chiefs had for some time been demanding stricter fire precautions in theatres, such as more emergency exits, an adequate water supply to fight fires and a fireproof curtain that could be lowered to divide the stage from the auditorium in an emergency.

Playing safe, the Bancrofts chose to start 1883 with a revival of a certain winner, *Caste*, which opened at the Haymarket in January, to run while *Fédora* was in rehearsal. This was to be their last-ever revival of Tom Robertson's best play, as their rights in it were to end the following year. Squire and Marie Bancroft were the only two members of the original cast, for the last time playing Captain Hawtree and Polly Eccles, the parts they had created back in 1867. Since the death of George Honey, this was the first time they had needed a new 'Papa' Eccles and they had cast an actor called David James, who had been in *The Overland Route*, in the part. Although they had feared that they might be unable to find the perfect Eccles, they were delighted to discover that David James was, if anything, even better than Honey.

As this was the last time they would ever produce *Caste*, it occurred to the Bancrofts that for the final night of the play, which was to be on the inauspicious date of Friday, 13 April – maybe Marie's many superstitions did not include a fear of Friday the Thirteenth – they would invite John Hare to appear for one last time as the gasfitter Sam Gerridge. Hare was delighted to be asked. He wrote to Marie:

> It will be to me a source of the greatest pleasure to be once more 'Sam' to your 'Polly' on the occasion of your last appearance in *Caste*, associated as that play is, in my mind, with such a host of pleasant and kindly memories. Those old times were indeed happy ones, and the recollection of them is not easily to be effaced.

There was an unprecedented demand for seats for the final night of *Caste* and there were queues outside the Haymarket from early in the day. There was prolonged applause as each of the originals first appeared on stage, and Hare and the Bancrofts were cheered and clapped at each entrance. Throughout the evening, flowers were being delivered to Marie's dressing room, including one enormous concoction that spelled her name in roses. When the final curtain fell, the flowers were all brought onto the stage and as the curtain calls began, the set of the Eccles's kitchen was carpeted with bouquets. In the following weeks Marie received countless requests for mementos of *Caste*, and she sent out many small items of clothing that she had used or worn during the various productions, keeping for herself a few things as reminders of the play. Squire remembered watching her looking sadly at an apron, with the name 'Polly Eccles' embroidered across the waistband, before packing it up and sending it off to its new owner.

It was around this time, early in 1883, that there were some changes on the administrative side of the Haymarket. Although Squire Bancroft was the manager, and took on the greater part of the responsibility of running the theatre, it had always been necessary to have people on board to help with the smooth running of a large, busy operation. (The best-known of such people in the theatre world of that time was Bram Stoker, the author of *Dracula*, who was for many years Henry Irving's close friend and business manager at the Lyceum.) From their earliest days at the Prince of Wales's, the Bancrofts had always relied heavily on their 'treasurer', the chief accountant who cared for much of the day-to-day business side of things. For the past seven years Charles Walter had been treasurer as well as business manager at both theatres. In May of 1883 he suddenly fell ill and died, aged only forty-eight. As he had passed away so unexpectedly, his wife and five children were left entirely unprovided for. A fund was immediately launched on their behalf and within just a few days a substantial amount was raised in subscriptions, headed by the Bancrofts who gave £100. Other generous donors included Henry Irving, John L. Toole, William Terriss, Bram Stoker, James Fernandez*, Johnston Forbes-Robertson and many others. Over £400 was raised on behalf of Walter's bereaved family.

Too late for poor Charles Walter, it was decided that his workload at the Haymarket was probably too much for one person and that it should be divided between two people. Edward Russell, who had for some years been Irving's treasurer at the Lyceum, came in to take charge of the finances, and the job of secretary, and responsibility for front-of-house management, went to George Bashford, who had previously been an army officer with the Scots Greys, and who had married Augusta Wilton, four years earlier, in 1879. Augusta had been with her sister's company from the earliest days at the Prince of Wales's. Her husband had been acting-manager at the Olympic Theatre for the past couple of years and later he went on to become a theatre manager himself. The Bashfords had two children. Their daughter, Olive, followed in her mother's footsteps and became an actress and their son, Geoffrey, joined the Royal Navy, but died in 1913, aged only thirty-three. A further change that took place around this time was that the Haymarket's musical director, Meredith Ball, left to join Henry Irving at the Lyceum. In those days, and for many

---

* James Fernandez, 1835-1915, had a long and distinguished career on the London stage.

years to come, a play would be introduced by an overture and accompanied throughout by incidental music.

The word around London was that the Bancrofts were now heading for a fall. No one could believe that *Fédora* would succeed without Sarah Bernhardt. The Bancrofts had engaged a talented, statuesque twenty-seven-year-old actress called Fanny Bernard-Beere[*] to play the heroine, Princess Fédora, and she travelled to Paris to see Bernhardt play the part. Whether or not she wore a hat on stage like the one made famous by Sarah Bernhardt in the Paris production is uncertain, but most probably she did, as Bernhardt's 'fedora' quickly became a fashionable accessory for women in London as well as in Paris, although by 1900 it had become more widely worn by men.

Squire Bancroft had complete confidence in Mrs Bernard-Beere's abilities. She did not pretend to be Bernhardt and, knowing it would be unwise to attempt to copy the great French actress, she determined to interpret the part in her own style. Squire told a friend that he had never before come across an actress so easy to direct and 'who would more readily listen to suggestions, or work harder to embody them with life and meaning.'

two Fédoras: Sarah Bernhardt, Fanny Bernard-Beere

---

[*] Fanny Mary Bernard-Beere (née Whitehead), 1856-1915. Born in Norwich, the daughter of a landscape painter, she was married three times and always used the name of her second husband as her stage name. Her engagement to play Fédora at the Haymarket established her as one of the leading actresses of her day.

Squire was warned that the rumours flying around London predicted that *Fédora* would be 'the direst failure on record'. These rumours went so far as to suggest that the Haymarket secretly had another play in rehearsal, ready to replace *Fédora*, which would surely have to be withdrawn almost as soon as it opened. Squire cheerfully asked his pessimistic friends not to contradict the rumour-mongers, saying that if the audience came along to the first night anticipating a dire failure then 'it will only add warmth to their reception of a success.'

Fédora opened on 5 May 1883, and was the hit that Squire had anticipated. *The Theatre* was full of praise for Mrs Bernard-Beere's performance: 'Never did [her] superb acting more absolutely command our admiration.' However, the reviewer did not care for the play as a whole and went on to say: 'No interpretation, however faultless, no reception however magnificent, no criticism however brilliant, will ever make *Fédora* a good play.' Charles Coghlan, who had been back from the USA for the past couple of years, played the part of Fédora's lover, Loris Ipanoff, and there was a large supporting cast that included both Bancrofts, all of whom had received advice from a diplomat at the Russian embassy on the pronunciations of Russian names and places.

Berkeley Square in the nineteenth century, with no.18 on the left, between the two carriages

Early in the summer of 1883, soon after *Fédora* opened, the Bancrofts moved to a fine, large house at 18 Berkeley Square, in the heart of

239

fashionable Mayfair, near the corner with Bruton Street. Their house in Cavendish Square had been quite dark, and they welcomed the light and sun that now poured in, and the great square was so full of tall trees that, with or without nightingales, birdsong could be heard all day long. At a time when the Lord Chamberlain's regulations stipulated that a theatre manager's address had to be printed on every programme, nothing could have demonstrated the Bancrofts' success more than a move to such a prestigious address. Behind the house lay South Bruton Mews, where the Bancrofts' horse and carriage were stabled, with a flat above for their coachman, George Clibbens. A few years later Clibbens was to marry Caroline Lambkin, George Bancroft's much-loved nursemaid from the St John's Wood days, who had remained with the family as a housekeeper. Caroline was forty-two when she married the coachman; they had no children of their own. Many of the old houses of Berkeley Square, including No.18, have long been knocked down to create hundreds of square feet of bland office space.

When *Fédora* had been running for two months, on the very appropriate date of the Fourth of July, a great banquet was held in honour of Henry Irving, who was soon to embark on his first tour in the United States of America, along with Ellen Terry and many of the Lyceum company. It was still both a professional and a financial risk for an actor to set off across the Atlantic, where even one such as Irving, whose reputation would have gone before him, might find himself facing failure. The dinner was held in the vast St James's Hall, one of London's principal concert halls, opening both onto Piccadilly and onto the Regent Street Quadrant. The banquet was presided over by the Lord Chief Justice, Lord Coleridge, and there were nearly five hundred guests, all male, of course. However *The Era* reported that nearly four hundred women were permitted to sit and observe the proceedings from the balconies above: 'Among the representatives of the fair sex who were privileged to look down upon the more privileged "lords of creation" at Wednesday's banquet was Miss Ellen Terry, who has so nobly shared in the Lyceum triumphs, and whose arrival was greeted with a ringing outburst of applause.' However, *The Era* did not say whether Ellen and the other women seated above were provided with any kind of refreshment while the men enjoyed their feast.

Squire Bancroft was appearing in *Fédora* at the Haymarket, a few hundred yards away, at the same time as the dinner. However, his part was a minor one and he was not required on stage until the first act was well underway. So, in full evening dress and stage make up, ready for his part of a French diplomat, he attended the soup course of the dinner, hurrying away before the fish. He was free again well before the end of the second act, which was followed by an interval, so he dashed back

240

again to St James's Hall just in time to hear the toast to the guest of honour, and to hear most of Irving's reply. Then he had to hasten back for the third act of *Fédora*. Once again, his part was concluded before the end of the play, so back he went once more, missing the curtain calls, in time to hear the concluding speeches.

Even though Bancroft could not have had much dinner, all his to-ing and fro-ing between the theatre and the St James's Hall enabled him to catch plenty of the speeches, which must have lasted for a couple of hours. The Lord Chief Justice proposed four toasts, each preceded by a speech. The first was to the Queen, the next to the rest of the royal family and then one to the United States of America, on its Independence Day. His final toast was to the guest of honour, Henry Irving, accompanied by his longest speech of all. Irving responded with a mercifully short speech and then there followed a succession of toasts and responses, from no fewer than five more people. 'Literature, Science and Art' were toasted together, each followed by its own response, with Lawrence Alma-Tadema RA[*] responding for 'Art'. Irving's close friend, John Lawrence Toole, then stood to toast the chairman, the Lord Chief Justice, who at long last closed the proceedings with a final speech of thanks. Between the speeches the guests were entertained by well-known singers. *The Era* reported each speech word for word, in a report that took up well over a full broadsheet page.

A short while later Squire Bancroft organised a more modest 'farewell supper' for Irving, at the Garrick Club, with a mere ninety guests. Dinner began at midnight as most of the guests were from the profession, and would have been unable to attend any earlier. The president of the Garrick, responding to Bancroft's request for this very late start, replied that the occasion would be 'an honour to the club'. The dinner was attended by almost every (male) name in the theatre of the day. When Bancroft stood to propose Irving's health, he joked that should his words fail him in his speech, he had the perfect understudy present, who 'not only could pick me up but take me off so well,' so that the assembled diners would be unable to tell the difference. This was a reference to the inevitable burlesque of *Fédora* that was being performed at the nearby Toole's Theatre[*], with Bancroft's part being brilliantly parodied by a young actor who was present at the dinner. A then very young

---

[*] Sir Lawrence Alma-Tadema, RA, 1836-1912, renowned for his paintings, mainly of classical subjects, was knighted in 1899.

[*] J.L.Toole was the first actor to have a West End theatre named after him. The Folly Theatre, renamed Toole's Theatre, near Charing Cross, was managed by him from 1879. It was demolished in 1895.

caricaturist, Phil May*, did a drawing of Irving, with Bancroft and Toole, all looking distinctly 'tired and emotional', staggering out of the Garrick Club following the dinner.

Irving, Toole, Bancroft: caricature by Phil May

John Hare then proposed the health of their host that night, Squire Bancroft. He spoke of the friendship they had held for each other over the years but he spoke as though they were both now elderly men, at one point referring to Bancroft being in 'the evening of his life' – he was, in 1883, only forty-two and Hare himself was still only thirty-nine. 'It seems to me a peculiarly fit and gracious thing that we should have been invited by the oldest and most successful manager in London to drink "bon voyage" and "God-speed" to its most distinguished and successful actor.'

Irving, accompanied by Ellen Terry, Bram Stoker and a large contingent from the Lyceum, departed for their six-month tour of the USA in October, returning in the spring of 1884, when late one evening Marie and Squire Bancroft were on their way to bed and heard a loud

---

* Philip William (Phil) May, 1864-1903, was to become famous for his work for *Punch* and other magazines.

knocking at their front door. A servant unfastened the door-chain and opened up and then a familiar voice was heard from below enquiring if Squire and Marie were at home. They both hurried downstairs again to find that Irving had arrived back in London that very evening and had called by in the hope that the Bancrofts would still be up. In the entrance hall he embraced Squire warmly, remarking 'How white you've grown, old fellow!' The three of them talked long into the night, with Irving telling of his travels and his experiences in America.

In 1883, legislation regarding public safety in theatres was introduced in response to the fire at the Alhambra, and an earlier, even more disastrous, fire at a theatre in Vienna in 1881, in which over six hundred people had died. Many London theatres were forced to end their seasons early in the summer of 1883, so that the necessary adaptations could be made. In the Haymarket this involved complicated building works, in spite of the major renovation only three years earlier.

That year the Bancrofts, for once forsaking their beloved Engadine valley, went instead to Bad Homburg, a spa and casino town in Germany, to see if taking the waters there might help relieve Marie's annual hay fever. The resort was full of wealthy English visitors. Squire Bancroft wrote that: 'Sometimes in the early morning the crowd of health-seekers was very largely Park and Piccadilly in its character .... We met and made no end of friends, and passed a pleasant "cure".' However, Squire was sceptical of the treatments offered by the different German watering-places:

> The waters may be laden with iron or charged with salt; the baths may be of pine, or perhaps of mud; still the life is much the same: there is generally a strong family resemblance between the Schloss, the Kursaal[*], the band, and the constant evidence of the Kaiser's vast army. Whichever the Bad you choose, the stall-keepers seem ubiquitous, and pursue their victims with their corals, their tortoise-shells, and their filigrees....

Following the extended summer break there were some changes in the cast of *Fédora*. Mrs Bernard-Beere stayed on in the part of the heroine but Charles Coghlan had decided to return to America and asked to be released from his contract, so, with some reservations, Bancroft took over the part of Loris Ipanoff himself, as he could not find any other suitable replacement for Coghlan. He was right to be anxious. On his return to London the building works were still in progress at the Haymarket and the stage was unusable for rehearsals, so he felt he was insufficiently prepared. *The Theatre*'s reviewer was critical of his performance,

---

[*] Kursaal: the public rooms, or entertainment hall, at a spa resort.

suggesting he had not the capacity for such a demanding part: 'To comprehend the passionate love Loris bears for Fédora is one thing; to portray this love, so as to make an audience believe in it, is entirely another – a power which Mr Bancroft evidently does not possess.' Squire felt that his performance did improve with time and that eventually it became 'among the best of my efforts as an actor'. Nevertheless, the resumption of *Fédora* failed to recapture the audiences it had pulled in earlier in the summer. Another reason for the falling off of interest in the play was that Marie was no longer in the cast. Even when she was playing a minor role, her presence in a play remained a major factor in attracting audiences. *Fédora*, although less of a success than Squire had anticipated, more than paid its way. It came off in November, when Pinero's new four-act play, *Lords and Commons*, was ready.

The son of a Sephardic Jewish solicitor of Portuguese origins, Arthur Wing Pinero had set out to follow in his father's footsteps by studying law, but soon put this aside to become an actor at the age of nineteen. 'Pin' first played under the Bancrofts' management in 1881 and had become a close friend. He was almost bald, with dark bushy eyebrows. A natty dresser, he invariably wore gloves. Pinero and Squire would often go cycling together and sometimes 'Pin' joined the Bancrofts in the Engadine where they would go for strenuous walks in the mountains. He was never tremendously successful as an actor but while he was acting he was also writing plays, mostly popular comedies. He was to become one of the leading dramatists of his time, and some of his work is still much enjoyed today.

John Hare and the Kendals produced several of Pinero's plays at the St James's Theatre, the first of these being *The Money Spinner* in 1881. Later that year they produced *The Squire*, concerning the lives of a beautiful young female landowner, the 'Squire' of the title, a dashing young officer and a loyal farm worker. This proved controversial: it had obvious similarities to Thomas Hardy's *Far from the Madding Crowd,* and Pinero was accused of plagiarism. Later in the 1880s and into the '90s came the plays touching on more socially significant topics, some of which remain familiar works today, notably *The Second Mrs Tanqueray* in 1893 and *The Notorious Mrs Ebbsmith* in 1895. Pinero was awarded a knighthood in 1909 and he died in 1934.

At the Haymarket Pinero shared in directing *Lords and Commons* himself. Bancroft considered he did this well, and reflected on the abilities of various playwrights as directors of their own work. Pinero 'rehearsed his play with great skill,' he wrote, 'giving all concerned a clear insight into the value of his characters: an art rarely possessed in the highest degree by author-actors, as, for instance, Dion Boucicault and T.W.Robertson and W.S.Gilbert. H.J.Byron, strange to say, was devoid of the power.' Indeed, Byron was well-known for detesting rehearsals.

Robert Reece, another writer of burlesques and comic plays, wrote of him: 'He would creep out of the theatre and walk around Covent Garden Market for a whole afternoon,' rather than be around while one of his plays was being rehearsed.

Pinero and Bancroft in the Engadine, 1898:
the scenery could be a studio backdrop

Lords and Commons was loosely based on a Swedish novel and was distinctly anti-aristocracy – a surprising subject to appeal to the Bancrofts, who loved nothing more than a good title. Complete with the usual lavish sets, interiors in a great ancestral hall, and a landscaped parkland exterior set, it told the improbable story of a pretty young woman who is thrown out by her husband's appalled (and appalling) family of English aristocrats, the Caryls, when they discover that she is illegitimate. She goes off to America, returning to England unrecognised many years later, having somehow acquired a fortune, and avenges

245

herself by buying up the now impoverished Caryl estate. Accompanied by an Englishman who had been prospecting for gold in California and a lively young American woman, played by Squire and Marie Bancroft, she proceeds to cause havoc among the Caryls who are first disdainful but then captivated by the transatlantic visitors.

Strangely, the very English daughter of the Caryl family was played by a young American actress called Eleanor Calhoun, whose own rags-to-riches life story would make a romantic novel in itself. Born in 1857, she spent her childhood in poverty, in a dirt-floored log cabin among the Californian goldfields. She was taken up by the millionaire Hearst family, and met their young son. They fell in love, but his family, as much or more snobbish than any English aristocrats, threatened to disinherit him if he married his 'Nellie'. The young man chose his inheritance over his love and went on to find fame as the newspaper magnate William Randolph Hearst. To get Eleanor out of the way, Hearst's mother paid for her to go to Europe, where she made a successful career as an actress. She eventually married a Serbian prince and lived to the great age of a hundred.

Lords and Commons was not one of Pinero's better works. Those were yet to come. Written early in his career as a dramatist, *Lords and Commons* barely features in lists of his works. It received mixed reviews, some of them very bad and, perhaps unsurprisingly, it was not well received in the stalls and the dress-circle, where the upper-crust were not amused by its theme. The first two acts were very slow and far too long, although it picked up towards the end. Only Marie Bancroft was a sure-fire hit on the first night. *The Theatre* reported that as the young American woman she 'elicits unlimited applause by her open and persistent flirtatiousness. She finds ample opportunity for the display of that irresistible fund of humour which is as genuine as it is inimitable.'

Surprisingly, the critic William Archer came to the defence of the play in January. Archer was not normally a great admirer of the Bancrofts but was known to be one of Pinero's closest friends, which may be why he sprang so enthusiastically to his defence. Although he considered that the most improbable point of the plot was '.... that a young nobleman in the nineteenth century should repudiate an innocent girl .... merely because of her inferiority of birth,' he nevertheless went on to say that he was pleasantly surprised at how much he enjoyed the play. 'The dialogue I thought admirable, the character sketches original.' Archer saw the play from high up in the 'gods', where the audience reaction was very different from that of the elite below. 'The audience seemed to have shared my feeling,' he wrote in *The Theatre*. 'I was too far aloft to notice the antagonism of the stalls, and I can answer for the interest and amusement with which the unreserved parts of the house followed the performance. My surprise was great, then, on opening the next week's papers, to find it treated on all hands with ridicule, contempt or indignation.'

The *New York Times* reviewer also approved, particularly the performances of the young couple: '…. it owes its success greatly to the really splendid acting of Mrs Bernard-Beere, admirably seconded by Mr Forbes-Robertson.' However, one performance the *NYT* did not appreciate was that of Squire Bancroft: 'The acting is most excellent all round, except, perhaps, in the case of Mr Bancroft, who …. has a part that does not fit him well.' *Lords and Commons*, although generally considered a failure, did in fact play to full houses, certainly for its first few weeks and was ultimately profitable for the Haymarket.

Also in the cast of *Lords and Commons* was a veteran actress, seventy-year-old Mary Anne 'Fanny' Stirling, who played the vindictive old mother of the young husband. Her performance was admired by the *New York Times* reviewer: 'Dear old Mrs Stirling, incomparable as an impersonator of *grandes dames*, plays the part of the aged Countess of Caryl with distinction.' She was not in the best of health but never missed a rehearsal or a performance. Marie Bancroft wrote of the devotion of Mrs Stirling and her like:

> It would be very interesting to an audience to be given now and then a peep behind the scenes, or in the green room; they would often see what good servants to the public are the actors; how often, when suffering acute pain, they have gone through their work so bravely that the audience has not detected even a look of it …. I have known that grand old actress, Mrs Stirling, when suffering from a severe attack of bronchitis, to go to the theatre in all weathers and at great risk …. when she ought to have been in bed. I have seen her arrive scarcely able to breathe, but insisting upon going through her duties. [Her] sight being impaired, she always dreaded stairs; unfortunately for her, in the hall of Caryl Court, there was a long gallery and then a tall flight of steps leading from it to the stage, while behind the scenes there was another flight to reach this gallery. Luckily she did not enter alone, but had the kindly help of Miss Eleanor Calhoun, who played her daughter in the piece …. One would imagine, to see her slowly and cautiously ascend the flight of steps, stopping every now and then to murmur 'Oh, these stairs!' that she would scarcely be able to get through her part; but although she has stood gasping for breath, the moment her cue came she seemed to become twenty years younger; vigour returned to her limbs, and she walked with such a firm and stately gait that the change was extraordinary.

The remarkable Fanny Stirling's long and distinguished career spanned a great part of the nineteenth century. Born in 1813, and first appearing in the early 1830s, she played mostly in comedy, but also, while in her twenties, played Desdemona, Cordelia and Portia. In 1852 she created the part of Peg Woffington in *Masks and Faces* that was later to be played by Marie Bancroft. The year before *Lords and Commons* at the Haymarket, Mrs Stirling first came out of retirement to play the Nurse in *Romeo and Juliet* at the Lyceum, with Henry Irving and Ellen Terry, and was said to have stolen the show from the two stars. When she died, in 1895, *The Times* obituary read: 'Mrs Stirling was beautiful, graceful, and indomitable .... one of the most vivacious and bewitching comedy actresses of her time.'

Mrs Fanny Stirling

11

EXEUNT

With 1883 drawing to a close, and *Lords and Commons* attracting reasonable but not huge audiences, Marie and Squire Bancroft were beginning to contemplate the unthinkable: retirement from 'the cares of management'. In the four years since they had moved to the Haymarket they had met with what Squire described as 'unthought-of success', financially and professionally. Indeed they had become seriously wealthy, while their reputation in the theatrical world, established long before they left the Prince of Wales's, was now confirmed as pre-eminent amongst the managements in London. Even the great Irving at the Lyceum regarded Squire Bancroft as the 'senior manager' in London as he had been in harness for some years longer than himself.

Initially the Bancrofts resolved not to speak openly of their thoughts of early retirement, fearing that they might regret it if they rushed into anything too soon; so for the time being they kept their thoughts to themselves. Having started out in management when they were both so young, Marie and Squire had been carrying the stresses and burdens connected with running a theatre for some eighteen years. The age they had now reached, their mid-forties, we would today regard as early middle-age. Back then, it would have been considered as approaching elderly, as Squire was reminded when John Hare, speaking of him at the Irving dinner a few months before, said he was in 'the evening of his life'. Certainly the strain was beginning to get to them. Squire wrote, 'Only those closely connected with the entire control of a popular and successful theatre can know the mental and bodily strain it means, and they alone can count the cost, in wear and tear, which buys its prizes.'

Meanwhile, the work at the Haymarket went on. As it turned out, *Lords and Commons* was to be the last original play that the Bancrofts were ever to produce. From now on, until they retired, they relied on revivals. A new production of *Peril* was to be accompanied by a curtain-raiser, *A Lesson*, a one-act piece by F.C.Burnand that they had used before. The small cast included Marie as a teacher of acting, with Eleanor Calhoun as her pupil, and Charles Brookfield and Johnston Forbes-Robertson in the two male parts. Marie was not in *Peril*, although Squire was, along with Fanny Bernard-Beere, Forbes-Robertson and Marie's sister, Augusta Bashford. It opened on 16 February 1884.

That spring was described by Squire Bancroft as a time when 'the King of Terrors was busy with his remorseless scythe'. In March Queen Victoria's youngest son, Prince Leopold, Duke of Albany, whose autograph book Marie had signed the previous summer, died as a result of the haemophilia he had suffered from all his life. He was just thirty-one. All London's theatres closed on the night of his funeral and a letter of condolence was sent to Leopold's brother, the Prince of Wales, signed by many of the leading actors then in London. Squire Bancroft, as the senior manager, was chosen to deliver it. Then, on Good Friday, 11 April, the playwrights Henry James Byron and Charles Reade both died on the same day. Reade was seventy and Byron was not yet fifty.

'Harry' Byron's early death distressed the Bancrofts greatly as their relationship went back to when Marie had first appeared in his burlesques at the Strand in the 1850s. Although their short-lived partnership at the Prince of Wales's had ended in disagreement, this had not soured their lifelong friendship, neither being the type to bear a grudge. Famed for his wit and charm, Byron was a much-loved figure in the world of the theatre, both in his early days as an indifferent actor and later as a popular playwright. Of his personality Marie wrote that he 'was the epitome of good nature; the most charming companion in the world, often keeping everyone about him in fits of laughter, when it was most amusing to see him laugh till he cried at his own jokes, and his laughter was so infectious that, no matter what humour one was in, a grave countenance was impossible.' 'Poor dear Byron!' wrote Squire. 'How the hours seemed to fly in his companionship! His very name meant fun. Perhaps no writer ever had a greater power in twisting his language into puns, while his intense appreciation of another's joke was delightful to see.' An obituary writer described him as 'the most lovable, most unselfish, the wittiest, brightest man of his time.'

The dramatist Charles Reade, author with Tom Taylor of one of the Bancrofts' most celebrated productions, *Masks and Faces*, lived a life as full of controversy as a novel. He neither drank nor smoked and was an ardent campaigner for such varied causes as animal rights and penal reform. His relationships with women, usually actresses, were often scandalous. When they were both young he was involved with the redoubtable Fanny Stirling and later he lived with another actress, Laura Seymour, until her death in 1879. He was also believed to have been in love with Ellen Terry – but then most men of his day were. His highly acclaimed novels and his plays probably earned him as much as almost any other writer of his time. Squire Bancroft wrote that his 'world-wide fame as a novelist and man of letters entitles his name to be enrolled among the literary giants of the age.' But he is now a fallen giant. By the end of the nineteenth century he was out of fashion, and today only one of his works, his best-known novel, *The Cloister and the Hearth*, is still occasionally bought and sold – if only in second-hand bookshops.

Undeterred by the failure of *The Merchant of Venice* nine years earlier, the Bancrofts, Squire in particular, had for some time been keen to try another Shakespeare comedy. He had *The Merry Wives of Windsor* in mind, as Marie would have shone either as Mistress Ford or Mistress Page. But this idea had to be put aside as they could not find the right Falstaff. Either John Clayton or the portly Arthur Cecil would have been ideal for the part, but these two were unavailable as they were now in partnership managing the Royal Court at Sloane Square. So they opted for another classic comedy instead, Sheridan's *The Rivals*, with the help of Arthur Wing Pinero, who undertook various revisions, mainly to avoid too many scene changes. Rehearsals had started before Christmas and continued for some months. The Bancrofts planned their usual lavish and meticulously authentic sets. *The Rivals* is set in eighteenth-century Bath, so their stage designer went there to make sketches and designs for recreating what was then 'the last century'. The Bancrofts, together with Pinero, 'tried the patience of those kind friends in the reading-room of the British Museum, who cheerfully devoted considerable time towards helping our researches to learn all we could of the fashionable resort of our forefathers.' Johnston Forbes-Robertson designed the costumes.

Forbes-Robertson had joined the Bancrofts' company in 1879, in *Duty* at the Prince of Wales's. Born in 1853, he was a gifted artist. Dante Gabriel Rossetti saw one of his early oil paintings, done when he was around fifteen, and advised that the boy should go to art school. This he did, studying initially at the Heatherley School of Fine Art, followed by three years at the Royal Academy. But in spite of this promising future as a painter he chose the stage as his career and was to become one of the best-known actors of his time, being a particularly renowned Hamlet in 1897. He was extremely handsome. Ellen Terry wrote of him: 'Everyone knows how good-looking he is now, but as a boy he was wonderful – a dreamy, poetic-looking creature in a blue smock, far more of an artist than an actor …. full of aspirations and ideals.' He did not give up painting entirely: his fine portrait of Samuel Phelps as Cardinal Wolsey is part of

251

the Garrick Club collection and he did a large painting of a great scene from *Much Ado About Nothing* at the Lyceum in 1882. It is packed with identifiable figures. As well as Irving as Benedick and Ellen Terry as Beatrice, it includes William Terriss as Don Pedro, Terriss's lover Jessie Millward as Hero, James Fernandez as Leonato and Forbes-Robertson himself as Claudio, as well as dozens of supers – priests, soldiers and ladies – crowding the stage. This painting is now in America.

Johnston Forbes-Robertson at his easel

The Rivals opened on 3 May 1884, Squire Bancroft and Arthur Pinero having jointly directed the play. Marie Bancroft might have played the lovely part of Mrs Malaprop, but this idea was abandoned, as the marvellous old lady, Mrs Fanny Stirling, was free and to make use of her services as Mrs Malaprop was an opportunity not to be missed.

In the event, 3 May turned out to be a calamitous first night. From behind the stage, during the opening scenes, the actors could sense hostility from the audience. Nevertheless Squire was totally unprepared for the moment when he made his first entrance. He was greeted by 'hooting and hisses' from the gallery, mingled with some rather sedate applause from the stalls, which entirely failed to drown out the clamour from above. This reception was totally mystifying. It was like the night of the 'pit riot' all over again, but with no apparent reason. It was not until after the final curtain that the cause for the antagonistic reception was revealed. The unfortunate occupiers of the gallery and upper circle seats, which were all unreserved, had to queue outside the theatre for each performance. On this occasion, while a long line of people was waiting patiently in the street, there had been a sudden downpour. As a result, many of them were soaked before they could get inside, even though the doors had been opened early so they could be admitted ahead of the usual time. A couple of years before Marie Bancroft had had a large awning installed above the pavement to protect the people waiting for admittance. This had to be set up and taken down each day and had worked well for many months. Then one day, while it was being erected, one of its metal struts fell on a passer-by. No serious injury was sustained, apart from wrecking the man's hat, but a large claim for damages was brought against the Haymarket. Rather than risk the huge expense of contesting the amount claimed, Bancroft agreed to settle out of court for £600 – the equivalent of around £30,000 in today's money. It is not just in our 'health and safety' conscious twenty-first century that claims for damages following minor accidents can – in this case literally at the drop of a hat – lead to huge financial penalties. Bancroft applied for planning permission to erect a permanent structure to shelter the Haymarket queues from the elements but this was refused; so, rather than risk any repetition of the accident, the use of the awning was discontinued and the patrons of the Haymarket once more had to take their chances with the weather.

This unfortunate start must have seemed like an omen as *The Rivals* did not go particularly well, although it more than paid for itself. As a whole the season of 1883-84 was the least successful of their entire time at the Haymarket. Bancroft put this down largely to the fact that for most of the season the theatre had lacked its star attraction – the only parts that Marie had played during the entire period had been limited to a small one in *Lords and Commons* and the lead in Burnand's short play, *A Lesson*. The reviews for *The Rivals* were not good: *The Theatre* thought that Pinero, who had virtually given up acting by this time, was an 'unfortunate selection' as Sir Anthony Absolute, complaining that he played the part in a 'tediously monotonous falsetto voice'. Nor did the reviewer like Forbes-Robertson as the young hero, Captain Jack Absolute, saying that he seemed 'to possess but little idea of the frank, careless manner of a dashing young officer', and they had no good words for Eleanor Calhoun as Lydia Languish. There was grudging praise for Mrs Bernard-Beere in the part that Squire described as 'the mawkish Julia', and also for Squire Bancroft himself, which must have pleased him, as his own part of Faulkland was not to his liking. The only person who received the wholehearted approval of the reviewer was Fanny Stirling: 'How admirable is the Mrs Malaprop of Mrs Stirling .... this true artist completely lapses personal identity in the part of this vain, ungrammatical old woman, whose extraordinary vagaries of speech elicit such unbounded applause and merriment.'

So the season of 1883-84 ended on a faintly unsatisfactory note and the Bancrofts headed for Pontresina for the summer to recover from their disappointments. This was followed by a fortnight in Brighton, where they relaxed with the many friends who were also staying there. They also had plenty of time to reflect and discuss their thoughts of retirement. They had made a fortune over the years of management and could afford to retire and live in comfort for the rest of their days. They decided that the forthcoming season would definitely be their last and that in the future they would limit their professional appearances to very occasional ones. On their return to London, before publicly announcing their intention, they began by writing private letters to inform close friends of their decision. After these had been sent, the news was released to the press: 'Mr and Mrs Bancroft beg to announce that this will be their Farewell Season. Soon after the twentieth anniversary of the opening of the Prince of Wales's Theatre on April 15th, 1865, they will retire from management.'

They were inundated with letters. There were hundreds of them, of mixed regret and congratulation. Arthur Wing Pinero wrote: 'When the history of the stage and its progress is adequately and faithfully written, Mrs Bancroft's name and your own must be recorded with honour and gratitude.' Francis Burnand, the editor of *Punch*, wrote humorously to Squire: 'You are a lucky man, and a wise one .... At *your* age to be able to retire! Wouldn't *I* if I could! But I shall *never* be able to retire; never free, never out of harness, until I lie down in the loose-box and am carried off to the knacker's, unless I go to the dogs by some shorter and cheaper route. Yours ever, F.C.B.'

The poet Robert Browning wrote: 'Are you too tired of being told how much everybody admires and loves you both? .... All happiness to you, from yours gratefully and affectionately ever, Robert Browning.' They had first met Browning some years earlier at a wedding reception when Marie Bancroft had mistaken the back-view of the poet for the bride's father. Taking him by the arm to turn him around to face her, she embraced him warmly and congratulated him before realising her mistake. Browning said he hoped that whenever they met in the future she would always greet him in the same way – which from then on she always did – 'more than once in the open street', Squire revealed. Their oldest and closest friend and colleague wrote warmly: 'You have both worked well and loyally, have done the stage the highest service, and well deserve your rest. That the same good fortune which has attached itself to you in your public career may follow you in all things in your private life is the very sincere wish of your old friend and fellow-worker, John Hare.'

Following the announcement in the press there were reports and articles in many newspapers. In one of these Squire Bancroft was quoted as saying that he hoped he and Marie 'had the .... good sense and resolution not to wait until they were superfluous veterans, a part few can play with grace.' One paper ran a long interview, in which Squire was asked why they were giving up management while still 'in the prime of life', to which he replied that they felt it was better to retire while they were 'still high in public favour, one iota of which we should be sorry to lose.' In other words, they had decided that they should get out while they were still on top, rather than wait until the theatre got on top of them. 'The management of a theatre involves a great deal of attention every day, to say nothing of the perpetual strain of always working months ahead ....' he went on. 'We do not complain. The public have repaid our liberality in management by yet larger liberality.' They were asked about their production methods, their determination that a play should be perfectly prepared and rehearsed throughout, not being just a vehicle for its leading actors but with every actor in the play important, in however minor a role. 'It was our ambition to have every small part in a comedy played as well as possible, and after continued preparation. We began with three weeks' rehearsal for a play, extended it to six, since to a couple of months, and in some cases longer.'

The subject of the pay and working conditions of actors was brought up. 'You are, I think, responsible in great measure for the present high salaries paid to actors,' the interviewer remarked. 'Salaries have risen, certainly, to an extraordinary extent,' Squire replied. 'During our career we have paid the same actor, for playing the same part, eighteen and sixty pounds a week, with an interval of ten years only .... When that great artist, Mrs Stirling, played in *Caste* at the Haymarket [in 1882], she received *seven times* the salary of the original Marquise de St Maur in 1867.' Asked what was the highest salary they had ever paid, Squire replied, without specifying to whom, 'For a special engagement, a hundred pounds a week .... No, it was not Mrs Langtry! When we induced Miss Ellen Terry to return to the stage in 1875 she was content with twenty pounds a week, which was considered a high price then. Our finding her, and bringing her back to the stage, is one of our brightest recollections. It was a victory which consoled us amply for an awful defeat.' This improvement in actors' pay, led by the Bancrofts, had in time been followed by most of the other London managements.

The original move towards better pay was driven partly by their objections to the system whereby actors and actresses were expected to supplement their meagre wages by having a 'benefit' on their behalf once or twice a year. In Dickens's *Nicholas Nickleby*, one of Nicholas's first tasks having joined Mr Crummles's troupe of players was to accompany the leading lady around town trying to sell seats for her 'bespeak', or benefit, which was shortly to take place. The Bancrofts believed that actors should be paid a proper wage and that benefits should only take place on special occasions, such as on the retirement of an old actor or actress or for members of theatre staff, or if they had fallen on hard times, for instance through sickness, on behalf of their widows and children, in similar circumstances. By the 1880s a benefit for a retiring actor could raise a sum well into four figures, enough money to allow the beneficiary to live out his or her days in some small comfort.

The Bancrofts took part in benefits for their colleagues for such special occasions, as in 1870 when there had been a star-studded benefit at Covent Garden for the popular actor Charles James Mathews, who was about to depart for Australia. The long, mixed programme included performances from Toole, Buckstone, Madame Celeste, Alfred Wigan, H.J.Byron and many others. The Bancrofts played a scene from Robertson's *School*, in which, Marie, as the schoolgirl Naomi Tighe, was asked, 'What do you consider the most valuable possession in Australia?' Marie's reply, to the delight of the audience, was 'Mr Charles Mathews.'

They had also been responsible for improving the conditions under which actors worked. They were among the first to provide costumes and accessories for their actors, rather than expecting them to provide them for themselves, as had been the norm in their own young days, and actors working for the Bancrofts had their pay packets brought to their dressing rooms at the end of each week. Until then all actors had been expected to queue up for their wages each Saturday outside the treasurer's office, a seemingly minor reform, but one greatly appreciated by actors.

It seems extraordinary today that the retirement of a couple of stage actors should make such headline news but the British public has always loved its stars and celebrities. The only truly visible stars and celebrities before the days of film, television, and the multi-million pound business that sport has now become, were the stars of the theatre and the music hall, which were attended by people from every level of society. The faces of stage stars were familiar from photographs, which were bought and collected by thousands, and actors were among those featured in the famous caricatures by 'Spy'* and 'Ape' in the magazine *Vanity Fair*. A 'Spy' portrait of Squire Bancroft appeared in 1891. Then there were stories and sketches in gossip magazines as well as long articles in publications dedicated to the theatre. The chief difference between these magazines and their equivalent today was that, with no paparazzi to

---

* The caricaturists 'Spy' and 'Ape' were Sir Leslie Ward, 1851-1922, and Italian-born Carlo Pellegrini, 1839-89. Their *Vanity Fair* prints are much collected today.

pursue the stars, there were far fewer pictures and far more text – and less salacious probing into their private lives.

the Bancrofts, around the time of their retirement

The Bancrofts' farewell season was unambitious. They decided it would be made up entirely of revivals of old favourites, starting with *Diplomacy*. The play, one of the Bancrofts' greatest successes at the Prince of Wales's, had not been seen in London since their original production seven years before. By 1884 no fewer than four of the original cast were now in management themselves, the Kendals, John Clayton and Arthur Cecil. Both the Bancrofts' earlier parts were now played by new members of the company: Marie's part of the wicked Countess Zicka was taken by Fanny Bernard-Beere and Squire handed on his part of Count Orloff to a visiting American, Maurice Barrymore. Born in India in 1849 to English parents, Maurice Barrymore was educated at Harrow and Oxford but had gone to America in 1874 where he made his name as an actor. The first of the great dynasty of theatrical Barrymores, he was the father of Lionel, Ethel and John Barrymore and great-grandfather of the film actress, Drew Barrymore. In 1884 Maurice was on a visit to England and joined the

Haymarket company for a few months. Johnston Forbes-Robertson and Eleanor Calhoun were also in the cast of *Diplomacy*.

Squire Bancroft did not usually make first-night speeches, but on the first night of the farewell season he was called for continuously until he went before the curtain to address the audience, saying, 'You will excuse my thinking your applause tonight to be a wish that I should break my rule. It would be an affectation not to know that part of that applause is provoked by the announcement of our intended retirement .... I will only say now that I have the opinion that no one in any walk of life should keep a position of command too long; and if my wife and I between us have held the reins of management for nearly twenty years, you must forgive us on the plea that we were both exceptionally young when we first took them up.'

In the spring of 1885, during a performance of *Diplomacy*, there was a narrow escape from catastrophe at the Haymarket when a piece of scenery caught fire. As theatre fires had until comparatively recently been alarmingly frequent – the Alhambra disaster had happened less than three years earlier – and could rapidly get out of control and spread through the entire building, the audience was instantly alarmed. Squire Bancroft, seeing that the flames were small enough to be dealt with quickly and easily, took Marie by the arm and walked onto the stage with her. The pair of them stood in front of the flames while the fire team tackled the blaze with buckets of water and the wet blankets that were always kept at the ready. The fire was extinguished, the relieved audience relaxed again and the play was resumed.

Diplomacy was followed by another old favourite, *Masks and Faces*, the Bancrofts once more playing their old parts of Peg Woffington and Triplet. The sentimental old comedy was again well received. One review made Squire Bancroft particularly happy: 'A very able and .... not too easily-pleased critic, Mr William Archer, did me the honour to write his opinion in these words: "There is no more delicate .... piece of acting than Mr Bancroft's Triplet on the English stage .... Such acting would move a heart of stone or an eye of glass. Everyone who has not seen it should see it forthwith, and everyone who has seen it once, twice, or thrice should see it again." The writer of those lines doubtless does not know how much they meant to me.' One day an afternoon performance of *Masks and Faces* was given at the Crystal Palace, where there was a large theatre. It was received with huge enthusiasm by the audience, mainly of women. After the show, when the Bancrofts left, they found a long line of ladies waiting for them outside. Marie had bouquets of flowers thrust into her hands and Squire shook many hands while they both spoke with as many as possible of their admirers.

After *Masks and Faces* the farewell season continued with a triple bill of *Sweethearts*, W.S.Gilbert's popular short romance, which was played along with Buckstone's *Good for Nothing* and *Katherine and Petruchio*, David Garrick's arrangement of *The Taming of the Shrew*, with Fanny Bernard-Beere as Katherine and Johnston Forbes-Robertson as Petruchio. The final season would not be complete without a Tom Robertson play so, the Bancrofts' rights having expired and with their last-ever productions of *Caste* and *School* having been done in 1883, the author's son gave permission for a final production of *Ours*, in which for the very last time the Bancrofts played Hugh Chalcot and Mary Netley.

All the while, rumours had been circulating that the real reason for the Bancrofts' retirement was that their Haymarket years had been less successful than those at the Prince of Wales's. A piece appeared in the press, headed, 'Plays at Popular Prices', stating, correctly, that 'Mr Bancroft was the pioneer of the dear stall. He abolished the pit at the theatre designed under his eye.' It continued less accurately: 'Eventually he had gracefully to confess to failure and it would be well if those who followed his lead admitted an error in judgment.' To begin with, Bancroft paid no attention but he eventually decided to correct the press rumour, writing: 'It is true that in 1874, owing to constantly increasing outlay at the Prince of Wales's Theatre, I instituted the ten-shilling stall .... But I never had reason to regret either being "the pioneer of the dear stall" or having "abolished the pit". I don't know to what failure I "had gracefully to confess".' He went on to deny that their resignation from management was because they had met with less success at the Haymarket than at the smaller theatre. 'I have always refrained from parading the profits and losses of management .... But briefly, our management of the Haymarket Theatre (notwithstanding the large amount expended in its reconstruction, which was borne entirely by us) resulted in almost doubling the sum we had realised at the Prince of Wales's Theatre.'

Later, in his memoirs, Squire Bancroft noted down some figures. 'Here,' he wrote, 'are a few final financial statements which will help to make theatrical history. The nightly expenses at the old Prince of Wales's Theatre never exceeded £70; at the Haymarket, when we began there, they reached £100, and had increased by the end of our stay to £120. £10,000 was spent at various times in altering and decorating the little old theatre; £20,000 in the same way at the Haymarket. The net profit on the twenty years' management exceeded the sum of £180,000.'

The Bancrofts' final night at the Theatre Royal, Haymarket was Monday 20 July, 1885. The policy of unreserved seats in the upper circle and gallery was rigorously adhered to, and those seats had to be queued for as on any other day. Thankfully it was a dry day, for by ten in the morning large numbers of people were queueing up with camp stools and sandwiches, prepared for a long wait. By late afternoon, those people who had been lucky enough to obtain ticketed seats started to arrive. Cabs and carriages began to congest the Haymarket and the police arrived to control the traffic. Inside the theatre the comfortable seats had been removed from the stalls and the dress circle and replaced with smaller chairs in order to squeeze more people in; every empty space that could be found – behind the back row, in front of the front row, in every corner and in every aisle – had been filled with extra seating. Marie wrote that the Haymarket was 'as closely packed as a box of sardines'. Not one more person could be squeezed in and there was scarcely room to breathe. Such 'health and safety' regulations as existed in the nineteenth century had been flouted entirely, and mercifully there was no calamity that might have involved an urgent evacuation of the theatre. Then, as now, there was a problem with ticket touts: as much as twenty guineas (more than £1000 in today's money) was offered for a seat anywhere in the house – any tucked-away corner at the back of the gallery, any spot with limited visibility – but no more than a handful of precious tickets were parted with.

The farewell night had been devised to incorporate the services of many of their old friends and colleagues. It consisted of extracts from three of the Bancrofts' best-loved plays, with the casts of *Money* and *London Assurance* made up entirely of past members of their companies. Several who were now managing their own theatres altered their programmes for the evening so that they could take part. Gifts were exchanged with all members of the company and the back stage staff presented the Bancrofts with a fine silver goblet inscribed: 'A grateful remembrance from the working staff behind the scenes.'

The audience crammed into the theatre included Albert Edward and Alexandra, the Prince and Princess of Wales, with their three teenage daughters, the Princesses Louise, Victoria and Maud. 'Bertie' had been a theatre lover all of his adult life, and not just because in the days of his youth it gave him the opportunity of meeting pretty young actresses. He had himself proposed the date for the Bancrofts' final night, so that he and the Princess could be present. Marie's son, Charles Bancroft, now twenty-two, was unable to be there because of his duties as a junior officer in the Royal Welch Fusiliers, but George, a sixteen-year-old schoolboy at Eton, was given leave to attend. His housemaster, Frank Tarver, was also sent a ticket and accompanied George to the Haymarket. Tarver was a keen theatregoer and an admirer of George's parents, and had been involved for years both in acting and producing drama at Eton.

The programme opened with the first act of Lord Lytton's *Money*. The cast included Ellen Terry, Lillie Langtry, Charles Wyndham, Arthur Cecil, Charles Coghlan (once again back in England for a while), John Clayton and Marie's brother-in-law, Charles Collette. This was followed by a scene from Boucicault's *London Assurance* with John Hare as Sir Harcourt Courtly and Madge Kendal as Lady Gay Spanker, and with Arthur Pinero and William Kendal also in the cast. The programme concluded with the second and third acts of *Masks and Faces*, performed by the present company, including Johnston Forbes-Robertson, Charles Brookfield, Maurice Barrymore, Henry Kemble, Eleanor Calhoun, and with Marie and Squire themselves for one last time in their old familiar parts. When the time came for Marie to make her entrance as Peg, Squire cut a small hole in the scenery so that with a pair of opera-glasses he could watch the audience's reaction as she walked on stage. At the reception she received she was almost overcome with emotion. Maurice Barrymore whispered 'Bear up' to her and she managed to pull herself together enough to carry on until the end. But her final words as Peg Woffington – 'Stage masks may cover honest faces, and hearts beat true beneath a tinselled robe' – 'seemed so appropriate to the occasion that I could fight against my emotions no longer; the tears came freely to my eyes, and I fairly broke down.'

Henry Irving then came onto the stage to read some fulsome verses composed for the occasion by the critic, Clement Scott, entitled 'A Valedictory Ode'. 'I take it as an act of extreme friendship to endow me with this "office of love",' Irving began. 'This compliment to me shows that you two, who are about my oldest friends, recognise that I have some place in the revivalism that you instituted. My sole fear is that, with all my earnest endeavours, I shall not be able to do full justice to a theme that is so dear to my heart, or to express with adequate enthusiasm what I really feel.' Of course, he read Scott's verses beautifully, all fourteen of them, which included the following:

A friend and neighbour from the busy Strand [Irving]
Warned by the summons of Fate's prompting Bell,
Has come to take two comrades by the hand,
And bid them both regretfully, 'Farewell.'

No age or sickness saddens this adieu,
No piteous cause I plead, no alms I beg;
My toast is 'Triplet, here's long life to you,
And years more laughter to delightful Peg.'

With kindly Robertson they formed a 'School,'
Rejoiced in 'Play' after long anxious hours;
'Caste' was for them, and theirs, a golden rule,
And thus by principle we made them 'Ours.'

Good-bye, old friends, it shall not be farewell;
Love is of art the birth and after-growth;
'Heaven prosper you' shall be our only knell,
Our parting prayer be this, 'God bless you both.'

Following this, the veteran comic actor 'Johnnie' Toole, who had been so supportive of Marie when she had first worked on the London stage as a teenager, spoke of his old friends with affection, at the same time reducing the whole audience to helpless laughter. In the course of his speech he said that 'This is my first appearance under the management of Mr and Mrs Bancroft, and also the first appearance of my friend Irving – a very short engagement, one night only. I hope it won't get in the papers that Messrs. Irving and Toole appeared for one night only under the management of Mr and Mrs Bancroft, after which they immediately closed the theatre.'

Henry Irving   *John Lawrence Toole*

After Irving's reading and Toole's speech, the curtain fell briefly. When it rose again the stage had been filled with the flowers that had been arriving throughout the day. One of these huge bouquets had 'brilliants' (simulated diamonds) among the flowers; another had been delivered in a silver bowl. The stage hands had arranged the flowers to form an aisle down which Marie and Squire Bancroft walked to the front of the stage, to take leave of their audience and to thank them for so many years of support. The whole house rose to their feet to applaud them. Squire was 'painfully agitated', as Marie put it, with the emotion of the occasion. As a writer in *The Theatre* put it, 'Triplet comes to say goodbye .... and the whole house rises, for there is Peg beside him. Hand-in-hand they join, and so the curtain falls upon them as they stand together between the banks of flowers. And so, farewell!' The curtain rose and fell many times, the audience cheering and waving handkerchiefs as the orchestra played 'Auld Lang Syne'. When at last silence fell, Bancroft spoke:

> We feel how far beyond our merits are the honours and compliments which have been showered upon us, and I am deeply conscious of the poverty of my attempt to acknowledge them. Robbed now of the actor's art, I must ask you to clothe my words with all the eloquence and wealth of thanks I mean them to convey .... It has been my privilege to spare Mrs Bancroft such labour and anxieties as should not be a woman's lot, how amply have I been a thousand-fold repaid! Most of us, I think, owe Mrs Bancroft something, but I am by far the heaviest in her debt. I alone know how she has supported me in trouble, saved me from many errors, helped me to many victories; and it is she who has given to our work those finishing touches, those last strokes of genius. .... I have now, in my wife's name and my own, to bid you goodbye. We do so with feelings of thankfulness, of great respect, and with feelings of deep affection.

When Bancroft finished speaking applause filled the theatre and the curtain rose and fell over and over again as he and Marie took countless bows. When at long last it fell for the final time a message came from the Princess of Wales, inviting Marie to come to the royal box, where the princess presented her with her own bouquet. When at last the time came for them to leave they found a huge crowd waiting for them outside the stage door. The street was blocked with hundreds of people waiting to bid them farewell. As they made their way through the crowd people called out, 'Don't go! Stay with your friends!' 'It mustn't be goodbye!' as they pressed forward to shake their hands and to wish them well.

Among the audience that night had been the millionaire banker Alfred de Rothschild[*], the Director of the Bank of England, who threw a party for Marie and Squire at the end of that long evening. Exhausted as they were, they were happy to go on to Rothschild's grand London house, after the emotional events of the evening, before returning to their silent home in Berkeley Square. Many of that night's audience, including young George Bancroft, had been invited to the party as well, and the Prince of Wales was also there, although Princess Alexandra and their daughters had already returned to Marlborough House.

When they did eventually reach home, in the early hours of the morning, Marie at last 'had a good cry'. She tried to describe her feelings: 'After all the noise, excitement, and suppressed emotion .... I sat alone in

---

[*]Alfred Charles de Rothschild, 1842-1918, a member of the prominent banking family, was, from 1869 to 1889, Director of the Bank of England, the first Jew to hold this office. A great patron of the arts, he donated large sums to acquire paintings for the National Gallery.

the silence of the night reflecting, looking back through that long vista of the past, with its hard work, many triumphs and bold achievements …. I thought of my early struggles in childhood and girlhood – which made the water very rough for me to wade – but now that I am safely landed, I cannot help looking sadly back upon the stormy sea through which I had to pass.'

It was a warm, moonlit night, so George and his father went out for a walk together. They strolled around Berkeley Square, reliving the events of the evening. Squire was in high-spirits. 'What a night!' he said, linking arms with his son. 'Has there ever been a greater tribute in a theatre? Ah! George, my dear, I'm very proud and very happy.' George, not yet seventeen and still with a year to go at school, decided this was a good moment to approach his father about something that had been worrying him. 'Serious, my boy?' asked his father. 'Terribly,' was the reply. 'At Eton – I, er – I owe twenty pounds.' There was an ominous silence, then George felt his arm gripped tightly, and his father burst out laughing. 'My boy – you should go into the Diplomatic Service.' It would be intriguing to know how a teenager at public school had managed to run up such an enormous debt, £20 being worth well over £1000 today. George did not reveal this information.

The next morning, the flowers that had filled the theatre were delivered to Berkeley Square. There were so many bouquets that every vase in the house was filled, and when there were no more containers to be found, the first floor balcony, overlooking the square, was filled with flowers. The arrival of the flowers attracted a small crowd of curious passers-by. 'What's all this mean?' one of them was heard to wonder. 'It's either a wedding or a funeral,' was the reply. 'Who lives 'ere? – Oh! I know, it's the Bancrofts' 'ouse; they've just had a heap of money left them by a relation wot insists on their leaving the stage!' 'Oh, then this is all for a party – it's more like a royal mausoleum!'

The Bancrofts had earned the right to relish this extravagant celebration. The theatrical profession that had just given them such a fond farewell was very different from the one they had joined, and many of the immense changes that had come about since 1865, when Marie took on the old Dust-Hole in Tottenham Street, must be attributed in no small way to their work, in conjunction with the work of T.W.Robertson. The Bancrofts and Robertson came together at the right time for all three of them: together they led a movement for change both in the content and production of plays. At the beginning of 1880 *The Theatre* wrote: 'The once-abused school of Robertson has sown good seed, and the playgoers of the present time are gathering in the harvest. The theatres based upon the Prince of Wales's system are increasing and multiplying, stage-management is recognised as an art, rehearsals are attended to with scrupulous regularity, and the results of good training may be observed in a hundred different directions.'

At the time of their retirement, Arthur Wing Pinero wrote of the Bancrofts: 'When the history of the stage and its progress is adequately and faithfully written, their names must be recorded with honour and gratitude.'

They have been accused of not moving with the times so far as their productions went, but by backing Robertson when previously his work had been rejected, and making his plays the most popular ones in London, they had in fact, for much of their careers, been in the vanguard of reforms. However, if they had remained at the Haymarket without making further forward strides, such as were already beginning to happen elsewhere, they would soon have begun to stagnate. Maybe this was at the back of their minds and they were content to leave the next leap forward to other, younger, people. Following their retirement, the London theatre was ready for the more challenging work of the later Pinero, Ibsen, Bernard Shaw, Henry Arthur Jones and Oscar Wilde. However, the Bancrofts' influence lives on, for the 'cup-and-saucer' realism of Tom Robertson, and their 'drawing-room' comedies, pointed the way directly through the years to the 'kitchen-sinks' of the mid-twentieth century and to later modernism. When Arnold Wesker's *Roots* was revived at the Donmar Warehouse in October 2013, several of the rave reviews it received reminded theatregoers just how revolutionary it had still been in the 1950s to see real potatoes being peeled at a real kitchen sink along with other menial kitchen tasks. The 'kitchen-sink' playwrights would have arrived soon enough anyway, but they arrived in a world that was ready for them. The Bancrofts had prepared the way.

After Robertson's early death the Bancrofts relied heavily on revivals of his work and other safe choices of production such as classic revivals and adaptations from the French, taking few risks and preferring to play safe and give their public what they wanted. This was the basis for their success, but also probably the reason, combined with their early retirement, that by the mid-twentieth century their names were largely forgotten, along with those of most of their contemporaries. Only the towering reputations of Henry Irving and Ellen Terry have survived the subsequent vagaries of time and taste.

Their contemporaries were always ready to acknowledge their contribution. *The Theatre*, again: 'Those who sneered at the "teacup-and-saucer school" have lived to see what it has done for art. [The Bancrofts have been] the pioneers of a new and true dramatic faith, for do not let it be imagined that an actor like Mr Hare would fail to acknowledge the debt he owed to his old master.' Indeed Hare himself, in proposing a toast to Bancroft following a dinner back in 1873, had said: 'His great ability as a manager is known to all, and it should never be forgotten that he was the first to originate and to introduce those reforms to which the dramatic profession owes so much of its proud position; although other managers have followed his lead, it should always be remembered that the lead was his.' He was speaking of Squire Bancroft, but all knew that his words referred as much to Marie as to her husband.

The Bancrofts' legacy contained, of course, far more than the fading, if influential, memory of the plays they produced. What mattered more was the radical style and setting of their productions. When Robertson came on the scene he demanded that his plays should be performed in a naturalistic way by actors representing recognisable people who spoke and behaved as people would in the real world. In the Bancrofts he met people who were in entire agreement with his vision. They developed further the box-sets introduced by Madame Vestris in the 1850s and gradually incorporated into those sets realistic scenery such as had not previously been seen. The front of the stage became what has been described as the 'fourth wall' of a room within which the actors would behave as naturally as if they were at home. None of this sounds innovative now, but at the time it was quite revolutionary and was quickly taken up at theatres throughout London and gradually further into the provinces.

Along with this, the Bancrofts specialised in ensemble acting, in which star actors, including themselves, would often play minor roles, on the over-riding principle that the chief aim of all members of the cast was to work closely together to create a balanced production. At the same time there was a significant, if slow, change in the direction of the plays themselves. When the Bancrofts first learnt their craft, there was limited direction, generally by the stage-manager, although sometimes an author would direct his own plays – Tom Robertson's plays always included lengthy and detailed instructions as to exactly how he wished the stage to be set and the actors' roles to be interpreted. Gradually, however, the influential actor-managers, such as Irving, the Bancrofts, Wyndham, the Kendals and Hare, assumed the directorial responsibility for productions themselves, becoming the 'producer' – a role that in turn, by the mid-twentieth century, would become the powerful director of today.

At the time of the Bancrofts' retirement, the days of the great actor-managers, the successors to David Garrick, were at their height. An actor-manager financed his or her theatre, directed it, and played on its stage, with Irving the acknowledged king of the actor-managers. Yet their days were numbered. There were already murmurings that they were too powerful as individuals and by the early part of twentieth century there were few left, and the few actors in charge of theatres today, such as Kevin Spacey at the Old Vic, have powerful promoters and managements to back and support them.

266

In his theatre Squire Bancroft was a strict disciplinarian, as were most of the other managers of those days. George Bancroft described his father's style of management: 'Father was always drastic in his control of his theatre. Today, I suppose, he would be called a dictator.' As a boy, George spent many happy hours behind the scenes at his parents' theatres during his school holidays, watching rehearsals and generally soaking up the atmosphere of the workings of the theatre. One day he was at the Haymarket when the young actor Charles Brookfield, fresh from Cambridge where he had been an enthusiastic amateur, had recently joined Bancroft's company as his first professional contract. That morning he was late for rehearsal. Everyone was expected to be present and on time, however small their part. Brookfield's cue came and he did not appear. There was a pause. 'Where's Mr Brookfield?' demanded Squire Bancroft. There was no answer. Then there was a sound of hurrying feet followed by a loud crash. A breathless 'Charlie' Brookfield hastily appeared, rubbing his head.

'You've kept the stage waiting, Mr Brookfield. Where have you been?' came the stern question.

Brookfield apologised: 'I'm sorry, sir. Before a mixed company, it's rather difficult to explain. I got here as fast as I could, but I met with an accident – I fell on the stairs – you may have heard – and am in considerable pain.'

'Ah,' replied Bancroft. 'I was afraid it was some of the scenery.'

Another miscreant was a handsome young actor called Harry Conway. He, too, was late one day for rehearsal. Again, anger from the manager, and more annoyance when he noticed that a rather windswept Conway had casually joined the rest of the waiting cast on stage in breeches and riding-boots. 'I'm sorry I'm late, sir,' he faltered, sensing the atmosphere was not in his favour.

'Understand, please, that it's the last time it will be overlooked. You've kept the entire company waiting and the act must be started again from the beginning – and you're not dressed properly.'

'I've been riding, sir. I've come straight from the Row*.'

'Mr Conway, in my theatre the company must be dressed suitably and treat their work seriously. Never let this happen again.'

What Squire Bancroft considered 'suitable' attire for rehearsals in those formal days consisted of respectable suits for the male actors, complete with necktie and polished shoes, and tidy day dresses for the women.

Strict though he could be, Squire was always ready to help out young members of his company who were in difficulties. George told how when

---

* Rotten Row: the fashionable riding track that encircles Hyde Park.

the actor, Henry Kemble, 'the Beetle', was young, he was often hard up, and had been known to ask Squire if he could lend him a small sum for a couple of months to see him through a difficult patch. Squire never turned him down, knowing that a cheque would arrive by the first post on the promised day.

Alongside the changes in the style of production came the Bancrofts' innovations within their actual theatre. With the introduction of plays performed in settings that audiences could recognise as not unlike their own homes, they provided them with new levels of comfort, with well-padded seats, carpets and extravagant décor along with improved refreshment and toilet facilities. It was becoming ever easier for people from outlying parts of London to get to the theatre. Since the first section of the Underground opened in 1863, carrying over twenty-six thousand passengers a day within a few months of its opening, the system had expanded rapidly throughout the sixties and seventies and beyond. Combined with the services into the mainline stations, by the 1880s this enabled people to get into central London with ease, and home the same evening, with the result that the middle-classes, attracted by the new respectability and comforts of the theatre, began attending in their droves. The gradual reduction in size of the pit and the rise in the price of seats drove the rowdier elements to the margins, but not away altogether. The Bancrofts have come to be looked upon as elitist, which in a way they were, with their changes in production and surroundings attracting middle and upper-class audiences, but their theatres remained as popular with audiences from the East End as from the smart parts of town and the suburbs. They had drawn the middle-classes in, rather than driven the working-classes out.

12

FAMILY MATTERS

There was only one place that Marie and Squire could go to unwind
following all the excitement and emotion of their retirement. 'When I get
to Pontresina,' wrote Marie to a friend, 'I shall lie down, look at my old
friends the mountains .... and not get up again for days.' For the first time
they did not have a deadline to hurry back for, so were able to relax in the
mountains for several weeks, and contemplate how they might spend their
retirement.

That retirement would turn out to be almost half of their lifetimes:
when they left the Haymarket, Marie was forty-seven and Squire was
forty-five and they were both to live into their eighties. During their years
of management they had accumulated a personal fortune of some
£180,000, an immense sum which would make them millionaires many
times over today. So money would not be a problem. Boredom might.
Half a lifetime is a long time to fill. As it turned out their retirement was
to prove anything but boring.

Almost immediately Marie and Squire Bancroft embarked on the long
task of writing their memoirs. *Mr & Mrs Bancroft: On and Off the Stage*
was a joint work. The first three chapters were Marie's, covering her
childhood and early days in London. Squire's recollections of his early
years followed. From the time of their marriage most of the story
connected with their productions was written by Squire, with Marie filling
in with more anecdotal material. Writing the book must have taken up
much of the three years between their retirement and 1888, when it was
published by Richard Bentley and Son, a London publishing house that
flourished through most of the nineteenth century. The original edition of
On and Off the Stage came out in two volumes. Then, in 1889, a one-
volume edition was published that ran to over four hundred pages. The

various editions must have sold well, as the book was reprinted five times in its first year, and eventually ran to seven editions before going out of print after many years. *On and Off the Stage,* along with a further book of memoirs they wrote more than twenty years later, *The Bancrofts: Recollections of Sixty Years*, form the basis of much that has been written about the Bancrofts since.

In many ways the early chapters of *On and Off the Stage* are the most interesting, dealing as they do with their early lives on the circuits, in the provinces, and in mid-nineteenth-century London. Marie Bancroft's descriptions of her early years as a child actress are full of anecdote and humour, though notably lacking much in the way of time or exact place – she seems to have regarded such details as unnecessary interruptions to her narrative. Augustin Filon, wrote: 'In her memoirs .... she has quite forgotten to give us the date of her birth.' Also this absence of dates might be a deliberate way of covering up some aspects of her early life: too many exact dates might give pointers to things that Marie preferred to keep hidden – such as her early relationships and the identities of the fathers of her first two children. Squire's account of the years of his own youth are more meticulous, with carefully recorded dates and locations. His writing, while elaborately Victorian in style, is descriptive and vivid, particularly when he is writing of his childhood days in London and of his travels. However, when detailing the productions of plays he is somewhat pedantic, though very informative, as almost every production is recorded, complete with its exact opening date, a list of who was in the cast and for how long it ran.

Inevitably autobiographies lack balance. Indeed they are often self-congratulatory and the Bancrofts' memoirs are no exception. Squire acknowledged as much in his preface to *Sixty Years*, saying: 'For the egotism displayed in the following story I offer no excuse. Egotism is inseparable from autobiography.' Both sets of reminiscences therefore are largely a tale of their successes. That is not to say they skim over their few failures, but to read their accounts you might believe that apart from those failures their reviews were consistently good. Often they were not, although on the whole they met with critical approval. Overall the picture they give is of a well-run business, for Squire was an exceptional businessman: he invariably had an eye to the profits, regardless of what the critics had to say. He wrote that if a production was running to houses that were just *over* half-full, that equalled profit, and it was allowed to run. If it was running to houses that were just *under* half-full, that equalled loss and it was time to get out.

The Bancrofts were both good storytellers, and some of their observations on their friends and colleagues throw vivid light on the darker corners of Victorian life, as in Squire's recollection of Wilkie Collins's severe addiction to laudanum, an opium derivative, then perfectly legal, indeed widely prescribed in Victorian times for a variety of ailments. More than once Collins tried to overcome his addiction. He failed. A mutual friend once told Squire of a time when he and Collins were travelling together in Switzerland, where the law was stricter than in England, and Collins ran short of his drug. 'I am in terrible trouble,' he told his companion when his laudanum ran out. He came up with a plan. There were several chemists in the town they were in and Collins proposed that he and his friend should separately approach each one saying they were doctors, and ask for the maximum amount of opium permitted by Swiss law. 'If we fail – Heaven help me!' said Collins. But the plan worked and the operation was repeated at each stop until they reached France, where the drug was easier to obtain. On another occasion Collins was dining with the Bancrofts one evening. Surprisingly, it might seem to us, for a Victorian dinner table, and no doubt after the ladies had 'withdrawn', the conversation over the port turned to drugs and addiction. Collins revealed just how much laudanum he was regularly taking. Another guest, astonished at the amount, suggested that it was surely enough 'to prevent any ordinary person from ever awaking'. A doctor who was among the guests confirmed this, assuring the company that Collins was clearly so accustomed to the drug that his current dose was perfectly safe for him, but that it would indeed be enough to kill every man at the table. (Opium forms a part of the plot of one of Collins's most famous novels, *The Moonstone*, in which he describes it as 'that all-potent and all-merciful drug'.)

Despite the fascinating glimpses of their contemporaries, and the historically important account they give of the theatre of the day, the Bancrofts' memoirs are deliberately, and tantalisingly, silent on their domestic life – crucially so in the case of their two sons, Charles, who was born in 1863, and George, born in 1868. For George's story any biographer can call on *Stage and Bar* (his own memoirs, published in 1939 during his own retirement) supplemented by official records, old photographs, and the family's oral tradition. Charles, however, does not appear in either his parents' or his brother's memoirs. For the story of his brief, but sensational, life, there are only family hearsay, a few puzzling official documents, and some even more confusing speculation that has been handed down successive generations.

The records show that Charles was baptised at the age of three, in Brighton. His mother had no known connections then with the south coast, so it seems possible that the little boy might have been living with foster parents while Marie pursued her career in London. However, by the spring of 1871, he was one of only nine boarders at a small school for boys in Hamilton Terrace, St John's Wood, just a stone's throw from Circus Road where Marie and Squire were by then living. The school was run by an eighty-year-old gentleman called James Bingley with the help of his wife Harriette, who was much younger, being a mere sixty-one. At seven, Charles was the second youngest child there. Although he had been registered at birth with the name of Wilton, at Mr Bingley's school he was known as Charles Bancroft. Clearly, after his marriage to Marie, Squire had accepted Charles as his own son. It was quite usual for small boys of seven, or even younger, to attend boarding school in those days: the fact that the Bancrofts had chosen a small school nearby would indicate that they wanted to have him close to home and for him to board would have solved much of the problem of daily and evening childcare while both his parents were at work till late at night.

George Bancroft, at around a year old, with his mother,
and aged around three, with his nursemaid, Caroline Lambkin

George, who was to give a picture of a happy childhood with indulgent, if preoccupied, parents, was to be sent further away when his time came to board. His earliest and fondest memories were of his nursemaid, Caroline Lambkin, whom he adored. It would seem that Marie was not particularly maternal, but there is a charming photograph of her, looking very young, in a gorgeous silk gown, with George, aged about a year, on her lap, wearing nothing more than a loose vest-like garment.

At four George was sent to a nearby day school until the very young age of six, when he was taken away from Caroline's loving care – he described it as 'a dreadful parting from her' – and sent to a boarding school in Brighton (the south coast connection again) where the first thing that happened was that his golden curly hair was cut off. Caroline was greatly dismayed at this when he returned home for the holidays and

272

George remembered that she declared it to be a shame. In the school holidays, much of the childcare of both boys was apparently left to Caroline and other servants, although George had memories of spending happy hours behind or beneath the stage at the Prince of Wales's Theatre, and he remembered the building itself well; he would have been eleven when his parents left the little theatre for their years at the Haymarket. For all of his life he treasured his mother's brick from the Prince of Wales's in its frame made of wood from the stage.

Although the Bancrofts never mention their boys accompanying them to Switzerland, George recalled spending holidays there. His first trip with his parents was in 1878, when he was nine. He described the train journey across Europe and remembered falling out of his top bunk in the sleeper carriage. He also told of long hikes in the mountains, in the company of his parents and Marie's sister, Ida. George grew to love Switzerland and mountaineering. 'I wanted to climb every mountain I saw .... climbing became a passion with me.'

Both boys went on to board at a school called St Michael's, in Slough, later to be renamed Hawtreys, after its founder, the Rev. John Hawtrey, an Eton schoolmaster who had established it as a preparatory school for Eton. Previously boys as young as eight had gone straight to Eton, until, with the full blessing of the Eton College authorities, Hawtrey took the youngest boys out of Eton and set them up in the separate school that he opened on St Michael's day, in September 1869. George started at Hawtreys in 1877, just before his ninth birthday. An exact contemporary there was Stanley Baldwin, the future prime minister. Charles and George Bancroft both went on to Eton when they were around thirteen, where they joined 'Tarver's' house. George loved his time at Eton and had fond memories of his housemaster, Frank Tarver. He related an episode in his schooldays when he and some Eton friends played truant one hot summer day, sneaking off to the races at nearby Royal Ascot. Returning to Eton they hitched a lift on the open top of a 'four-in-hand' carriage. Suddenly they realised they were about to be overtaken by an Eton master driving a fast, light 'dog-cart'. 'Look out, brollies up!' George urgently told his friends, and up went their large black umbrellas, in the hope that these would hide them. The dog-cart sped on by and they thought they were in the clear, until the next day after house prayers, when Mr Tarver summoned George to his study. With sinking heart, he presented himself. 'Were you at Ascot yesterday, Bancroft?' demanded the housemaster. 'Yes, sir,' admitted George reluctantly, fearing an imminent beating. There was a moment's pause, then, 'Whom did you see there? Anybody?'

'My father, sir. He was on Lord Londesborough's* coach.' There was a longer pause, then the theatre-loving Frank Tarver said, 'The next time you go to Ascot on a blazing June day, *don't* put up an umbrella.'

George Bancroft ready for Eton

As was usual in the nineteenth century, their parents, Squire possibly more than Marie, seem to have been a major influence on both their boys' choice of career. Charles went into the army and George, although he

---

* William Henry Forester Denison, 1st Earl of Londesborough, 1834-1900, a Liberal politician and an enthusiastic follower of sports of all kinds.

wanted to follow his parents onto the stage, was apparently prepared to go along with whatever his father might suggest. It would seem that having been so instrumental in making the stage 'respectable', Squire nevertheless preferred that his son should go into one of the more conventional professions. At seventeen George was sent off to live in France and Germany for two years, in order to learn both languages, with a view to entering the Diplomatic Service. He had a good ear and was soon fluent in both. He had an allowance of £100 a year – which should have been ample to keep himself entertained for his time abroad, although following a visit to Vienna with a friend, where the delights of the beautiful city proved too much for him, he had to confess to his father that he had overspent and had to ask for some more funds. He told Squire about everything that he had got up to there and begged him not to tell his mother. It cannot have been too outrageous, as George reported that his father 'shouted with laughter' at his escapades.

While living in Paris George spent many evenings at the Comédie Française, which served to strengthen his love for the theatre. He also joined his parents at St Moritz for three weeks of winter sports, as Squire and Marie now had time to visit Switzerland in the winter. Skiing had yet to be introduced as the main alpine sport but there was plenty of skating and tobogganing. The famous Cresta Run had been constructed not long before. It may have held fewer terrors in its early days than now, but even then it was three-quarters of a mile long and had, among its many hazards, the fearsome bends 'Battledore' and 'Shuttlecock'. They were given those names by Marie Bancroft in the mid 1880s: she was watching one day as two intrepid young English women, perched on a low, lightweight toboggan called a schlittli, sped towards the first bend. They misjudged the bend and shot over the edge, to a drop of six feet. The two ladies and their schlittli parted company and they flew through the air with their long skirts and petticoats flying around their heads and their underwear on display. This astonishing sight reminded Marie Bancroft of the feathered shuttlecocks that were used in the popular indoor game of battledore and shuttlecock (before long to evolve into badminton). She immediately christened the bend, and the one that followed it, after the game, and so they are still so called today. Apart from a few bruises to their bodies and to their dignity, the two ladies fortunately suffered no harm.

At 'racing pace' in those days the Cresta Run could be covered in a minute and a half, but it was a long haul back up again on foot for another run. George and Squire tackled the famous run together. As they hurtled towards the dreaded 'Shuttlecock', Squire put his weight on the wrong side of the toboggan and they – like the two ladies before them – flew over the icy bank. Picking himself up, George was relieved to see his father emerging unharmed from a mound of snow, his monocle miraculously intact.

On his return to England, George's future was still undecided. The idea of the Diplomatic Service was soon discarded as his father was advised that without powerful influences in the right quarters George would have little chance of progressing to the heights he had in mind for his son. The possibility of a clerkship in the House of Commons was his next suggestion, but this idea was also abandoned. Finally it was decided that George should become a lawyer. He was accepted into Brasenose College, Oxford, where he spent three happy years reading law and enjoying undergraduate life.

One of George's closest friends at Oxford was Henry Irving's son, Harry, who went up in the same term as George, to New College. Harry Irving was a couple of years younger than George, whose two 'gap' years had delayed his arrival at Oxford. He and the two Irving boys, Harry and his brother Laurence, had known each other all their lives. Harry was a prominent member of the Oxford University Dramatic Society, but George decided not to join, fearing that, having made the decision that his future was to be in the law, an involvement with OUDS might reignite his passion for the theatre which he had regretfully decided must be put aside. Harry too was reading law as his father also attempted to discourage his son from a theatrical career. However, both Irving's sons would go on to make names for themselves in the theatre, Harry as an actor, using the name H.B.Irving, to distinguish him from his illustrious father, and Laurence as an actor and as a playwright. Both died before they were fifty: Laurence was drowned, with his wife Mabel and more than a thousand other people, when the liner *The Empress of Ireland* sank in May 1914 in the St Lawrence River. Harry died in 1919 following a long illness.

Another of George's university friends was Max Beerbohm, who was to become a famous caricaturist and essayist, author of the novel *Zuleika Dobson*, and described by Shaw as 'the incomparable Max'. Squire Bancroft paid frequent visits to his son at Oxford and Beerbohm drew a caricature of George and his father walking together in the High. The handwritten caption reads: 'Mr Bancroft on a visit to Mr George Bancroft at Oxford, in the Summer Term of 1891.'

In 1893 George was called to the bar at the Inner Temple, and in April of the same year he married Effie Hare, the daughter of his parents' great friend, John Hare. His career at the bar started out well, but he still had hankerings for the stage and he did, briefly, become an actor. In 1896 he appeared at the St James's Theatre in a stage version of Anthony Hope's famous novel, *The Prisoner of Zenda* and in the following year in a Pinero play, *The Princess and the Butterfly*, which also had his friend H.B.Irving in the cast. He made no great impact in his minor roles, so it would seem that his father was right to discourage him from a stage career.

Max Beerbohm's caricature of Squire Bancroft and his son George, in Oxford, 1891

Meanwhile, on leaving Eton in 1881, Charles Bancroft had joined the army. He went through officer training and was commissioned into the Duke of Cornwall's Light Infantry in 1883, but soon he transferred to the Royal Welch Fusiliers. Despite George's strange omission of any reference to his brother, the two Bancroft boys must have remained good friends as they grew up, as Charles was George's best man at his wedding in 1893 and two years later, when Charles married, George was one of the witnesses. Charles, like George, had fallen in love with a daughter of a famous theatrical couple who were friends of his parents. She was Margaret Catherine Grimston, the daughter of Madge and William Kendal and the eldest of their five children. (The Kendals always retained the name Grimston in their private life and it was the name always used for their children.) Charles would have known the children of Madge and William Kendal through most of their childhood, although the Grimston children were several years younger than the Bancroft boys. As the children of both families grew older the age gap would have appeared less wide and by 1895, when Charles Bancroft was thirty-two and Margaret Grimston was twenty-four, they fell in love and in September 1895 they were married. Nothing, surely, could have been more appropriate and welcome to both families.

At this point, however, a mystery begins: out of the four parents of the happy couple, only one was present at the wedding. After appearing on stage in Hull on the evening of Saturday 14 September, Madge Kendal hurried to the station as soon as the final curtain fell and took an overnight train to London, arriving in time to play a key part in her daughter's wedding the following morning, a day on which Madge was free, theatres being closed on Sundays. The ceremony took place under special licence at All Souls Church, Langham Place, immediately following matins on Sunday 15 September.

It was not a large wedding, although it was colourful enough to attract descriptions of the event in the press. There was a short report in *The Times,* headed 'A Bancroft-Kendal Wedding' and longer piece in *The Era,* which described the event in considerable detail. *The Era* informed its readers: 'The proceedings were of a private nature, only the nearest relations and schoolfellows of the bride being present.' It went on to describe the bride's dress, which was of cream-coloured satin, with fresh orange blossoms in her hair, her veil fastened with diamond clasps. Carrying a bouquet of white roses and trailing pinks, Margaret was led up the aisle by one of her brothers, nineteen-year-old Harold Grimston, who at the altar passed her hand to Madge Kendal, who gave her daughter away. This must have been quite unusual for those days: as a rule, if a father was unable to give his daughter away, a brother, an uncle, or some other male relative would do the honours. Mrs Kendal was 'richly-gowned in pale heliotrope' and her elaborate hat included a spray of marguerites 'as a compliment to the bride'. The single bridesmaid was Margaret's youngest sister, fifteen-year-old Dorothy, in a cream silk dress to which was pinned the bridegroom's gift of a gold brooch of entwined hearts. The best man was one of Charles's fellow-officers, and the guests included Charles's brother, George Bancroft, with his wife Effie and Barbara, their eighteen-month-old daughter, who threw a posy of marguerites in front of the happy couple as they walked together down the aisle. The signing of the register was witnessed by four people, Marie Bancroft's sister Ida, George Bancroft, and the best man, along with Mrs Kendal herself, signing her name as Madge Grimston. *The Times* reported that 'the presents were most handsome and costly'. On the marriage certificate the bride's father's profession was entered as 'actor'. In Charles's entry, a line was drawn through the blank space for his father's name and profession.

Charles Edward Bancroft   *Margaret Catherine Grimston*

The only discordant note in the arrangements for this small but colourful wedding lay in the absence of three out of the four parents of the bride and bridegroom. William Kendal was unable to attend and had remained in the north. The Bancrofts were away on holiday. It does seem most surprising that the occasion could not have been arranged to fit in with the schedules of two such prominent couples. The Kendals were still busy working actors, which might explain the absence of the bride's father, but it could not have been impossible to plan the event for a time when *both* were free for their eldest daughter's wedding and William

Kendal must have been looking forward for years to walking his adored daughter down the aisle on his arm. As for the Bancrofts, they had been retired for years, so should have been able to attend their son's marriage at almost any time. It therefore seems that the wedding might have been deliberately arranged to take place while they were out of the country – and out of the way.

The ceremony was followed by a reception at Mrs Kendal's house in Portland Place, after which the bride and groom departed for Lake Como in Italy. On the face of it, this would seem an unremarkable destination for a young couple to choose for their honeymoon. However, *The Era* mentioned that the Bancrofts were away in Italy – and when in Italy they always stayed at their favourite village of Cadenabbia on the shore of Lake Como. It seems that Charles and Margaret were headed for the very place where his parents were staying, possibly to surprise them with the news of their marriage and to ask for their blessing. Madge Kendal went straight back to Hull on the evening of the wedding.

In spite of its seemingly happy start, there was very soon something badly wrong with Charles and Margaret's marriage. Barely nine months after their wedding Margaret was back at her parents' London home, and on 23 June 1896 she applied to the High Court for an annulment. The petition states that, 'By reason of the malformation or frigidity of the said Charles Edward Bancroft your petitioner's said marriage has never been consummated.' On 12 August the decree nisi declared that the marriage was ' …. absolutely null and void to all intents and purposes in the law whatsoever by reason of the impotence of the said respondent and the said petitioner be pronounced to have been and to be free from all bond of marriage.' On 27 November Charles was ordered to pay costs of £123.10s.3d and on 22 February 1897 the decree absolute was passed.

Was Charles's impotence the real reason for the annulment, or could there have been another, even more hideously embarrassing, reason? Of course it is perfectly possible that Charles really might have been impotent at that time. However, this does seem unlikely, as in the year following the annulment of his marriage he was to father an illegitimate daughter, and in 1901 he was to remarry and have another daughter. At the time of the petition for annulment the court had ordered that two doctors should conduct physical examinations of the couple. Maybe, if for some reason Charles could have been persuaded to admit to impotence, it might then have been unnecessary to conduct an actual physical examination.

Another possibility could have been that Charles was gay, although this seems unlikely in view of an affair the following year, a second marriage and two children. Homosexuality was a serious issue in those days. Only a few months before Charles and Margaret's marriage in 1895 Oscar Wilde had been convicted of 'gross indecency' and jailed. An annulment on the grounds of homosexuality would have spelled the end of Charles's career in the Royal Welch Fusiliers. If that had been the true reason for the non-consummation, then an admission of impotence might have been preferable to accusations of homosexuality, being thrown out of his regiment in disgrace, and possible imprisonment.

A third possibility is that Charles and Margaret could, while being totally unaware of it, have been close blood-relations. If, for instance, soon after their marriage, they discovered that Margaret's father, William Kendal, was also *Charles's* father, then this would make them half-brother and half-sister, so their marriage would be incestuous and would have to be ended immediately. This could explain the absence from the wedding of the only three people who would have known of his paternity (assuming that Squire Bancroft knew the identity of his stepson's father). Madge Kendal, however, the only parent who was at the wedding, would almost certainly have been kept in ignorance of any pre-marital affair her husband might have had with Marie Wilton. This most upright of Victorian ladies would have been devastated at the revelation of a liaison of her husband with a woman she had known as a friend for decades. At the same time, Charles and Margaret themselves would have had no idea why three of their parents appeared to frown upon a relationship between them, and this could also explain why they arranged for their marriage to take place in the Bancrofts' and William Kendal's absence, so that none of the three people who had opposed their relationship would know that it was taking place. If Kendal *was* Charles's father, and if either he or the Bancrofts had been aware that the marriage was about to take place, they would have had to take immediate steps to prevent it going ahead. 'Just cause or impediment' indeed.

There are, however, strong arguments against Kendal being Charles's father. Records show that William Kendal and Marie Wilton were hundreds of miles apart nine months before Charles's birth on 20 October 1863. Kendal was acting at the Theatre Royal, Glasgow, while Marie Wilton was in London. However, there was a disastrous fire at the Theatre Royal at the end of January 1863, and although Kendal quickly found work elsewhere in Glasgow, he could have spent a few days in London before that work began. Also, at nineteen, William was almost five years younger than Marie, which must have seemed very immature to a worldly young woman of twenty-four, even though he was certainly an attractive young man: Squire Bancroft described him as being 'very fair and handsome' when they first met in their youth.

One of the witnesses at the wedding was Marie Bancroft's sister Ida. Close to her sister, Ida would probably have been one of the very few people that Marie might have confided in at the time of Charles's birth. *If* Ida had been aware that Kendal was Charles's father she would surely have alerted her sister urgently and would certainly not have witnessed the

281

marriage. A further argument against would be that Kendal's devoted wife, Madge, would never have gone against her husband's wishes if he had made it clear that he was opposed to any romantic involvement between Margaret and Charles. On the other hand, he might not have wished to arouse his wife's curiosity and so played down his opposition. Certainly, there was a rift between the Bancrofts and the Kendals from that time: in Madge Kendal's autobiography, published many years later, in 1933, she referred to an 'estrangement' between the two families. She did not elaborate on this estrangement.

For a young man at any time to admit to impotence would be deeply distressing, but if Kendal was revealed as his father Charles would have had to be persuaded that the grounds for the annulment of his marriage should be non-consummation. The unthinkable alternative would have been for his and Margaret's parents, all pillars of the Victorian social and theatrical establishment, to have their most intimate affairs made public. Even without the tabloid sensationalism of today, innuendo and word-of-mouth tittle-tattle would have spread, resulting in huge embarrassment for both families. Mrs Kendal referred to the unhappy time of her daughter's brief marriage as 'my Margaret's so-called marriage' – without naming any names. 'She had ills to bear,' she wrote, 'and she bore them with strength, for when the time came for her to be married to the man of her choice, the marriage had to be annulled.'

She also wrote that Margaret would not hear a word spoken against her unnamed husband or his family: '…. that event overclouded my daughter's life and still overclouds mine, for she never recovered from the shock, her loyalty to the family of the man she married never wavered.' Madge Kendal as well as her daughter appears to have been totally shattered by the annulment of the marriage. Margaret had been a sweet-natured child who grew up into a sweet-natured young woman, ready to forgive whatever caused the tragedy of her marriage to Charles. Distressing as it would all have been, if either Charles's impotence or homosexuality had been the true reason for the annulment, it would have been humiliating for Margaret but maybe not so devastating as to ruin the rest of her life. Still young and attractive, she could have recovered from the heartbreak and the Kendals could have encouraged their daughter to put the sad episode behind her and look forward to seeking a happier relationship. If, however, she had been torn apart from the man she loved soon after her marriage for a reason quite beyond the control of herself or of Charles, this could indeed have blighted the rest of her life.

Word of the annulment must have got around and even into the press. Inquisitive friends would call on Mrs Kendal and her daughter and attempt to discuss the delicate subject. Whenever her mother appeared to be about to reply Margaret would interrupt and firmly change the subject. Even the Duchess of Teck, mother of Princess May (later to become

Queen Mary, wife of King George V) was curious, asking Madge whether it was indeed her daughter that was the subject of the gossip going around. 'It is a subject on which we must always be silent,' Margaret insisted.

There is a further piece that needs to be fitted into the puzzle. Some of Dame Madge Kendal's papers are held in the North East Lincolnshire Archives, in Grimsby. Among them is a scrapbook containing a photograph of Charles when he was a boy aged around eleven or twelve. His name is written beneath the photograph in Madge Kendal's handwriting and on the same page as the photograph, near the end of the album, is a cutting from *The Times* announcing Charles's death in 1906. The handwriting of the caption looks as though it might have been written late on in Madge Kendal's life. It was surely unusual back then to have a photograph of another family's child in an album. Why would the Kendals have a photograph of Charles as a boy – unless Marie Bancroft had sent William a portrait of his young, growing son? If William was the boy's father, how did he explain to his wife how he came to have a photograph of the young Charles? Kendal died some years after Charles: maybe Madge found both items among her husband's papers when he died and pasted them both into her scrapbook at that time, towards the back of her album. Interestingly the youngest Grimston daughter, Dorothy, always maintained that her father, William Kendal, was also the father of Charles Bancroft. This belief Dorothy passed on to her own descendants: one of her daughters, as recently as 2008, in her late eighties, stated verbally that it had always been believed in her branch of the Grimston family that her grandfather, William Hunter Kendal, had been the father of Charles Bancroft, and that this had been the reason her aunt Margaret's marriage had had to be annulled. This granddaughter of William and Madge Kendal died in 2009.

Margaret spent most of the rest of her short life living quietly with her parents. Then, in 1902, she contracted rheumatic fever and died on 31 October, at her parents' home in Filey, on the Yorkshire coast, around the time of her thirty-first birthday. Her body was brought to London and she was buried in St Marylebone (now called East Finchley) Cemetery.

The Kendals had other sadnesses in their lives, becoming estranged one by one from all their four surviving children. Mrs Kendal wrote sadly that '....we gave up all hope of any sign of affection from our family.' She also wrote: 'As my husband and I stood together one day by [Margaret's] grave he said to me, "All the children that loved us, Madge, lie here under this stone."' When William Hunter Kendal died in November 1917, his wife wrote: 'My beloved husband died of a broken heart and wounded pride.' Madge Kendal herself lived until 1935, having been awarded a DBE in 1926. She and William were buried in the same grave as their beloved Margaret. Before her own death, Madge had an inscription engraved around the plot with the words 'Mater Afflicta'.

283

Charles Bancroft's paternity remains a mystery. Brought up as Squire Bancroft's son, it is not beyond possibility that he could actually have *been* Bancroft's son, but it seems almost certain that Marie and Squire had no opportunity to meet before 1864, after Charles's birth in October 1863. Other possibilities include Marie's cousin, Charles Wilton – the name Charles could be a pointer here – but this is unlikely in view of the fact that this Charles was in love with yet another Wilton cousin. The 'Mr Underwood' referred to in Charles Wilton's diaries was around at the right time, but absolutely nothing is known of him, not so much as his first name. Then there is the draper Alfred Shoolbred, whose probable involvement with Marie Wilton has been referred to earlier. Being around at the right times, Shoolbred is a distinctly strong contender for being the father of Charles and also of Marie's little daughter, Florence.

A further possibility, one that was for years dismissed as an improbable myth among the Bancrofts' few descendants, was that Charles's father was the Prince of Wales, later King Edward VII, who was famously attracted to pretty young actresses. 'Bertie' sowed plenty of wild oats during the years of his young adulthood and in March of 1863 the twenty-one-year-old prince married the Danish princess, Alexandra. In the first couple of months of that year Bertie could have been enjoying his final flings around London before Alexandra arrived in England for their marriage. Then as recently as 2009 some evidence came to light that there might after all be some truth in this family legend.

In 1898 Charles Bancroft suffered an illness and on 25 June a brief announcement appeared in *The Era* that reported that Mrs Bancroft was 'to be congratulated upon the complete recovery from his late illness of her son, Captain Charles E. Bancroft of the Royal Welch Fusiliers, who is under orders to rejoin his regiment in Egypt. Captain Bancroft is very popular in his regiment.' Charles's popularity in the regiment certainly seems likely: in the regimental archives of the RWF there is a caricature of him entitled 'Night Club King', suggesting that he must have been something of a party animal. It has to be wondered just why *The Era* considered such an insignificant event as Charles's recovery from illness was worthy of a mention. The short report referred to 'Mrs Bancroft' and 'her' son, with no mention of Squire Bancroft. It could be that the paper was hinting at a skeleton in the Bancroft cupboard.

Later that year, on 31 October 1898, a baby girl was born to a young woman in London. No father was named on the birth certificate but the little girl, Grace, was given Bancroft as a middle name. (Her first name has been changed here, and her mother's name omitted, in respect for her descendants' privacy.) Grace inherited papers of her mother's, among them letters that revealed to her the identity of her father. Late in her long life, in the 1980s when she was getting on for 90, Grace corresponded with a relative telling of her own father's, and of *his* father's, identities.

'My father was Charles E. Bancroft ....' she wrote. 'I have his letters to my mother when I was born.' The letter went on to say that, 'Rumour in London insisted that Charles, my father, was Edward VII's son.' Grace indicated that her interests had been looked after by a lawyer, suggesting that Charles contributed financially to his daughter's maintenance.

In 1898 Charles saw active service with his regiment both in Egypt and in South Africa in the second Boer War; then the regiment was sent to China at the time of the Boxer Rebellion in 1900. While he was stationed in Hong Kong, Charles met and married Ellie Moses, the daughter of an Australian politician, Henry Moses MLC (Member of the Legislative Council) of New South Wales, whose own father, Uriah Moses, had been a convict, transported to Australia in 1800. Uriah must have been a remarkable man as, after receiving his ticket of leave and eventually his pardon, he had made good, becoming a successful businessman in Windsor, New South Wales, and the founder of a large family.

Ellie Moses and her sister Lurline were visiting Hong Kong in 1901, and there both girls fell in love with and married officers of the Royal Welch Fusiliers. Charles and Ellie Bancroft sailed for England in October 1901. Back in England, they rented a small London flat in Gloucester Place. Here they enjoyed warm relations with the rest of the family, as evidenced by an exchange of jocular messages between the young couple and Charles Collette, the husband of Marie Bancroft's sister, Blanche. Collette, as well as being an actor, produced numerous caricature drawings, many of which are in the archives of the Royal College of Medicine. One of these drawings, sent to Ellie and Charles at Christmas 1902, shows the young couple hand-in-hand, crammed on to a sofa in their tiny apartment, a dog and a cat beside them, with most of their bulky belongings piled up on the landing outside. The caption, a quote from one of Ellie's letters to him, reads: 'My dear Uncle Charlie, now that we have got settled in our new home we hope you will pay us a visit. Our place is small but cosy – we have been obliged to leave my piano and boxes and Charlie's organ and helmet case outside. But we have managed to get in a sofa, and if we sit <u>very</u> close together, which Charlie says he does not mind, we can both sit down in the same room, which is very nice.' Charles and Ellie had one child, a daughter, Primrose, who was born in December 1902.

In 1906 Charles contracted meningitis and died on 6 October, just two weeks short of his forty-third birthday. His remains were interred at Brompton Cemetery in London in a mausoleum that had been constructed in 1879 for William Fletcher, the first husband of his aunt, Ida. Also interred in the same tomb were Ida's second husband, John Elmes, and Francis Ashton Drake, Emma Wilton's husband, who years before had lent Marie Wilton the £1000 that enabled her to take on the lease of the Prince of Wales's Theatre. Eventually there was to be a fifth and final person in the mausoleum, Ida Fletcher Elmes herself, who died in 1920. Of all the five people in the tomb, the only name to be commemorated is that of W.F.H.Fletcher, engraved over the door. It seems very strange that Marie and Squire Bancroft did not have Charles buried in a grave of his own. The name of Charles Edward Bancroft is not commemorated anywhere. Ellie remarried in 1911, becoming Lady McMahon, her second husband being a baronet, Sir Horace McMahon, who was also an officer in the Royal Welch Fusiliers. She remained on close terms with Marie and Squire Bancroft for the rest of their lives.

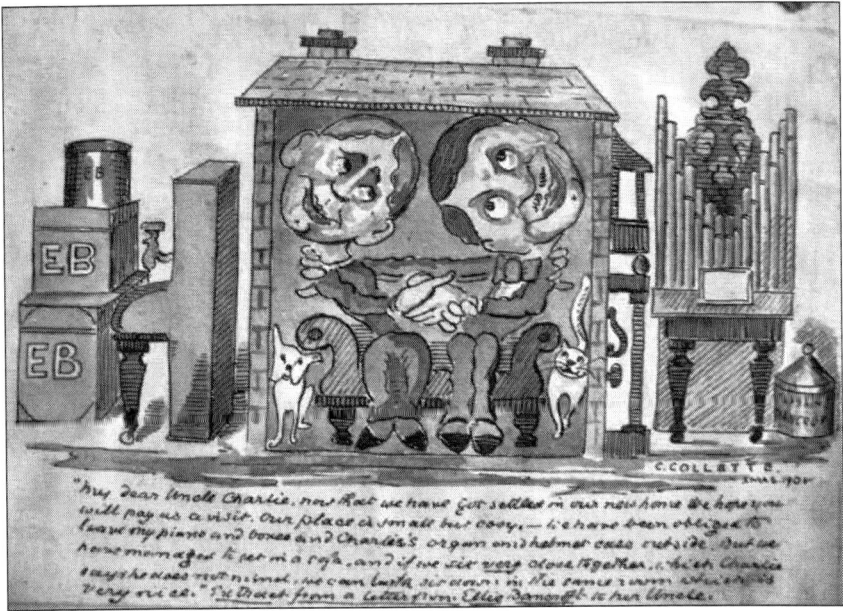

caricature of Charles Bancroft and his wife Ellie, by Charles Collette

There are so many conflicting answers to the riddle of Charles's paternity, but just one thing is certain: the only person who knew the true identity of Charles's father was his mother. When Marie Bancroft died, that knowledge died with her.

13

BACK ON THE BOARDS

Following their retirement, the Bancrofts at first resisted any temptation to return to the stage. However, Marie spent some of her new spare time training and preparing inexperienced young actresses for parts they were to play. One of these was Julia Neilson[*], who went on to become an acclaimed actress. She also became part of the Terry theatrical dynasty when she married Fred Terry, Ellen Terry's youngest brother: Julia and Fred often played together in many romantic 'cape-and-sword' dramas. Years later, in her own autobiography, Julia recalled that Marie Bancroft, '.... was exceedingly kind to me, coaching and helping me in every way. The lessons I had from her were really the first I ever had in the art of acting.' She was another of the many to be struck by the sound of Marie's voice: 'She was an elegant little figure – she had wonderful grey eyes and one of the most lovely voices I have ever heard.'

We do not know what parts the Bancrofts may have been offered after leaving the Haymarket, but we do know when one offer was made and how it was accepted. In 1889 Henry Irving approached his old friend 'B' with an offer of a major part in *The Dead Heart*, a drama by Watts Phillips set during the French Revolution. Irving was keen to produce the play to mark the centenary of the storming of the Bastille but said he

---

[*] Julia Neilson, 1868-1957, and Fred Terry, 1863-1933. Fred's first stage appearance was in *Money*, the Bancrofts' opening production at the Haymarket in 1880, when he was sixteen. Their daughter Phyllis Neilson-Terry, 1892-1977, and son Dennis Neilson-Terry, 1895-1932, continued in the family tradition, becoming well-known actors themselves.

would only go ahead with the production if Bancroft accepted the part of the dastardly Abbé Latour. Irving clearly saw villainous possibilities in Squire that he himself had never previously explored.

The two friends uncomfortably discussed the embarrassing subject of terms, neither looking directly at the other but both gazing abstractedly out of a window. Irving was determined that he should pay the going rate but Bancroft insisted that he would only accept the part 'as a labour of love'. After a lengthy discussion it was agreed that the payment suggested by Irving would be donated to charity. Squire was nervous at the prospect of returning to the stage after so many years. In a letter to Clement Scott he wrote, 'I am going to act in the autumn – the mere telling you so makes me tremble, but it was impossible to resist the manner in which Irving has wished me to play the Abbé Latour in *The Dead Heart*.'

The Dead Heart was a play with a history. It had first been produced by Benjamin Webster at the Adelphi in 1859. Squire Bancroft had seen the production when he was a boy of eighteen: 'The splendid performance of that fine actor Benjamin Webster …. is vividly imprinted on my mind.' When the play was first seen in 1859 the French Revolution was a not too distant historical event: still within the living memory of older people, it was no further back in time than the Second World War is from us now. Its subject grabbed the imagination of the British public uneasily. Followed as it was by the rise of Napoleon Bonaparte, the scary bogeyman whose name could be used to frighten small children into obedience, the terrifying events of the Revolution were seen as ones that could be repeated here.

The plot is centred on the character of the handsome, debonair Robert Landry, the part created by Webster, now to be played by Irving. In the untroubled days of 1771 Landry was in love with a beautiful young woman, Catherine Duval. However the wicked Abbé Latour plotted with his dissolute friend, the Comte de St Valery who wanted Catherine for himself, to compromise her virtue and to have Landry framed, arrested and incarcerated in the dreaded Bastille. Many years pass and the Revolution breaks out. Among the emaciated prisoners that are released at the storming of the Bastille is Landry who emerges, a broken man, to find that his Catherine has married the Comte, who has since died. Her young son, Arthur, is now being groomed by the villainous Abbé to follow in the ways of his father. Landry becomes a high-ranking Revolutionary official, hardened and embittered by his experiences. He has the *aristos*, the Abbé and the young Comte de St Valery, now aged eighteen, arrested. Both are condemned to die on the guillotine. Catherine pleads with Landry for her son's life, but he cold-heartedly rejects her, still believing she betrayed him when they were both young. He orders Abbé Latour to be brought to him and challenges him to a duel to the death. On a table are papers that ensure the Abbé's safe-conduct out of France if he should win. They fight with swords and, too late, a mortally wounded Abbé reveals Catherine's innocence with his dying breath. But the young Comte's execution is imminent and irreversible. The play ends in a dramatic scene at the guillotine. The boy's name is called – and, as the curtain falls, Landry nobly mounts the scaffold to die in his place.

So – it was a far, far better thing he did .... The ending of *The Dead Heart* obviously chimes closely with that of *A Tale of Two Cities* and Watts Phillips was duly accused of stealing Dickens's plot. But things were not so simple. The original Adelphi production of *The Dead Heart* opened on 10 November, 1859, so had to have been written well before that date. *A Tale of Two Cities* had been appearing since April of that same year in serial form, but its final dramatic instalment would not be published until 20 November, ten days *after* the play opened. Nevertheless accusations of plagiarism flew around in both directions. Dickens's supporters suggested there had been a leak of the entire, closely-guarded plot and accused Phillips of stealing the ending; Phillips's supporters asserted that Dickens had seen the play in time to re-write his ending.

However, Benjamin Webster's claim that he had been in possession of a manuscript of Watts Phillips's play for three years was later backed up by Dickens's biographer, John Forster, and Webster insisted that Phillips had been urging him to produce his play throughout that time. In a letter Webster wrote, 'It is well known, and I can immediately prove it, that *The Dead Heart* was written and paid for years before *A Tale of Two Cities*, or the periodical in which it appeared, was dreamed of.' In reality it seems likely that the powerful closing scenes of both *A Tale of Two Cities* and *The Dead Heart* might have originated before either work had been written. Several earlier writers had come up with the same theme of self-sacrifice, including Alexandre Dumas, in his novel *Le Chevalier de la Maison Rouge*, published in 1845, and Edward Bulwer-Lytton in an 1842 play, *Zanoni*, which may explain why neither Dickens nor Phillips themselves appear to have taken much part in the subsequent furore – which anyway would have done no harm to the sales either of *A Tale of Two Cities* or of tickets for *The Dead Heart*.

By the time Irving produced *The Dead Heart* in 1889 Dickens and Phillips were long dead, but the new production of the play revived the thirty-year-old controversy and there was much press speculation as to whose was the original idea of Robert Landry's/Sydney Carton's noble self-sacrifice on the scaffold. It all helped attract publicity for Irving's lavish new production and the play was well received. Irving wrote to Ellen Terry, who was to play Catherine, of his plans for a huge cast of extras, particularly for the Bastille scene: 'We must have a starving crowd – hungry, eager, cadaverous faces ....' A vast crowd there was: at the taking of the Bastille 'the stage was filled with a surging and howling mob, a spectacle that haunts the mind,' reported *The Times*.

Ellen Terry was not much inspired by her own part of the beautiful but insipid Catherine, whom she described as 'a rather uninteresting mother'. But she was more than compensated by the fact that her son, Edward Gordon Craig, known as Teddy, played the young Comte de St Valery. She proudly wrote that he 'had such a big success that I soon forgot that for me the play was rather "small beer".'

Squire Bancroft's return to the stage was greeted with enthusiasm by press and audiences alike but his performance as the dastardly Abbé received mixed reviews. Several critics said he appeared uncomfortable and stiff in the part and suggested he needed to regain his confidence following his years away from the stage. It was also said that he appeared anxious that his voice was not carrying. Others were kinder. One critic congratulated Bancroft for his portrayal of a 'cynical, treacherous courtier' with its 'splendid audacity, its biting sarcasm, its utterly corrupt and depraved selfishness.' Squire was later to admit that it was the one play in which he invariably felt nervous before going on stage. The *Pall Mall Gazette* carried an interview with him. When asked about his apparent lack of confidence on the first night, Squire gave a surprising explanation: he was suffering from a severe head cold and was not feeling at all well, which might explain his fear that his voice was not carrying as it should. He went on to tell the reporter that to ensure that he would not break his record of never missing a call in his entire professional career, he had 'taken an injection of cocaine in the nose' shortly before going on stage. Cocaine being easily, and legally, available over the counter, it was an accepted remedy for many conditions and ailments, including the common cold. A best-selling preparation called Ryno's Hay Fever and Catarrh Mixture was very popular. It was 99% cocaine. It is highly improbable that Squire actually injected the drug by needle – he had more likely 'snorted' it like snuff in powder form and used the word 'injection' to describe the process. There is no evidence to suggest that he was ever a regular cocaine user, or that he was in any way an addict like his friend Wilkie Collins, but it is interesting that Squire had no compunction over speaking openly of his use of the drug – to a reporter, at that.

The Dead Heart ran until May of 1890, more than one hundred and eighty performances and, although there remained some criticism of Bancroft's performance in general, his big duel scene with Irving was riveting and universally admired. 'Very striking is the duel scene between Landry and the Abbé,' wrote *The Times* reviewer, 'the one cold, implacable, pitiless, the other haughty, contemptuous and cynical, with a perceptible undercurrent of deadly hate and treachery.' Both Irving and Bancroft were accomplished fencers and their fight was so convincing that audiences were alarmed – with good reason. Both actors were in real danger, as both were very short-sighted and it would seem that their swords did not have safety tips. As they could not fight wearing their glasses, there was a genuine risk that one or other of them might have been seriously injured. When they first started rehearsing the scene, Irving, who stood at well over six feet, said to Bancroft, 'I had no idea you were so much the taller.'

Irving and Bancroft in **The Dead Heart,** *1890, by J.Bernard Partridge*
(caption in Squire Bancroft's handwriting)

One night, after they had taken their curtain calls, Irving and Bancroft were walking together off stage. 'What a big name you might have made for yourself,' said Irving, putting his arm around Bancroft's shoulder, 'had you never come across those Robertson plays – what a pity – for your own sake – for no actor can be remembered long who does not appear in classical drama.' Bancroft was entirely undisturbed by this remark. Indeed, he believed that Irving was absolutely correct. 'While the names of actors of tragedy survive,' he wrote, 'those of comedians live on if at all, but feebly …. in the records of the rare student of the stage.' It did not bother him that his own name and those of other great actors of comedy such as Toole and Hare would before long be entirely forgotten except by theatre historians, whereas the names of Henry Irving and Ellen Terry would live for ever.

Much has been written about Henry Irving, both during his life and over the century since his death. He was a giant within the theatrical world, but the Bancrofts were privileged to know him also as a close friend. George Bancroft first knew him in his own childhood, and

described him as 'a wonderful person, a towering man among men ....
The personality of Irving was by far the most arresting and magnetic that I
had ever met or seen. He seemed to possess all the qualities that make for
greatness – repose, dignity, charm, simplicity, sympathy, strength.'
Physically, Irving's appearance was curious. He was well over six feet
tall, with spindly legs and ungainly movements. He had a strange way of
speaking, possibly connected with overcoming a childhood speech
impediment. George described him vividly: 'His long hair, which seemed
right and not the least affected .... a remarkable pair of eyes, at one
moment aflame, at the next as soft and captivating as a child's; a beautiful
and finely chiselled aquiline nose and a strong, thin-lipped mouth. In
repose the rather drawn pale face would be called, I think, ascetic, and
when it smiled it was irresistible.' In personality he was reserved. Squire
Bancroft wrote that 'without being in the least distant or proud, he was
reticent and secretive; yet such was his peculiar force and magnetism that
many thought they were intimate with him who were never really allowed
to be so.'

One of George Bancroft's fondest childhood memories was of a
Christmas Day when Irving turned up unexpectedly at the Bancroft home
in time for some Christmas pudding. George was keen to show the great
actor his model theatre in which he had created a famous duel scene in the
snow from *The Corsican Brothers**, which he had been taken to see at the
Lyceum. He had made his snow out of salt and had cut out pictures of the
duel between Irving and William Terriss, positioning them carefully on
the tiny stage. His audience of three applauded enthusiastically as the
curtain rose on the little tableau. Irving then, on his knees in front of the
small theatre, solemnly advised George on how, with some minor
adjustments, he could make his 'snowdrifts' more realistic and made
suggestions as to how the boy might arrange his two 'actors' so that they
showed up better in the lamplight.

When, as a boy, George Bancroft first saw *The Bells**, the play in
which Henry Irving had established his reputation as the finest actor in
London, he was deeply affected and frightened by it. 'For nights I feared
the darkness and was haunted by it. Nightlights had to be provided.'

Irving first appeared in *The Bells* in 1871. Set in the early 1800s, it told
of Mathias, innkeeper in a small town in Alsace, who robs and kills a
traveller for his gold, disposing of the body in a lime kiln. Years later
Mathias's guilt returns to haunt him. He comes to believe that the ghost of
his victim has returned, the sound of the traveller's sleighbells ringing in

---

* *The Corsican Brothers*: Dion Boucicault's 1852 adaptation of an Alexandre
Dumas novel of revenge.
* *The Bells,* by Leopold Lewis (1828-90), from a French play called *Le Juif
Polonais* (*The Polish Jew*).

the snow outside being audible only to the guilty man – and to the audience. Irving's performances as the tormented Mathias, a part he played many times during the rest of his career, was invariably truly frightening for his audiences, not just for an awestruck boy.

Henry Irving as Mathias in **The Bells**

Irving was personally warm and generous: he always tipped generously and George Bancroft wrote that he 'was never known to give a tip that wasn't gold'. He often helped members of his profession who were down on their luck. George recounted an incidence of this legendary generosity: Irving was concerned about the health of a young actor in the company and asked his stage-manager, Harry Loveday, about him. 'I don't think he looks very strong. What's his salary?' 'I think it's three pounds a week,' was the reply. Irving then asked for the actor's name and address. The next day the young man was eating his midday meal in his lodgings when there was a knock at the door and to his amazement he found 'The Guvnor' on the threshold. Irving explained that he just happened to have been passing by and thought he would look him up.

'Won't you sit down, sir,' asked the young actor. 'I can't, my boy. No time.' Peering at an old print of Mrs Siddons, Irving remarked that with his poor eyesight he could not make out its faint caption. The young man crossed the room to the picture and read it out for him. Soon Irving took his leave. 'Take care of yourself – I must hurry on. No, no – don't see me out. God bless you my boy.' Returning to the table, the actor lifted up his glass to take a drink. Tucked beneath the glass was a folded bank note.

Irving was known to be a tardy correspondent, but as a stage-struck teenager George found him the opposite: he would often write to his hero begging for a seat at the latest Lyceum production: a ticket would arrive by return of post, accompanied by a handwritten note from Irving telling George to be sure to go round and visit him in his dressing-room after the play. This way he saw many of Irving's productions. Writing of his portrayal of the 'Martyr King' in *Charles the First**, George described Irving as 'a Van Dyck that had stepped out of its frame .... Will anyone who saw that performance forget the final scene? It was almost unbearable. And when you remember that the Queen was played by Ellen Terry you can realise what the combination of the two great artists meant.'

With plenty of time now for leisure pursuits, the Bancrofts continued with their frequent visits to Europe. They still regularly visited Pontresina, and now they could spend more time there and could go in the winter as well as in the summer. Once or twice they even spent Christmas there. Like all people who want to keep 'their' favourite place a secret from the wider world, they watched with regret as the tiny Alpine village grew and changed over the years from the remote and isolated place it had been when they first went there. 'It is all, alas, very different now, with its railway, its tramcars, and hotel omnibuses,' wrote Squire. The tourist trade as we know it was on its way. Cadenabbia on Lake Como also remained a favourite destination. They sometimes visited Monte Carlo, either in the spring or the autumn to avoid the heat of high summer, although Marie did not much care for the busy town. When they spent the Easter of 1893 at Monte Carlo, their hotel was having a large extension built, and noisy, dusty work was being carried on from the early hours of the morning and all through the day, so that it should be complete in time for the busy summer season. This will sound all too horribly familiar to many twenty-first-century package holidaymakers. Squire, however, always enjoyed Monte Carlo: although not a betting man himself, he liked watching the activity of the gamblers at the gaming tables. Marie's dislike of Monte Carlo was confirmed once and for all one day when she was

---

* *Charles the First:* play by Irish dramatist, William Gorman Wills, 1828-91.

walking near their hotel while a pigeon-shooting contest was taking place nearby. A bird fell dead close by her, splattering her with its blood. The animal-loving Marie insisted that she would not stay a moment longer and they departed the same day. From then on they stayed at quieter Mediterranean spots and any further visits made by Squire to Monte Carlo were on his own.

In 1890 and in 1900 they visited Oberammergau, for the world-famous Passion Play that is performed every ten years by the residents of the Bavarian village, also famed for its centuries-old tradition of wood-carving. It was first performed in 1634, during an epidemic of the plague that was sweeping Europe. The villagers had then vowed to re-enact the Passion every ten years if they were spared. Spared they were, and the Oberammergau Passion Play quickly became famous, with pilgrims from all over Europe flocking to the village to watch the performances. By the nineteenth century thousands of people were coming from all over the world to see the play and now it is invariably booked out years ahead. It used to be performed in the open air, as it was at the time of the Bancrofts' first visit, but by 1900 a new covered theatre had been built to seat the audience of hundreds. Also, between their two visits, the village had become accessible by train whereas previously it could be reached only by horse-drawn transport – or on foot – from Munich.

The Oberammergau Passion Play was then, and still is, a marathon performance, lasting eight hours, with long intervals. Squire could not resist watching it with a director's eye and casting it in his mind, with Henry Irving as Judas, Herbert Beerbohm Tree as Pontius Pilate, and Johnston Forbes-Robertson, with his beautiful voice, as Jesus. He was impressed by 'the work of tradition carried out at the hands of peasants ….' and he was moved to tears by the scene of the Last Supper, although he felt some unease about it, feeling 'that there are still some things which should not, however reverently, be mimicked.'

Marie Bancroft became an enthusiastic writer now that she had time to spare. After co-authoring their joint autobiography with Squire, she tried her hand at writing plays. She wrote three in all, the first called *A Riverside Story*. It had a sentimental plot, based on a story she had been told by a young boat-builder she had met many years before. While staying near Broadstairs in the summer of 1868, she and her sister Ida had come across the young man on the shore where he was breaking up a boat which had the name 'Alice' painted on its bow. They got talking to him and he told them his sad story. He had fallen in love with a pretty village girl called Alice who had promised to marry him, but she was seduced by the heartless, philandering son of the lady of the manor. She ran away with him, leaving the young boatman heartbroken. Inevitably she was abandoned when she became pregnant and, destitute, returned to the village with her baby. Our hero gave Alice and her child the cottage that was to have been their home but, he said, 'I've never spoken to 'er, and I never will, but so long as I live she shall never want.' Driven to drink and with his life in ruins, he was breaking up the boat he had named for her as she had broken up his life – and they all lived unhappily ever after.

A Riverside Story was played for just one matinée performance at the Haymarket, on 22 May 1890, in aid of an orphanage in Scotland, with a cast of minor professional actors and 'stage-managed' by Squire Bancroft. Unfortunately, Marie's talents did not stretch to the writing of plays and it received some very bad reviews. The *Dramatic Notes Yearbook* suggested that the only excuse for it was that Mrs Bancroft must be blind to the faults in her work that were painfully clear to others; it expressed surprise that Squire Bancroft had not dissuaded his wife from the production. The play, the review observed, was far too long, its slight storyline, which should have lasted for no longer than an hour, 'dragging out to two long and wearisome acts.' The two leads 'prolonged the agony of the situation to an undue extent,' and the scoundrel was far too 'bright and honest-looking' to be capable of betraying the girl who had trusted him. There were too many 'chattering, spiteful village girls.' One of these bucolic wenches, all with names like Hetty, Kitty, Polly and Tilly, was played by Marie's niece, nineteen-year-old Mary Collette. The review grudgingly admitted that 'some of the dialogue was well written', and went on to report that when the curtain fell the author was called for but it doubted that this would have happened if it had been a normal evening production. Marie wrote a further couple of even more insignificant plays. One of them, *My Daughter*, written in 1892, was an adaptation from the German, and the third in 1903 was called *A Dream*.

When not wrapped up in her writing, Marie involved herself in various forms of charity work. A few years after her retirement, to raise money at a fête held to mark the silver wedding of the Prince and Princess of Wales, Marie wrote in advance to all her theatrical friends enclosing photographs of themselves that she had purchased, along with the request that they sign them and return them to her so that she could sell them in aid of the Victoria Hospital for Children. She sent several to Ellen Terry, which were promptly returned, duly signed, and also to Henry Irving. In her accompanying letter to Irving, notoriously slow at dealing with his correspondence, she begged him not to 'keep her waiting for a year', before returning them to her. She took her commitments seriously: on the same evening as the fête Henry Irving was holding a supper party at the Lyceum in honour of Sarah Bernhardt, to which he had invited both Bancrofts. 'B' attended, but Marie declined as she would be busy selling her photographs at the same moment and she would not contemplate putting her charity work to one side for a social event, however tempting.

Following Bancroft's return to the stage in *The Dead Heart*, both he and Marie made occasional appearances during the 1890s, usually in charity benefits, as in 1897 when they took part in a performance at the Lyceum in aid of the Royal College of Music. Others involved included Henry Irving, John Lawrence Toole, Ellen Terry, James Fernandez and William Terriss. The main play, a melodrama called *Robert Macaire* had a good, swaggering part for Irving as a vagabond thief 'blessed with the impudence of the devil and the manner and appearance of a gentleman.' However it was 'Johnny' Toole who stole the show. He and Irving were the greatest of friends but had not worked together for years, Irving being the great tragedian and Toole specialising in high comedy. In *Robert Macaire* Toole made the most of his part, ad-libbing outrageously throughout. 'The more Mr Toole gagged,' read one report of the occasion, 'the more the audience laughed.' *Macaire* was followed by Marie Bancroft and Arthur Cecil, the old friend from the Prince of Wales's days, performing their popular scene from Lord Lytton's *Money*, in which a flirtatious middle-aged Lady Franklin attempts to entice the mournful widower Mr Graves out of his melancholy. The evening raised over £1000 for the Royal College of Music.

In 1893 John Hare, by now managing the Garrick Theatre, decided to revive Sardou's *Diplomacy* and invited Squire Bancroft to play his old part of Count Orloff. Hare did not originally offer Marie a part in the production, as being now in her mid-fifties she clearly would not be able to play either of the two younger female parts, the heroine Dora or her old part of the scheming spy, Countess Zicka, and Hare did not feel he could ask her to take on the minor role of an older woman, Lady Fairfax. However, Marie herself offered to play the part for fifty performances. Hare accepted delightedly. Tickets for *Diplomacy* sold out fast; it played to packed houses for months and Hare persuaded Marie to remain in the cast after her fifty performances were up. Others in the play included John Hare's son, Gilbert 'Bertie' Hare, Arthur Cecil and Johnston Forbes-Robertson. The other women were popular actresses of the day, Kate Rorke, Olga Nethersole and Maria Louisa Monckton.

At Marie's first entrance on her return to the London stage she was greeted with a rapturous ovation from the audience. 'The cheering,' wrote Squire Bancroft, 'began as soon as her merry, musical laugh was heard in the wings.' Lady Fairfax's opening words, spoken as she made her entrance were, 'You have not forgotten me, then, after this long absence?' The words were greeted with roars of applause. One newspaper reported that, 'Rarely within the walls of any theatre had there been witnessed so overpowering a demonstration .... The moment she entered the room she seemed to brighten everything in it.' After the final curtain, John Hare led his dear friend and one-time manager out in front of the curtain and spoke words of appreciation of her. Then the audience called for Marie herself to speak. John Hare's prompt-book from this production of

Diplomacy, complete with illustrations and set arrangements, is in the Theatre and Performance Collection of the Victoria and Albert Museum.

Diplomacy, *1893. Clockwise, from top left: Arthur Cecil, Maria Louisa Monckton, Squire Bancroft, John Hare, Johnston Forbes-Robertson, Kate Rorke, Marie Bancroft, Gilbert Hare, Olga Nethersole*

Unfortunately, on 11 July, a few days before the end of the season, Marie was injured in a street accident when the cab in which she was riding was involved in a collision in Jermyn Street. She was thrown out, her head was badly cut, and a wheel ran over her leg, an injury from which she never entirely recovered, suffering pain in that leg for the rest of her life. The accident was reported in *The Times* and other papers, and Marie received many letters and messages of sympathy from friends and also from total strangers. She even received a message from Queen Victoria, who expressed her sympathy and asked to be kept informed of her progress. The Bancrofts' plans for a holiday on the continent that summer had to be abandoned and instead, after lengthy treatment, they spent a few weeks in Norfolk once Marie was fit to travel. While in East Anglia they visited some of the places where Marie remembered

298

performing as a child.

That autumn John Hare took his production of *Diplomacy* on tour around the country with the full London cast. Fortunately Marie had recovered enough from her injuries to join the tour. They played in Birmingham, Liverpool, Manchester, Edinburgh and Glasgow. When they reached Edinburgh an invitation arrived from Balmoral inviting the company to perform the play there for the Queen and those of her family who were staying there. Queen Victoria had not set foot inside a theatre since the death of Prince Albert in 1861. Squire Bancroft once pointed out, in an after-dinner speech, that he had never enjoyed the privilege of appearing before the Queen as 'Her Majesty ceased to go to the play in the year I went upon the stage.' However, the Queen never lost her love for the theatre, and often invited London's leading managers to bring their companies to Windsor or Sandringham for Command Performances, although she apparently never invited the Bancrofts. It was rare for her to invite a company to the more remote Balmoral.

At this Royal Command Performance the Queen, now in her seventies, entered the room in a wheelchair pushed by her Indian attendants and was escorted to her seat by gentlemen-in-waiting. The members of the company were then presented to the Queen. Squire wrote that the Queen had 'perhaps the most beautiful and winning voice I ever listened to, although I have lived in the company of a strong rival to it for more than forty years.' Squire was not the only person to compare Marie's voice to that of the Queen – Ellen Terry also made a similar comparison, describing it as 'one of the most silvery voices I have ever heard from any woman except .... Queen Victoria, whose voice was like a silver stream flowing over golden stones.'

After the play the Queen was heard to say regretfully: 'What an evening! And now it is all over!' After she retired the actors were entertained to a supper hosted by Princess Beatrice and her husband, Prince Henry of Battenberg, after which the princess presented gifts chosen by the Queen. Marie Bancroft received a ruby and sapphire brooch and Squire was given a gold cigar-case. Late in the evening, the nine-mile drive back to Ballater, where they were staying, was long and cold, as so far in the north of Scotland there was already snow on the ground.

The following year, 1894, Marie Bancroft returned to the Garrick Theatre to appear in her old part of Lady Franklin in Hare's production of another favourite, Lord Lytton's comedy *Money*. Several of her friends were in the cast, including Hare himself, Forbes-Robertson and Arthur Cecil. *Money* also ran for some months. A sad event took place on the first night. The Bancrofts' old friend, Edmund Yates, was in the stalls. He had greatly enjoyed the play and after the final curtain, when the applause had ended and the national anthem had been played, he turned to his companion,

Clement Scott, saying, 'Did you ever hear such a laugh as Marie's? Isn't it enough to rouse the dead to life again? The "Old Brigade" – nobody will ever beat them.' Then, preparing to leave, Yates reached down for his hat. He had a seizure, fell between the seats, and never recovered consciousness. He died the following day.

Marie Bancroft's last appearance on a stage, apart from occasional charity performances, was later in 1894, when she was invited by Herbert Beerbohm Tree to take part in his production of *Fédora* at her old home, the Haymarket. Tree's *Fédora* was the first since the Bancrofts' production more than ten years before and it ran for fifty nights. Mrs Patrick Campbell was in the leading part and Tree himself in Squire's old part of Loris Ipanoff. It was the first time that either Bancroft had worked with or for Tree, who had taken over the Haymarket in 1887. In the two years following the departure of the Bancrofts, the great theatre had not thrived under the management of Augusta Wilton's husband, George Bashford, but Tree quickly restored its fortunes, and ran it successfully for many years, accumulating a large enough fortune to rebuild Her Majesty's Theatre, almost directly opposite the Haymarket. Her Majesty's opened in April 1897 and was renamed His Majesty's in 1901 when Edward VII came to the throne. Since then its name has changed according to the sex of the reigning monarch, so is now once again Her Majesty's. The great theatre is four storeys high, and lavishly designed, inside and out. It features tall Corinthian columns on its opulent facade and is topped with a dome, which held Tree's own private apartment.. One morning, shortly before building was completed, Tree ran into Squire Bancroft who was walking along the Haymarket. They chatted in the street and Tree, pointing to his magnificent new theatre, said. 'Look, B, don't you think it's fine?' The more cautious 'B' adjusted his monocle and solemnly surveyed the new building before replying, 'Yes, it certainly is. But all those windows will somehow have to be kept clean.'

During the early years of his retirement, Squire Bancroft was inevitably invited to serve on many bodies connected with the theatre. He was, for instance, often called upon to arbitrate in disputes that sometimes arose among members of his profession, and he served well into the twentieth century as a member of the Lord Chamberlain's Advisory Board for the Licensing of Plays. Until the Theatres Act of 1968 abolished censorship, all plays had to be submitted to the Lord Chamberlain's office for approval. Any hint of obscenity, blasphemy or anything that might be considered indecent, could be banned, with no reason having to be given, and portrayals of living people, in particular politicians, came in for close scrutiny: there must be times when many of today's politicians might wish the Board was still operating. The work of many famous playwrights was often rejected at first, including that of Shaw and Ibsen. Few of Squire's fellow members of the Board had any connection with the theatre, often being retired military men or civil servants; so he must have been one of the few who could contribute some real knowledge of the theatre, even if from an era that was itself passing into history. One of his obituaries was to read: 'Although he brought to this committee the Victorian's point-of-view, no one could ever have accused him of being narrow-minded,' and the novelist Max Pemberton* considered 'he showed a praiseworthy breadth and tolerance of judgement.'

He also played a key role in the early days of the Actors' Benevolent Fund. In the spring of 1882 Henry Irving had invited several of his friends, among them Toole, Wyndham and Bancroft, to dinner in the 'The Beefsteak Room', his private dining room at the Lyceum. There the Fund was established, with Irving himself as its first president and with Bram Stoker acting as its first secretary. Its object was initially described as being for 'the relief of distressed and decayed actors', a description that was quickly changed to something less insensitive. It was financed largely by the theatrical profession, who each undertook to subscribe £100 annually. Members of the dramatic profession were invited to subscribe to the Fund, which aimed 'to grant annuities in deserving cases, when the funds allow of it being done.' Among the original subscribers were John Toole, Squire Bancroft, Marie Bancroft, Charles Wyndham, John Hare, William Kendal, John Clayton and Dion Boucicault.

Tuberculosis then being a widespread scourge, a bed was sponsored at the Royal National Hospital for Consumption and Diseases of the Chest at Ventnor on the Isle of Wight, specifically for beneficiaries of the Fund. Supporters did not simply sign their cheques: they also donated their talents, and regular charity matinées were produced in aid of the Fund, the first being at Drury Lane in May 1883. It was the usual mixed bill, the highlight being Henry Irving and Ellen Terry in the trial scene from *The Merchant of Venice*. It also included a scene from Bulwer Lytton's *Money*, with the Bancrofts, the Kendals, Arthur Cecil and John Clayton. The Actors' Benevolent Fund is still active today, more than 125 years later, its role still 'to care for actors and theatrical stage managers unable to work because of poor health, an accident or frail old age.'

Squire Bancroft was a member of the Freemasons and in 1892 he was elected Worshipful Master of the Drury Lane Lodge, a post that is held for the period of one year. The last quarter of the nineteenth century saw an enormous growth in Freemasonry, membership more than doubling from the 1860s. Prominent masons included members of the royal family and people in positions of power in government and the professions, including many members of the theatrical profession, among them Henry Irving. Squire Bancroft and John Hare had both long been masons, members of

---

* Sir Max Pemberton, 1863-1950, was a popular novelist and journalist. His wife was a granddaughter of Madame Tussaud.

the Drury Lane Theatrical Lodge. In February, Bancroft's immediate predecessor as Worshipful Master was James Fernandez, who had been a well-known and popular figure on the stage for many years and a member of Irving's company at the Lyceum. Fernandez performed the ceremony of installing his successor as the new Master. Bancroft then presented his predecessor with the ceremonial 'Pin', a jewel worn in the cravat that was traditionally presented to the immediate Past Master by his successor.

Then, in July 1895 Squire Bancroft was chosen by the theatrical profession to preside over the celebrations at the Lyceum to mark a very special occasion. In the Queen's Birthday Honours of that year, Henry Irving became the first actor ever to be honoured with a knighthood – a sign that at last the acting profession was recognised as being entirely respectable and as worthy of recognition as the arts of music or painting. Gladstone, a great admirer, had wanted to recommend him for a knighthood back in 1883, but had been dissuaded, largely because of Irving's complicated personal life. In 1869 he had married Florence O'Callaghan, who considered herself his social superior. The marriage was unsuccessful from the start. Their first son, Henry, was born in 1870. Then, in November 1871, following the triumphant first night of *The Bells*, the powerful melodrama in which Irving made his name, they were on their way home from the theatre when a row broke out. It was very late and Florence was eight months pregnant with their second son, Laurence. She had been in a bad mood all through the party that followed the performance, and in the cab she taunted Irving: 'Are you going to go on making a fool of yourself like this all your life?' Irving stopped the cab and got out. He never returned home and never spoke to Florence again. Irving's subsequent long-term professional relationship with Ellen Terry was a constant subject for speculation and it is almost certain that they were intimate personally as well as professionally, although they never lived together openly. Certainly it may have delayed the knighthood he was eventually awarded. However, Queen Victoria was reportedly delighted to have been able at last to honour the great actor. She never normally spoke to those being knighted, but as Irving knelt before her and she touched his shoulder with the sword, she was heard to murmur that she was 'very, very pleased'.

There was a remarkable gathering on the stage at the Lyceum to honour Irving. The large theatre was packed, with every seat taken. More than four thousand signatures from the profession had been gathered on an address composed by Arthur Pinero, which was presented to Irving in a gold and crystal casket designed by Johnston Forbes-Robertson. In his speech Bancroft described the thousands of names on Pinero's address as 'a roll-call of the British stage .... the names of those "who have done honour to our calling in the past .... those who are its most distinguished ornaments now, and .... those whose destinies lie in the future."' Among the names were those of the veterans Helena Faucit, who had acted with Macready, Mrs Fanny Stirling, whose last appearance on any stage had been with Irving and who was to die, aged eighty, in December that year, and a man believed to be the oldest living actor, James Doel, under whose management Squire Bancroft had worked in his youth at Devonport.

When a deeply moved Irving rose to reply he was received with prolonged cheers. 'There can be no greater honour to any man than the appreciation of his efforts by his comrades and fellow workers,' he said. '….I rejoice at the honour conferred upon our art. I have been always proud to be an actor; but I have never been so proud as now.'

During that same year, 1895, Squire Bancroft was walking near Piccadilly one day when he was hailed from a passing carriage. 'Hi, Bancroft,' – a greeting closer to 'ahoy there' rather than the casual 'hello' of today. It was an elderly clerical gentleman of his acquaintance, the Reverend William Rogers, rector of St Botolph's Church in the City of London. This dynamic and reforming clergyman, popularly known as 'Hang-Theology Rogers', had set up schools and other facilities for the poor of his parish, including bathhouses, libraries and playgrounds. Now he was raising funds for the Bishopsgate Institute, an educational organisation he had helped launch which is still active today in the East End as a cultural centre. He had plans for a series of fund-raising lectures and, spotting Squire walking along the street, asked if would take part by giving a talk. When Squire replied that the only thing he knew anything about was the stage, Rogers answered that he could think of no better subject. Squire then asked if a reading would be acceptable rather than a lecture and Rogers replied, 'Anything you like – only come.'

After much thought, Squire came up with the idea of reading from *A Christmas Carol*. Charles Dickens himself had given readings of his much-loved tale years before. These had proved hugely popular and Squire believed they might well turn out to be so again. He spent many hours studying the *Carol* in depth and annotating a copy of the book. The success of the event exceeded expectations and raised much needed funds for the Bishopsgate Institute. Sadly the Rev William Rogers did not live long after the reading. In his late seventies, he still invariably went around in an open carriage, in all weathers, and towards the end of 1895 he caught a chill and died early in the new year. Bancroft described him as 'one of the best men it has been my privilege to know.'

It seemed to Bancroft that it would be a shame if all the work he had put into preparing for the reading should be for just the one occasion and he came up with the idea that he might repeat it in aid of hospitals and medical charities. Thus began an undreamed-of phase in his life which was to last for almost twenty years. Once the word got around, invitations began to pour in from charitable organisations all over the country. In

1897 he read in aid of a Catholic institution, the Sisters of Nazareth, in Hammersmith, west London. Nazareth House had been founded in 1857, and is to this day providing residential care for older people. In the nineteenth century the Sisters also cared for sick children. Squire told a story of a friend of his who was visited by two of the nuns. On their arrival they were announced by a servant as two 'Sisters of Lazarus'. 'What, Martha and Mary!' he exclaimed. 'Show them in!' The Sisters overheard, and were much amused. Although Squire was not himself a Catholic, both Bancrofts were sympathetic to the faith and shortly after her retirement Marie had been received into the Roman Catholic church; the Bancrofts referred scarcely, if at all, to religion in their memoirs. The reading at Nazareth House was presided over by the Lord Chief Justice, Lord Russell of Killowen,[*] the first Catholic for centuries to be appointed Lord Chief Justice of England.

Shortly after the death of the Rev William Rogers, funds were raised for a memorial to commemorate his life. There was a shortfall of around a hundred pounds. Squire was invited to do a reading to make up the amount and he was asked if he would approach his friend, the Lord Chief Justice, to see if he might preside. Squire pointed out that, as a devout Catholic, Lord Russell might not be prepared to help commemorate a Church of England clergyman. Lord Russell proved him wrong and accepted, saying that as Squire had gone out of his way to support a charity of his faith, he was delighted to return the favour.

As the popularity of Bancroft's readings grew, he found himself more and more in demand. On one occasion he read in aid of a Jewish hospital, the evening presided over by the Chief Rabbi. Bancroft wrote: 'The audience, which comprised many of the most prominent followers of that great faith, was one of the most responsive I have appealed to – for the Jews are well known for their wide knowledge and true appreciation of art in all its branches.' He went on to relate a story, possibly apocryphal, of a luncheon at which the Chief Rabbi was seated next to a Cardinal. The Cardinal, on being served a plateful of ham, turned to his neighbour asking, 'When will the day come when you, sir, will partake of ham?' to which the Chief Rabbi replied, 'At your Eminence's wedding.'

In the first season of readings of *A Christmas Carol*, Squire Bancroft raised large sums for hospitals in London and throughout the country. Over the many years he performed the readings he invariably paid all his

---

[*] Charles Arthur Russell, Baron Russell of Killowen, 1832-1900, an Irishman and an illustrious Lord Chief Justice.

own travelling and accommodation expenses so that every penny raised went to the charities concerned, whose overheads were thus minimal, just the hire of a hall and some publicity costs, and maybe an advertisement in the local newspaper – every town of any size had its own newspaper in those days. Energetic ladies from hospital fund-raising committees enthusiastically sold tickets. Readings were presided over by the great and the good, dukes and bishops, mayors and lord mayors, the Deans of Windsor, Westminster, Lincoln and other cathedral cities. The largest sum raised in any one evening was £800, from a reading Squire performed in the Egyptian Hall of the Mansion House in London, a splendid venue offered by the Lord Mayor of London. It was in aid of the Earlswood Asylum, a psychiatric hospital in Surrey.   .

During the early years of the readings Bancroft was invited by the Prince of Wales to present *A Christmas Carol* at Sandringham at Christmas. The ballroom was packed: the royals were present, together with their neighbours and guests, the royal household and the servants. For the occasion Squire slipped in an ad-lib that had Scrooge taking a 'real *Norfolk* turkey' to the Cratchits for their Christmas dinner, an addition that attracted extra laughter and applause. Later, over drinks in the billiard room, Bancroft produced the gold cigar-case presented to him by Queen Victoria at Balmoral a few years before and, showing it to the Prince of Wales, said that this was the first time it had been away from the safety of his home. 'Perhaps you would like me to be the first to take a cigar from it?' the Prince replied

The Prince of Wales had always been a good friend to the theatrical profession. Not long before he became king, he and the Princess of Wales attended a fête in aid of an actors' orphanage at which the Bancrofts were also present. The previous day a story had appeared in the papers headed 'Lady Bancroft's Lost Lovebird', referring to a small parakeet of Marie's that had escaped. A reward of ten shillings was offered for the bird's safe return. At the fête the Prince produced a cutting from his pocket saying, 'I believe I have Lady Bancroft's lost bird.' A small green bird had been spotted flying around the gardens of Marlborough House and a gardener had managed to catch it. 'Mind,' said the Prince, 'I shall claim the reward.' 'Certainly, sir,' replied Bancroft; 'it is small, but appropriate – *half a sovereign.*' The joke was impromptu, informal, but perhaps more easily made as Bancroft and the prince had met very informally a few years earlier – in rather unusual circumstances.

One bitterly cold afternoon in March 1892, with unseasonable snow falling, Squire Bancroft set out from his home in Berkeley Square for the Garrick Club. As he left his house he spotted a figure walking ahead of him that appeared familiar, enveloped in a large cape and hunched against the cold. Squire followed, struck by the resemblance of the cloaked figure to the Prince of Wales. He dismissed any idea that it might actually be the prince, as the heir to Victoria's throne would surely not be walking around the streets of London unaccompanied, but a moment later the figure ahead stopped and glanced behind him. Bancroft was now able to see that it was indeed the Prince of Wales. He crossed to the other side of the road, so the prince could retain the privacy he must be seeking, but the prince called out his name. So he crossed back towards him and, removing his hat, bowed to the future king, who begged him to replace it as it was such filthy weather. The two men walked along together and the Prince of Wales, who seemed in very low spirits, explained that he had desperately needed to get out and be on his own for a while. He began to talk of the many sadnesses and troubles that were distressing him at that time. Over the past few months, his eldest son, the next heir to the throne, Prince Albert Victor, Duke of Clarence, had died in January, aged only twenty-eight, during an influenza pandemic that had been sweeping the world. Prince Louis of Hesse, the husband of his sister, Princess Alice (the great-grandparents of Prince Philip, Duke of Edinburgh) was seriously ill and not expected to live: he too was to die shortly afterwards. Then there had been a devastating fire at Sandringham that had destroyed part of the house. As they walked on, the prince talked for some time about these sorrows and of other problems that he feared were looming. Then shaking Bancroft's hand he turned up Hay Hill, saying, 'I am so glad to have had this talk with you.' It was clearly unusual even then for a senior member of the royal family to walk unescorted around the streets of London. Today it would be unthinkable.

Invitations to read *A Christmas Carol* were now pouring in from so many charitable organisations that Bancroft decided he would have to restrict his readings to raising funds for hospitals and medical charities or he would never have had a spare day. In Liverpool a local newspaper reported on his visit in aid of the Home for Blind Children at Wavertree:

> For two hours he held the audience in the hollow of his hands [as he] drew tears and stirred to laughter .... The tragedy of the *Carol* was developed with power, and its pathos with infinite tenderness. Indeed the treatment of the story throughout – it was, by the way, given from memory – was a triumph of the art of the actor.

Another newspaper wrote that:

> he neither read nor declaimed .... but by his voice and gesture and attitude .... made Dickens's characters live and move and suffer and enjoy. One *saw* a gentleman in evening dress; but, by the alchemy of art, he became Scrooge, and the ghost, and Bob Cratchit, and Tiny Tim – each and every character in turn ....

Bancroft's *Carol* readings involved extensive rail travel. One winter tour involved eight readings in twelve days. It began in Newcastle-on-Tyne on a Tuesday, and the following evening he was in Glasgow. Most of the Thursday was spent travelling southwards, in order to reach Southport and Liverpool for the Friday and Saturday. He went home for one day before setting off on Monday for Bath. On Tuesday it was on to Torquay for an afternoon reading and immediately following this he moved on to Plymouth to be ready for the following day. While there he visited his old manager, James Doel, by now believed to be the oldest living actor. After reading in Plymouth on Wednesday Bancroft immediately took the London train for a reading at the Inner Temple Hall on the Thursday. Then just two days later he set sail for Canada, where he had accepted an invitation to perform his *Christmas Carol* in aid of hospitals there.

It was a tour that Bancroft must have relished. Most of his theatrical contemporaries had visited North America many times, with lucrative but gruelling tours that took them all over the continent. Bancroft, who was once described as the only actor since David Garrick who managed to make a fortune without at least one tour in America, would have dearly loved to do the same, if only Marie had not so dreaded the prospect of the long ocean crossing. Now at last he was to go, with her blessing, on his own. It was to be a gruelling trip, but one that he greatly enjoyed.

The St Lawrence River was frozen over, so, unable to go directly to Montreal, Bancroft sailed to New York, continuing by train, a journey of many hours. As ever, he had insisted on paying all his own travel expenses, including his Atlantic crossing . He was 'treated like a prince' in Canada, being invited to stay with notable figures in the cities he visited. In Ottawa he stayed with the Governor-General and in Quebec with the Bishop. In Toronto he stayed with the Governor of Ontario, who, when Squire mentioned how much he would love to see Niagara Falls, immediately arranged a visit for him.

Travel was difficult in Canada in the depths of winter. On his opening night in Montreal there was a blizzard and Squire suggested that surely no audience would turn up in such conditions. His host roared with laughter, saying that if they waited for the weather in Canada they would go nowhere for months on end. They set off through the blizzard in a horse-drawn sleigh and sure enough, the hall was packed. The day after the Montreal reading he met a Scotsman, then resident in Canada, who told him, 'You know, you made me cry last night.' 'Well, that'll do you no harm,' replied Squire. 'No, and it won't do the hospital no harm, either,' said the man as they parted. Later Squire was told that the unidentified expatriate Scot had donated a million dollars to the Montreal branch of the Victorian Order of Nurses, the charity for which, along with the Montreal Maternity Hospital, the reading had been raising funds. The following day, the train from Montreal to Quebec was stuck for hours in a snowdrift and, when he eventually reached Quebec, Bancroft crossed the frozen river in a sleigh. In all he performed seven readings, in the cities of Montreal, Quebec, Ottawa, Kingston, Toronto, Hamilton and London, Ontario, with long train journeys between the cities.

He then returned to New York, where he stayed near Greenwich Village. He wrote that he found the place where he had lodged as a boy, an old house in downtown Manhattan, greatly changed:

> I found, instead of pleasant private dwellings, lofty warehouses and towering cranes; the same with Houston Street and Bleecker Street close by. Between them Laura Keene's theatre had stood, while Wallack's theatre was then below Canal Street .... Down by the City Hall I went up a tremendous 'sky-scraper' – a strange, Gilbertian, topsy-turvy form of architecture – which extinguished everything below. The spire of Trinity Church .... and the churchyard of St Paul's, hard by, seemed very small and insignificant.

In New York Bancroft met with many actors he knew who had over the years spent time in England. He received much kindness and hospitality from these old friends 'in an old-world remnant of the city – Washington Square.' Among these was Maurice Barrymore who had been with the Haymarket company more than ten years earlier. Of course, while in New York, he went to the theatre, seeing Ada Rehan[*] in *The Country Girl*, David Garrick's 'cleaned-up' 1776 version of William Wycherley's Restoration comedy *The Country Wife*, which was for around 250 years considered too indecent to put on stage.

Another colourful American whom Squire had met in London was the flamboyant Augustin Daly[*]. In New York Daly called him in his hotel room by telephone but Squire found this piece of new-fangled, modern technology alarming: 'Being unfamiliar, then, with that useful but aggravating instrument, I dictated my share of the task to a diminutive Yankee boy with a powerful twang. When Daly asked, "How is your dear wife?" I prompted the boy to say, "Splendid; heard from her this morning."' To Squire's amazement, the answer came back at once, 'So glad to hear it, and so glad to hear your voice again!'

Bancroft sailed for home in the Cunard liner, the *Umbria*, which, when she was launched in 1884, was the largest liner then afloat. She had two large funnels but still carried three great masts with a vast expanse of canvas sail – one of the last liners still to carry sails. Three years after her

---

[*] Ada Rehan, 1859-1916, a distinguished American actress, born in Ireland. She toured successfully in Europe.

[*] John Augustin Daly, 1838-99, an American theatre manager and impresario, and drama critic. He ran the popular Daly's theatres in New York, with Ada Rehan as his leading actress, and, for a time, in London.

launch she won the coveted 'Blue Riband' for the fastest liner across the Atlantic, completing the westbound crossing in six days plus a few hours. On his arrival home when the figures were calculated, Squire discovered that his readings to date had raised the remarkable total of £7,000, which would be getting on for a million pounds today.

***Squire Bancroft** reading* **A Christmas Carol;**
*caricature by **L.J.Binns***

Back home the *Carol* readings continued for many years, with Bancroft visiting towns and cities all over the country. He told of a near-disaster when he was due to perform in Bradford. Two trains left London for the north at 1.30, one from Euston, the other from King's Cross. Squire went to Euston and too late he realised that his train was not going to Bradford. There was nothing he could do until he reached Crewe. Here, 'I ordered a special train .... I was prepared to pay anything demanded of me, for never once in my life had I failed to keep an appointment with the public.' It sounds quite extraordinary today that anyone, however wealthy, could order 'a special train' at a moment's notice. Waiting anxiously in Bradford, the chairman for the evening was the Bishop of Ripon, who, with no idea when, or if, his speaker would arrive, was preparing to give the waiting audience a lecture of his own – on Dante. He was surely most relieved – or maybe disappointed – when his speaker arrived with minutes to spare. Squire hurriedly changed into his evening clothes, downed a quick cup of soup, and went on stage only fifteen minutes late.

He performed his *Christmas Carol* for the undergraduates and dons at the universities of Oxford and Cambridge, and also for the boys and staff at the great public schools, including Eton, Harrow and Winchester, where wealthy parents were happy to come and listen along with their sons, and to contribute to those less fortunate in need of health care. Occasionally an evening's takings would be boosted when members of the audience would sign up for annual subscriptions or maybe leave a sum to the charity in their wills. The *British Medical Journal* often ran reports on the readings, raising, as they did, much-needed funds for hospitals and medical institutions all over the country, hospitals that had constantly to raise funds in order to exist – the National Health Service was still more than half a century in the future.

It was at the busiest period of the Bancrofts' charitable fundraising, in 1897, that the nation celebrated Queen Victoria's Diamond Jubilee, marking the sixty years of her reign. She had ruled for longer than any other monarch and there had been more changes during her long reign than during any other period of British history. Vast areas of the world had been coloured red as the British Empire expanded to become the largest the world had ever known. At home there had been the still-developing Industrial Revolution, the Chartist movement, and technological advances unimaginable when she came to the throne in 1837. Since then the Queen herself had survived assassination attempts, rail travel had spread across the land, and the age of the motor car was about to dawn. Sound recording was in its infancy – the voice of Henry Irving can be heard today, his words from *Hamlet* just about audible via an early wax cylinder now digitised – but the telephone was already transforming communications, and the established art of photography was about to revolutionise the world of entertainment, with the era of film just around the corner.

In the week before the Diamond Jubilee celebrations, on 16 June 1897, Squire and Marie Bancroft returned home from an afternoon engagement to find a letter addressed to Squire awaiting them. It was from 10 Downing Street, from the Prime Minister, the Marquess of Salisbury. It read:

> I have the honour of submitting to the Queen that the Honour of Knighthood should be conferred upon you on the occasion of the approaching Jubilee; Her Majesty having been pleased to approve of my recommendation, in recognition of the high position which you occupy in

the profession to which you have rendered such notable service, it becomes my duty to acquaint you with Her gracious intention.

Believe me, yours very faithfully, Salisbury

So, Squire Bancroft became the second actor to receive the honour of knighthood. Following the knighting of Henry Irving in 1895, this was a signal that the gates were at last well and truly open for the acting profession to be so recognised. In 1902 Charles Wyndham would become the third actor to be knighted, and John Hare the fourth, in 1907. The DBE, Dame Commander of the Order of the British Empire, was not introduced until 1917, twenty years after Bancroft's knighthood. The first actress to receive the honour was Dame May Whitty[*], in 1918, although she received her award for her charitable work during World War One. Three years later Dame Genevieve Ward[*] became the first actress to be honoured specifically for her services to the dramatic profession when she was created a DBE on her eighty-fourth birthday in March 1921. Then at long last, in the New Year's honours list of 1925, Ellen Terry's great contribution to the theatrical profession was recognised, when she was awarded the DBE. Today, no honours list would be complete without representatives of men and women from the acting profession.

Everyone recognised and accepted that the honour conferred upon Squire Bancroft was as much for Marie's contribution to their profession as for his own. Joseph Knight, in *The Stage in the Year 1900*, wrote that 'she shared the honour conferred by Queen Victoria upon her husband' at a time when the only way that a woman could be honoured was by receiving the title of 'Lady' through her husband. For the Bancrofts it was therefore a joint honour in recognition of their years of work together and for the charitable work both had undertaken since their retirement from acting. Bancroft would himself have readily admitted that he was never a truly great actor, but he treasured this tribute to their joint achievements in management and in raising the status of actors and the theatre to a level unimaginable when they each set out as fledgling players so many years before.

---

[*] May Whitty, 1865-1948, was to appear in several films, including Hitchcock's *The Lady Vanishes* in 1938.
[*] Genevieve Ward, 1837-1922, started out as an operatic singer, later becoming a distinguished actress.

14

CURTAIN

Squire Bancroft continued his readings of *A Christmas Carol* well into the twentieth century, raising the equivalent of over a million pounds in today's money. In 1905 the *Tatler* reported that a very large sum was raised in one night for the National Hospital for the Paralysed and Epileptic – at that time specialist hospitals had no problem with spelling out exactly the conditions of the patients they cared for. That particular hospital must have been close to the hearts of the Bancrofts: Marie's sister, Georgina, a sufferer from epilepsy, had died in 1893. She had always lived, after the deaths of her parents, at the homes of one or other of her sisters, but many epileptics spent their lives in institutions.

The Bancrofts marked the early years of the new century by supporting two other causes close to their hearts. The first of these was the welfare of the London cab drivers to whose labours theatres had been indebted over many years. Their work involved driving their horse-drawn cabs long distances in all weathers, with no covers to their driving seats, to bring people, including theatre staff, actors and audiences, into the West End. Then they would have to wait around, often frequenting the public houses, which was regarded as an undesirable risk in that they might be less than capable drivers when it came to delivering their patrons safely home. As early as 1874 a charity was set up by the Earl of Salisbury to install shelters for cabbies, where they could get 'good and wholesome refreshments at moderate prices' during their long waits, while their patient horses waited nearby, the lucky ones with a nosebag full of hay attached to their harness.

Once there were over sixty elegant green timber Victorian and Edwardian cabmen's shelters around London. Just thirteen remain, still in use today. One of them stands in Russell Square, a plaque on its door indicating that it was donated by Sir Squire Bancroft in 1901. This shelter was originally positioned in the Haymarket but when motor traffic increased, making such a structure, with its waiting cabs and horses, an obstruction to through traffic, it was resited in the more spacious area of Leicester Square, opposite the Odeon. Years later, when Leicester Square was going through one of its many facelifts, it was again moved, to the western corner of Russell Square, where there is plenty of space for today's drivers to park their black cabs while they take a well-earned break. In the 1980s it was restored by the Heritage of London Trust, the former Greater London Council and other bodies, along with help from Brenda Bancroft, a granddaughter of Charles Bancroft. The thirteen surviving shelters are now carefully tended as Grade II listed buildings[*].

Squire Bancroft's cabmen's shelter, now in Russell Square

---

[*] In 2012 the shelter in Russell Square underwent a further restoration. The pavement it stands on has been widely extended and the shelter now faces the garden of the square, a pleasant aspect for the cabbies.

The Bancrofts and most of the leading actors and managers of the late nineteenth century believed that their profession should strive for two goals above all others: that Britain should have its own National Theatre and that there should be an establishment devoted to the training of new recruits to the acting profession. Despite their enthusiasm, however, it was not until the 1960s that Britain's own National Theatre was finally established, and it was 1976 before it moved into its own home on the South Bank. A national drama school came about sooner, but only after several false starts.

The cause had a long history. In July 1860 *The Era* carried a report of a fête that was held at the Crystal Palace, in aid of the Royal Dramatic College near Woking. (The foundation stone of the college had been laid by Prince Albert in June that year.) Among the theatrical ladies involved in the 'Fête and Fancy Fair' of 1860 was Miss Marie Wilton, along with Ada Swanborough and other colleagues from the Strand Theatre, and Mrs Fanny Stirling, then in her forties. Some theatrical gentlemen also took part, including John Baldwin Buckstone, John Lawrence Toole and James Rogers, manning attractions that included 'Aunt Sally, Sticks and Snuffboxes, and a Mystery Tent'. Sadly, it was not enough. The College was opened by the Prince of Wales three years later but from the start it struggled. In spite of generous financial backing from T.P.Cooke*, an actor who went on to leave the college a large bequest in his will when he died in 1867, it was always in serious need of funds and depended entirely on public support and fundraising events. The Royal Dramatic College closed in 1870.

Then in 1875 someone came up with the idea that there should be a 'Shakespeare Theatre' in Stratford-upon-Avon – an idea that was itself to come to fruition in the distant future – and that a school of dramatic art should be established there at the same time. This was opposed by those who insisted that any such institute could only be set up in London, at the heart of the profession. Meetings and discussions were held over many years, yet it was not until 1904 that Herbert Beerbohm Tree, by then the leading actor-manager in London, had the courage to bring this ideal to reality by launching the Academy of Dramatic Art within his own theatre, His Majesty's, in the Haymarket. George Bancroft, now aged thirty-five, was appointed its secretary and administrator.

Putting his legal career on hold for the next five years, George was immediately inundated with applications. For all of its first year the Academy was based at His Majesty's, which George described as being

---

* T.P. (Thomas Potter) Cooke, 1786-1864, was among the original members of the Garrick Club. Before becoming an actor, he served in Nelson's navy, fighting at the Battle of Toulon in 1796 – at the age of ten – and at Cape St Vincent in 1897. He was the first actor to play Frankenstein's monster.

314

like a rabbit warren, full of half-lit rooms and passages, with young men and women scuttling around the building to and from their studies in whatever spare spaces had been taken over for teaching. The theatre's foyer was used as a rehearsal area during times when the public were not around. Then in the following year, 1905, the Academy moved to its own quarters in Gower Street, eventually becoming the Royal Academy of Dramatic Art. At the same time a Council was set up to administer the Academy, with Squire Bancroft being elected its first President.

RADA has gone on from those early days to become one of the most prestigious drama schools in the world. Right at its beginning Squire Bancroft endowed its most coveted prize, the Bancroft Gold Medal, awarded annually to the outstanding student of the year. From 1905, for eighty years, until the medal was discontinued in 1985, the names of the winners were listed on an honours board at RADA. The first winner was Robert Atkins, who went on to become a successful actor and director, eventually founding the Open Air Theatre in Regent's Park in 1932, and no fewer than thirteen of the first twenty Gold Medals were awarded to women. Among the many well-known actors of today who won the Bancroft Gold Medal in their youth are Siân Phillips, Gemma Jones, Alan Rickman, Trevor Eve, Timothy Spall, Fiona Shaw, Kenneth Branagh, Mark Rylance and Juliet Stevenson; and countless other famous names have graduated from RADA over the years.

BANCROFT GOLD MEDAL

Year	Winner	Year	Winner	Year	Winner
1905	ROBERT ATKINS	1935	DOUGLAS MATTHEWS	1966	KENNETH CRANHAM
	REGINALD OWEN	1936	GEOFFREY KEEN	1967	JOAN MEREDITH
1906	MARY BARTON	1937	KATHLEEN LAURIE	1968	DESMOND McNAMARA
1907	H.G. BENTLY	1938	EDWARD BURNHAM	1969	JAMES HURDLE / STUART WILSON
1908	ATHENE SEYLER	1939	HUGH GRIFFITH	1970	LYNN DEARTH
1909	RUPERT LUMLEY	1940	ALAN MACNAUGHTAN	1971	CHARLES LUTZ / REBECCA SMITH
1910	GRACE CROFT	1941	ALAN BADEL	1972	JONATHAN HYDE
1911	DOROTHY WOOD		HAROLD LANG	1973	LINDA JANIEC / TREVOR EVE
1912	LEONARD NOTCUTT	1943	JACQUELINE MAUDE	1974	ALAN RICKMAN
1913	OLIVE DAVIES	1944	PATRICIA LAWRENCE	1975	STEPHEN DAVIES / KEVIN McNALLY
1914	GLADYS YOUNG	1945	JEAN WILSON	1976	ANDREW SEEAR
1915	NORAH BALFOUR	1946	DAPHNE SLATER	1977	ANTON LESSER / JULIET STEVENSON
1916	JOAN TEMPLE	1947	PATRICIA KNEALE	1978	TIMOTHY SPALL
1917	MEGGIE ALBANESI	1948	BREWSTER MASON	1979	DAVID BAMBER / KIERON JECCHINIS
1918	ANNE TURNER ROBERTSON	1949	BARBARA JEFFORD	1980	MARK RYLANCE
1919	IRENE WARD	1950	PETER FAWCETT	1981	MARY JO RANDLE / KENNETH BRANAGH
1920	JANE AMSTEL	1951	GABRIEL WOOLF	1982	FIONA SHAW
1921	JOAN SWINSTEAD	1952	ROSEMARY HARRIS	1983	JANET McTEER / SARAH WOODWARD
1922	GUY PELHAM BOULTON	1953	MARGARET WHITING	1984	GERARD LOGAN
1923	MERVYN JOHNS	1954	JANE DOWNS	1985	IAIN GLEN / PAUL RHYS
1924	CARLETON HOBBS	1955	BRYAN PRINGLE		
1925	MOLLY RANKIN	1956	GILLIAN MARTELL		
1926	CHARLES LAUGHTON	1957	SIÂN PHILLIPS		
1927	JOAN HARBEN	1958	CHARLES KAY		
1928	PATRICIA HAYES	1959	BARBARA BARNETT		
1929	GEORGE CROSS	1960	DEREK SMITH		
1930	JOHN BOXER	1961	JENNIFER HILARY		
1931	BETTY LYNNE	1962	GEMMA JONES		
1932	GRIFFITH JONES	1963	PHILIP GILLARD		
1933	VIOLA KEATS	1964	SUSAN FLEETWOOD		
1934	JACQUELINE CLARKE	1965	BARBARA EWING		

board at RADA showing the winners of the Bancroft Gold Medal

George Bancroft was to hand on the administration of RADA in 1910, when he resumed his legal career, but his father remained a key member of the Council. Some years later a silent film of *Masks and Faces*[*] was made by Ideal Films to raise funds at a time when RADA's future was uncertain during the First World War. It was released in March 1917 and the star-studded cast included Johnston Forbes-Robertson as Triplet, and Irene Vanbrugh as Peg Woffington. Other characters were played by Gerald du Maurier, Dennis Neilson-Terry and Gladys Cooper, along with many other famous names of the time, who all appeared for free. The film opened with a prologue in which members of the Academy's Council, appearing as themselves, can be seen seated around a table, with Sir Squire Bancroft in the chair. Sir Arthur Pinero, unmistakable with his bald head, is seated next to the actress Irene Vanbrugh, who years later, in 1941, was to become a DBE. Also unmistakable is George Bernard Shaw, on Bancroft's left, with Sir John Hare, the small man next to him. Others around the table include the playwright Sir James Barrie, Sir Johnston Forbes-Robertson and Sir George Alexander. Noticeably missing from the gathering is Sir Herbert Beerbohm Tree, the inspiration behind the Academy: he died in July that very year, having received a knighthood for services to his profession in 1909.

scene of the RADA Council in the 1917 film of **Masks and Faces**

In October 1905 the English theatre lost its brightest star, Henry Irving. Early that month he set off to tour the north. He was so ill that his devoted

---

[*] It is still possible to see the film of *Masks and Faces* today, by appointment, as there is a copy in the archives of the British Film Institute.

staff became more and more alarmed at his condition. On the night of 13 October he appeared at the Theatre Royal, Bradford, in Tennyson's play *Becket*, when he played the part of Thomas à Becket more movingly than ever before. In the final dramatic moments, when the king's knights burst into Canterbury cathedral with drawn swords to slaughter the archbishop, Irving's final words on stage were 'Into Thy hands, O Lord, into Thy hands', as he fell at the steps of the altar. He just managed to take a few curtain calls and in his dressing room he bid an unusually fond goodnight to Bram Stoker. Harry Loveday, his stage-manager, assisted him into a cab and he was taken back to his hotel, where he was helped up the steps and into the hotel hallway, where he collapsed and, moments later, died.

Henry Irving as the Archbishop in **Becket**

In one of the many tributes that poured in at the time of Irving's death John Hare wrote: 'A great man, indeed, he was, not only as an actor and manager, but great by reason of his humanity, his heroic courage in times of stress and suffering, and his gentle tenderness of heart to all men. Other actors have in the past died and left an honourable record of great

317

achievement. None, from Garrick onwards, has left such a legacy of love and deep respect as the dear friend we have lost. The best tribute the stage can pay to his memory is for its members to follow his example of noble, high endeavour; the only one the country can pay is to accord him a last resting place in …. Westminster Abbey so that amongst the roll of our illustrious dead may be inscribed the honoured name of Henry Irving.'

Irving's ashes were indeed buried in Westminster Abbey, in Poets' Corner close by David Garrick and the statue of William Shakespeare. Among the pall-bearers at his funeral were his fellow-actors Squire Bancroft, John Hare, Herbert Beerbohm Tree and Charles Wyndham along with the playwright Arthur Pinero and the Royal Academician Sir Lawrence Alma-Tadema, and on the day of his funeral London's cabbies tied black ribbons to their whips to mark the day. Hare went on to chair a committee that was set up to commemorate Irving's life and it was he who unveiled the statue of Irving by Sir Thomas Brock that still stands outside the National Portrait Gallery in London.

Among George Bancroft's most treasured possessions was the wooden cross that Irving, as the murdered Thomas Becket, was carrying as he fell at the steps of the altar. A stage prop, of little intrinsic value, the 'Irving Cross' is a theatrical relic beyond price. George kept it in a glass case for the rest of his life. It is now safely in the keeping of RADA.

The year 1906 marked Ellen Terry's Jubilee – fifty years since she made her stage debut at the age of nine in *A Winter's Tale*. She and Irving had hoped and planned for a joint 'monster performance' as his own jubilee fell in the same year. Now she resisted any thought of a celebration: 'I did not want to think about it, for any recognition of my jubilee which did not include his, seemed to me very unnecessary,' she wrote, but her colleagues in the profession would not hear of such an occasion passing unmarked and a lavish celebratory programme was planned at Drury Lane. Crowds began queueing outside the theatre the night before in the hope of seats in the pit or the gallery. They brought camp stools, food and reading matter to occupy themselves during their long wait and buskers helped entertain them while they waited. Ellen herself visited the patient queue at two o'clock in the morning.

It was a star-studded programme. There was a performance of *Trial by Jury* with W.S.Gilbert himself taking part, along with well-known figures as spectators in court or on the jury, among them Sir Arthur Conan Doyle and Anthony Hope, the author of *The Prisoner of Zenda*. Twelve 'tableaux vivants' included Lillie Langtry as Cleopatra, and other well-known actresses posing as famous paintings or dramatic episodes from history, many of them designed by Royal Academicians such as Luke Fildes RA and Sir Laurence Alma-Tadema. There were scenes from *Much Ado about Nothing*, with Ellen herself as Beatrice and Herbert Beerbohm

Tree as Benedick. Johnston Forbes-Robertson and Gerald du Maurier were also in the cast as were Henry Irving's two sons, Harry and Laurence Irving. Gordon Craig (Ellen's son Teddy) designed the set and an elaborate masked dance was performed by the twenty-two members of the Terry family who were present, partnered by London's leading stage stars. Other performances included a song from the celebrated Italian tenor, Enrico Caruso. The event closed with a speech delivered by Marie Bancroft on behalf of the profession, and when at last the celebrations were all over, before going home Ellen drove to Berkeley Square to present Marie, 'one of my best and oldest comrades', with a bouquet of flowers.

photograph given by Ellen Terry to
George Bancroft when he left school in 1886

In 1906 Squire Bancroft was elected chairman of two more charities. The first was of the board of governors of the Foundling Hospital*, then still

---

* The Foundling Hospital was established in London in 1739 by Captain Thomas Coram. William Hogarth was a governor and George Friedrich Handel gave performances there to raise funds. It is now the moving and fascinating Foundling Museum, in Brunswick Square.

caring for abandoned children in Coram's Fields, London, before relocating to Berkhamsted, Hertfordshire, in 1926. His name is among those commemorated in a stained glass window that was in the original Coram's Fields chapel and is now in the chapel at Berkhamsted. The second chairmanship was of the Actors' Association, which had been formed in 1891 by the actors Frank Benson* and Robert Courtneidge*, originally with the object of protecting actors from unscrupulous managers who absconded without paying them and to raise the pay and status of actors generally. Irving was its first president. Bancroft's election was opposed by several younger members of the Association who thought Bancroft and his contemporaries represented the old, Victorian outlook that no longer fitted with their vision of a forward-looking organisation. This new generation of actors was pressing for the Association to become a fully-fledged trade union, raising pay and improving conditions for its members. The Actors' Association was eventually replaced by British Actors' Equity in 1929.

In 1909 Marie Bancroft turned seventy, and Squire was sixty-eight. That year their second set of reminiscences, *Recollections of Sixty Years*, was produced by the prestigious publisher John Murray, some twenty years after their first memoirs. Murray, established in Albemarle Street in 1768, had been the publisher of Lord Byron, Jane Austen, Walter Scott, and Darwin's *On the Origin of Species*. The original edition of *Sixty Years* was a handsome volume printed on heavy paper, with facsimiles of both Bancrofts' signatures on the title page and illustrated with photographs and drawings of themselves and of their theatrical colleagues. It is predominantly the work of Squire Bancroft; nevertheless his dedication is an acknowledgment that the success of their career was due to Marie's talents. It reads: '*I dedicate my share in this book to a comrade and friend, my wife, but for whose name and fame there would be small need for it – S.B.*' Much of the material in *Sixty Years* – the first forty of those years – had already been covered in *On and Off the Stage*, but this did not appear to deter the book-buying public and a reprint was soon needed. Then in 1911 a cheaper 'Popular Edition', on thinner paper and without the illustrations, was published by Thomas Nelson.

---

* Sir Francis Robert (Frank) Benson, 1858-1939. His first appearance on the London stage was with Irving at the Lyceum. He went on to become one of the foremost actors and producers, primarily of Shakespeare.
* Robert Courtneidge, 1859–1939, actor and theatre manager, father of actress Dame Cicely Courtneidge, 1893-1980.

Again their recollections covered only their professional lives; personal matters, whether concerning themselves or their children, were kept strictly private. This leaves the reader at a loss to know what faces lay behind the masks of two such very public, and popular, figures, especially as few personal letters have come to light. Their son, George, in his autobiography, *Stage and Bar*, is more revealing, though even he gives very little intimate detail. However, from George it is possible to deduce that he had a close and affectionate relationship with his father and that he adored his mother, describing her as warm-hearted and bewitching. 'She possessed great courage and tremendous strength of character,' he wrote. 'A tiny figure but a real rock – immovable if she had made up her mind. Temperament? Like quicksilver; up one moment and down the next. But never down for long. Difficult? Ye-e-s, sometimes; but you would not have had her different. Impulsive? She could be, but she was generally right. Her spontaneity was, I think, one of her greatest charms ....'

Squire and Marie Bancroft in retirement

When she was well into her seventies, Marie tried her hand at a novel, *The Shadow of Neeme*, which was published in 1912, also by John

Murray. It is a romance, with hints of the supernatural, set in an old manor house inherited by a rich but melancholic young man who lives there with his widowed mother and his spirited younger sister. Hanging in the house is a mesmerising portrait of a lovely, unknown young woman from an earlier era. He becomes entranced by the girl in the portrait. Living nearby is the penniless local rector, with his wife and daughters. The beautiful younger daughter rarely leaves the rectory where she devotedly cares for her invalid mother. When eventually our hero meets her, he finds that she is identical in appearance to the young woman in the portrait and, inevitably, he falls in love with her. Overcoming many setbacks, eventually all turns out well. The novel is quite well-written, in spite of being sentimental and predictable. The most interesting character is the sister, a 'modern' young woman, who uses the sort of slangy language that makes her mother feel quite faint with dismay and who, horror of horrors, smokes – when her mother can't see her. Marie clearly relished creating a character in many ways similar to her own younger self.

When the Bancrofts were in London Squire would go to one of his clubs on most days; generally it would be the Garrick, but also among his favourites were the Green Room Club and the Athenaeum, probably the most prestigious of all the London gentlemen's clubs. When he had first applied to become a member of the Athenaeum in 1893 his application was rejected. This caused much indignation amongst his friends, including the artist Frederick Leighton who wrote to Henry Irving, expressing his 'disgust' that 'a parcel of nobodies' had blackballed their friend. Irving too wrote to a friend saying that he was 'very grieved' and Bancroft himself, in a letter to Irving, expressed his hurt that there was still such prejudice against actors. However, he applied again some years later and this time he was elected, possibly because he was now 'Sir' Squire Bancroft: his and Irving's knighthoods opened many doors that had previously been closed to their profession.

Squire Bancroft was diligent about visiting sick friends, invariably bringing grapes. With morbid humour he would tell the invalid he was visiting that 'I'm bringing you white grapes because I am sure you are going to get better. I only bring black grapes when there is no hope.' He also had what one friend described as 'a perfect mania' for attending funerals, those of close friends and of more distant acquaintances – or even when he did not know the deceased at all. The novelist Max Pemberton told of an occasion that he admitted was almost certainly apocryphal, when a train in which 'B' was travelling was held up at a lonely country station, with no chance of moving for some time. Spotting a funeral cortège passing the station, he got off the train and joined the followers. 'Whom are we burying?' he asked the sexton at the lych gate of the village church. 'History does not record the answer,' wrote Pemberton. Squire himself had a sense of humour about his enjoyment of funerals: he once said that 'if the ghosts of all those whose interment ceremonies I have been present at were to assemble at my own funeral, the wraiths would completely fill a church as large as St Margaret's, Westminster.'

In retirement the Bancrofts gradually substituted holidays at home for those they had for so many years enjoyed on the continent. They became increasingly fond of Kent, and bought a house by the sea, White Lodge in Westgate. Their granddaughter, Naomi, remembered that when she was small her grandparents had a parrot that could speak its address. It would squawk: 'Eighteen Berkeley Square – I prefer Westgate.' Squire would take a daily swim in the sea when it was warm enough; in August of 1902 he mentioned his daily dips in a letter to Bram Stoker, describing how he would go 'bathing like a boy, throwing my clothes on the sands – not bad for 61!' He also enjoyed cycling, as a recreation with friends rather than as a means of transport. There is a photograph of him with Sir Arthur Pinero, 'B' looking casual in plus-fours and a cap, 'Pin' rather smartly suited, leaning on their bicycles while out for a jaunt.

Bancroft and Pinero – cycling jaunt

323

In 1911 the Bancrofts handed over White Lodge to George and Effie, and moved to a smaller house at Sandgate, close to Folkestone, then a pleasantly quiet seaside town, which thrived on holiday visitors in the summer. They lived in a pretty house called Underlea, to the west of the town, overlooking the sea. The Bancrofts both involved themselves with Folkestone life and in 1914 Squire was invited to lay the foundation stone of the Chichester Memorial Hall in Sandgate, a fine building that is still in use today. Squire became president of the local Folkestone amateur dramatic club and both he and Marie gave their support and encouragement by attending its performances.

During the First World War the holidaymakers disappeared from Folkestone, to be replaced by troops awaiting transport across the Channel to France. Camps were built for them nearby and many were billeted in requisitioned hotels and boarding houses around the town. Hundreds of refugees began to arrive, fleeing the conflict raging just across the Channel. Folkestone became a dangerous place. Being so close to the continent it suffered several air raids during the war. In the worst of these, in 1917, more than seventy civilians were killed and almost a hundred injured. Being literally the first ports of call for wounded soldiers, the Channel ports soon began to receive an ever-growing number of casualties into their hospitals.

The Bancrofts involved themselves as best they could in helping the war effort, mainly by taking part in fund-raising entertainments in aid of the Royal Victoria Hospital in Folkestone and the wounded soldiers they cared for. One Christmas during the war years Squire gave a reading of *A Christmas Carol* at the Pleasure Gardens Theatre in Folkestone. The local paper reported that the theatre was packed with an audience that was 'thrilled and charmed with the eminent actor's wonderful diction and the artistry with which he made the characters live.' They took part in entertainments put on for the casualties at various hospitals in and around Folkestone. Marie also volunteered her help in 'performing hospital duties' for the wounded soldiers, probably by sitting to chat with them and maybe read to them. It is unlikely that she would have been much help in writing letters for those who were too injured to do this for themselves, as her handwriting would, if possible, have become more indecipherable than ever with old age. It saddened Squire, in his mid-seventies, that he was too old to do more for the war effort. He was saddened too by the loss of so many of his young successors in the acting profession. 'The Great War dealt severe blows to the stage, many a young life of promise being taken,' he wrote.

Happily for the Bancrofts there was one new production to celebrate, even in that traumatic time of war. Their son George, who had never entirely abandoned his theatrical yearnings – he had written about eight plays, mostly unmemorable – had at last come up with a notable success. This was *The Ware Case*, which he adapted from his own novel, published by Methuen in 1913. It was first produced in 1915 at Wyndham's Theatre, with George's close friend Gerald du Maurier*, the manager of Wyndham's, directing as well as playing the lead. It being wartime, among the advertisements in the programme for cigarettes, alcoholic drinks, and even for 'Wm.Pierrepont, Inquiry Agent to the Nobility and Gentry, Entrusted with Divorce and Delicate Negotiations in all parts of the World. Go to him if Blackmailed .... ', there were appeals for young men to sign up. The London Rifle Brigade – 'The Office Man's Corps' – proclaimed that 'recruits are urgently needed', and the Finsbury Rifles were being formed, providing 'a good opportunity for smart men to "do their bit".'

The Ware Case was a legal thriller with a memorable courtroom scene, in which, for the first time ever, the stage was arranged so that the audience was in the position of the jury box; thus the counsels for the prosecution and for the defence, and the judge in his summing up, would turn and address the audience as 'Gentlemen of the Jury' (women were not allowed to serve on juries until a few years after the war ended). Du Maurier insisted that George, with his legal expertise, should assist him in directing the trial scene. Daphne du Maurier, in her biography of her father, wrote that 'the trial scene in *The Ware Case* was faultlessly produced and acted'. One night during the original London production there was a Zeppelin raid over London. A distant drone and a thud were heard, followed by another, closer, explosion. From the stage it could be seen that the audience, which that night included George Bancroft's parents, was becoming uneasy. There was restless fidgeting and much fluttering of programmes. In an undertone du Maurier instructed the rest of the cast to raise their voices and carry on. The audience calmed, the play went on and the air-raid passed. At the end of the act, when the curtain fell, there was tremendous applause and calls for the cast. Du Maurier led his company to the footlights where they all applauded the audience in return. 'Gerald addressed them, in his characteristic, airy way,' wrote George. '"Ladies and gentlemen," he said, "it's all right. That tiresome little trouble just now has gone away."'

---

* Sir Gerald du Maurier, 1873-1934, one of the most popular actors of the early years of the twentieth century, created the dual roles of Captain Hook and Mr Darling in *Peter Pan*. He was knighted for services to the stage in 1922. His daughter, the novelist Daphne du Maurier, wrote a biography of her father, *Gerald, a Portrait*, published in 1934.

Later *The Ware Case* was to be filmed – three times. There were two silent versions, then in 1939 Michael Balcon* produced a version at Ealing Studios, directed by Robert Stevenson*. A radio version of the play was broadcast by the BBC in the 1960s.

George Bancroft's legal career was long and distinguished and he became Clerk of Assize of the Midland Circuit in 1913, a position he held for over thirty years. In the days of legal circuits and regional assizes, the Clerk of Assize was responsible for the smooth running of trials and assisting and advising the judge: 'I am the judge's stage manager in court,' George would reply when asked to describe his position. On his retirement in 1946, a Birmingham newspaper quoted a judge as saying, 'Without him, the Midland Circuit is unthinkable. There is no judge on the Bench who has not found him a wise, patient and faithful adviser – practical, resourceful and considerate.'

George and Effie Bancroft's first child, a daughter, Barbara, was born in 1894, followed by a son, Squire John, born in 1899. Sadly this baby died of pneumonia around the time of his first birthday. Two more daughters followed, Diana Marie and Naomi. In the 1930s George bought Elibank, a beautiful early eighteenth-century house in the village of Taplow, Buckinghamshire. It is a Grade II Listed Building. Elibank was full of mementoes and signed photographs of George and Effie's parents and other theatrical legends, alongside photographs of bewigged judges and other eminent legal figures. Both Effie and George died at Elibank, Effie of cancer in 1934. George died in 1956, at the age of 87.

Despite the agonies of war, celebrations were organised on 2 May 1916 at Drury Lane, in the presence of the King and Queen, to mark the three hundred years since the death of William Shakespeare. The committee that organised the event was headed by Sir Herbert Beerbohm Tree and Sir George Alexander, supported by a large assembly of actors and managers, among them Squire Bancroft, W.H.Kendal, John Hare, Johnston Forbes-Robertson, John Martin-Harvey*, H.B.Irving and Gerald du Maurier.

---

* Sir Michael Balcon, 1896-1977, film producer, famed for his work at Ealing Studios. He was knighted in 1948.

* Robert Stevenson, 1905-86. His long career as a director included many films for Disney, notably *Mary Poppins* in 1964.

* Sir John Martin-Harvey, 1863-1944, actor and manager, who was for many years at the Lyceum under Irving. Later, his most celebrated role was Sidney Carton in *The Only Way*, a stage adaptation of *A Tale of Two Cities*, in which he performed countless times; in 1925 he appeared in a silent film version of the play. He was knighted in 1921.

Squire Bancroft, about to turn seventy-five, was invited to deliver 'A tribute to the Memory of Shakespeare'. He would seem to be an odd choice for this task, with so many great Shakespearean actors available, his only venture into Shakespeare having been a dire failure. His address concluded with words still relevant today: 'The lustre …. Shakespeare's transcendent genius has shed upon the world marches down the ages undimmed by time.' The performance then opened with scenes from *Julius Caesar* which was followed by 'A Shakespeare Pageant', extracts from nine more Shakespeare plays, with dozens of celebrated actors and actresses taking part. Among these were George Alexander, Marion Terry, her brother Fred and his wife, Julia Neilson, Gerald du Maurier, H.B.Irving, Gladys Cooper, Mrs Patrick Campbell and Sybil Thorndike[*]. In the course of the evening the actor Frank Benson, still in his costume as Julius Caesar, was called to the royal box, where he was knighted on the spot by King George V. The climax of the evening was an excerpt from *The Merchant of Venice* with Ellen Terry, now nearly seventy, once more entrancing the audience as Portia. The Shakespearean performances were interspersed with a musical programme of songs, dances and instrumental pieces arranged by the composers Sir Hubert Parry and Sir Alexander Mackenzie, while other composers, such as Edward German, Eric Coates and Sir Henry Wood, conducted settings for Shakespeare's words that they had composed specially for the occasion.

A year or two after the end of the Great War Squire took part in a theatrical gala, 'Warriors' Day', at Drury Lane, organised by the theatrical profession in aid of ex-soldiers. The event was attended by the then Prince of Wales – one day to reign, briefly, as King Edward VIII – along with a host of military figures and stage celebrities. Sir Arthur Pinero presided over the event and introduced Squire Bancroft as 'the Grand Old Man of the English stage,' at which 'B' jokingly shook his fist at him, before going on stage to read some extracts from *A Christmas Carol*, still as fresh as ever in his memory.

There seems to have been much real affection from succeeding generations for both Bancrofts, who by the end of the war had outlived so many of their friends from the past. Marie in old age was described as 'a tiny Dresden-china old lady, lace ruffles and pale pink powder, dancing mischievous eyes', although her youngest granddaughter Naomi recalled that she could also be quite formidable when she chose. Squire cut a striking figure with his 'shining silver hair, his monocle, his morning coat …. sitting down to bridge at the Garrick Club with John Hare, Hare volatile, impatient, snapping his fingers: "Come on, B!" and "B" not to be

---

[*] Dame Sybil Thorndike, 1882-1976, DBE 1931. In 1924 she was Shaw's original *Saint Joan*.

bustled.' Squire Bancroft has sometimes been described as 'pompous' by writers from later generations, writers who never knew him. He certainly tends to look haughty in photographs, but people usually did look somewhat rigid in photographs back then: a sitter for a portrait had to remain motionless while the photographer, enveloped in a large black cloth, his flash held aloft, timed his exposure. Squire's great height, his invariably impeccable attire – to the end of his life he would never set foot outside unless meticulously turned out – with his gold-topped cane, his monocle, his silk top hat, might give the appearance of pomposity to a later generation. His many friends knew him as kindly, considerate and generous. At over six foot two – a very considerable height in his time – there was no point in attempting to disguise his conspicuous appearance, so he consciously accentuated his style with a theatricality which could be perceived as pomposity. In the last photograph taken of Marie and Squire together, a grainy old newspaper shot, their difference in height is evident. Marie is standing on a flight of steps. Squire, one foot on a lower step, still has to stoop to bring himself down to her level.

the last picture of Marie and Squire Bancroft together

Towards the end of the war, Marie Bancroft's health, which had been failing for some years, began to deteriorate seriously. Her decline was painful and her once lively mind was beginning to fail her. Squire was finding it more and more difficult to manage, even with plenty of help, and finally he was forced to accept that she needed more care than was practicable at their Sandgate home, so they moved into a fine suite of rooms at the nearby Burlington Hotel. Overlooking the Channel, it is a vast Victorian pile, with a magnificent oak staircase and fine stained-glass windows.

On 12 January 1919, two months after the end of the Great War, Marie turned eighty, a milestone that passed without attention, as the wider world never knew the exact year of her birth. (It has only been possible to confirm the date with the help of a passing mention by the ever-superstitious Marie that many of the milestones in her life took place on a Saturday, her 'lucky day', starting with the day she was born, and in 1839 the twelfth of January fell on a Saturday.) However Squire's eightieth, two years later, on 14 May 1921, did not go unnoticed. There were stories in the newspapers and messages of congratulation from all over the world, including a telegram from the King and Queen. Then, just eight days later, the letters of congratulation merged with messages of condolence when Marie's health finally gave out and she died of cardiac failure at the Burlington Hotel on 22 May. Her beloved 'Bogie' wrote to one friend, 'I can say with Carlyle, "the light of my life has gone out."' Among the hundreds of letters that he received following Marie's death, was one from Queen Mary, in which she recalled that the first time the Bancrofts had visited her had been more than forty years before when her mother, Princess Mary Adelaide of Teck, was still alive. The Queen recalled that at the time her mother had been in very low spirits and rarely smiled. When the Bancrofts left, Mary Adelaide had said to her daughter, 'What a wonderful woman. She has made my sad heart like a bright garden.'

Following Marie Bancroft's death, Arthur Pinero in particular was an enormous support to Squire and to George Bancroft. At Marie's own request, the time and place of her small, intimate funeral service were not announced. Apart from Squire, just their family members and four close friends from the world of the theatre were present. Pinero was one and the other three were the actors Johnston Forbes-Robertson and Gerald du Maurier, and a theatre manager and friend of George's, Arthur Chudleigh[*]. A few days later there was a memorial service at the great Anglican church of St Martin-in-the Fields on 28 May. The service was

---

[*] Arthur Chudleigh, 1858-1932. Born Arthur Lillies, he took the name Chudleigh from the Devon village where he was born. In 1888 he became joint manager with Mrs John Wood of the Court Theatre; later he   managed the Comedy.

conducted by the Rev W.H.Elliott, the vicar of Holy Trinity Church, Folkestone. (Although Marie had converted to Roman Catholicism, Squire had remained an Anglican and they had both become close friends with Elliott.) The 121st Psalm, 'I will lift up mine eyes unto the hills ....' was sung, with the hymns 'Lead Kindly Light' and 'Abide With Me'. Tennyson's poem, *Crossing the Bar*, was sung as an anthem, to the music composed by Sir Frederick Bridge for the poet's own funeral in Westminster Abbey in 1892, with its final words:

I hope to see my Pilot face to face
When I have crossed the Bar.

Marie's remains were interred in a mausoleum that Squire had built in Brompton Cemetery. A few years later Squire wrote, as the closing words of his final book, *Empty Chairs*, that this was where '.... all that is left of her in this world is at rest and where there is room for me.' Into the wall of the mausoleum was set the stone inscribed '*Mary's Place, Fortune Gate*,' that Marie's mother, Georgiana Wilton had seen on the row of cottages in 1865, on the day that the old Prince of Wales's Theatre first opened its doors under its youthful new manager, Miss Marie Wilton.

Even after so many years out of the public eye, Marie Bancroft's legacy to the theatre of the twentieth century was acknowledged. Squire Bancroft never failed to remind anyone and everyone that 'Our success was largely due to the gleams of genius in her.' One newspaper later summed up what she and her husband had achieved so long before:

The present-day theatregoer, seated in a comfortably-appointed theatre, watching a well-staged comedy of ideas which does not affront his intelligence, presented by well-dressed and well-bred artistes, owes this and much more largely to the labours of the Bancrofts. The state of the English theatre and drama at the time they commenced their management can be estimated from the reforms these pioneers initiated. The Prince of Wales's Theatre was the first which had a carpet. It was here the modern stalls appeared; it was here that the play became reasonable instead of theatrical and bombastic, that it was mounted with care for correct detail, that the actors gave up ranting for ordinary conversation; it was here that 'matinées' were instituted, and other now established reforms initiated. It was here also that all connected with the playhouse ceased to be 'rogues and vagabonds', 'bohemians', people apart, their places being taken by a professional class whose standard of manners and intelligence would compare with any other .... At one time or another most of the actors and actresses who in the last years of the 19th century dominated the London stage owed much of their training and their success to the Bancrofts' management. Their influence was decisive upon the drama of their time. Their story is one of the romances of the stage. The brilliant art of Marie

Wilton, linked to the managerial skill of Squire Bancroft, and the fresh sparkling gifts of Tom Robertson – there was a wonderful combination of qualities with which perhaps only the Gilbert and Sullivan-D'Oyly Carte combination is comparable.

After his wife's death, Squire Bancroft moved back permanently to London, where he settled down to a life at 1A, Albany, with his dogs and his parrot for company. The Albany is a fine eighteenth-century mansion designed by Sir William Chambers. Early in the nineteenth century it had been converted into elegant apartments, many of them then – and now – inhabited by public figures and celebrities in pursuit of some privacy. Originally, but rarely now, known as 'Albany', with no article, the building is set back off the north side of Piccadilly, next door to the Royal Academy, with Fortnum and Mason's as its 'corner shop' directly opposite, and Hatchard's, the royal bookshop, close by. There Squire was cared for by a devoted housekeeper, Amelia Nutt, who had been with him and Marie for many years.

Squire had always been a keen collector of antiques and objets d'art and was well-known as a connoisseur among the antique shops, sale rooms and curiosity shops of London. This passion continued following Marie's death, and in true Victorian style every inch of his home was filled with treasures accumulated over the years – antique furniture, clocks, porcelain, silver and books. Both Bancrofts were especially fond of marquetry furniture: they dined at a beautifully inlaid table with matching sideboard, and slept in an enormous marquetry double bed, with their entwined initials inlaid in the headboard.

Bancroft also had a fine collection of paintings, including many theatrical portraits, of himself and Marie and of other actors. One of his paintings was a life-size, three-quarter length portrait of David Garrick, believed to be a Zoffany[*]. Both Bancrofts sat for portraits themselves. Among these, in the Garrick Club's fine collection, is a life-size, rather severe oil painting of Squire from around 1900 by Hugh Goldwin Riviere. The Garrick also has a pair of marble busts of the Bancrofts from about 1880, probably done to mark their move to the Haymarket Theatre. These are by Count Gleichen, a talented sculptor with numerous first names: a minor German royal, he was a relative of Queen Victoria. The National Portrait Gallery has, along with many photographic portraits of both Bancrofts, a life-size, three-quarter length portrait in oils of Marie by Thomas Jones Barker that was bequeathed to the gallery by her husband.

---

[*] Zoffany, Johann, 1733-1810. Born in Germany, he found fame in England, where he was especially admired for his theatrical works, of which the Garrick Club has an important collection. In 2012 the Royal Academy staged an exhibition of his works.

The artist who, above all others, Squire Bancroft wanted to paint his wife was John Everett Millais, one of the founder members of the Pre-Raphaelite movement. As early as 1874 Bancroft implored the painter to accept the commission and offered him the then vast sum of £1000 to do it. Millais declined, writing: 'I know no face that it would be more difficult to tackle; it lives entirely upon expression, which is ever changing, both on the stage and off it. No, my dear fellow, the job must be done either in seconds or left alone for ever.'

Squire Bancroft in his study. Val Prinsep's painting of the minuet from **The School for Scandal** *is clearly visible over the fireplace.*

Some of his friends remarked that living on his own after Marie's death, although lonely, 'B' was never morose. However, he appeared to become more reserved than before, even shy, and his friends became ever more important to him. Although so many of his contemporaries had already passed on, he forged close friendships with members of the younger generation of actors. One friend wrote of him that 'When "Old B" came into a room he would sit down beside the youngest actor present and delight him by the knowledge he showed of all that the young man was doing.' When asked to speak at a twenty-first birthday dinner in 1925, when he was eighty-four, 'B' said: 'Age has its privileges, and I suppose its drawbacks, although I don't admit it has drawbacks – I feel I can go a yard or two farther. But our greatest privilege is to welcome youth. It is youth that does things, that carries on. Let us always give welcome and hope to youth.' It upset him when his younger friends had rows with each other. The actor Fred Kerr[*] told of a time when he and Gerald du Maurier had a falling out, the story of which had somehow spread around. Kerr had invited Squire to dine with him and, in accepting, 'B' had remarked to Kerr how delighted he was 'that you and Gerald have buried the hatchet'.

He himself was a fine example of growing old gracefully. 'You just live to be old,' he once said. 'It comes naturally. Plenty of exercise every day and an interest in life. I do not allow my mind to grow old.' On another occasion he said, 'We Victorians are considered highly respectable by you moderners. That is only because we were wise enough to conceal what we thought might get us a bad name.' Although he was in many ways a relic of another era, he was happy to see the way the theatre was progressing, and often remarked that methods of production were constantly improving.

Marie's death in 1921 was soon followed by that of the Bancrofts' oldest and dearest friend, John Hare. Hare had been their closest colleague in those critical early years at the Prince of Wales's, where he had established his reputation as a brilliant character actor, with a unique talent for the portrayal of elderly eccentrics, thanks to an exceptional skill with makeup. He had gone on to become a highly successful actor manager, first in partnership with the Kendals at the Court and the St James's theatres, and then on his own at the Garrick, built for him by W.S.Gilbert at the huge cost of over £40,000.

John Hare was a small, dapper man, always well dressed. His son-in-law, George Bancroft, described him as 'highly strung and sensitive but "peppery" too …. with a resonant voice and the power to dominate a scene in spite of his smallness.' He was famed for his irritability, but in

---

[*] Frederick 'Fred' Kerr, 1858-1933, actor and stage director.

spite of this the actors and staff at his theatres loved him. Madge Kendal told how, on his birthday one year, she and some others clubbed together to give him a present.

The day's rehearsal had not gone well, and Hare was in a foul mood. The young actress who had been chosen to present the gift nervously asked if she might have a word with him. 'Certainly not,' snapped Hare. 'The rehearsal's been very bad and we've got to go through it all again.'

'But it's your birthday, Mr Hare, and the members of the company wish to present you with this little remembrance,' stammered the girl.

Hare was overwhelmed and his eyes filled with tears. 'How sweet of you all to remember my birthday. What *can* I say to you? I'll *never* be in a temper again.'

ink sketch by W.H.Kendal of John Hare in Pinero's **The Money Spinner**, *1881, at the Royal Court*

334

Alice Comyns Carr confirmed that Hare 'was an extraordinarily temperamental creature .... but the changing moods only seemed to add to his attractiveness.'

Hare and his wife Mary had three children, two daughters, Effie and Molly, and a son, Gilbert, or 'Bertie', who enjoyed a long and successful stage career, although he never became a household name like his father. Hare adored his family and they could do no wrong in his eyes. One morning, he was standing at a window watching his young son riding a pony outside. Arthur Pinero was with him. 'Here, Pin, quick!' called Hare urgently. 'What is it?' asked Pinero, hurrying to the window. 'Look – Bertie! He's riding! Wonderful seat, what? Part and parcel of the horse, eh? Damn it, he's off!'

'Hare radiated enthusiasm in all things,' wrote George Bancroft, 'especially in politics. Gladstone was a god to him – and games.' He particularly loved cards and golf. However, he was hopeless at cards – it was 'easy to read in his face the nature of his hand' – and even worse at golf. He played at Cromer, on the Norfolk coast, where he had a house called The Grange at nearby Overstrand. His son-in-law, also a golf enthusiast, wrote that he 'dressed in breeches, stockings, heavily nailed boots, a boiled shirt with stiff white cuffs and a stand-up collar .... around it there would be an MCC tie! Any outfit more incongruous it would be hard to imagine.' Once when they were playing together, the pro who was Hare's partner played a beautiful shot. 'Superb!' exclaimed Hare. 'I would give the world to be able to do that.' Then Hare's turn came:

> We all watched with keen amusement and genuine anxiety. Earnest concentration, nervous apprehension upon his every feature .... Crash! The ball scuttling into a bunker! Hare's club raised jerkily towards heaven, his agonized voice ringing out: 'God, I would drag *Braid*[*] down!'

Alice Comyns Carr wrote of Hare that 'with the exception of Henry Irving, none could claim the personality of Hare. Johnny was ever the best of company .... alert and full of energy, and with an inexhaustible fund of good stories; his presence at any dinner party was sufficient to ensure its success, and he was acclaimed everywhere with open arms.'

Friends would often come to stay at The Grange. Possibly the last photograph ever to be taken of Henry Irving was a snapshot taken by the Hares' younger daughter, Molly, in August 1905, just a few weeks before Irving died. It shows the two friends seated companionably side by side

---

[*] James Braid, 1870-1950, a great professional golfer who won the British Open five times between 1901 and 1910.

enjoying the summer sunshine in spite of their heavy coats and waistcoats.

Henry Irving and John Hare at The Grange, Overstrand, 1905

John Hare was knighted in 1907, the fourth member of his profession to be so honoured. He died in December 1921, just after Christmas, aged seventy-seven, following a bout of influenza that turned into pneumonia. His wife, Mary lived for another ten years. Squire Bancroft described her in old age: 'She is as beautiful as ever. I recall the time when we were all in love with her, as young men. She still retains her beauty in an astonishing way.' In 1893 Millais, a friend and fellow-member of the Garrick Club, had painted a fine portrait of John Hare. Hare left the portrait to the Garrick Club collection in his will.

In 1924 King George V and Queen Mary were present at a special Royal Command Performance in aid of King George's Pension Fund for Actors and Actresses. The king and queen had asked that George Bancroft's play, *The Ware Case*, should be performed in aid of the charity, and an all-star matinée production was put on for the occasion. Gerald du Maurier reprised his leading role of Sir Hubert Ware, nine years after he had originally played the part, and even the small parts had star actors in them, such as Gladys Cooper and Owen Nares[*]. Sir Johnston Forbes-Robertson played the small part of the judge in the court room scene. The king and queen were greeted at the door of the theatre by the 83-year-old Squire Bancroft, with Bancroft tactfully positioned at a lower level than the king, so as not to tower over him.

***Squire Bancroft welcoming King George V to
Command Performance of* The Ware Case, *1924***

Squire was clearly fond of children although he rarely mentions them in his memoirs. His granddaughters adored him. In his old age, one of his friends had a little girl of around five who was often taken to visit 'B', who would always give her some chocolate. One day she boldly asked him to double her ration. He declined, pleading that he had no money left. After that the little girl always referred to him as 'Sir Squire Bankrupt'. He once said, 'It seems to me that I have arrived at an age when I can say that I knew nearly everybody's grandfather.'

---

[*] Owen Nares, 1888-1943, a matinée idol, and star of stage and silent films.

Ever since living in St John's Wood during the early years of his marriage, Bancroft had loved watching cricket at Lords, although with his poor eyesight he must have found the distant play hard to follow. He continued to visit Lords right up until the year before he died. He rarely missed going to Epsom on Derby Day. He kept himself busy during his last years by working on his final book entitled *Empty Chairs*, which was published by John Murray in 1925, recounting memories and anecdotes of the many friends who over the past decades had dined at the Bancrofts' table, or they at theirs, and who would no longer fill a chair at any table. The final chapter, with additional contributions from his closest friends, is about the emptiest of all those chairs – the one that was once filled by his beloved wife, Marie.

The tall, handsome figure, with the head of thick white hair, the white moustache, the silk top hat, the frock coat, the monocle on its black ribbon and the gold-topped cane, was one of the most instantly recognisable figures around London. Distinguished, picturesque, debonair – those were the sort of words used to describe him. His unusually tall silk hat was often remarked upon: he had several top hats which were carefully kept for him by a Bond Street hatter. Each day he would call in at the shop where one of them would be waiting for him, ready ironed. It would be exchanged for the previous day's hat. The hatter described how Sir Squire would often strike his gold-topped walking stick on the ground exclaiming, 'I like a topper!' He walked almost everywhere: the park, his clubs and his bank were all within walking distance.

The great twentieth-century actor John Gielgud[*] was to recall that, as a young man in his twenties, he could remember seeing the tall, elegant, figure walking along Piccadilly. He would call in at his bank each day on his way to lunch at the Garrick, Gielgud wrote, where he would enquire about the state of his balance. Most evenings he would set out again, dine at the Athenaeum, then walk back to the Albany. With all his walking, Squire Bancroft kept fit and well almost to the end of his life. On his eightieth birthday, in 1921, to the astonishment of a reporter who had come to interview him for a local Folkestone paper, he suddenly produced a skipping rope, saying that a hundred skips each day kept him reasonably fit.

'Old B' invariably took a daily walk along Piccadilly to Green Park with his dogs. He and Marie were never without dogs in their home. As well as the giant St Bernard, Monk, who had lived with them in the '70s, there is a photograph of Marie, in matronly middle-age, holding a black Pekingese. Charles Bancroft's second wife, Ellie, who often spoke of her memories of the Bancrofts to her granddaughter, Brenda, recalled Squire

---

[*] Sir John Gielgud, 1904-2000, one of the finest actors of the 20th century. He was a great-nephew of Ellen Terry, being a grandson of her sister, Kate.

in his old age taking his two dogs – then an Old English sheepdog and a long-haired dachshund – on their daily walk to Green Park. In most of the informal photographs taken of him in old age, he is shown with one or two dogs. When Squire returned to London the long-lived parrot that had preferred Westgate to Berkeley Square came too, to live with him in his apartment in the Albany where friends would hear him talk to it 'crooningly and lovingly' as it hung in its cage in the window.

Squire Bancroft with his dogs and his parrot, c.1914

'Porters, commissionaires, newspaper sellers would run to do him small services, which he acknowledged with old-world courtesy and they felt themselves fully rewarded,' a friend wrote of 'B'. Each day, as he passed St James's, Piccadilly, he would stop for a few words with a blind man whose regular spot was outside the church. 'B' would greet him and drop a coin in his tin. The man always recognised his step and his voice, and would say, 'Thank you, Sir Squire.' Then he would carry on to the Garrick Club for lunch, where he liked to order mussels – so long as there was an 'r' in the month.

He was a regular at the frequent luncheon parties given by the widow of Sir Charles Wyndham at her house overlooking Regent's Park. Madge Kendal would usually be there, and, among the older guests, there would be younger actors now in their prime such as Henry Ainley[*] and Sybil

---

[*]Henry Ainley, 1879-1945, Shakespearean actor.

Thorndike. The Irish MP, T.P.O'Connor*, was also often at the lunches. One of O'Connor's favourite stories was one Bancroft told of a gathering many years before at a rather grand house. During the festivities a valuable silver cake-knife went missing. Only one of the guests present could be responsible. Someone suggested that if the lights were turned out, surely when they were turned on again the knife would be back in its place. 'But when the lights went up,' said Squire, sonorously, 'the cake-dish, as well as the knife, was missing.'

Above all, Squire Bancroft loved going to the theatre. 'No first night was complete without his striking presence,' one of his obituaries was one day to read, '.... a picturesque figure, tall and lithe, with a crown of thick white hair surmounting a long face, a monocle in his alert, searching eye, haughtily jaunty in bearing, always spruce and debonair. He never looked his age.' He enjoyed the arrival of the movie era. 'I do like the films,' he would say. 'One doesn't have to think.' He and Marie certainly lived to see several of their friends appearing in silent films. Ellen Terry was in several, which they would have surely seen, and in 1913, the year he received his knighthood, Johnston Forbes-Robertson played Hamlet on film, with his wife, Gertrude Elliott* as Ophelia. In 1914 Herbert Beerbohm Tree played Svengali, in the film version of George du Maurier's phenomenally successful *Trilby*, and in the following year he starred in D.W.Griffith's spectacular silent screen version of *Macbeth*, although *The Times* did not consider that brief extracts from Shakespeare's text projected onto the screen were any substitute for 'the grandeur of the spoken word'. In 1915, John Hare, by then over seventy, appeared once more as old Eccles when Tom Robertson's *Caste* was filmed.

Squire Bancroft took a keen interest in a revival of *Diplomacy* at the Adelphi in 1923, and would turn up at rehearsals in the hope that he could be of help in the production. It has to be wondered whether the company entirely appreciated these visits and well-meaning advice from the old gentleman from another era. He had made his last ever appearance on a stage eight years before, at the age of seventy-seven, in his old part of Triplet at a charity performance of *Masks and Faces*. Triplet was clean-shaven so, determined that his appearance should be right for the part, for that one single performance Squire shaved off his luxuriant moustache. In May 1922 he was awarded an honorary LL.D at St Andrew's University,

---

*The Rt.Hon.T.P.O'Connor, 1848-1929, a journalist and newspaper editor. He represented a Liverpool constituency as an Irish Nationalist MP. He was president of the British Board of Film Censors from 1917.
*Gertrude Elliott, 1874-1950, American actress, married to Johnston Forbes-Robertson.

the same year that he made his last speech at the annual dinner of the Actors' Benevolent Fund.

Near the end of Alice Comyns Carr's *Reminiscences*, written when she was in her seventies, she imagines a fantasy party. It is 1925 and in her mind she has gathered together all her old friends who are still living, all now advanced in years. Among her imagined guests are Ellen Terry, Johnston Forbes-Robertson, Arthur Pinero and many others, recalling as they chat together friends long gone and times long past. Among them, 'Sir Squire Bancroft, upright and hearty at eighty-four years of age, enters on the arm of his still beautiful daughter-in-law, John Hare's daughter.'

Bancroft with his granddaughters Naomi (left) and Diana, c.1925

Squire Bancroft retained his good health and vigour almost to the end of his life, until in April 1926, when he had a bout of influenza, then a dangerous virus and still to be feared today, especially by older people. He appeared to have recovered well enough to accompany his old friend, Arthur Pinero, to Bath for a few days. While there he became ill again. 'Pin' telephoned George Bancroft to tell him that he should come at once. George hurried down to Bath, motoring through the night, a journey that in the 1920s, with no fast roads, must have taken several hours. On his arrival George found that his father was indeed very ill and that a doctor had been sent for. Squire only wanted to be in his own familiar rooms and

341

begged George to take him home. The doctor agreed that he could travel and he was helped to dress, ready for the long car ride to London. A 'wheelchair was brought to his room, but Squire took one look at it, adjusted his monocle, and demanded, 'What's this?' Insisting that he was not a Guy Fawkes, he walked, without any assistance, to the lift and then out to George's car for the long drive home to the Albany.

Back home, the failing Squire Bancroft was cared for by his devoted housekeeper, Amelia Nutt. During part of the evening of Sunday 18 April he appeared to be unconscious, but by the next morning he seemed to have recovered enough for Amelia to feel that some company might be beneficial, so she telephoned an old friend of his who came round for a short visit that afternoon and they chatted amiably over a cup of tea. Later that evening he slipped into unconsciousness and George was sent for. At ten forty-five on the evening of 19 April Squire Bancroft died peacefully in his apartment at the Albany.

The very next morning, newspapers all over the country reported the death of the man whom many of them described as the 'Grand Old Man of the Stage'. The basic outline of Squire Bancroft's life and career was related in every paper, as obituaries for prominent figures are usually prepared well ahead of their deaths to be held on file ready for when they are needed. *The Times* obituary ran to three full columns and the one in the *Daily Telegraph* to four and a half. The report in the *Stage*, published on 22 April, filled almost seven full columns. Obituaries appeared in dozens of the daily local papers of towns where Squire had acted in his youth, such as Birmingham, Cork, Liverpool and Plymouth, and in those cities all over the country, such as Gloucester, where he had more recently performed his readings of *A Christmas Carol*, raising much needed funds for their hospitals, and, of course, Folkestone where he and Marie had lived during the last years of her life. More remarkably, papers published in places where he had never set foot also carried reports of Squire Bancroft's departure.

Over the following days long appreciations of his life were run, again in papers from the national dailies to those from all over the country, from Aberdeen to Brighton, from Belfast to Ipswich, Nottingham, Coventry, Cardiff, and countless other places, and also unexpectedly in journals such as *Horse and Hound* and the *Sporting Times*. 'The Pink 'Un', as the *Sporting Times* was generally known, reported that the previous year Sir Squire, who had rarely missed an Epsom Derby, had been a guest of honour at the paper's Diamond Jubilee dinner. In his reply to a toast to 'The Stage', he had informed everyone there that his first appearance on the London stage had coincided with the first publication of the paper. The report concluded with the words: 'Sir Squire Bancroft was in the best sense one of the sights of London.'

'His passing is to me a great personal loss and a heavy blow,' Sir Johnston Forbes-Robertson was reported to have told one columnist. 'I believe I am the only man now alive who actually worked with him and knew him intimately in those early days at the Prince of Wales's Theatre and at the Haymarket, when he surrounded himself with all the greatest actors and actresses of his day. He was one of the most considerate, one of the most kindly men I have ever known .... Again and again at the Prince of Wales's he used to take subordinate parts because his mind was set upon the achievement of a finished product and not upon any personal success or prominence. Never was a man more popular and more liked than was Squire Bancroft.'

George Bancroft summed up his father's character: 'He was big and generous; always on the search for the good points in a man, never the bad ones. He was able to put himself into the position of the other fellow. And in the quarrels of others he was slow to condemn.' On hearing an unhappy story being spread around regarding one couple's private affairs, he would say: 'Aren't you condemning without knowledge? *No one* knows anything about those things except two people – the man and the woman.'

A few days later, once again more than a hundred newspapers ran the story of Squire Bancroft's funeral. As such a connoisseur of funerals, he would have relished his own. It took place on Friday 23 April at St Martin-in-the-Fields, where a great crowd had gathered outside to watch the arrival of the cortège. The Victorians and their immediate successors took death and funerals very seriously indeed. From the distance of 1940, Julia Neilson wrote that they 'carried the signs of mourning .... to astounding lengths'. As the cortège moved slowly from the Albany towards Trafalgar Square, passing the Haymarket Theatre en route, buses and cabs stopped as it passed by, men removed their hats, and people stood with their heads bowed in respect. Shops in Piccadilly had closed their shutters. Large crowds gathered around St Martin's to watch the arrival of the funeral procession. The service was conducted by the Dean of Westminster and the vicar of Folkestone, who had been such a comfort following the death of Marie. Squire had requested 'family flowers only' but this did not prevent the arrival of bouquets from the highest in the land to the most humble: among them there was a wreath sent by King George V – and there was one from the cabbies of London.

It was a gathering of 'the great and the good'. The twelve pallbearers were mostly from the world of the arts: they included Squire's old friends and colleagues, Sir Johnston Forbes-Robertson and Sir Arthur Pinero, both now in their seventies, the theatre manager, Arthur Chudleigh, and from the next generation, John Hare's son, Gilbert, and Gerald du Maurier. There was the composer Sir Alexander Mackenzie, aged nearly eighty, the sculptor Sir George Frampton RA, creator of the Peter Pan statue in Kensington Gardens and the monument to Edith Cavell that stands near the National Portrait Gallery, and General Sir Nevil Macready, a son of the great actor William Charles Macready.

Squire Bancroft's funeral at St Martin-in-the Fields

The large congregation included young and old. The *Western Mail* described 'old actors with silk hats, painfully ironed to look spruce, and shabby green-black coats, deftly patched .... old men with trembling hands, heavy white moustaches and long hair.' Sir Johnston Forbes-Robertson was described as looking frail and distressed, with tears in his eyes, at the loss of his old friend; he himself was to live for another eleven years. But there were not just old men and old women present: there were students and ex-students from RADA and among the later generations of actors, whose careers would take them into the world of radio and film, were Nina Boucicault, daughter of Dion and the first 'Peter Pan', Allan Aynesworth, the original Algernon Moncrieff in *The Importance of Being Earnest* and Ronald Squire, who had been in George Bancroft's play, *The Ware Case*, in 1915.

Most of Squire's contemporaries were long gone but the widows of Sir Charles Wyndham, Sir Herbert Beerbohm Tree and Sir George Alexander were there (knighthoods came thick and fast for actors after

Irving's and Bancroft's). The first theatrical DBE, Dame May Whitty, was there as were future Dames, Irene Vanbrugh and Lilian Braithwaite. Others from the world of the arts included the poet John Drinkwater, the novelist Hugh Walpole and the prolific writer E.V.Lucas along with the actor Aubrey Smith, remembered by cricket historians as the man who introduced what was then England's national sport to Hollywood.

There were politicians present, members of the medical profession, and plenty of lawyers, as Bancroft had many friends in the legal profession. These included Sir Edward Marshall-Hall KC, the renowned trial barrister, and Sir Edward Clarke KC, who had appeared in the scandalous 'Baccarat Case' of 1890, in which he cross-examined the Prince of Wales, and who had represented Oscar Wilde in his 1895 libel action against the Marquess of Queensberry. Mr Willy Clarkson was there, the most famous wigmaker and theatrical costumier in London: a blue plaque adorns the restaurant in Soho that was once his premises. The king was represented. One figure still living who was sadly absent was Ellen Terry. The 'incomparable Ellen' had been made a DBE the previous year, 1925, but at the age of nearly eighty and frail in mind and body, she now rarely left her home at Smallhythe in Kent, where she was to die two years later. There were representatives from the Garrick and other clubs to which Squire had belonged and from the many charities and hospitals he supported and there were young actors and actresses, back-stage staff of theatres, Squire's and Marie's personal servants, and many London cabbies.

The vicar of Folkestone spoke from the pulpit: 'The man we mourn was a friendly man. Friendship meant much to him …. He knew all sorts and conditions of men, who loved him and gained inspiration from him. He lived his life debonairly, and to live debonairly is often the expression of fine qualities of heart and mind. He faced life with a smile and when age laid heavy hands on him, he bore himself with gallant dignity to the end.' As at Marie's memorial, *Abide With Me* was sung, and the 23rd Psalm, and Tennyson's poem *Crossing the Bar* was once again sung as an anthem.

More crowds lined the streets near Brompton Cemetery, where the remains of Squire Bancroft were laid to rest alongside his beloved wife. On the front of the mausoleum were inscribed just their names, and around the gothic arched rim the words, 'From shadows and fancies to the truth.' During the Second World War the mausoleum, which stood just inside the north entrance to the Cemetery, was destroyed by a bomb and only its front remains, now lying horizontal on the ground, forming a large, flat tombstone, surrounded by small, granite obelisks. The stone that read 'Mary's Place, Fortune Gate', which had been set into the mausoleum, vanished, and must now be buried deep with Marie and Squire Bancroft.

Brompton Cemetery is a peaceful place to wander, as are all London's great cemeteries. They are fine places to be laid to rest. Full of wild flowers and great trees, they are wildlife havens in the midst of the city. The sound of the nearby traffic fades, birds sing in the trees and you might meet urban foxes, foraging squirrels, maybe a lone dog-walker. Wandering around the cemetery, its long footpaths lined with more than thirty thousand monuments to people the vast majority of whom no one today would remember, you come across familiar names. Among them are Emmeline Pankhurst, the suffragette leader; George Borrow, the traveller and writer; the great tenor, Richard Tauber; the controversial journalist, Bernard Levin; John Wisden, the cricketer who founded the Almanack. Many of the monuments are vast: a group of River Thames watermen stands guard around a large tomb that holds the remains of a champion oarsman and a massive stone lion tops that of 'Gentleman' John Jackson, a famous pugilist of the early nineteenth century. There are mausoleums the size of small chapels and a host of ivy-clad marble angels.

The Bancrofts lie among friends and family. Marie Wilton's son Charles is close by, with her sister Ida. So is her brother-in-law Francis Drake, who showed his faith in Marie by backing her in her first step into management. Charles Dillon, who brought the young Marie Wilton to London is buried there. The Swanboroughs, in whose theatre she first found fame, lie in a large family tomb. The great actor-manager Benjamin Webster is there. So too are many old friends. Among them are Marie's one-time partner, the playwright Henry James Byron; the actor-manager John Clayton, one of the company at the Prince of Wales's Theatre; the much-loved William Terriss, cut down at the height of his fame; the Pre-Raphaelite painter Val Prinsep, who designed the act-drop for the Haymarket. At Brompton they are all back on stage.

Squire Bancroft left £173,894 in his will, the largest part of it to his son George and his family. That figure today would be the equivalent of several million pounds. In addition to individual annuities and bequests to relatives and servants, he left £1000 and his many books on the theatre to RADA, and sums to various charities, mostly connected with the theatrical profession. In the words of the will, these were 'in remembrance that my late wife and I have owed all our worldly possessions to the calling which we have served and loved, neither of us having ever inherited or received money in any other way.' The treasured personal possessions that meant most to him – the gold cuff links that had been his first gift from Marie, his father's gold pocket watch, the cigar case that Queen Victoria had presented to him – he bequeathed to George, along with all his private papers, with the instruction that George destroy any of these that he considered should not be preserved. He also asked that George select a gift from his collection of objets d'art for each of twenty-nine 'comrades of the stage, all members of the Garrick Club', including Johnston Forbes-Robertson and Arthur Pinero, 'in grateful remembrance of their friendship'.

The passing of Marie and Squire Bancroft marked the end of a theatrical era. Some words from the great Henry Irving sum them up. Spoken of Squire, but with minimal adaptation these words can apply equally to both Squire and Marie: 'They popularised a system of management which has dominated our stage ever since, and the principle of which may be described as the harmony of realism and art. Their management is associated with the early successes of notable artists. In the old Prince of Wales's Theatre John Hare became famous. It was there that Ellen Terry's Portia first charmed the world and it was there that Marie Wilton and Squire Bancroft became identified with types of character which have not lost their hold on the public. I am quite certain that the people of whom such things can be said are sure of a remarkable place in the history of the stage.'

The work of later generations of great actors is preserved for posterity on film but from the Bancrofts' era and before, only legends survive – of David Garrick, of Sarah Siddons and the Kembles, of Kean and of Macready, of Henry Irving and of Ellen Terry. None of their names mean much to the vast majority of people today. We can look at their portraits in galleries, and a few of the later ones, whose careers extended into the twentieth century, can be glimpsed in surviving clips of silent film. We can hear a few of their voices, on crackling old recordings, and we can see their faces in faded old photographs, but the Bancrofts and most of their contemporaries now live on only in the work of theatre historians.

It seems appropriate to close Marie and Squire Bancroft's story with Squire's own modest words. Without any regret, he was seemingly content that in his time an actor's legacy would die with him or her. In *On and Off the Stage* he wrote: 'Even with the mightiest actor .... how fleeting is his renown, how far less lasting his hold upon posterity than that enjoyed by the followers of every other intellectual calling in the world. When the last words of his part in the play are spoken, their tones are buried by the remorseless curtain as it falls. £70,000 may enrich our National Gallery with the magic art of Raphael, but ten times that sum could not buy for us one performance by David Garrick. The path the actor treads is laid but with sand, and his footmarks can in a moment be washed away by whatever wave may be the fashion of the hour.'

MARIE WILTON AND SQUIRE BANCROFT

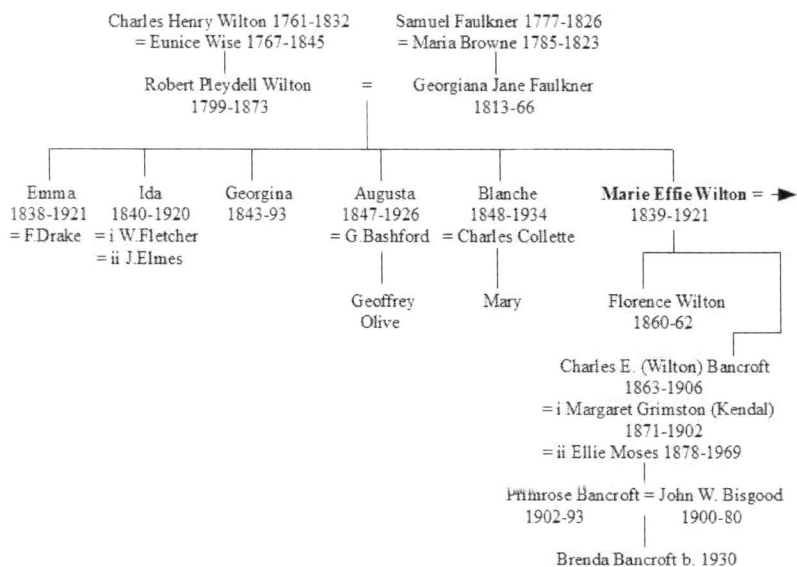

Charles Henry Wilton 1761-1832   Samuel Faulkner 1777-1826
= Eunice Wise 1767-1845   = Maria Browne 1785-1823

Robert Pleydell Wilton   =   Georgiana Jane Faulkner
1799-1873   1813-66

Emma	Ida	Georgina	Augusta	Blanche	**Marie Effie Wilton** = ➤
1838-1921	1840-1920	1843-93	1847-1926	1848-1934	1839-1921
= F.Drake	= i W.Fletcher		= G.Bashford	= Charles Collette	
	= ii J.Elmes				

Geoffrey   Mary   Florence Wilton
Olive   1860-62

Charles E. (Wilton) Bancroft
1863-1906
= i Margaret Grimston (Kendal)
1871-1902
= ii Ellie Moses 1878-1969

Primrose Bancroft = John W. Bisgood
1902-93   1900-80

Brenda Bancroft b. 1930

FAMILY TREE

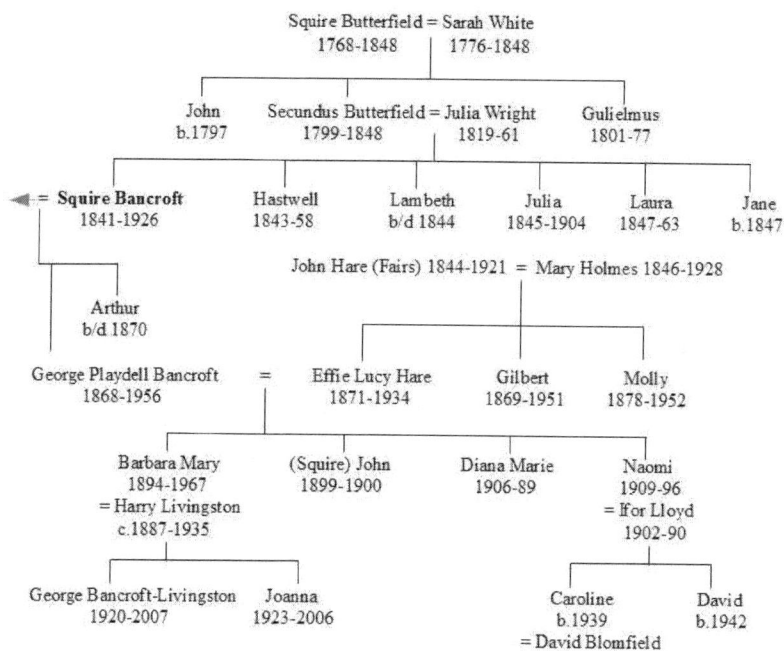

BIBLIOGRAPHY

Arthur, George: *From Phelps to Gielgud, Reminiscences of the Stage through Sixty-five years* (1936)

Auerbach, Nina: *Ellen Terry, Player in Her Time* (1987)

Bancroft, George Pleydell: *Stage and Bar* (1939)

Bancroft, Marie and Squire: *On and Off the Stage* (1888)

Bancroft, Marie and Squire: *Recollections of Sixty Years* (1909)

Bancroft, Squire: *Empty Chairs* (1925)

Blanchard, E.L: *The Life and Reminiscences of E.L.Blanchard*, 2 vols. (1891)

Baker, H.Barton: *History of the London Stage and Its Famous Players 1576-1903* (1904)

Baker, Michael: *The Rise of the Victorian Actor* (1978)

Barker, Kathleen: *The Theatre Royal, Bristol: Two Centuries of Stage History, 1776-1966* (1974)

Beerbohm, Max: *Mainly on the Air* (1946)

Booth, Michael R: *Theatre in the Victorian Age* (1991)

Brook, Donald: *The Romance of the English Theatre* (1945)

Brookfield, Charles: *Random Reminiscences* (1902)

Burley, T.L.G: *Playhouses of East Anglia* (1928)

Burnim, Kalman A. and Baskett, John: *Brief Lives: Sitters and Artists in the Garrick Club Collection* (2003)

Burnim, Kalman A. and Baskett, John: *Pictures in the Garrick Club* (1997)

Carr, Alice Comyns: *Reminiscences* (1926)

Clarence, Reginald: *'The Stage' Cyclopaedia, a bibliography of plays* (1909)

Coleman, John: *Players and Playwrights I Have Known* vol.2 (1888)

Cook, Dutton: *Nights at the Play, a View of the English Stage* (1883)

Crispe, Thomas: *Reminiscences of a KC* (1909)

Dickens, Charles: *The Life and Adventures of Nicholas Nickleby* (first published in serial form 1838-39)

Filon, Augustin (tr.from French by Frederic Whyte): *The English Stage: Being an Account of the Victorian Drama* (1897)

Findlater, Richard: *The Player Queens* (1976)

Fyfe, H.Hamilton: *Arthur Wing Pinero, Playwright* (1902)

Gielgud, Kate: *Kate Terry Gielgud, an Autobiography* (1953)

Goddard, Arthur: *Players of the Period* (1891)

Hartnoll, Phyllis (ed.): *Oxford Companion to the Theatre* (1983)

Hibbert, H.G.: *Fifty Years of a Londoner's Life* (1916)

Holroyd, Michael: *A Strange Eventful History, the Dramatic Lives of Ellen Terry, Henry Irving and Their Remarkable Families* (2008)

Hooper, W.Eden and Knight, Joseph: *The Stage in the Year 1900* (1901)

Irving, Laurence: *Henry Irving, the Actor and his World* (1951)

Jackson, Russell: *Victorian Theatre* (1989)

Kendal, Madge: *Dame Madge Kendal by Herself* (1933)

Kerr, Fred: *Recollections of a Defective Memory* (1930)

Macqueen-Pope, W: *Ladies First, the Story of Woman's Conquest of the British Stage* (1952)

Maude, Cyril: *The Haymarket Theatre, some Records and Reminiscences* (1903)

Morley, Sheridan: *The Great Stage Stars* (1986)

Neilson, Julia: *This for Remembrance* (1940)

Nicoll, Allardyce: *A History of English Drama 1600-1900,* vol 4: Early 19th Century Drama; vol .5: Late 19th Century Drama (1946)

Pascoe, Charles E. (ed.): *The Dramatic List* (1880)

Pemberton, T.Edgar: *John Hare, Comedian* (1895)

Pemberton, T.Edgar: *The Kendals, a Biography* (1900)

Pemberton, T.Edgar: *The Life and Writings of T.W.Robertson* (1893)

Powell, G.Rennie: *The Bristol Stage – Its Story* (1919)

Reid, Erskine and Compton, Herbert: *The Dramatic Peerage* (1892)

Robertson, T.W. *Six Plays*, introduction by Michael Booth (1980)

Rowell, George (ed.): *Nineteenth-Century Plays* (1953)

Rowell, George: *The Victorian Theatre, a Survey* (1956)

Savin, Maynard: *T.W.Robertson, his Plays and Stagecraft* (1950)

Scott, Clement: *The Drama of Yesterday and Today* (1899)

Scott, Clement (ed, magazines): *The Stage Door* and *The Green Room* (1880)

Scott, Mrs Clement: *Old Days in Bohemian London, recollections of Clement Scott* (1919)

Short, Ernest: *Introducing the Theatre* (1949)

Short, Ernest: *Theatrical Cavalcade* (1848)

Steen, Marguerite: *A Pride of Terrys* (1962)

Tanitch, Robert: *London Stage in the Nineteenth Century* (2010)

Taylor, George: *Players and Performance in the Victorian Theatre* (1989)

Terry, Ellen: *The Story of My Life* (1908)

Whyte, Frederic: *Actors of the Century, a Play-Lover's Gleanings from Theatrical Annals* (1898)

Williams, Montagu, Q.C. *Round London: Down East and Up West* (1894)

Wright, Thomas 'The Journeyman Engineer': *Some Habits and Customs of the Working Classes*, Ch.10: *Among the Gods'* (1867)

Yates, Edmund: *Edmund Yates: His Recollections and Experiences* (1885)

INDEX

management 110; Robertson's *Caste* 110-14,*112,114;* MW and SB marry 114; SB change of name 115,*115;* Boucicault's *How She Loves Him* 116-19; 'Bancroft parts' 118; Robertson's *Play* 119,120; first visit of Prince of Wales to the PoW 119; SB first meets Henry Irving 119; their dislike of benefits 120; MW's first trip abroad 120; revival of *Society* 121; engagement of William Terriss 121; birth of George B. 123; failure of *Tame Cats* 124-25; Robertson's *School* 125-28; first matinées 127; move to Grove End Road 128; joint managers of PoW 128; SB elected to Garrick Club 129; refurbishment of PoW 130-31; birth/ death of Bs' second child 132; revival of *Ours* 135; illness/death of Robertson 136-38; Bs' relationship with Robertson 137; revival of *Caste* 139; Lytton's *Money* 140-41; SB's continental trip with Coghlan 141-43; Lambs Club 145-46, *Caste* in the East End 146-47; holidays abroad 147-48,156,163-64,181-82,187-88, 195,216-18,230,243,*245,*254,269, 275, 294-95; death of Robert Wilton 148; *School for Scandal* 148-54; seat 154-55; researching the *Merchant* in Venice 156-57; Ellen Terry invited to play Portia 157,159, ET's description of MB 159; Gilbert's *Sweethearts* 159-61,*161;* failure of *Merchant* 161-63; revival of *Money* 163; *Masks and Faces* 164-68, *166, 167;* revival of *Ours* with Ellen Terry 169;further refurbishment of PoW 171; Sardou's *Peril* 171-73;MW charity reading of *Bleak House* 174; SB sees Sardou's *Dora* in Paris/ buys rights 175; Boucicault's *London Assurance* 176,*177;* MB first billed as 'Mrs Bancroft' 177; Dutton Cook on *London Assurance* 180; *The Vicarage* 179-80,*179;* Sardou's *Diplomacy* 183-187,*184,187;* SB visits Sardou 188; use of non-English plays 189; profile in *The World* magazine 190-92; Gilbert's *Sweethearts* 193; Buckstone's *Good for Nothing* 193; considering move from PoW 194; lease Haymarket 195; Sardou's *Duty* 195; renovating Haymarket 195-197; last night at PoW197-98; MB opens Scala Th, 199-200; Haymarket history 201,*202;* new décor 202-03,*204;* abolition of pit 203; opening night/Lytton's *Money* 205,211-12,*212;* pit protest

205-07; 'pit question' 209-11; Robertson's *School* 213-14,*213;* road accident 218; *Masks and Faces* 219-21,*220;* SB's Mediterranean journey 221-24; Sardou's *Odette* in Paris 225; Lillie Langtry at the Haymarket 225-28; Sardou's *Odette* 228-30; casting themselves 229; Sardou's *Fédora* in Paris 232-33; last revival of *Caste* 236-237; admin at Haymarket 237; *Fédora* at Haymarket 238-41; move to Berkeley Square 239- 40,*239;* farewells to Irving first USA tour 240-43; SB's friendship with Pinero 244; Pinero's *Lords and Commons* 244-50; considering retirement 249; deaths of Byron and Reade 250; *The Rivals* 251-53; retirement announced 254; improved conditions and pay for actors/benefits 255-56; farewell season 257-259; last production of Robertson's *Ours* 259; SB's defence of his 'reforms' 259; last night at Haymarket 259-64; their collabora-tion with Robertson 265-66; the Bs' legacy 266; SB as manager 267; their absence from son Charles's wedding 279; possible paternity of Charles 284-85; Julia Neilson's on MB 287; SB in Irving's production *The Dead Heart* 287-91,296; Passion Play, Oberammergau 295; MB's plays 295-96; MB's plays 296- 97; MB's charity works/benefits 296-97; Bs return to stage in revival of *Diplomacy* 297-98; MB's road accident 298; *Diplomacy* at Balmoral 299; MB in Hare's *Money* 299; MB in Tree's *Fédora* 300; SB on Lord Chamberlain's Advisory Board 300; Bs and Actors' Benevolent Fund 301; SB and Freemasonry 301-02; Irving's knighthood celebrations 302-03; SB's *Christmas Carol* readings 303-07, 309-10,312,324,327,342; 303-10,312; in Canada/New York 307-09,*309;* SB's knighthood 310-11;MB's 'share' in honour 311; London cab shelter 312-13; campaigns for a national theatre and drama school 314; RADA, Bancroft Gold Medal 315,*315;* film of *Masks and Faces* 316; Irving's funeral 318; Ellen Terry's jubilee 318-19; Foundling Hospital, 319-20; Actors' Association 320; *Recollections of Sixty Years* published 320; MB's novel *The Shadow of Neeme* 321-22; SB's clubs 322; at Westgate 323; physical fitness 323; in Folkestone/ WWI 324; Shakespeare tercentenary

358